Shannon

Shannon

a novel

William Vincent

To: Phoebe —
With my best
wishes -
William Vincent

IG

International Graphics

A C K N O W L E D G E M E N T S

My deepest thanks to everyone
who made this book possible.

Cover: *Storm Coming, Ireland* Oil, 24 x 30" © William Vincent

Back cover photograph: © Chris Corrie

Cover and book design: John Cole GRAPHIC DESIGNER

Produced by: Dennis Kirk / International Graphics
Scottsdale, Arizona

Printed in U.S.A. by Bang Printing

Library of Congress Catalog Card Number: 98-71468

ISBN: 1-889741-24-8

International Graphics
11923 E. Beryl Avenue, Scottsdale, AZ 85259
1 (800) 887-2108

1 2 3 4 5 6 7 8 9

For my children
Royanna, Alena, Deanna and Teresa

BOOK ONE

"Oh, who would not welcome
that moment's returning,
When passion first wak'd a new
life through his frame,
And his soul, like the wood that
grows precious in burning
Gave out all its sweets to
love's exquisite flame."

Thomas Moore
(1779 - 1852)

Chapter One

"Céad Mile Fáilte," the sign read. "A Hundred Thousand Welcomes." Jack Murphy smiled to himself when he saw it.

A light rain swept across the inlet, passed over the ferry and vanished against the green slopes of Ireland. At the gangway, one of the officers was shouting orders to the hands. A few people were standing at dockside, waiting to pick up friends or relatives.

Jack kept his eyes on the dock. He was watching for the driver who was meeting him with a car from Dan Doolittle's Auto Rental. Sure enough, there he was, standing under an umbrella, carrying a placard with the name of the company in big, bold letters. At the same moment, Jack also saw his luggage being placed on the dock. A sigh of relief. Everything was in order.

"Good morning, sir," Jack greeted the driver.

"Good morning. You must be Jack Murphy."

"Yes, I'm Jack Murphy," he said as he studied the old man.

"How are you keeping?" the man asked him.

"Oh, fine. Just fine. It was a very nice trip. The water was calm most of the way. That is, until we reached the Irish coast."

The man gave him a nod and an understanding look. "Aye, it can be stormy in late winter. This way, Mr. Murphy."

"And what is your name?" Jack asked.

"O'Sullivan, sir. Jim O'Sullivan. Tell me, are ye on holiday, then? Is it business or pleasure brings ye here?"

O'Sullivan had noticed over the years that most Americans answer more than they are asked. Jack proved to be no exception.

"I'm here on business, though my business is always a pleasure. I am a writer. I've had two books published, with modest success. But they did well enough that the publisher gave me another three-book contract. And I wanted the next book to be set in Ireland, so here I am."

"Ah, what do ye know about that?" exclaimed O'Sullivan, his wise old eyes lighting up at the prospect of a good story. "A writer! Well, you've come to the right place, lad. This is the land of writers, you know. Swift! Yeats! Wilde, Joyce and Shaw, to mention a few."

Jack watched him as he warmed to the subject. He could not place O'Sullivan's age, although he guessed he was a good deal older than himself. The man walked with a pronounced limp, which made him seem somewhat more elderly despite his healthy appearance.

As the two men went about getting acquainted, Jack learned that O'Sullivan had been a fisherman as a young man. When he was thirty-five, his boat had been driven up against the rocks during a storm off the coast of Dingle. One of the fishermen in the boat had been killed, and another had suffered disabling injuries. O'Sullivan was lucky. He he was able to recover and get about eventually, but the accident ended his fishing days. Now he could only recall the rhythm of the water and the ways of the boats and the fish, and tell the tourists some of his tales of the seafaring life.

Jack's rental car, a small, black Toyota sedan, was just across the street. O'Sullivan placed the luggage in the trunk and motioned Jack to get in the car.

"The other side, sir," the old man said with a wry grin. Of course, Jack thought. The driver's side is on the right in Ireland. He felt a little foolish as he climbed into the car.

"The office is just around the corner, sir. We'll fill out the paperwork and you'll be on your way."

"How far is County Kerry?" Jack inquired.

"Depends."

"Depends on what?"

"Where it is you are going in Kerry. County Kerry is a big area."

"I have a meeting this afternoon in Kenmare," Jack told him.

"Well, then. You should be getting to Kenmare just around lunch time, I should guess."

With that admonition in mind, Jack set forth into the Irish countryside. He was filled with eagerness and just a little apprehension, for he knew that a great deal of beauty and a few surprises lay in store. What he could not know is that he would be changed forever.

Ireland!

This is the island of roaring water, magical castles, immense in antiquity and the weight of time. A land ancient in all respects, wild in its myths and its daily joys and sorrows. A nation of small farmers and fishermen keeping to the old ways. And many, by their very steadfastness, having a hard time surviving in this modern age.

As Jack continued to drive, he thought with pleasure of the coming of Spring, celebrated on February first with St. Brighid's Day, in honor of a Celtic goddess of poetry and learning. Spring does not rush in on Ireland. It comes very gradually, a slight shift from winter rain to spring rain. It rains almost any time of year, for that matter. Perhaps Jack, like so many before him, would never have come to Ireland at all if he could have heard a long range weather forecast.

Ah, but summer always arrives with a smile, and in summer Ireland is miraculous. It is filled with the colors of festivals and picnics and fairs, with regattas and horse racing, with sports such as football and hurling and golf—and, most of all, courting!

Jack watched the unfolding scene before him. Every story that had been told to Jack by his Irish grandfather, all the books he had read and the visions he had stored up about Ireland took hold of his mind now.

The quality of his memory need not be challenged, for he was here at last, driving through the open countryside. Imagination became reality. In his mind, he was traveling on a cultural fault line, with Ireland and Europe on one side and North America on the other.

This parade of vivid sounds, smells, colors, shapes, and stories blazed a trail through his being, tumbling together in a kaleidoscope of impressions. The central lowlands, heavily cloaked in woods. A warren of small roads and old churches, monasteries and manor houses. The great open spaces of The Curragh with its deep green pasture lands and its hedge-lined roads. Scattered small villages, their stone dwellings watched over by some isolated ruin. The River Shannon, the Blasket Islands and the Aran Islands, the great Cork Harbour, and mighty Bantry Bay. St. Patrick. The broad and beautiful Kenmare River, the lakes of Killarney, the coast of Dingle. The vast southland of County Mayo with its untamed woodlands and bogs.

Suddenly, a sharp memory of his young manhood came to him. He tried to evoke it clearly, for here it was before him, all the promise and freshness of unspent youth in these utterly familiar and common things of Ireland. Everything fit together into an indelible whole. The look of an old stone wall, the boom of the ocean, the distant click of a train. The low sounds of a muddy Irish stream, the bellow of a cow, the slow clopping of a nearby horse. He was only just arrived, yet he realized that he knew it by heart.

Jack inhaled deeply, feeling as if he were coming home in a way. He wondered if he might be a descendant of the Druids, those men of passion whose stories preserved the history and the customs of the place. In another, ancient lifetime, maybe he had been a "file," who was expected to recite at least three hundred and fifty tales. If he were, then perhaps in his present incarnation he would find fame and fortune like Finn, who slew a giant by the Sionna, which was the early name for the River Shannon.

These observations crowded Jack's mind as he made his way along the unfamiliar route. He was not yet adept at driving on the left side of the road, so he was not making very good time on the highway. He was a bit worried about being late for his meeting. But, this is Ireland, he thought. They won't mind.

At length, the rain stopped and a sunbeam came dancing down the road. This made Jack feel better. Now he could pick up the time a little as he drove through the Golden Vale. A bit west of Cork, the land became rocky. The wild countryside alternated with farmland, thick undergrowth, forests and lakes. Here is where villages keep alive the Irish culture, and where many first time visitors may lose their way because the signs and signposts are in Old Irish.

Just south of Macroom was a signpost that read "Site of Ambush." It was the spot where the Irish hero Michael Collins had been shot dead in 1922. Jack was tempted to stop and look around, but he was watching the time. Perhaps he would return for a visit once he settled in, and see how this place might fit into his grand vision of Ireland.

Kenmare was exactly as it had been described to him. Its two main streets were several blocks long, with a park and a magnificent church at one end of town, and many small shops, pubs and restaurants. There were no parking meters and no signs as to how long one could stay. Jack took the first parking space he came to, and went looking for The Bank of Ireland. It couldn't be far.

Jack Murphy had always had a way of making what he was doing, or was about to do, seem much more important than it was, though it would be difficult for anyone to uncover the reason. As it happened, this day was to be of vital importance to him, as he would soon begin to discover. Just now, he strode purposefully toward the center of town. Kenmare felt good to him.

Suddenly, it felt even better as he noticed a stunningly beautiful young woman standing and looking into a store window. Jack felt as if an Irish myth had come to life right before him. Her hair was a pale, clear shade of red. It tumbled to her shoulders with highlights of golden amber and depths of smoky brown playing hide and seek with the sunlight. The young woman turned from the shop window and looked up at him with a lively yet serene expression. She had dazzling green eyes. Gracious, charming Irish eyes.

Her lovely presence caused Jack Murphy to take stock of himself before he spoke to her. He felt that it was important to present himself in a favorable light. He was acutely conscious of how he was dressed, and whether or not his hair was combed, and if he had a pleasing look about him. Not that he was worried, for his sister had always said that he knew he was a good looking man, and that he looked much younger than his forty-six years. Having played sports as a kid, and never having been one to put down a lot of sweets and fatty foods, Jack was in pretty good shape. There was not a trace of gray in his thick, dark hair. His clear blue eyes and high cheekbones lent him a star quality, though his personality was anything but theatrical.

His soft spoken manner gained him respect from people who didn't even know him. Women simply liked him. Strangers were apt to treat him as someone important, someone whose name and rank escaped them for the moment, but whose presence made them take notice. Most people would tell Jack that they felt as if they had met him before.

Now the young woman standing before him was looking at him in the same way, as if she were trying to place him.

"Pardon me, miss," Jack said, raising his hand as he spoke.

"Yes, sir," she smiled a small smile.

"Can you direct me to the Bank of Ireland?"

"I can, yes. It is just there, around the corner about one half block. However, it is closed until two o'clock."

Jack wanted to continue to talk with her, to look at her, but he could sense that she was on her way someplace. He had read somewhere that when the Irish are asked directions, they tend to go to extremes to be certain that you know exactly where you are going. Oftentimes they will take you to your destination in person.

This day was an exception to that rule. The young lady was not rude, just matter-of-fact and to the point. She turned to walk away. Jack called to her, hoping to delay her going. "I'm sorry to bother you again, but where is the best place in town to get good pub grub?"

"They are all good. It would be hard to say which is the best."

"Well, is there a pub near the bank?"

She gave a little laugh. "There is one, yes. It is just next door." She smiled again and turned and walked away. Jack watched after her until she was out of his sight, wondering if she could possibly be interested in someone his age.

Then he made his way down the street and found the Bank of Ireland. Sure enough, there was a pub right next door. He saw the sign and a small shiver of delight ran through him. "Murphy's Pub," Jack said out loud. "Murphy's Pub!"

He walked over and glanced in the doorway. The pub looked as though the noon rush had just ended. It was nearly empty, but the room was filled with smoke, and glasses were still sitting about on the tables. Jack entered and found a place to his liking in the corner. It was a small table with low, stool-like chairs without backs. A young girl approached.

"Good afternoon, sir. What would you be having?"

"Good afternoon," Jack replied. "Can I get a Guinness?"

"You can, of course. Would that be a pint?"

"Er, yes. A pint would be fine."

He took in the dark walls and the musty flavor of tobacco. If this pub could speak, he thought, it could tell many tales. It had been there a long time, and was not a touristy kind of place. He was to learn that this pub was just one of many throughout Ireland, all of them frequented by the locals, all with very much the same atmosphere.

The young girl returned with a glass in hand.

"Now. Your Guinness, sir. Would there be anything else?"

"No, thank you."

Jack looked down at the chocolate-like liquid moving like molten lava in his glass. The beer was alive. He waited a minute and then took his first sip of Guinness. It was different than any other brew he had ever tasted.

It put him in a thoughtful mood. He considered his destiny that had led him from Miami to Kenmare, thus to encounter a stunning woman who had directed him to Murphy's Pub. That chance meeting gave him a kind of hope that he had not allowed himself for many years.

The women Jack had been associated with in the past were not the type to embrace life and love each minute of it. Rather, they seemed to escape from it. Now, seeing the village of Kenmare and meeting such a self-possessed beauty, he allowed himself to dream. He smiled inwardly, sensing that a significant journey was beginning. It would turn out to have a far greater impact than he could have predicted.

Jack felt his destiny all around him. The sounds of Kenmare fell familiarly on his ear. He looked at the massive stones carved by the weather, and thought of the River Shannon coursing through the heart of Ireland and emptying into the ever-changing sea. He could sense the million moments to come in his life. He could feel the lures and sense the pitfalls.

He was willing to unravel and repair the fabric of lost time, of the years before he had come to this place. He was more than ready to accept the living light that Ireland was offering him now.

He took another long swallow and set his glass down. Looking deep into the umber colored drink, he considered the workings of fate that had brought him from his crowded, fast-paced existence in America to this pristine Irish village.

His memory ran back down the years to a time far removed, to a love that had marked his early life. His mind returned inevitably to Helen. A vision of her began to fill his being, until she was all that he could think about.

Chapter Two

Texas, early 1960's

"Come on, Jack! Get dressed. I'm taking you to the best damn country nightclub in Texas." Sam Bennett took Jack by the arm and motioned for him to get up.

"Okay, okay, Sam," answered Jack. "I'm coming."

Sam Bennett had been Jack's roommate for just one week, since his arrival at the military base in Victoria, Texas. Jack considered Sam an all right kind of a guy, tall and towheaded and good looking. A little spoiled, maybe, coming from Texas oil money and oil patch society. It made for some pretty unsophisticated attitudes, even considering that times were simpler then, and they were, after all, just kids.

Sam always told Jack that the best way to pick up women was first to be totally rude to them, and put them down even to the point of tears. Once Sam had told a waitress that she had the biggest feet he had ever seen on a girl, and wondered how any guy could ever want to take her out. Sam did, of course, take her out. Then he came back to the base and bragged about getting her into bed. That was what guys in the service talked about—drinking, gambling, fighting, and getting women into bed. That was what it was like.

Jack Murphy, young as the rest and no more worldly wise, was different even then. His mother always said that her boy was not the kind to go out and look for trouble. In a certain way, he was a man already, and his interest in women ran deeper than trophy hunting.

"We'll find us one tonight, Jack, ol' boy. And, like the song goes, don't expect too much at three in the morning." Sam laughed, lit a Camel and offered one to Jack, who waved it away. "I'm gonna stop smoking one of these days," he laughed again, "that is, when I die."

The first thing Sam did when they got into his car, a new Chevy his folks had given him, was turn on the radio. A George Jones song was playing and Sam started to sing along. He knew every word by heart.

Jack watched what little scenery there was. "There's your Texas," Sam slapped Jack on the shoulder. "I know some parts don't look too pretty, but don't let that fool you. We've got the most beautiful women in the world. You know what they say about Texas? It's a bad place to live and a good place to die, and if you don't like Hank, you ain't shit."

The sun had set by now, leaving just a dim glow in the sky. A Texas-sized billboard on the side of the highway proclaimed: "Spurs! The Best Damn Country Nightclub In Texas! Two miles." Sam turned off and sped down the narrow, winding road. He pulled into the parking lot and jumped out of the car, all the while shouting to Jack to hurry up.

Jack expected very little from the evening at hand. Probably a tiny, run-down nightclub with pool tables, a jukebox, and a smoky roomful of drunks and wild Texas cowboys. He was surprised to find a barn of a place, bright and lively and even interesting. They entered and found a table by the dance floor.

"Make it two long neck Falstaffs," Sam said to the young waitress in tight jeans and a low cut pullover blouse. She was, as they said hereabouts, stacked.

"Wow," breathed Sam. "Would you just look at that? What I wouldn't give for an hour in bed with her."

"More like ten minutes," Jack replied genially. Sam gave no sign of having heard him.

There was a pretty good hillbilly band, and it was playing a Texas two-step. Sam picked up some girl at the bar and danced away with her. Jack looked over at the floor, filled on a Saturday night with kids from the military base, local cowboys, and especially those famous small town Texas girls. They kept themselves up so well that even the plain ones came off looking just fine.

A tall cowboy danced by, wearing jeans and boots, a black Stetson, and the largest gold belt buckle Jack had ever seen. He was probably a rodeo star. He did not seem to be having a very good time. It looked like an argument was going on. Jack waited for him to turn with his partner so he could get a look at her.

That was the first time he ever saw Helen. Helen in the bright red dress. Helen with her blond hair falling over her shoulders. Her long legs and statuesque figure made her look taller than she was. She was obviously upset, yet she danced with spellbinding grace.

The cowboy snapped a couple of cuss words, let go of Helen and bolted off the dance floor. A moment later he was out the door and in his pickup truck. Jack could hear the gravel flying and the tires squealing as he raced out of the parking lot and hit the paved road. Helen ran after him, just to the door, and stood watching him go. Another girl approached and gave Helen a sisterly hug.

Jack felt like he was in an old movie in slow motion. Through the smoke of the nightclub, he saw the action but couldn't hear the words. If he had ever felt the urge to get up and go ask anyone to dance, or to have a drink, or just to talk, this was it. But, of course, he didn't. She was still upset, and he had a certain sensitivity to such feelings. So he just kept looking at her. After a few minutes, she calmed down and went with her friend to their table. As the dancers went by, Jack could catch a blimpse of her glowing blond hair now and then.

The song ended. Sam stayed on the dance floor talking and laughing with the girl he had found. Now Jack could see Helen clearly. She sat with such poise, moving ever so slowly, seeming relieved that the fight was over and the cowboy was gone. The music started again, and the dance floor began to fill up. Again, Jack caught a glimpse of her between the couples moving by.

The waitress asked Jack if he wanted another beer. "Sure, bring us two more. By the way, do you know that girl sitting over there in the red dress? The blond girl?"

The waitress looked past the crowded dance floor. Then smiled and said, "Oh, yes, that's Helen. All the guys ask me about Helen. She's here every Saturday night. Sometimes with her boyfriend Chuck, but when they're fighting she comes alone. It seems to me that she comes alone more often than not, lately. Must be going through something. Know what I mean?" She laughed at her own cleverness.

"What's her last name—where does she live?" Jack asked in a single question.

"Well, honey, her last name is Baker. Helen Baker. She lives about ten miles up the road. A real country girl."

"Has she lived here a long time?"

"Not really. Not by local standards, anyway. Her Pa works cattle for this big rancher. They live in a small house out on the ranch, not much of a place. The last family to live there moved to Austin about four or five years ago. So I guess Helen has lived here for about that long. There's nothing else out there but a bunch of damned cows and another old ranch house for the guy that bought the place when the last of the Campbells died. He's rich, lives back in Dallas, never comes around much. Don't even know his name."

The waitress turned to walk away. "Miss, one more question. Are Helen and this guy Chuck engaged, or anything like that?"

"Lord, no, honey. Who in their right mind would marry that asshole?" The waitress turned again and moved to the next table, calling out as she left, "Back in a minute with those two Falstaffs."

Helen was still sitting at the table with her friend. Every few minutes or so, she looked up and shook her head with a polite smile at someone asking her to dance. Jack was dying to go and ask her to dance with him, but he was certain that she would say no to him as well. Besides, he was not a very good dancer to begin with, and certainly was not a two-stepping cowboy. He had been in Texas a grand total of eight days, counting the bus ride from Houston.

The waitress returned with the two beers. At the same moment, Jack saw two patrol cars with flashing red lights in front of the door of the club. The county sheriff got out with his deputies and stopped to talk with someone in the parking lot, then came in the door.

The music stopped. Everyone stood on the dance floor, some still clinging to each other. A few milled around, walked toward the door or returned to their tables. After a moment, the officers approached Helen's table, spoke to her briefly, then took her to one of the cars and drove away. The place buzzed for awhile, then the music started up again. Everything went back to normal, as if halftime were over and the football game had started again.

Sam came back to the table. "Damn," he called out to Jack as soon as he was in earshot. "Did you hear what happened?" Jack actually wanted very much to hear what happened. Sam plopped down at the table, grabbed his beer, and raised it to say thanks to Jack for buying it. "That girl's boyfriend," he began. "The girl in the red dress, that he was dancing with. He hit a telephone pole about a mile or so down the road. Killed him on the spot."

Jack could not speak for a minute. Finally, he gasped, "What?"

"Yeah. Killed him dead." Sam was almost smiling as he spoke.

Jack jumped up from the table and walked toward the bar. He found his waitress, the talkative one, and asked her what had happened. Just as Sam had reported, Helen's boyfriend, Chuck, had been driving at a very high rate of speed. Evidently, he had lost control of his pickup and hit the power pole with enough force to total the truck. The police reported that he had died on impact, and they had come to take Helen into town to identify him.

Something moved Jack to press the waitress for information. He had to find out where Helen lived, and he had to go see her. "Tell me," he asked, not hiding his concern. "Where does Helen live, exactly?"

"Boy, honey, you are hung up on this gal. Well, if you must know, you go back to the main highway and turn left. Drive seven or eight miles and you'll see a 'Texas Ford' billboard. Right past that is a dirt road. Turn in there and drive two miles or so and you'll see an old farmhouse, no paint on it. That's it."

"Thanks," Jack smiled at her, grateful that she understood. "Thanks a lot."

Tomorrow was Sunday. Jack was off work. He could borrow Sam's car and drive out to Helen's house. That was what he was going to do.

Chapter Three

"Now. Would you be wanting another pint of Guinness, sir?"

Jack brought himself back to the present, to Ireland, from where his mind had taken him to another place, another time long, long ago. He glanced at his watch and then smiled up at the waitress.

"No, not a thing. Thank you."

"That would be two pounds, sir, for the pint." Jack sat waiting for his change and reflected on his arrival in Ireland and his drive to Kenmare. Most of all, he thought of the lovely lady who had directed him to Murphy's pub. He took the last sip of his Guinness, warm by now. He saw several Guinness posters around the pub. One said, "Guinness For Strength," and another, "Guinness Is Good For You."

Behind the bar he noticed many brands of whisky which he had never heard of before, except for Jameson and Bushmill, which he had seen many times in America. Two men were sitting at the bar, cracking British jokes and laughing uproariously. Jack noticed that they would take a sip of Guinness and then chase it with Irish whisky.

The waitress returned. "Now. Your change, sir." Jack thanked her, looked at his watch again, left a tip on the table and headed out the door. It was just after two. He turned in to the Bank of Ireland, feeling relaxed after the beer. He was surprised and delighted to see, sitting at a desk just inside the bank, the very lass who had directed him there a short while earlier. The nameplate on the desk read "Shannon Kelly."

For a moment, Jack was struck with a sense of déjà vu. He had just been remembering how he felt the first time he saw Helen, and here was the same impression, the same intensity that he had not experienced in all the years since. He was just a little unnerved, but he pulled himself together and walked toward her desk.

"Well, hello again. Remember me? I was the person who asked you for directions earlier today."

Shannon smiled. "I do, yes. I recall that you also wanted the best pub in Kenmare."

"Yes. And it is a good one, the one you told me was just next door. Would you believe, Murphy's Pub. That's my name, Jack Murphy."

Again she smiled, acknowledging the coincidence. Then, in a professional manner, she replied, "Very nice, sir. Now. How can I help you?"

Jack felt vaguely disappointed to be on the subject of bank business so quickly. He expected a more sociable interlude, and he wished she would not call him "sir." However, he kept it to himself and smiled back at her. My God, how utterly beautiful she was—even more than he had realized when he met her on the street.

He noticed that she was waiting. "I have an appointment with Mr. Clark," he finally said. Shannon picked up the phone and rang Mr. Clark's office. In a few moments, the banker came out to greet Jack and escort him into his office. Jack had already arranged by mail to set up an account and make a rather large deposit. He planned to use the account to get a small house in the area.

Now, in the banker's office, Jack was having a great deal of trouble keeping his thoughts on the business at hand. He kept shifting in his chair and glancing out the large window toward Shannon's desk on the main floor of the bank. Somehow, Jack thought, I must get to know this lady. I must ask her to dinner tonight, he continued to himself. I must, he thought again.

Business concluded, Jack thanked Mr. Clark and started toward the front of the bank. Shannon was not at her desk. Jack panicked briefly, then stopped at a teller window to exchange his American money for punts. And, not incidentally, to ask the teller where he might find Shannon.

"Oh, she left early today," the teller replied.

Damn, he thought to himself.

Jack collected his money and left the bank. Just outside the doorway he stopped, as if he didn't know what to do next. He turned and headed for the nearest door, into his namesake pub. He was absorbed with this beautiful girl, this Shannon Kelly. He found a table and ordered a pint of Guinness and a whisky chaser.

He took a long swallow. Then, as a scene unfolds after the intermission in a half-remembered play, his thoughts took him back in time once again. From thinking about the young woman he had just met, he drifted as in a waking dream to the girl he had known in another lifetime, in a faraway country called Texas.

Chapter Four

Texas, early 1960's

It was a beautiful Texas morning, and the shadows were getting shorter as the day opened onto noon. Sunday morning traffic was light. Jack felt great driving his friend's stylish Chevy. He glanced up ahead and saw the big red billboard, "Texas Ford, Home Of The Best Deals In Pickups and Sedans." Just as the waitress had described, there was the dirt road. He turned in and headed past the fields. He could feel his heart thumping.

Jack had made certain to look his very best. He wore clean, freshly pressed pants and a yellow pullover shirt. His hair was combed and his shoes were polished. He felt ten feet tall in Sam's shiny new car. Off to his left he could see the old farmhouse as he expected. He pulled in, stopped the car and got out, and opened the gate onto a bare yard. He was greeted by a small black dog, barking energetically.

"Come, boy. Come." Jack put his hand down toward the ground. The dog stopped barking and came closer so that Jack could rub under his chin. Pretty soon the dog's tail was wagging, and he and Jack were old friends. A woman came out the screen door and onto the porch, stopped for a moment, then came slowly down the front steps.

"What can I do for ya?" she asked, sizing him up, not unfriendly but not rolling out the red carpet, either.

"Good morning, ma'am. My name is Jack Murphy, and I was wondering if I could speak to Helen."

"Well, I don't think so..." the woman's voice trailed off as she turned to glance back toward the door.

She appeared much older than Jack figured she really was, as if she could be Helen's grandmother. But he felt sure that she was her mother, so he asked, politely, "Are you Helen's mother?"

"Yes, I am, I reckon."

"Well, Mrs. Baker, if you don't mind, I would just like to tell Helen how sorry I am to hear the news about Chuck." The woman started to speak when Helen appeared, standing half in and half out of the screen door.

"What is it, mama?" she called out.

"It's a friend of yours, or Chuck's, who wants to see you."

"It's okay, mama. Go on in." She held the door for her mother, then came out into the sun. "Hello. Do I know you?"

"Well, no, not really," Jack admitted. "I was at Spurs the night of the accident. Last night."

"Are you a friend of Chuck's?"

"Well, no. I just felt so bad for you last night, when I found out what had happened, that I wanted to come and meet you and tell you so."

"I never heard of anybody doing anything like this before," Helen said in a long, flat Texas drawl, softened only slightly by the sweet quality of her voice. "I think it's awfully nice of you to drive all this way just to tell me something like that."

Jack smiled, relieved that she accepted his sympathy but somewhat taken aback by her manner of speaking. She moved like a legend, but she sounded like all the local girls. The two traits did not seem to go together. But charming she was.

Helen was even more attractive to Jack without her Saturday night makeup and her fancy red dress. Today her dress was plain blue cotton, cut straight, rather tight fitting through the middle, with a white collar off the shoulders. The sun picked up the outline of her shapely legs through the light fabric. "Come on up and have a seat," she motioned as she spoke.

The two of them sat down in an old swing. They did not speak for what seemed to Jack like a long time. Finally he said, "When is the funeral?" Then he paused. "I'm sure you're going—?"

"No," said Helen firmly. "I can't stand funerals. I'm afraid if I go to a funeral, then I'll be the next one."

Jack just looked at her.

She went on with her explanation. "I had this dream once. A dream where I went to a funeral and the next day I fell off this high cliff into the ocean and...that was it. It was all over. I was dead." She paused again and looked at him, seeming perfectly confident that he understood what she was saying. "I have never forgotten that dream, and I know that I could never go to a funeral."

Jack did not reply. He knew intuitively that she was getting into an area that seemed dark and strange to him. He decided to offer to take her for a drive. With total confidence he suggested that they get in the Chevy and go into town for an ice cream or a cup of coffee. It would make her feel better to get out of the house for awhile, he said, and Helen agreed.

This was Jack's first date with Helen. He would remember it always, the sun on her hair, her easy conversation, the things she told him. Some of them were a little surprising coming from a pretty girl. They talked and laughed, talked some more, walked through the park eating ice cream.

Jack learned that Helen had not been all that crazy about Chuck. She had even considered breaking it off with him, but never did. Sure, he was childish and moody, she said, but in some ways she had liked him. Chuck had gotten her off the "dirt road," as she called the ranch. He had given her a chance to go out to the movies, or dancing.

Helen had never had much, and in fact was considered by Texas standards to be dirt poor. But, as she told Jack, she had her dreams and held onto them with all her being, despite a deep premonition that they would never come true. Her mother had confided her own regrets and mistakes, and always told her she wanted more for her daughter.

Helen felt real good about Jack taking an interest in her, as if a small portion of her dream were coming true. She felt lucky for this chance to make a new friend and to get acquainted with someone like Jack. She had never known a young man who treated her so courteously. Who, if he wanted to grab her like the rest of them did, certainly kept it to himself and put her at ease. He was a gentleman, even if he was only in his early twenties.

Helen had never been one to go off with just anyone who came along. Even Chuck, the local rodeo star, had been an achiever of sorts. Helen was choosier in that way than any of her school friends, and her taste and bearing underscored her determination to rise above her surroundings. Deep inside herself, safe from mockery and disappointment, she was a queen. A gorgeous, tragic queen.

Jack had a very pleasant time with Helen that afternoon. She seemed comfortable with him. She knew she had the same effect on him that she had on everyone else. But she also saw that he was a reliable young man with his own sense of who he was. He seemed to have some imagination, and was not easily put off by her odd combination of worldly thoughts and country manners.

Now, as they pulled up to the front of her house and got out, Jack's mind was reeling from the glorious day. As if to top it off, Helen reached over and kissed his cheek. "Thanks for a great afternoon," she said with a smile. "This has been one of the best ever."

Jack felt that he should respond in some way, perhaps return her kiss or give her a hug. Instead, he just stood by the car looking at her.

"What is it?" Helen asked as she pushed her shining golden hair back from her face.

"Oh, nothing. I was just thinking how beautiful you are." Helen blushed a little, and looked at the ground.

In that late afternoon, in the unforgiving climate of south Texas, in the middle of the twentieth century, Jack had a deep sense of possibility. Overhead a flock of birds filled the air with high, staccato murmurs as they flew against a gathering sunset. A hint of autumn ruffled the clouds. Cattle made plaintive sounds in the distance. He took Helen's arm and walked with her toward the front gate. They moved slowly, as if to draw out every moment of this day together.

"Helen, I want to see you again." Immediately, she smiled. Rising on tiptoe, she kissed Jack quickly on the lips, then walked up to the porch. For both of them, it was a beginning, though they did not know it then. It was the calm before the storm, the doorway opening onto one of the most turbulent periods either of them had ever known in their young lives.

Chapter Five

Murphy's Pub was beginning to fill up with the early afternoon local crowd. Jack finished his second pint of Guinness and drifted back to the present. He could not understand why he had been thinking of Helen so much since arriving in Kenmare. He asked himself what was the connection between that long lost love, now turned to dust, and today's brief encounter with a young woman named Shannon.

She was so different from Helen, who had been a real Texas girl. Shannon was elegant and reserved. She sparkled with mysterious depths like this land, this Emerald Isle, this Ireland. Nothing about the two women was alike, and yet his feelings upon meeting each of them bore an uncanny resemblance. He could not help feeling a little bit afraid.

Jack seldom allowed himself to probe too deeply into his own feelings, but here in Murphy's Pub, now into his third pint of Guinness, it seemed safe at last to do so. Here, feelings were respected, even transformed into poetry. Here, he could think on a deeper level, with no one to elbow his ribs in false conviviality.

He considered that perhaps there had always been an inherent desire for a more tender relationship, a warmer woman in his life. In his early manhood he had thought it possible, but it had turned out to be a bubble of illusion that burst and left him empty. Had he built an armor around himself for so many years that now it was nearly impossible to let anyone in?

Had he not unconsciously picked superficial women who would not challenge his fortress? Had he ever singled out a truly gentle lady, one with whom he could have built a quality life?

He realized that he had been living under a self-imposed indictment of guilt, one he had not earned by anything he did or failed to do. His one crime had been youthful inexperience. He could not go back and change anything that had happened as a result of that, and his regret consumed him. A common reaction, surely, but it had bound him up in desperation for many years. He had had women in his life simply in order to avoid being alone, but always there was a grim refusal to lower his shield.

Today, seeing Shannon on the streets of Kenmare and later in the bank, something had stirred within him. For the first time since the carefree days with Helen, he felt his weighted spirit begin to lift. He began to sense a change of fortune brewing in his life. He sincerely begged the powers that be that the fire under the cauldron would not go out.

Jack, old boy, he said to himself, you had better keep that thought, for it has been a long time coming. You had also better turn in. It's been a big day.

He paid his tab and began rummaging in his pocket for his itinerary and reservations. The address of his hotel indicated that it was just at the end of that very street, so he set out to find it. As he walked along, his thoughts returned to Shannon. If only he could have asked her out to dinner, could have begun getting better acquainted with her at once. He felt like a schoolboy. It was puppy love all over again, vivid and real, something he had not experienced for decades. He desperately wanted to see Shannon, to visit with her.

But this evening, it was not to be. This evening he would check into his hotel, get a good night's rest, and start adjusting to the change in time from America to Ireland. He had read somewhere that it takes one day for each hour of time change. True, he had taken a boat from London to Ireland, but that was merely the last leg of a long trip, a gentle way to approach this mythical land. Before that, he had flown over the ocean into the rising sun and gotten a half day ahead. That meant his internal clock would not be on Irish time for at least a week, even allowing for the soothing effect of a few pints of Guinness.

He was here to write his next book, but there was no rush to start. First, he needed to secure his living quarters, then stock up on food and supplies. Then he could get into the rhythms and the ways of the Irish countryside and people he was going to write about.

Perhaps Shannon would help him locate a place, or at least show him the area. He caught himself up short. Was this something that truly could come about? He knew his tendency to spin daydreams, the more improbable the better. This is different, he told himself firmly. I know I am going to get to know Shannon. I will, he said under his breath.

The following morning, Jack pulled the drapes back from his hotel window to be greeted by a glorious early morning mist. It had stopped raining and the sun was beginning to break through the fog, turning it to a fine golden glow that picked out the shapes of people going about their daily work. It was going to be what they call in Ireland "a bright day." His thoughts immediately turned to Shannon, wondering if she, too, were on her way to work at the bank today. He wondered if she might have lunch with him, or dinner, or if she would even consider such a thing with a total stranger. Maybe she was engaged or something. Of course not, Jack told himself. Shannon was going to be his, was his already. Period. He was not being rational. He knew that. And he didn't care.

He got dressed, walked over to the bank, and looked into the window to see Shannon sitting at her desk. Some inner vision just then, some insight past understanding, gave him a clear look at the hidden meaning of this girl. She was more than lovely. She was beyond ordinary. She was magical. Shannon was not just Irish, she was Ireland itself.

His thoughts became lyrical. As the rain in spring is unpredictable, he mused, so is Shannon. As the golden yellow and orange of buttercups herald the summer, so do Shannon's vivid curls promise warmth and laughter. The golden Irish spurge and St. Patrick's cabbage and brilliant violets and small lacy flowers cling to the rocks and run along the ground for all to enjoy. All this is County Kerry. All this is Shannon.

Jack stood without moving for a few minutes, letting his thoughts wash over him, letting the images and words flow along in his mind and assume their own shapes and directions. This was more than the writer within him, feeling his way along into a new story. This was something else entirely. This was Ireland itself taking hold of him in the person of Shannon. This was Ireland pouring its literary soul into his veins, taking him over, carrying him to unknown places of bleak magic and heightened realities.

All this Jack realized in an instant, and in an instant more it was gone. He straightened up, took a deep breath, walked into the bank and approached the desk as Shannon looked up to greet him with a smile.

"Good morning," he fairly sang out. Steady, now, he reminded himself. She'll notice.

"Good morning, Mr. Murphy. And how are you keeping?"

"I'm keeping well, thank you." Jack had learned the typical Irish greeting.

He felt it was time. Right now. Say it. He asked her to help him locate living space and to show him the area. To his surprise she agreed to do so with no hesitation. She had already been asked by her boss, Mr. Clark, to be of service to their new customer. Being unaware of this, however, Jack felt that she welcomed the idea, even wanted the opportunity. So a date was set for the day after tomorrow, which would be a Saturday, which meant that Shannon would be off work. He was inwardly delirious at this whole turn of events. Could he make it until Saturday? Whatever would he do in the meantime?

It was agreed that he should come to her house, for he should meet her parents and visit with them before taking her out—even though she would tell them that this was bank duty, to show a new client the area and help him get settled in. It was better to handle it this way, she told him.

Inside herself, Shannon was looking forward to the outing. She had not met anyone interesting since she had broken her engagement with Bruce six months before. Somehow, the idea of becoming an ordinary housewife on a small farm fifteen miles outside of Kenmare just did not sit well with her. There had been a time in her life when she felt that that was exactly what she wanted, or was supposed to want. But as she grew into adulthood, she realized that she wanted more. She had seen enough poverty and hard times in her own family, and to marry into the same thing scared her. She did not want to watch her dreams turn to ashes.

None of this was Bruce's fault, she realized. He was honest, hardworking, and a man who loved all things. Shannon knew he would always try his best for her, but it was just not enough. So she had broken it off, to the surprise of all Kenmare.

Her family had taken it the hardest, for her mother and father liked Bruce and wanted Shannon to marry him and settle in County Kerry. Now they feared that she might one day move to Dublin or, God forbid, London. With her banking knowledge and her outstanding abilities, she could get herself a quality position just about anywhere. Her mother, especially, knew this. She was wary of any man who threatened to take her beautiful daughter away from Kenmare.

Shannon's father was a farmer, though he did not want to be. He had always loved the sea, even as a boy, and had wanted to join the Navy and see the world. Instead, he had tilled the rocky Irish soil and made a meager living for his family.

Meeting him, Jack thought of his own life in past years. He, too, had felt that life was passing him by, but in a different way. Despite the writing, the adventures, the serious times, there was an inward sense of missing something. Now he felt the gates opening. Was he leaving an old life behind and entering a new one?

He observed Shannon's parents and reflected on his past even as brief introductions were made. He was careful to give the impression that he was with Shannon for business reasons only, and that seemed to go well with them. They said goodbye and Jack drove down the highway in the direction Shannon indicated, glancing at her as she watched for landmarks.

"Go to the end of that road and turn right," she motioned with her hand as she spoke. "About a mile farther is a very nice farm. A wonderful man and his wife live and work there. I would like for you to meet Mr. and Mrs. Mullins and look at the cottage on their land. As late as last week it was for let. It has only one bedroom, but a nice big kitchen and living area. There are two fireplaces, one in the main room downstairs and one in the bedroom, which is just overhead."

"It sounds perfect. I hope it is still for rent."

"I would guess that it is," replied Shannon. "News travels fast in Kenmare, and we haven't heard a word at the bank about anyone moving in."

"How long have you been with the bank?" he asked, looking at her.

Keeping her eyes on the road, she answered, "I've been at this position here in Kenmare for about three years. I was the Assistant Bank Manager in Limerick. Then, when my mother became very ill, I asked for a transfer to Kenmare. I had to take a lower position at the bank here, but I was able to be with her and see her through."

Jack nodded appreciatively. "How did you get into banking?"

"I didn't even want to, not at first. I wanted to study history, for it's Ireland I love more than the business of money. But banking is more practical and I've grown used to it." Then, changing the subject, she asked, "What kind of books do you write?"

"Novels, fiction, literary work if I can call it that. My first book was set in America, in the deep South just after the War Between the States."

"Is that where you are from?"

"Yes. I'm a Southern gentleman. I was born in a small town in North Carolina."

"You don't seem to have a Southern accent," Shannon observed.

"That's because our family moved to Florida when I was young," he explained. "Florida is a mixed bag of people from all over America. You don't get those slow Southern drawls you hear in other parts of the South."

Jack lowered the window a little and glanced out, relishing the sounds and smells that came in on the breeze. A man and his dog were standing by the roadside with several large cans of milk, waiting for the milk truck to pick them up. The dog barked at their car as they passed.

Shannon motioned again to turn in at the next lane. Jack looked at the house that lay ahead and saw a woman in an apron sweeping the front steps clean. "Mrs. Mullins, how are you keeping?" Shannon called out as they came to a stop. She got out and Jack followed.

Mrs. Mullins gave her a big hug. "'Tis my darling little Shannon. And who might this be?" she asked, looking over at Jack.

"Mrs. Mullins, this is Jack Murphy. He's from America, and he'd like to inquire about your cottage. Would it still be for let?"

"It is, yes," she greeted Jack with a smile. Taking Shannon by the hand, she added, "I looked after this little lady since she was a child. Any friend of Shannon's is a friend of ours, indeed. And what brings you from America to County Kerry, Mr. Murphy?"

"I'm a writer, Mrs. Mullins, and I'm here to work on my book."

"A writer! Well, what do you know about that? Have you books in print already?"

"Yes, ma'am. Two."

"That's grand, just grand. I'd be mighty proud to have a writer on the place. I guess you know by now that Ireland invented writing," she smiled at them cheerfully. "Now. Won't you both come in for a wee bite to eat? It's not a bother."

"Oh, no, thank you, Mrs. Mullins," said Shannon. "We must be getting on. Another time."

"All right then, off with you. You know where the cottage is. It may be a bit dusty, mind you. I haven't cleaned in a spell. Been put up with a cold, but I'm better now. Be off now, and mind the muddy road. The door is unlocked."

The cottage was hard to see from the main house. If one did not know just where to look, it would be easy to miss the roof lying behind the trees. It was a hefty walk, and the narrow lane was indeed quite muddy, so Shannon suggested they drive. The car slipped a bit as it turned the last curve in the lane. There, before them, was a rock cottage nestled securely under the trees. A long green lawn fell off toward the shoreline, where there was a dock and a small boat. Across the water, Jack could spot a small fishing village. He guessed that the inlet made its way to the ocean.

"This is truly one of the garden spots in the whole of the 'Ring of Kerry,'" Shannon told him. "This is where the Kenmare River moves deep into the Kerry coast. The warm Gulf Stream waters kiss these shores, and that is why there are subtropical yuccas, palm trees and bamboo all mingled with the blazing yellow gorse."

Jack interrupted. "You could be a storyteller, Shannon."

She warmed to her subject then, obviously enjoying the chance to tell a stranger about her homeland. "The old name for Kenmare, Ceann Mara, means the head of the sea. Kenmare is at the head of the Ring of Kerry, which is a circuit starting in Killarney, going through Kenmare and then several other villages. Then it dips and rises through the mountains along the coast, all the way to Dingle and beyond." She waved her hand toward the horizon as she spoke. One day, Jack thought, Shannon and I will explore the Ring together.

They reached the cottage door, and Shannon worked at the handle to get it open. Jack suggested he give it a try.

"Oh, Mr. Murphy, I can manage," she said with a smile.

"Please. Call me Jack, or anything but sir."

"Fine, Mr. Murphy. I'll call you Jack, if you like." And just then, the door yielded. "Now," Shannon said in a low, calm voice as the door swung open.

Jack tried to look more interested in the cottage than in Shannon, though in truth he could tell at once that the cottage would be perfect for him. Off to his right was a kitchen with a big fireplace, as she had described, and a smaller fireplace in the main room to his left. There was a chimney at each end of the cottage, with fireplaces above and below, four in all. The upstairs was bigger than Shannon had remembered, with two bedrooms and a bath between. As Jack walked about the hardwood floors of the cottage, he could hear the chiming of church bells in the distance.

"Come, look at this," Shannon called from the kitchen. He went to her at once and saw her kneeling, looking at a stone just at the corner of the fireplace. Carved into the stone was a word in Old Irish: Sláinte.

"What does it say?"

"Health," Shannon replied.

Then, to his surprise, she took his hand and led him upstairs. "Come," she told him. "Just look at the view of the water from the bedroom." Then, as if she had just realized that she was holding his hand, she let go and moved back from the window to allow Jack to have a better view.

His eyes moved toward the inlet, where a small boat lay perfectly still at the water's edge. The sun moved behind some passing clouds as Jack stood silently staring out the window. He turned and looked at Shannon standing a little way across the room. Almost against his will, his eyes glanced down her body, at her light blue sweater and white wool skirt. He wanted to hold her, hug her, kiss her intimately.

He turned back and stood at the window with an intent look, hoping she would not guess his feelings. "Shhh," Shannon said, now just behind him. He could feel her presence, smell the perfect beauty standing near. "There," she whispered in his ear. "See it?"

"What? Where?" he asked softly.

"There, next to that tree. A baby duck. I wonder where the mother is."

He blinked, then nodded as he saw it. Soon there were several baby ducks, and then the mother waddled into view. Jack and Shannon stood for a moment, watching, sharing this small event.

He turned to her. "I'll take this place," he said in a quiet but forceful voice. "It's perfect. Let's go tell Mrs. Mullins."

"No," said Shannon. "That's not the way to do this." She paused. "First, we thank Mrs. Mullins for letting you look. Then we tell her that you would like to think about it, and that you would like to come back tomorrow and visit with both Mr. and Mrs. Mullins about the cottage."

Jack understood. For some reason, having nothing to do with his own experience, he knew what this was about. He instinctively understood what Shannon was about, and all of Ireland, for that matter. He nodded in agreement. Tomorrow he and Shannon would return to meet with Mr. and Mrs. Mullins.

Chapter Six

Texas, early 1960's

Helen was sitting close to Jack in the front seat of Sam's Chevy. They had had several dates, and that Sunday evening they were on their way home from town. They cruised along slowly, listening to the country radio station, being quiet together.

"Jack," said Helen in a low voice, "I'm falling in love with you." He was taken totally aback, and did not know how to reply. He pulled the car to the side of the road and kissed her tentatively, gently, then sat there on the side of the road for a long while, just holding her in his arms. Nothing like this had ever happened to him before. He wasn't sure how he felt or what he was supposed to do.

"Jack, please don't hurt me. Promise that you will never hurt me," Helen whispered.

Jack was silent and did not answer while he wondered what was behind her plea. He decided that it did matter, mattered a great deal in fact, that she was crying, but that he would probably not know why for a long time. He brushed away the tears and said he would never do anything to hurt her. He promised. At that, all of her doubts seemed to vanish. She displayed complete trust in Jack. He kissed her again, and then again, and kept his arm around her as they drove on.

When they reached her house, none of the lights were on. Her father's pickup was gone. Worried, Helen asked Jack to come in with her. Almost as soon as they walked in the door, the telephone rang. It was Helen's father calling to say that he and her mother had gone into San Antonio to look at some cattle for his boss, but the truck had broken down and they were going to have to spend the night. He said they would get the repairs done in the morning and be home in the afternoon. He told her not to worry.

Helen hung up the phone and turned to Jack, biting her lip, her body tense. Knowing what she wanted. Half afraid, half not afraid. She told him of the telephone conversation. "Jack, stay the night, will you? Please stay with me."

Jack nodded wordlessly. She kissed him, and kissed him again. And so they made love for the first time, alone on a Texas ranch, in this old house at the end of a dirt road, in the middle of nowhere.

Helen felt as if she were floating. The excitement built up inside her body. She had never felt a real desire for any man. Sure, it felt good, at least after the first time, and it certainly got them excited. But until now, she had not known the same urgency, the same rise in temperature, the same headlong rush to tear away the clothes and melt into each other. She had always wondered how it felt to a man when his feelings exploded, when she felt him move within her, when he fell back exhausted and satisfied. Tonight she found out. She learned her own desire, learned the almost unbearable pleasure that strung itself out in soft bursts that she could feel in the soles of her feet and the depths of her mind. At long last, she understood why everybody made such a big thing of it.

As for Jack, he thought he already knew a good deal. He did, at least enough to concentrate on Helen, respond to her rising excitement, hold back his own until she was spent, then pour himself into her. That much he had picked up from previous experience, and from the literary works he was always reading. Poetry and fiction had told him more than a biology text about the rhythm and ecstasy and subtle danger of a man and a woman making love.

The next morning, just before dawn, Jack started out for the military base, all the while thinking of Helen with her sweet laughter and how she looked in the dim light of the bedroom. And how her naked body looked as she approached the bed, revealing and tantalizing, as if calling for him to surrender to her warmth completely. And her firm breasts rising to meet him as she, in turn, surrendered to him. All this he would remember forever.

Over the next several months, he spent as much time as possible with Helen. He would get a ride into town and take the local bus, which would drop him at the head of the dirt road. From there, he would walk to Helen's house. By now, Jack was almost a part of her family. He would often stay over for the weekend, and now and then Mr. Baker would allow him to drive his old pickup truck and take Helen into town for a movie.

On several occasions, when Sam had to work over the weekend, he would let Jack take his car. Then Jack would take Helen on a real holiday. They went to the beaches along the Gulf Coast, and once the two of them even went to Mexico for the weekend. They were madly in love, so it seemed to them like a trip to Europe, even though it was just a drab little border town.

Helen had never been happier in her life. She lived for Jack. From time to time, he would have to work through the weekend and the next week, and that would mean two weeks before they could be together again. Those were endless hours for Helen. Everything good about her life revolved around Jack, and their days together, and their nights together making love. She had never dreamed that being in love could be so grand, or that lovemaking could be so perfect.

As the weeks passed, they talked about everything imaginable except the one subject Jack would not discuss. That was marriage. Helen would bring up the idea from time to time, and try to talk to Jack about their future. At those times, Jack would become very quiet and ask Helen not to talk about it. This troubled Helen. She could not understand why Jack would never approach the idea of marriage, or even their future together, when it was clear that he loved her deeply. Finally, one evening when they were alone at her house, she forced the issue.

"Jack, I must know where we stand, where you stand on our future together." She paused and took a deep breath. "What happens when you get out of the service next year? To us, I mean?"

Jack knew he could not avoid Helen's questions any longer. He had dreaded this moment, but in his heart he was certain that one day he must tell her the truth. He did not mean to keep it from her. In fact, he had wanted to tell her many, many times. But somehow, he felt deep within himself that when he did finally own up, their relationship might be over. He could not bear the thought. She was a dream come true. He could not lose her.

Somehow, he had to find a way to tell Helen the whole story, and tell her in such a way that she would not walk out of his life forever.

Jack had not had an easy life. He was just fifteen when his father died. He was sent to live with his uncle Ted, while his two sisters stayed at home. His mother died of a stroke a few years later. There was no warning, no lingering sickness. Jack was just out of high school, working for a small town newspaper and going to college part time. He could see no real future there, but he was gaining experience in the only thing that truly interested him: writing. He knew, when he looked back, what had led him to his decision to join the Air Force. It was the combination of his newspaper job, his mother's death and the idea that he might be drafted into the Army.

And there was one other thing. While working for the newspaper, he had met a girl there, a fellow reporter. They were young and foolish, and, as kids do, they did a young and foolish thing. They got married and had a child.

The marriage did not last long. They separated, but were still legally married. Jack felt that if they stayed married while he was in the service, he might get better duty assignments, and would for certain get additional allotments for a wife and child. His plan was to get a formal divorce just prior to getting out of the service. His young wife was in total agreement, as she had a boyfriend and they planned to get married one day.

So far, Jack's plan had worked just fine. Now he had served most of his hitch, with only a little over a year left. He had not given a single thought to where he wanted to live or what type of work he would pursue, but he knew it would have something to do with writing.

He had thought many times how to tell Helen about all this. At night, at the military base, he would go over and over again the way he planned to address the subject. He would often find himself awake at two in the morning, with no answer in sight. Each time this happened, Jack would postpone the day that he would tell her, would put it off one more time.

In one respect, he felt she would understand totally, except for why he had waited to give her this news. Surely she would know that he had been afraid of losing her. Jack knew he must tell her everything and hope for the best, but he was unable to find the right time and the right place.

Helen was watching him as he struggled to find something to say. Now she asked him a second time, "What happens when you get discharged? Where are you going to live, and work?" She held Jack's hand in both of hers and looked into his eyes. A tear was falling from her cheek. "And me? Us?"

"Helen, I promise you that next week, when I come over, we will talk about all of these things. I promise."

Helen seemed to accept Jack's reply. At least, she acted as if it were acceptable to her. He kissed her long and tenderly and headed back to the base.

Chapter Seven

"Mr. Murphy," Shannon said in a light tone of voice as they drove back to town from the stone cottage by the river.

"Mr. Murphy?" he echoed. "Mr. Murphy?"

"Jack," she said in mock penitence. "Would you be wanting lunch, now? I know where to find the best pub grub in Kenmare." They both laughed out loud.

"Why, yes, I do believe I could do with a bit of lunch," he replied.

Today was market day in Kenmare, and the town was crowded with horses, cows, sheep, goats, and a little bit of everything. Jack had never seen anything like this before. Local farmers who had livestock they wanted to sell or trade actually drove them right down the highway and into town. At one end of the street a man might have five or six cows, just standing around, while a little way down the block would be several horses. The local traffic simply moved around them. Down near the square were farmers who had come to town with butter, fruit jam and preserves. From out of town, some tinkers had come in with clothing and other useful items which they were selling right out of their wagons. Jack loved it. This, to him, was Ireland.

As he and Shannon walked the streets of Kenmare, Jack could not help thinking that he belonged here, in Kenmare, with Shannon. She was such a delight to be with. As she spoke to all the locals, it made Jack feel very proud to be her escort for all the world to see.

"Shannon! Shannon Kelly!" a girl called out.

"Hello, Meg. How are you?" Shannon said as they crossed the street to meet her. Giving her a hug, Shannon placed her hand on Meg's stomach. "Would you look at this now. Seven months?"

"It is. Not long now."

"Meg, I would like you to meet Jack Murphy. Jack, this is an old school friend, Meg Kissane." They shook hands. "Jack is from America," Shannon continued. "He's going to be staying in Kenmare. He's a writer."

"You've come to the right place, Mr. Murphy. Welcome to Ireland. It is nice to meet you."

"Thank you. It's my pleasure."

"Well, I should be getting on," Meg said, turning to go. Then, as an afterthought, "How's your brother Brien?

Shannon paused. "Fine. He's fine. Living in Dublin, he is." She looked away, almost as if she were hiding something.

"Grand. Tell him I said hello," said Meg as she walked away.

"Nice girl," said Jack.

"Oh, that she is," Shannon said smiling. "We were good friends in school. Then I went off to college, and she got married. This will be her second child." She stood in the middle of the sidewalk for a moment and watched Meg.

Jack was interested in finding out more about Brien. "So you have a brother?

"Yes. Two years younger," Shannon answered tersely. It was obvious she didn't want to discuss it. Changing the subject, she asked, "Are you hungry?"

He nodded and said no more. Continuing along the street, they turned into a pub and found a table. It was very crowded, being Saturday and market day besides. The place was buzzing with conversation and laughter.

Jack could not believe how well he and Shannon were getting on together. He was beginning to think that she truly enjoyed his company, and that there might be more to come in this relationship than house hunting.

"Tell me, Mr. Murphy. Jack. How do you come by the name Jack Murphy?"

"Well, Shannon, I'm happy to say that I came by my name honestly. My great-great grandfather Murphy moved from Ireland to America. I am 100% Irish on both sides, as my great-great grandmother was also from Ireland. In fact, she was with child, my grandfather, while en route to America. He was born in America."

"Where were they from? Which county?" asked Shannon.

"I'm not altogether sure," replied Jack. "I can recall my aunt talking about County Clare, so perhaps my father's side of the family was from there. But I think my mother's side of the family was from Northern Ireland."

"Northern Ireland," Shannon repeated. "Such a beautiful part of the country."

Jack glanced her way and smiled. "And tell me, now, how did you get the name Shannon? Is that your mother's name, or your grandmother's?"

"I can tell you, yes. Shannon is not really my name. My name is Mary Ruth Kelly. My father used to call me his little Shannon, I guess after the Shannon River, for he loved it so. As time went by the name continued with me."

"I love the name Shannon," Jack told her sincerely. "I think it is you. There is something very romantic about the name Shannon, so very Irish." She just glanced at him without comment.

After a quiet moment, Jack said, "You know, I expected to see tanks and soldiers in the street when I arrived in Ireland."

She rose at once to the defense. "That's American media, Jack. They really don't do a very good job of explaining our plight. You see, many years ago when Ireland gained independence from England, the agreement allowed England to keep six counties to the north, which is now Northern

Ireland. The rest of it is the Republic of Ireland, where we are now. All the trouble is over one group wanting those six counties to join the Republic of Ireland, and the other, the English group, wanting to keep things the way they are."

"I see," Jack said soberly. "I understand by your explanation that the fighting is in Northern Ireland only."

"That is correct. We try not to pay too much attention to it here in County Kerry. We are one of the most southwesterly parts of the Republic, a long way from Northern Ireland."

"Perhaps we could go there one day," Jack was thinking aloud, "and even look up some of my relatives, if that is possible."

"It is, yes." Shannon said. "I would love the idea of helping you locate your relatives, both in Northern Ireland and elsewhere in Ireland proper." Jack could see by the expression in her eyes that she was excited by the prospect.

After lunch, they strolled the streets of Kenmare, taking in the fun and excitement of the market. A light rain began to fall, and Shannon pulled out her umbrella. Jack had not learned as yet to keep an umbrella handy, but was secretly delighted at the thought of sharing Shannon's with her. The two of them huddled under the small umbrella and made their way about town. Feeling Shannon next to him moved Jack to slide in just a little closer. She did not move away. Rather, she took his arm and pulled herself tightly against him. This was a magnificent day, Jack thought to himself. Walking the streets of Ireland with Shannon, in the rain. A grand day, indeed.

"Perhaps one day I'll take you over to Bantry," Shannon suggested. "Bantry is a rather short drive from here. 'The Flower of the Gulf Stream,' it's called. Bantry Bay is one of the world's largest and most beautiful harbours. In May, they have the famous Bantry Mussel Festival. We can visit some really nice small villages nearby, like Castletown, Glengarriff, Mizen Head, Skull..."

"Skull?" Jack interrupted.

"Skull is a yachting harbour at the foot of Mount Gabriel. The village, whose Irish name means 'school,' was founded in the tenth century. It's little more than a single street with small shops and bars."

"Tell me more. I love to listen to you speak, love your Irish accent. Please go on."

Shannon smiled warmly at him. "Well, not far from there, we'll find Three Castle Head and the ruins of Dunlough Castle, with three hundred foot cliffs on one side, dropping straight to the sea. On the other side, there is a lake. Dunlough was built by the O'Mahoney clan, a warring bunch who lived back in 1200."

"I can't wait. When do we go?"

Shannon laughed. "Oh, we'll be getting there soon enough, I suppose."

"I've noticed that you speak Old Irish very well."

"It's the law. Everyone in school must learn Old Irish. It's our first language."

"Can you teach me?"

"I can, yes. I suppose we could be getting on with a little Old Irish now and then."

"Teach me to say something now. How about the Old Irish phrase for 'How are you'?"

"Conas tá tú."

"Say that one more time."

"Conas tá tú."

"Conas tá tú," Jack repeated.

"Very well done, Mr. Murphy." He did not correct her this time, for he could tell by her tone of voice that she was using the formal term in jest.

"Give me another word. How about 'love'?"

"Another time. I need to be getting on."

The rain had let up. Shannon moved away from him, closed the umbrella, and glanced up to meet his eyes. She smiled. A soft smile, just like the one he had seen in her mother. A beautiful smile. Oh, God, how he wanted to kiss her at this very moment. How he wanted to hold her in his arms and tell her that he was crazy for her, that he wanted her to be his lady, his Irish lass, his lover. He looked at her for a long moment, his eyes betraying his feelings. But what he said to her was, "Thank you for a lovely day, Shannon."

Chapter Eight

That night, pacing about his hotel room after dinner, Jack could see Shannon's face in vivid flashes of memory. He could recall every detail, every move, every color of the day. He had been so happy in her company.

Now, in the blue violet night of Kenmare, he could not sleep. He decided not to fight his feelings, and so he allowed himself to think only of Shannon. When would it happen? Would it come swiftly, and would they both realize at the same time that they were in love? When would he lie beside this fantastic woman, neither of them able to hold back the lovemaking, that breathless, shivering, eager thrill of making love for the first time? Would it be on an Irish carpet of green, still damp from the overnight mist? Perhaps a field of wildflowers, or buttercups. Somewhere during these flights of imagining and desiring, Jack fell asleep, and his wishful thoughts became dreams.

The next morning, he awoke early. Looking at his watch, he saw that it was six o'clock. He was to pick Shannon up at eleven, just after she returned from early Mass. Six o'clock! What on earth was he going to do for the next five hours? He looked out the window for awhile, watching the light come up. He splashed himself clean, put on his favorite new wool Irish sweater and went over to the window again, thinking about Shannon, remembering yesterday. Then sat down on the edge of the bed, pulled a notebook out of his briefcase, and began to write a poem. He did not know where it was coming from and, indeed, gave it no thought whatever. Paying no mind to form, or meter, or style, he just began to write.

> Silver white flames
>   were the flowers in blossom
> I saw her appear
>   amid the colors
>   of the soul…
> But she did not see me.
> I was in love
>   in a garden by the sea
>   and by a woeful chance
>   she passed by…
> She moved toward the strand
>   and my love was vanishing.
> Her streaming red hair
>   danced in the wind,
> Teasing away
>   in my eyes, a lover's gaze
>   and I dreamed of her
>   clasped in my arms.
> But from this paradise
>   she will fly
>   and I shall forever cherish my
>   silent love, forever
> with no word spoken…
>   but in my heart.

Jack read over what he had written, convinced at last that he was in love with Shannon. Indeed, he was lovesick. Steady, boy, steady—give this thing the best you've got, he told himself. Not for you to be weak and crazy at a time like this. She's worth more than life itself, so you will love her as she deserves.

He walked once more to the window. Looking down at the streets of Kenmare in the early morning of an Irish Sunday, he knew at once how he could throw a harness on his passion for Shannon, how he could find his way to her. He would immerse himself in the small village life and ways of Ireland, and thus learn more about Shannon. He wanted to come to her whole and awake.

And he did that. Without asking a lot of questions, just by observing and listening and putting together bits of information, he began to breathe and live the life of the Irish. He learned that before beginning a journey, one must say three Hail Marys for a safe arrival. Well, he thought, if ever there was an important journey in my life, this is it, and I don't mean just the roads.

Granted, the roads were a caution. As Jack was to learn on his outings with Shannon, Ireland is a country without freeways except a few near the larger cities. Even "major" roads connecting Killarney and Kenmare and Bantry are unreliable, and a few Hail Marys couldn't hurt.

He found some nice similarities between small town America, especially the southern and western states, and the Irish way of life. In both places, people still wave to you on the road. In the typical Irish household, just as in a small town American one, there is always something on the stove to eat. It is rare indeed to go into an Irish home, such as Shannon's mother's cottage, and not be asked to sit down and have a bite. It may be a hot scone with homemade butter and homemade jam, or something more filling like a good Irish soup.

The houses are warmed by peat, which is burned in the fireplaces. In the smaller villages, it is common to see the local men cutting chunks of it out of trenches in the peat bogs. Jack would also learn of the Irish tinkers, some of whom still live in horse drawn caravans. There is a difference, he found, between tinkers and Irish gypsies, though they may appear to be one and the same. The tinkers are the people who went on the road in the time of the Famine, and never came in again.

Then there was the Irish pub, and here the resemblance to small town America ended. In no other place on earth is the pub so alive and well, such an important part of the life of the town. The smaller the village, the more essential it becomes. The Irish pub is a meeting place, a brotherhood of locals who gather and tell tales and read from their latest writings, for every Irishman has a literary turn of mind. They talk politics and religion, and argue about both, but most of all they visit with each other. They know each other well.

The Irish have a marvelous way of giving great significance to this small out island of only three and a half million people. Ireland is a land with thousands of tales and myths. It differs from other English speaking countries in its enormous range of memories, from great victories to great sadness. It is eternal, unchanging, the same in many ways as it was a millennium ago. Since the Celts, the Vikings, the Normans and the English coursed through Ireland, the unifying force has been *cara*, the Celtic word for friendship. Out of all this history has come some of the world's finest minds, and in particular some of the greatest writers ever to live. Everything that Jack saw in the local people of Kenmare, and in Shannon and her parents, reflected the way they live their heritage, all of it, every day.

Jack felt a sense of pride, and, at the same time, was humbled by the fact that he himself was Irish, and a writer to boot. Perhaps, he realized, this was what Shannon saw in him.

In turn, what he saw in her was all of Ireland. To him, she was the Trinity College Library and salmon fishing and Guinness beer and modern Dublin and the Blasket Islands. She was the green fields and the stormy coast and the soft, misting rain. Jack was half in love with Ireland and half in love with Shannon, and had no wish to distinguish between them.

The morning moved ever so slowly until it was time to pick up Shannon. She came walking out to meet him as he drove up to her parents' house, stepping lightly down the path in her wool cape the color of burnt sugar. She got in the car and gave him a smile. The rest of the day was as near perfect as Jack could have wanted. It was made perfect by Shannon, by her beauty and mirth, by her willingness to be in his company.

They rode out to meet with Mr. and Mrs. Mullins and to see the cottage once more. It had looked totally different yesterday in the bright sunlight, just before the rain shower moved in. Today's visit offered a foggy coastline, a light drizzle interspersed with heavy rain. Once inside the stone cottage, Jack felt the cold from the stone walls begging for the fireplace to be lit, for the chill to be off, for human conversation, for quiet days of writing, thinking, and perhaps loving. It was so beautiful despite the cold and the rain. Jack Murphy had no wish for anything beyond this perfect moment.

A price was set and agreed upon, and Jack could begin moving in at any time. Of course there was no lease, only a handshake between Jack and Mr. Mullins. Naturally, Mrs. Mullins offered hot tea and scones, which topped off the arrangement. It was now Jack's cottage, for as long as he desired to stay.

Chapter Nine

Texas, early 1960's

The Texas wind had been slashing about all morning. Jack had about an hour before he was to meet Helen. Thanks to Sam's nemesis, the first sergeant, Sam was on call at the base and Jack had his Chevy for the entire weekend.

Texas Sam, as Jack now referred to him, had turned out to be a good friend. The two young men had developed a close bond, in spite of the fact that Jack was a sensitive, romantic writer-poet and Sam was the perfect all-American jock. Sam carried on a constant quest for women, while Jack lived for the opportunity to be with one woman, Helen.

Sam would occasionally complain about having to go out to the night-clubs without Jack, but he didn't put any real pressure on him to go "out juking," a favorite expression of his. Jack's thoughts remained on Helen, and he wanted to spend every available minute with her. Sam understood this about Jack. Loaning him the car was what friends did.

On this day, Jack drove through the blowing tumbleweeds to Helen's place, and they walked down to the river together. It was a favorite spot of theirs. They had a special tree near the riverbank where they would sit, protected from view and from the hot Texas sun and wind, and just talk.

It had been three weeks since they had seen each other. Jack had been called in for special duty. He and six others had a short TDY, military parlance for "temporary duty assignment." The TDY took Jack off the base and out of town for a training session. Jack was concerned, for he had heard a rumor that the Government had made a decision to close the base. That meant he would be sent to another location to serve out his remaining months or, as in some cases, would be let out of the military with an early discharge.

He was wondering how to bring up the subject with Helen, but what she had to tell him proved to be even more unsettling.

"Helen," he asked, "What was that sign I saw at the head of your road? 'For Sale'?"

"Yes. It's true. The owner has put the whole ranch up for sale. The sign went up this week, right after he phoned us. My pa can stay on with the owner if he wants to, but we'll have to move to another ranch he owns, a big spread in East Texas.

"Really! What did your dad say? About moving?"

"Well, we don't have a whole lot of choice. We don't have much money, and now no place to live and no work. My Pa said yes, he'd take the work and move there. You know, for a man like my Pa, his age and all, work is pretty hard to come by."

"When is all this going to happen?"

"Well, they want him to get ready to move pretty soon now. They'll send trucks to get the cattle in a week or so. After they're loaded up, I guess we'll just head on out to East Texas. It's 'way up, almost to the state line." For the first time, her voice wavered a little.

Jack took her in his arms and held her. Then he gave her a gentle kiss. She returned the kiss with tears filling her face.

"Jack, tell me that we won't have to be apart. Tell me that you will marry me and keep me here with you. We can set up a small apartment near the base and I can find work. There's this lady who owns a cafe in town who says I can have a job anytime I want to."

She looked so hopeful, so in love, and just a little bit frightened. Do it, Jack, he told himself. Tell her the truth.

"Helen, we can't do that." He took a deep breath. Finally he managed to choke it out. "Helen, I'm married. It's not what you think, but I am married." He tried to continue, but Helen was gone, running up toward the house. She did not stop until she reached the house, with Jack running and calling after her. When she reached the front porch, she collapsed on the steps and broke down. She could not speak and could not stop crying. Jack tried to hold her, but she pushed him away and continued to cry.

In time, the tears let up enough for her to ask Jack to tell her about his wife. He went into all that had happened, explaining everything in detail, leaving nothing out. He told her that he had intended to clear it up long before now, but it had been so hard to find a way to tell her. Helen walked the length of the porch, stopped, turned, and went down the steps into the yard. Jack stood motionless.

After a backward glance, Helen turned her back and let out a long sigh. With a weary slowness, she sat down on a log. A restless breeze was blowing, kicking up the dust. Helen absentmindedly ran her hand through her hair, shaking the sand away. In the distance, storm clouds were building up. Now and then, a streak of lightning dashed across the horizon in silence, followed in a minute or so by a low rumble of distant thunder.

"No one else will ever make love to me, Jack. No one. Ever." Finally, she turned to face him, steadier now, but still trembling from the shock of what she had heard. She had absorbed it. She had decided what to tell him.

"I am yours," she said. "I belong to you. I don't ever want anyone to touch me, ever again, but you."

She paused. "...and if I have to wait for you until you get your divorce, I will. I knew from the very first night we made love that I was meant to be yours. And I will be, for as long as I live."

Jack went to her then, and took her in his arms. He kissed her. For a long time after that, he just held her close. She began to cry again. He could feel her heart beating wildly against him. Clinging to his neck, she whispered in his ear, "Jack, I want to make love with you. Right now." She held onto him with all her might. "Jack, I feel so afraid. I'm so scared."

"It will be all right," he tried to soothe her.

"I feel as if this will be the last time we will ever be together. That feeling just now came over me. I don't know why, but I'm so afraid."

Jack did not speak. He did not know how to reassure her.

"Jack, I can see myself in a coffin."

"Helen! Don't talk like that," he pleaded.

"Hold me. Please hold me. I feel so afraid."

Chapter Ten

Texas, early 1960's

The next week turned out to be a disaster for Jack and Helen. Jack was given short notice orders for a special TDY, and he did not know how long he would be away. When he called Helen to tell her this news, her reaction was surprisingly cool. She made distant remarks. She seemed to be immobilized, totally withdrawn into a state of deep depression.

He tried to console her, but nothing he said made any difference. There was no way to get a positive reaction, no way to help her figure out how to deal with her family's move, no way to get a response of any kind. She just kept repeating how scared she was, and how alone she felt.

Jack had to leave for his TDY not knowing what he would find when he returned. He was gone for three weeks on a training mission to a base in Washington State. He tried to call Helen, only to get an operator saying that the telephone was no longer in service. He felt certain that the family had already moved to East Texas, and wondered if Helen had simply gone with them.

He called Sam, thinking perhaps that Helen had left an address or telephone number with his friend. Sam said he had not heard a word. Jack asked him to drive out to the ranch in hopes that someone might still be around, or to stop by the nightclub to see if any of Helen's friends knew anything. Hearing the panic in Jack's voice, Sam said he would do that. When Jack called back a few days later, Sam reported that he had tried everything, but that no one knew when she had left, or exactly where in East Texas she had moved.

When Jack returned to the base in Texas, he took up the job of finding her. He did everything he could think of to find out information or news of Helen or her family. He sent a letter to her old house and it came back, no forwarding address. He asked around at the Texas Cafe and at Spurs. He could not find a single clue. It was as if she had vanished from the face of the earth. As the weeks rolled into months, he hoped for a phone call or a letter from Helen, anything that would tell him how to reach her. Nothing.

Jack had totally lost contact with Helen.

The next month, an announcement was made at the base. The decision everyone was expecting had been made. The base was being closed. The wheels ground in slow motion. Sam was assigned to stay on and help pack it in. Jack received orders to be transferred to a base in the West, and then the orders were withdrawn. Another wait. Finally, he was granted an early discharge. He took care of the divorce details with his estranged wife, who was more than ready to marry her boyfriend and seemed relieved to have Jack out of her life. She said a few polite words about keeping in touch, but Jack knew he had seen the last of her and their baby daughter.

And still no word from Helen.

He planned to go looking for her as soon as he was mustered out, but at the last minute he had to go to Baton Rouge to take care of his ailing uncle Ted. He would decide what he wanted to do and where he wanted to live while he tended to his uncle, the one who had looked after him when he himself was young.

But Ted died a month later, and there were details to be taken care of. Ted's wife had died a few years back, and they had had no children, so he left what holdings he had to Jack and his two sisters. He had not been rich, by any means, but he was financially secure. Jack inherited a comfortable amount of money and stocks. There was no longer any rush to get located and get a job. He decided to look for Helen.

He traded his uncle's old car for a dependable Buick and headed out toward East Texas. It had now been well over eight months since his last, anguished night with Helen. He must find her. The base had closed and everyone he knew had scattered. He asked around in many of the smaller towns near the Texas-Oklahoma border, which was the only clue he had. He was hoping to learn anything, anything at all of Helen or her family. Nothing came of the project.

Jack gave up.

Miami, early 1970's

A decade had gone by. Jack had found a job as a reporter at the Miami Herald, and had begun to be a serious writer in his free time. His first book was about to be published, so he had dug out his military records and had sent the news to the last addresses he had for his old buddies at the base in Texas. He wanted them to know he was an author now.

He was sitting on the deck of his apartment, going over notes for a story and enjoying the sea breeze as it ruffled the tall palm trees, when the telephone rang. It was Sam Bennett, calling to say that Jack's letter had just caught up with him the week before, after his mother forwarded it. "And Jack, would you believe I'm in Miami on business this very minute?" he boomed in his familiar, expansive way. "Let me take you out to dinner. Best restaurant in Miami." Same old Texas Sam.

Over dinner at Joe's Stone Crab, Jack filled Sam in on the details of his activities since getting out of the service. There wasn't much to tell besides years of being a reporter, which had been grueling but had at least taught him to write a good story. Writing was his main interest in life, and it was paying the bills, "which is pretty unusual," he admitted. As for social life, he had very little, being caught up in his writing. He had pretty much withdrawn into a solitary existence since he left Texas. Still, he was reasonably happy, he told Sam.

"You don't have some special squeeze?" Sam asked.

"No, not really," Jack answered. "Oh, I've had a few women in and out of my life. You know. A date here and there."

"Getting any?" Sam grinned.

"God. You haven't changed, Sam," Jack was laughing in spite of himself.

"Hell, man can't live on beer and barbecue alone."

"You seem to have plenty of all three, Sam. What have you been up to?"

"Well, Jack, ol' boy, I've hit it lucky. I've been taken into my dad's oil business, which I knew was bound to happen, and I've made a lot of money. Now a group of local businessmen in Houston want me to run for state office. I'm going into politics! What do you think about that?"

"Sam, you are perfect for Texas politics," Jack told him sincerely, lifting his glass in a toast to Sam's career. "Who knows? One day you may run for Governor or Senator. Or, hell, who knows, even President! I'll vote for you." They both laughed and took a sip of wine.

It was just like old times, Jack thought, when he and Sam spent time together in Texas, being kids, having fun. He had a vivid flash of Helen, and he almost expected to see her walk into the room and sit down with them, as she had done so long ago.

"You've suddenly become quiet, Jack, ol' boy," said Sam.

"Oh, sorry. My thoughts were back in time, to the days in Texas, the military days. I was thinking of the first time I saw Helen at Spurs, and about how you used to lend me your car to take her places. You were real decent to do that."

"Aw, it was nothing. That was some really bad shit about Helen, I guess."

"You know, Sam," Jack did not bother to hide the pain in his voice, "I never did hear from Helen. Not a word. We were so close, and then I totally lost contact with her, just like that."

Sam was speechless, looking at him in shock. Finally he spoke.

"Jack. You don't know?"

"Know what?"

"Oh, God, I don't believe this. I thought surely you knew. Helen committed suicide. Oh, man, I'm sorry."

"What? How do you know? How did you find this out? I looked all over East Texas for her, never found her. What happened to her?"

"Well, my last night at the base, I decided to go out to Spurs and have a few beers and say goodbye to all my old girlfriends. You'd already gone by then. I ran into Martha what's-her-name, you know, one of Helen's good friends. I asked her about Helen. She told me Helen's mother had called her from Clarksville, up in the Red River Valley, where they'd moved. She was real worried, trying to find Helen, and thought she might have come back looking for you. She called Martha back the next day and said they had found Helen in a motel room right in Clarksville. She had taken a bunch of pills. And on top of that, she was going to have a baby."

Jack just sat motionless. He did not speak, but stared into his glass for a long time. Finally he excused himself and told Sam that he would be back. Once outside, he broke down.

Chapter Eleven

Shannon was standing outside her house when Jack pulled up. The Irish sun was shining on her face and hair as she talked to her mother. It had not rained all week, and Jack was edgy because the relentless sun stirred up fleeting memories and unsettling dreams. He was relieved at the sight of his beautiful Shannon and her solid Irish family.

Shannon and her mother smiled as Jack got out of the car and approached. "Good morning, Mrs. Kelly. How are you keeping?" he asked.

"Very well, and you, sir? How are you keeping?"

Jack loved this greeting. He loved hearing it, and he especially loved saying it to people when he met them.

They stood for a short while, mostly talking about the weather and how bright the days had been. "It's been very dry, if ever there was a dry spell," Mrs. Kelly declared, looking up at the sky toward the west. "It's near time for another storm. Powerful altogether, I'd say. I feel it coming on."

Jack knew that she knew what she was talking about. In her quiet way, she was an amazing woman, the gentlest he had ever met. She had the kindest eyes. Her expression always looked as if she were about to smile, as if she could see inside a person and liked what she saw.

Mrs. Kelly was a strong woman, though. He had seen that right off. He recognized that one could not work a farm in this part of Ireland and live to be her age without being strong. She had had a very hard life, with little in the way of worldly goods. But in Ireland, as Jack had learned, not to have money did not mean that you were poor. It simply meant that you did not have money.

Mrs. Kelly never went on about "woman things," not even to her husband. Perhaps, he thought, this was why Shannon kept her dreams to herself. She had told him that never once could she remember her father telling her mother that he loved her. Still, one afternoon, in the back of the family Bible, she had found a poem he had written when they were courting. Shannon remembered one line especially: "I wish I could send you armies of swallows, and the swallows will sing your name."

Shannon had realized at a very young age that women kept their dreams to themselves and rarely acted upon them. Why was this? she asked herself. Men had such privileges, and women seemed to live in caution. Men could speak with candor and bluntness, but women must obey a certain decorum.

It seemed to Shannon that the minutes of her mother's day became lost in the hours, which became weeks, then months and finally years, until the canvas beneath the painting rotted away to nothing and the painting itself lost its luster. She saw that dreams became her mother's harbor, her refuge from a legacy she had not chosen but might not have changed even if she could. Shannon became aware as she matured that a major part of her own dreams came from her mother, and she was determined to make at least a few of them come true.

Yet, Jack noted, she had many of her mother's ways. They were very much alike in their manner and movements, even their size. Mrs. Kelly had truly raised an outstanding child in Shannon, he thought. At twenty-eight, she was much more mature than her years, yet she looked younger. She could have passed for a princess or a woman of wealth, for she had a way about her that Jack had only witnessed in the movies. But Shannon had not been fabricated by some studio executive. Shannon was real.

Mrs. Kelly looked at Jack. "I suppose a cup of tea wouldn't go straight?"

"Oh, no thank you, Mrs. Kelly. I've had a lot of coffee this morning."

Jack was impatient to get on the road for their drive to Bantry Bay, happy at the prospect of getting Shannon alone. He had only spent an hour with her all week, having met her at Murphy's Pub after the bank closed one afternoon. The rest of the week Shannon reported home right after work to help her mother, who had not been feeling well. Her father had suggested she spend extra time at home. Shannon's father never gave orders. He always suggested. Everyone always followed his suggestions.

Mr. Kelly never raised his voice and he never used foul words, nor would he allow anyone in his presence to do so. He always attended Mass on Sunday, and it was his habit to invite someone home from church to sit down and have a bite to eat. Mrs. Kelly just automatically fixed extra food on Sunday.

The most angry Shannon ever saw her father was when a tinker struck one of his horses. He had given the man some work helping him plow, and Shannon watched from her window as Mr. Kelly bolted out into the field yelling, "Stop that! Don't you dare lay a hand on those animals." He grabbed the tinker by the front of his shirt, lifted him so hard his feet left the ground, and said, "Get off my land. Never show your face here again, understand? And don't let me catch you beating anyone else's horse either, mind you. I'll take my blackthorn cane to you, I will." He never spoke of it afterwards.

Mr. Kelly was a big man. His arms and hands had been worked hard for many years. He was very strong in both his manner and his presence. He didn't talk a great deal, and at first, Jack had thought it was because he didn't like him. Later he came to see that Mr. Kelly spoke only when he had something worthwhile to say. Jack could not engage him in idle conversation.

On this day, Jack and Shannon did not linger in the kitchen as they sometimes did, but departed at once for Bantry Bay. As they drove, they discussed many subjects, mostly small talk until Shannon asked about his past. Did he have brothers and sisters? Had he been married? Normal questions, to be sure.

Jack told her most of his background, except for two things. He did not reveal that he had been married many years ago and that he had a child. Nor did he mention Helen. He had an uncomfortable feeling that Shannon might be put off if he told her, and an equally clear memory of what had happened so long ago when he delayed the telling for too long.

Back then, he told himself, he had been a boy in love with a girl. Now he was a man. His feelings for this woman, Shannon, went far deeper, encompassing the whole of Ireland from which she sprang. The stakes were higher. Now, as then, he was in fear of saying the wrong thing. And so, once again, he said nothing.

Instead, he kept his comments mostly to general conversation about school and work. He told her about his mother and father, and how he had gone to live with his uncle Ted after they had died. He told Shannon of his two sisters in some detail, that one lived in California and was very happily married. The other, Terri, lived in Las Vegas and had been married twice, but had no children.

The car reached the summit of the mountain and they turned into a large parking area, an overlook as Jack called it. In Ireland it was called a standby. They stopped, got out and walked to the mountain top. The view was magnificent. Standing, looking down at Bantry Bay, Jack slipped his arm around Shannon's waist. She did not seem to mind.

"God, this is beautiful!" Jack exclaimed. "This is one of the most beautiful places I have ever been."

"It is, yes," she replied. "I love this spot. When I was a child, my papa and my mother would bring me and my sister and brother here for picnics. We would climb on the rocks and tease the sheep." She pulled away and walked toward the car, calling out that she was going to get the picnic she had made for this day.

She returned with a blanket and a basket of food, and began arranging the setting. Jack helped, and they sat down and started to eat smoked salmon, raw carrots, and fresh scones with homemade butter and jam. Shannon had also made cookies, and had brought a big jug of fresh milk.

"You said your brother lives in Dublin?" asked Jack, resuming the conversation.

"He does, yes," Shannon said, with no further comment. Jack had an odd feeling that there was more to it than that, but she wasn't saying.

"And your sister?"

"She died, Jack. She was only twenty-one at the time. It was a sudden kind of thing. I was just fifteen."

"I'm sorry. It must have been hard on your family."

"It was, yes. It was hardest on my mother." She paused. "I don't think she has been the same since. She had a difficult time bearing children—two miscarriages at first and a stillborn child a year later. Finally my sister Bridget was born. My mother had me and my brother Brian rather late in life. She had great hopes for all of us, but especially Bridget." Her face was calm, but Jack could see the hurt in her eyes.

He sat quietly for a moment. "Shannon, I don't think anyone ever gets over the death of a relative or close friend. Not totally."

At that moment, he wanted very much to tell her about Helen and about his young and foolish days, his marriage and child. Somehow, he could not. That was a very long time ago, he rationalized yet again. It could serve no good to bring it up now. There was enough pain already, with the story of Shannon's sister.

"I guess you're right, Jack," Shannon said now. "'Tis the kind of thing that stays with you, just a little. It's always there, always occupies a small place in your heart."

She smiled. "But, come now. My sister would want us to smile and be happy, here in this place where we used to play together. A toast to my dear sister Bridget." She lifted her glass, still smiling.

How lovely she was at that moment. Jack reached into his pocket and pulled out the poem he had written while in his hotel room. "Shannon, may I share a poem with you?"

"You can, of course. I would like that."

He handed her the poem, explaining when and how he had written it. She sat motionless and read the poem. She paused, then read it again. She looked up. Her eyes met Jack's. Softly she said, "Is this poem about me?"

"Yes."

"Jack, that is so sweet."

Jack leaned toward her. His face was almost touching hers. Then he kissed her very gently. Shannon returned the kiss. He took her hand and they sat for a long while, without a word spoken between them. Now and then they would look at each other, and then back toward the mountains and Bantry Bay.

Finally, they gathered up their picnic supplies and walked to the car. Jack opened the door for Shannon. At that moment he put his arms around her and pulled her tightly to him. He kissed her cheek and her forehead, lightly, then found her lips. This was not a soft, gentle kiss as before. There was passion behind it. Jack and Shannon released their warmth to each other in this kiss.

Finally Shannon pulled back, breathless and smiling, and suggested that they should be getting on. The rest of the day was glorious. Shannon could not get the words out fast enough, knowing that she was drawing closer to this man, knowing that she was revealing a great deal of herself in her stories of her homeland. Between her storytelling and the sightseeing, Jack would steal a kiss, a hug or just an opportunity to be close to Shannon. He was deeply happy.

It was well after dark when they returned to Kenmare. Jack walked Shannon to the front door, gave her a quick kiss on the cheek, and asked if he could see her the next day. She suggested that he call her at the bank.

Shannon walked in and was greeted by her parents and Father Mulvany, who had been invited to eat with them. At dinner the conversation was light. Her father and the priest talked about various subjects until Mrs. Kelly brought up Jack Murphy. "We wanted to talk with you serious, about Mr. Murphy," she said to her daughter. "We don't want you to make a mistake."

"Joking me, you are," Shannon said, but inwardly she was furious. She did not show any emotion, but inside she could not believe it. Merciful God, she thought. It had been hard enough to move back into her parents' home. She loved them and was glad to be able to help her mother, but to return home as an adult, after living alone in Limerick, had been difficult. She felt like jumping up and running out of the house, but couldn't quite bring herself to do so.

"'Tis no joke, Shannon. I could tell right off that you like this Mr. Murphy. I saw the way the pair of ye looked at each other. But we want you to consider his age and yours, and take into account that he is from America. This can only cause you trouble and heartache, child."

Shannon sat very still, but her fury was building. She simply could not believe this maddening conversation. Finally Father Mulvany moved into the conversation in his angelic manner.

"When this lad returns to America, and you're left here in the village, then where will ye be?"

It was too much. Shannon interrupted him. "Everyone is entitled to their view. I thank you for your concern for my well being. But I really don't think this conversation is necessary."

"No?" her mother asked.

"That's right. I've just met Jack Murphy. At the bank's request, I might add, I've shown him around Kenmare and introduced him to Mr. and Mrs. Mullins." She paused, wishing she didn't have to defend herself.

Shannon's father had not said a word, but sat quietly looking down at the table listening. Father Mulvany went on in a parental manner as if he had not heard a word she had said. "What happens when Mr. Murphy gets tired of you, or you him?" he asked, raising his eyebrows.

Shannon felt cornered. She stood up, walked to the sink, and got herself a glass of water. Turning and looking at the three of them, she finally said,

"I think everyone has built this all out of proportion. Yes. I like Jack Murphy's company. He is an interesting person, and very kind. I think you should all give me a little credit. This kind of talk is an injustice to Jack."

"Oh, Jack, is it?"

"Mother! I'm a grown woman, for God's sake."

"Watch your tongue," her mother said quickly.

Shannon controlled herself, but only out of respect to her family and Father Mulvany. None of them could understand the magnitude of the sacrifice she had made in moving back to Kenmare, nor the hurt and loneliness she had had to endure.

Either they would believe her or they wouldn't. She knew this. She decided to appease them as best she could, and not aggravate the situation any further. In order to calm her mother, she took a diplomatic approach, something that had become a habit with her since she moved back home.

"I fully understand, I do," she began. "Jack Murphy is much older than I. And yes, he is from America and will be returning. And 'tis true, I don't know him all that well. But there are some things in life that are my choice alone, so you'll just have to trust in me and," she added quickly, "in God, that I will make wise decisions concerning Mr. Jack Murphy."

Finally Mr. Kelly stood up, walked over to his daughter, and put his arm around her. "Let's have a little faith," he looked pointedly at his wife and Father Mulvany, "in Shannon."

Chapter Twelve

Jack stepped out of his cottage to be greeted by a crisp Irish morning. A light wind fanned over the distant hillside, ruffling the clouds. His mind was preoccupied with Shannon.

As he walked under the shadow of the trees and into the lane, he saw Skip, Joe Mullins' black and white dog, coming around the bend. Joe would not be far behind, and sure enough, there he was. Jack called out, "Good morning, Mr. Mullins."

"Top o' the morning to you, Jack, and a fine day it is." He put out his hand to Jack's. "And how are you keeping?"

"I'm keeping well," Jack answered.

"Going to be a bright day, it is."

"Yes, sir, Mr. Mullins. I think you're right. A very bright day." He reached down to pat Skip on the head. "I wonder if I could use your telephone? Mine is still not working."

Joe nodded and tapped his pipe on the heel of his shoe. Using it as a pointer, he motioned toward his house. "Mrs. Mullins is readying herself for some shopping." He always called his wife Mrs. Mullins. "We are just on our way into Kenmare."

"I was wondering if I could make a long distance call? I'll pay the charges."

"Not a bother. Help yourself." They walked to the house, Skip leading the way. "Mind the door when you leave."

Mr. and Mrs. Mullins set out for town in their car and Jack went inside to place his call. Finally the connection was made.

"Sylvia, how are you? I called to wish you a happy birthday."

"Jack, is that you? My God, how are you? And thanks, but my birthday was yesterday. Do you have any idea what time it is over here?"

"How are the kids, Sylvia? And Dr. Rob? Is he as busy as ever?"

"The kids are great. Dr. Rob is keeping very busy at the hospital. I've gained at least ten pounds and I'm on a strict diet. How is Ireland?"

"Ireland is beautiful. I'll tell you all about it, but first, what have you heard from our sister?"

"Not much, Jack. About as usual. You would think she'd come for a visit or at least call more often. You know, Las Vegas is not that far from Los Angeles."

Sylvia and Jack had always been close, but it was different with Terri. Conversations with her were always just a little strained and somewhat distant. Sylvia changed the subject, something she often did when the topic was Terri.

"So tell me about Ireland. How are you doing?"

"Sylvia, I'm in love with the most beautiful woman in the world. Her name is Shannon, and I met her here in Kenmare my first day in town."

"In love! Well, Jack, I think that's terrific. It's about time you met someone you could be with beyond one movie, two dinners and three nights in bed. Does she like you?"

Jack was in his glory to be able to tell someone about Shannon. Ah, that fantastic feeling of letting a person in on your secret. "I think so. She acts like she likes me a lot, and wants to spend time with me. It's all so new to her, to us both. But, yes. She likes me."

"What does Shannon do? How old is she?" Jack stared out the window, thinking how to answer. "Jack, are you there?"

"Yes, I'm sorry. Shannon works here in Kenmare at the bank. And she is twenty-eight."

A pause. "Twenty-eight? Isn't that a little young? You'll soon be forty-eight yourself. Jack, what have you gotten yourself into?"

Jack corrected her. "I'll be forty-seven in July. And it's not what you think. We get on so well, as they say here in Ireland. Shannon is much more stable and mature than any twenty-eight year old you'd ever meet in America. Besides, she says our age difference is no problem."

Sylvia did not press the issue. She changed the subject back around to their sister, and her voice got lower. "I'm truly concerned for Terri," she confided. "This guy she married, this entire Vegas scene, the booze, the drugs, all of it." A long pause. "Jack, when are you planning to be in the States? Perhaps we could both visit her in Las Vegas."

"Well, I'm just now getting deep into my new book. And there's Shannon."

"I know, Jack. I was just hoping you'd be back soon. I'm really worried this time, that's all. I know I, we, haven't been all that close to Terri."

"She wouldn't allow us to be close," Jack reminded her.

"I know. But you're better with her than I am. And I have a feeling that she needs help, now."

"We'll see, Sylvia. We'll just have to see."

This ceremony was not a new one. The same conversation about Terri had taken place many times before. They both felt great pity and sympathy for their sister and her plight, and sometimes even anger. They would talk from time to time, but as the months and sometimes years passed with no word from Terri, they saw little hope of saving her.

Neither of them could understand Terri. She was bright and attractive, maybe too attractive. She had a college degree and a winning personality. But her choice of friends and husbands, her lifestyle, her self-destructive ways belied her talents. This was a standard litany during these conversations, and neither of them ever had an answer to the problem.

This time, however, Sylvia said something that shocked Jack into petrified silence. She told him that Terri had spent a night in jail, busted on possession of drugs. She managed to get off with probation because it was a first offense. Jack took it hard. He assured Sylvia that he, too, was alarmed. He would think about making the trip, he told her.

Finally the conversation turned back to Ireland, Jack's book, and Shannon, the very things he loved to talk about. He filled Sylvia in on a few more details.

"Well, sister dear, even if I'm a day late, happy birthday to you," he said at length. "Get a pen, now, and I'll give you my address. It's very simple. Jack Murphy, Kenmare, County Kerry, Ireland."

"That's it?" asked Sylvia.

"Yep. The people at the post office know me by now, and they all know I live on the Mullins' place. That's all you need."

"Jack, thank you for the call. I love you and miss you. And Jack, good luck with your new love. I mean that."

"Thanks, Sylvia. I miss you and love you too."

Jack hung up the phone in a pensive mood. He was moved by the vote of confidence from Sylvia, for their close bond meant a great deal to him. He was uneasy about his sister Terri. Aloofness and wild living were one thing, but this latest event was ominous. He couldn't sit idly by, for he was her brother after all. He would at least call or write, and maybe go in person. Talk to her, ask what was driving her to harm herself. Probably he couldn't help, but he could certainly try.

He thought it over as he walked down the lane to his cottage. How far away it all seemed now, and after such a short time in Ireland at that. Remembering how very different it was in America, how crowded and consumer-crazy, yet how vital, he decided to talk to Shannon about it. She was so intelligent, so profoundly sensible, that her viewpoint was becoming very important to him. He was to meet her at the bank at noon on this day. If he could keep his mind off her sheer loveliness, he would try to tell her something of America.

Every time Jack met Shannon it was as if it were the first time. Today's luncheon was no different. The meeting turned out to be another stitch in the slowly weaving fabric of their wonderful relationship.

Shannon looked across the table with a smile. "Tell me. When did you first know that you wanted to become a writer?" Then, after a moment's thought, added, "As a professional, I mean. To devote your life to writing."

Jack glanced up from his plate. "Believe it or not, I thought I wanted to be a painter. Of course, that was after I pitched in the World Series and won the Super Bowl, which followed my earlier careers as a fighter pilot and then a race car driver." They both laughed. "I was a dreamer as a kid. Guess I still am."

"A painter?" Shannon picked up the one serious note. "I loved art, too. I painted some in college, but more for the making of it than looking toward a career. I had to be practical."

"Really? Do you have one or two paintings you could show me?"

"I do, yes. Under the bed someplace, or in the closet." Her tone was light

"Great minds run together. I'll call you Minerva, ruler with Jupiter and Juno, goddess of the arts and all intellect, symbol of wisdom. Of course we'll have to get you a helmet, which symbolizes her role as warrior goddess." He was teasing her now, and her eyes sparkled at the fun of it.

"Come, Jack, be serious. You wanted to be an artist?"

"Yes, back when I was a cub reporter I would sketch and paint every day. But little by little I found myself being drawn to serious writing. I started spending more time at it, and less time painting." He added, almost apologetically, "I can't say just when or how. It sort of evolved."

"What writers or books influenced you most?"

Jack thought for a moment, then started to rattle off some of his favorites. "Huxley, Thomas Mann, and of course Tolstoy. And F. Scott Fitzgerald.

"I like *Gone With the Wind* because it was such an important work back then, not just because I'm from the South. Do you realize that today, if a book sells 50,000 copies, it gets on the best seller list? If it sells 250,000, it is a smash hit. Well, when *Gone With the Wind* was released, it sold more than 175,000 copies in the first three weeks, 750,000 in the next few months, and nearly a million and a half by the end of the year. By now, it's up to twenty-two million. Isn't that something?"

Shannon thought about the numbers he was reciting, and how they might relate to the content of the book. "I've never read *Gone With the Wind*," she said. "What was it about the story that made it do so well?"

He paused. "I think it touched a chord in people," he answered. "Like poetry does, in a way. The truth of it is, poetry is my first love, especially the Irish poets."

"Kidding me, you are, just to get along with me," Shannon said reprovingly.

"No. It's true. I remember reading once that if a young man has not memorized long passages of poetry by the time he is twenty, he has wasted a good portion of his life."

She knew he was serious. "Jack, I don't have to tell you this, but you are a very good writer. No, you are an excellent writer. I loved your first two books. I did, truly." Jack smiled at her. "When may I read some of the new one?" she asked.

He saw that she was sincere, and didn't want to put her off by what he was about to say. "Please don't take this wrong, Shannon, but I have this...this superstition about allowing the book to be read before it is published. I almost feel that if we talk about the story, we will talk away the creativity. Does that make sense?"

"It does, yes. I understand completely. I can remember that I never liked to show my paintings to anyone during the working stages. Not until they were finished. Questions, or even praise, would have gotten me off my train of thought." She was gazing out the window, remembering. Now she looked at him, almost shyly. "I'll get the paintings out and show you my work. One day."

The noon time crowd filled the pub with noise. Jack had come to know and enjoy these sounds of music, laughter, Irish joke telling, dishes rattling and glasses clicking together in salute. Shannon leaned forward to be heard. "Tell me about America, Jack."

"Hmm," Jack squinted his eyes and put down his fork. "America. Where to start? America is so many things. It can be the best country in the world, and it can be the worst."

"What do you mean, exactly?"

"Well, like a lot of the world today, America seems driven by greed, especially when you look at the media. It's all about buying more, consuming more. The poor are treated harshly, as if it were a crime to be without. It is a disgrace to have so many homeless people on the streets of a nation that gave prosperity a whole new meaning."

Shannon frowned. "Jack, you make your country sound so awful."

"Well, part of it is. And it's woven together with what is beautiful beyond telling. America spans the two major oceans of the world, and in between is everything from mountain forest to flat desert to Arctic tundra to tropical jungle. And the best highways in the world for seeing it all." Jack grew enthusiastic as he talked. "Our fine colleges and universities are available to all, as is our first-rate medical care. And our systems! Our airports are more efficient, and our telephones and banks run more smoothly, than anywhere else I know. Even the lines of people going into a concert, a ballgame or a movie theater are orderly."

He paused, thinking about the down side. "But we have lost something precious along the way, a quality of life. Many of our family-owned businesses have been swallowed up by discount stores. The Mom and Pop restaurants are almost gone, and fast food places are everywhere, each with worse food than the next."

"I know what you mean," Shannon agreed. "I've not met many Americans, beyond saying hello at the bank and things like that, but I have noticed that most of them seem to be in a hurry whether there's a reason or not." She leaned back, took a sip from her glass and wiped the corner of her mouth with a napkin.

"True, Shannon. Americans want things now. Right now! I can't stand the fast food joints and what they represent. My God, people rush in and grab their food, and oftentimes it is consumed by the time they get out of the parking lot. And that's not to mention what happens at the drive-through window!"

Seeing Shannon's dismay, he hastened to balance his diatribe. "But listen. We have a great deal to be thankful for, too. We have unparalleled opportunity, and freedom like no other country in the world. You know what that is all about."

She nodded. "I do, yes," she replied. "That is why so many people want to move to America, after all."

Jack took her hand in his and then put his other hand on top of it, as if to keep her from getting away while he made his case. "Shannon, I would love to show you America. My America, which is made from the bones of Ireland, Italy, Greece and so many other places. Why, there are no true natives except for the Indians, and they are a minority. The rest came from other places. Which, I might add, does not keep the majority from ridiculing everyone else. America is a gigantic puzzle. None of the pieces are exactly square and none are exactly round. It can be the happiest place on earth at times, and the most appalling. That is what makes it wonderful, I guess."

"I would like to see your country," Shannon said matter-of-factly.

Jack stared at her in surprise, doubting she could have made up her mind so swiftly. She looked straight into his eyes, becoming sure of herself.

"Yes, Mr. Murphy. I would like for you to show me America."

Still somewhat doubtful that she meant it, he said, "Well, we'll just have to do that one day. I'll show you the deep South, God's part of America. We'll see New York, Florida, California, the Grand Canyon, Santa Fe, New Orleans." He stopped. "You're not serious? Would you really go to America with me?"

The pure light of Irish mischief shone in her eyes. "Well, Mr. Murphy, we'll just have to see now, won't we?"

Jack beamed and repeated obediently, "Yes. We'll just have to see."

Chapter Thirteen

The next couple of weeks Jack continued to organize his new cottage and arrange his work space. He even managed from time to time to work on his new book.

He and Shannon saw each other almost every day for lunch. Sometimes they met after the bank closed for a drink at the pub. If Jack was fortunate, she was able to stay for dinner with him, but most of the time they saved dinner outings for Saturday night. Saturday had become their special day, a day for cherished moments together.

For the very first time, Mr. Kelly actually carried on a conversation with Jack one Saturday morning while he was standing outside waiting for Shannon.

"There was this lad who came to Kenmare, a blow-in, you might say," Mr. Kelly began. "Shannon was just a wee thing then." He held his hand about three feet off the ground.

"They said this young man was a cousin of the late President Kennedy. 'Tis hard for me to believe now, but I believed it then. With my own eyes I saw him. He looked like a Kennedy, all right. And you know what happened? He came down the road, there, the same road you came yourself. He walked up to me and said that he wanted to buy my place. Said that he wanted to retire here and write a book. I could make nothing of it, him being a stranger.

"I will not deny that I found him interesting, so I invited him in for a wee bit of whisky. I was never one to drink much, but this was a special occasion. 'Tis true, a Kennedy in my home. He spent a long time sitting by the fire with me. He was a likable lad, he was. We sat there and told stories to each other for at least two hours."

Mr. Kelly tapped his pipe on his hand and knocked out some ashes, then took out a match. He did not light the pipe at first, but stood with the pipe in one hand and the match in the other as he continued. "I can't swear to the exact words, but he said that when he got back to America he was going to send me a photo of himself and President Kennedy."

"Did you ever get the photo?" Jack asked.

"I didn't, no. I never received the photo." He paused, struck the match on the heel of his shoe, and lit his pipe. "Tell me, Mr. Murphy, how long do you expect to be in Ireland?" he asked with a penetrating look. There was a small silence while Jack waited for other questions, but none came.

"I'm not sure, Mr.Kelly. I guess it depends on how fast my new book comes along. I haven't really set a timetable."

"I see. Are you getting on well in Kenmare?"

"Oh, yes, sir. I like the village, and the people. They are great."

"And Shannon. How are you and Shannon getting on?"

Jack was disconcerted. He could see the point Mr.Kelly was making with his stories and questions. He didn't know exactly how to answer the last one, and was relieved when the postman came riding up on his bicycle just then.

"Morning, Mr. Kelly," he called out. "I have something in the post for you today," handing him a small letter. Mr. Kelly looked at it for a long moment. He did not open it at once, but shoved it into his coat pocket. Jack glanced at the front of the envelope. It was from Belfast.

"Time for me to be getting back to work," Mr. Kelly said matter-of-factly.

"Nice visiting with you Mr. Kelly," Jack called out as Mr. Kelly headed toward the barn.

"Good day to you, sir," the postman said, adding under his breath, "What an old grump he is today." Jack watched each of them go off in different directions, thinking to himself that the letter must have been from someone very important to Mr. Kelly, since he seemed disturbed by it. He mumbled an old saying to himself. "If you want to be happy in life, mind your own business."

Jack turned his thoughts to this day, when he and Shannon would journey off on a day trip and she would show him some more of her Ireland. He was beginning to learn that it was a magical island, filled with wonder, history, and a world of quiet time.

On one such outing, near Dingle, Jack had come face to face with his ancestors. Far out beyond the world of normal living sits a small group of islands known as the Blaskets. It is deserted today, but at one point in 1840, one hundred and fifty people lived there. Jack learned that the people of the Blasket Islands had left a great literary legacy. Almost all of them had been writers, poets, and artists. He had been so fascinated, in fact, that Shannon suggested they return this very day for another visit.

His reverie was interrupted when Shannon came briskly out the front door, looking directly at him with a shy, pleasant smile in her eyes. Jack watched her as she walked closer. There was a slight breeze and her hair flowed as she walked. She was dressed simply for their outing, in comfortable shoes and heavy stockings. Her dark blue dress was cut loosely, for ease of motion, and would have been quite modest on a lesser woman. But on Shannon, it simply pointed up the generosity of her womanly body, her supple waist and delicious curves, the fluid grace of her stride.

He would never get used to the sight of her, or so he devoutly hoped. Each time she appeared, he wanted to grab her and kiss her wildly. Today, his desire for her almost made his knees buckle, though he maintained his composure with an effort. My God, he thought, she is so absolutely beautiful today!

He beamed at her as she drew near, and inhaled her clean, healthy scent. Her eyes took the morning sun and gave it back in shades of emerald and gold. In this glorious moment, Jack wanted only to love her, to make love to her and feel her body melting into his own. It was all that he could do to contain his hunger for her. The sheer joy of being with her filled his heart like a flood tide crashing onto the shore. He wanted to shout out to her that he loved her madly, that he wanted her to be his own. But decorum prevailed. He took her by the arm and walked her to the car, placing the basket in the back seat.

As they drove along the narrow roads, Jack continued to ask himself what had happened to him. He couldn't believe his own feelings and his frenzied emotions over this woman. He was not sane. He was impassioned, enchanted, caught up in something he could not explain. This magnetism that she possessed, so irresistible and ever so seductive, was driving him mad. He wanted at least to speak more directly about his feelings, but contained himself. Finally they reached their destination, and found a picnic spot on the edge of the water looking out at the Great Blasket Island. Shannon began to fix the luncheon she had brought.

"Jack," she said, turning her head up a little toward him.

"Yes." There was a long pause. Somewhere very far away across the silent green fields, Jack heard the sound of a steeple bell.

"How long will you be in Ireland?" she finally asked.

"I'm not sure. A year, perhaps. A year and a few months. I'm not sure," Jack answered, struggling with his response. It was the second time today he had been asked that very question, and he wanted to be honest.

"Where will you go when you've finished your book?" She felt oddly detached as she asked, although her mind was preoccupied with past experience. She wondered if Jack would be another Stal, and if she were being overly cautious. Perhaps she was afraid of replaying that painful incident, of falling in love and then losing that love.

Jack did not want to answer her question. He was afraid of saying the wrong thing. A hundred scenes from these past few weeks filled his mind. He desperately wanted to foster this growing relationship. The idea of perhaps staying longer in County Kerry was becoming more attractive as he got to know this lovely Irishwoman.

"Well, I still have a condo in Miami," he finally said, waving his hand toward the sea.

"But, Shannon, I'm in no hurry to leave Ireland, and I'm especially in no hurry to leave you."

She shook her head. "Jack, you barely know me." Her tone was calming, yet her voice trembled just a little. She did not take her eyes off him as she listened to his outpourings.

"Shannon!" He knew he had to tell her now. His face glowed warmly. "I think—no, I know that I fell in love with you that very day I saw you in Kenmare. I was overcome by you the first time we met." Her eyes lit up and a faint blush colored her cheeks. "I knew then that we would be together," he went on, more confidently than he felt. "Shannon, it's true. I'm in love with you. There. I've said it. I love you."

Then there was a very long silence. Her eyes welled up with tears. Finally she spoke as she reached up and touched Jack's face. "Jack. Oh, Jack." Her throat tightened. "I don't know what to say." Then, with more assurance, she said, "This is all going so fast."

Jack said nothing. Then, without warning, he grabbed her around the waist and pulled her to into his arms. They both rolled over on the damp earth. "Look at me," he said, and she did. Her heart beating so fast it frightened her. She suddenly felt so vulnerable.

"Shannon, I can't believe how wonderful you feel in my arms," Jack kissed her gently. "I love you. I know it. I love you." A careless rapture overcame him. He kissed her once more, this time with unabated longing, and a wave of emotion crashed in on him. Shannon returned his kiss with a passion to match his own, pressing closer to him, just as he had dreamed.

Then she pulled away, gracefully as always, and sat up and looked at him tenderly. Jack was in awe of her. He'd never met a woman like this in his life. He gripped her arm, wanting to hold her yet giving her room to collect herself. She glanced up and away, then back at him. Softly he asked, "What is it?"

She shook her head. "We hardly know each other, and we have all of these complications. Lord knows, I've thought of them over and over again."

"What complications?" Jack tried to sound agreeable.

She gave out a distracted glance toward the bay and then looked at him quizzically, as if he had asked a foolish question. "Jack," her voice was rising a little, "You are from America and I'm Irish. I'm from a small village and you are from a big city. And you'll be going back to America when your book is finished."

Jack ventured a thought. "But, Shannon, if we have love, we can work all that out." He let that register, then went on insistently. "I won't let you go. That's all there is to it. I won't allow you to break off this relationship."

Shannon had a very serious look. "What about the difference of age?"

"Age? We are not that far apart. You're talking as if I'm ready for the grave. I'm only forty-six. You're what, twenty-eight? That's only a few years."

"Eighteen, Jack. Eighteen."

"Shannon, you are strong and wise beyond your years. I am, well, maybe a little less mature than I would wish. That makes us about the same age in real terms." He was smiling now, trying to lighten her mood, but she would say what was on her mind.

"There is my mother and father." They sat on the blanket looking at each other, as she told him of their opposition, and of their unwillingness to respect her freedom, and of the sacrifices she had already made for them. Shannon held Jack's hands in hers. The peaceful setting, there by the sea, was underscored by the sounds of seagulls and an occasional lone cow off in the distance.

"You must know by now that I enjoy your company," she continued. She looked away toward the islands, then back at Jack. "And that…well, that…" she stopped. "Oh, God, this all sounds so formal."

She looked down at the ground, thinking, then turned to him again. Her voice softened as she said, "I like you more than a little. That's the problem."

"Problem?" Jack beamed delightedly. "It's the most wonderful problem a man could ask for." Shannon tried to remain serious, but he would not wait for her to continue.

"Listen to me," he demanded. "Why don't we just be friends, or lovers, or be dating, or whatever you want to call it? Not worry about every little detail. Enjoy each other. Laugh. Dance. Go out to dinner. Walk in the park. Just be together and allow time to work everything out." He found himself talking faster. "We don't have to make any decisions today, or tomorrow for that matter. I have just now begun my book and it will be a long time before it is completed. It's a major project for me, and will take a great deal of time and effort."

She considered his words, but did not answer directly. Instead, she asked, "Jack do you believe in fate? Do you believe that there is a reason for everything?"

"I'm not altogether sure," he replied. "I used to believe everything the Catholic Church told me. I used to believe that there is this master plan, and in some ways, I guess I still do."

"You do believe in God?"

"Yes, I believe there is a God. And you? I know you must, being Catholic."

"I do, indeed." She reached over to touch Jack's hand. The blood rushed up into her cheeks. "We could not have this closeness without Him. All good comes from God. My mother used to tell me to look for the beauty in all things, and to shy away from anything that was not of God."

"True," he nodded thoughtfully, "but can you have joy without knowing pain? In this tragic web of life, don't we find our greatest joy following bitter sorrow?"

"In other words," Shannon replied, "An existence of loneliness can be redeemed by a life of love. Does that mean heaven can be found here on this earth, through love?"

"This is getting pretty philosophical, Shannon," he smiled at her fondly, and she relented.

Changing the subject, she continued, "Speaking of love, I think I was in love once. I had this boyfriend when I lived in Limerick. His name was Stal. That was about three years ago. Anyway, the relationship did not work out. Then, when my mother fell ill, I asked for that transfer and moved back to Kenmare. Kind of on the rebound, I guess, I started dating Bruce again. We even talked of marriage. Then I realized that I did not want to be married to Bruce, so I broke it off. But even while I was seeing Bruce, I was never truly happy. My life was not what I thought life should be. I never let go of my old boyfriend, Stal, and I never accepted Bruce. I was miserable…until I met you.

"You have given me reasons to want to go on a picnic to Bantry Bay, or to the Blasket Islands. I look forward to getting off work and seeing you at the pub. Going out to dinner, or just for a walk by the water's edge. Jack, I truly enjoy being with you. I find myself out of sorts when we are not together. I even worry for you, like your coming trip to Cork."

Jack listened quietly, beaming inside his mind with her every word. Shannon began to sense that she was contradicting herself. She suddenly realized that she had just verbalized what she had been afraid to feel. She smiled at him tentatively, touched his face, then leaned forward and kissed him quickly.

"You're right, Mr. Murphy," she admitted sheepishly. "I've just said exactly what you said, only backwards. We shouldn't worry about when you are going to finish your book and where you will live and when will you return to America. We should live this day, for this day we know for sure that we have. None of us is sure what will come tomorrow."

Jack saw with great pleasure that she had reached a resolution. She appeared calm and happy now. He looked at her long red hair in the sunlight, and at her soft delicate hands. He marveled at her elegant manner in all things, and realized once again how rare Shannon truly was.

On the horizon, there was a slight rain passing, but the skies over the Blaskets were clear washed and as bright as Jack had yet seen in Ireland. The sun smiled at the two of them, giving a little wink in Jack's direction as if to say, "Not to worry, my lad. You've got your lady."

Chapter Fourteen

Jack put himself deep into his novel, and he was very pleased with his progress. The book was filled with romance, and his portraits of the feature characters in the book were coming to life. The theme remained constant, and the settings, language and images were clear. He had read the last four completed chapters yet again, and now he rubbed his eyes, stretched his back and raised his arms high above his head. He went to the front door and looked out at the water beyond. A ripple was forming. He thought perhaps a fish had jumped. He looked hard but could see no trace of anything.

Jack walked out of the house, leaving the door open. He strolled the front grounds a bit and then started walking up the road toward the main house. He could see Mr. Mullins sitting out front on an old bench. Mr. Mullins had a pocket knife in his hand and was whittling something.

"What are you paring?" Jack called out as he approached.

"Ah, 'tis you, Mr. Murphy. Good evening to you. A fine afternoon it is, too." He smiled. "What did you say?"

"I said, what are you carving?"

"I'm whittling. I'm not making anything a'tall. I just like to whittle. And think." He glanced up at Jack as he brushed some shavings from his sweater. "Try it some time, lad. 'Tis good for the soul."

“Yes, I will, Mr. Mullins. I really will.”

“Sit down.” Mr. Mullins patted the bench with his hand. “How are you finding Ireland, Mr. Murphy?” he inquired.

“I love it. I’m feeling more and more at home each day that passes.”

“And little Shannon, how are you two getting on?” he looked over at Jack.

There was so many answers to this question, Jack did not know where to start. He decided to not respond at all, but answer the question with a question. “How long have you known the family?”

“My whole life, I guess. We were all born in County Kerry, grew up right here in Kenmare. I can remember the day each of their children were born. A happy day, every time, it was.” His expression softened at the memory. It was plain that Shannon was beloved in Kenmare, was a source of pride to all, and that any false moves in her direction would invite trouble. They gave each other a clear look, as if both knew perfectly well what Mr. Mullins was talking about.

“Mr. Mullins, are you trying to tell me something?”

Mr. Mullins shook his head, saying, “You’re a very wise young lad. Do ye know the writings of Sterne? Laurence Sterne?”

“I’ve read a little,” Jack answered, glad to be on safer ground.

“How about this one. ‘What is the life of man? Is it not to shift from side to side, from sorrow to sorrow? To button up one cause of vexation and unbutton another?’”

Jack stared thoughtfully out toward the pasture. A cow was grazing nearby. He looked back at Mr. Mullins, who stroked his chin and said, “Here’s another from Oscar Wilde. ‘One’s real life is so often the life that one does not lead.’”

Jack wiped his brown shirt sleeve across his forehead, carefully choosing his moment. “I have one for you Mr. Mullins. Another of your countrymen, Sean O’Casey. ‘A lament in one ear, maybe, but always a song in the other. And to me life is simply an invitation to live.’”

"Well done, lad, well done!" Mr. Mullins fastened his large hand around Jack's.

Jack smiled. "I must be getting on down the road, Mr. Mullins. I have work to do. The typewriter is calling, speaking of writers."

"Very well lad. It was good visiting with you. I like to be challenged by a strong, sound mind such as yours. You come up anytime, do ye hear?" Jack walked down the path, stopping to look back at the old man, still sitting, whittling the same stick. He waved, but Mr. Mullins did not look up.

The sun was setting and the air was beginning to cool. The door to Jack's cottage had blown closed. He went inside and began to build a fire. The phone rang, and he laid down the matches and answered with a rushed hello.

"Mr. Murphy," a cheery Shannon called out. "You have an invitation to join a certain Ms. Kelly tomorrow afternoon for lunch. Would you be caring to go along with that?"

"I'm not sure of my social calendar. If you'll hold one moment I'll check with my secretary and see if I'm free tomorrow." They both laughed.

"Good afternoon, my love," she said softly. "I miss you. Are you working?"

"Not right now, though I got a lot done earlier today. I was just down the road talking with Mr. Mullins. I was about to build a fire, have a bite to eat and return to my typewriter. But I could be talked into putting all that aside and picking you up for dinner. Do you want to go to the Old Boat House?"

"I would love it. Let's do it. Give me thirty minutes and I'll be ready."

Jack beamed as he hung up the phone and dashed upstairs to change clothes. Standing unclothed in front of the mirror, his hands hanging naturally to his sides, he took a deep breath and looked at himself. His body was all right, he supposed, but it had lost its definition. He was getting a bit of a gut. He noticed a little roll of fat, and with that he lifted his shoulders to raise his waist as high as he could, pulling it in and extending his chest. He took out a mirror and turned around to look at the back of his head, holding the mirror just right so he could see the top as well. Thank God, he thought, I'm not losing any hair. Well, not much, anyway. But he was still uneasy about the whole business of aging, and knew he should take better care of himself.

He felt a sudden resentment that he had wasted so much of his life with transient, meaningless relationships. Mostly, he felt cheated. He had allowed so many years to pass since Helen's death that youth had passed him by. All those years had been buried under the weight of guilt and a certain feeling of betrayal because he had not been allowed to help her. Was he now regaining the youth he had lost then? Was he getting a second chance, and was it not too late after all? If that was true, he told himself, then he had better not blow it this time. He took a last look in the mirror, got dressed and headed to Shannon's.

She was standing out front of the house when he arrived and she looked stunning. Her hair was piled atop her head and secured with a wisp of black silk, setting off a simple dress in a jewel-toned print of deep red, blue, green and black. Pulling the car very close to her, Jack stopped the engine and got out to greet her. Shannon gave him a nice hug and got into the car. After they had pulled off onto the main road, she reached over and kissed him. "Hi."

"Hello," he said. "You look ravishing. Lovely. Radiant".

"Wow," she said. "And all I did was change my dress."

"Shannon," Jack grew more serious. "I've got to go to America."

"No. When?" Shannon frowned.

"Soon. I must meet with my publishers, so I thought I would go a few days early and see my sister in California, and even try to see my sister in Las Vegas. It can't be helped. I must. It's business."

"I'll miss you. I wish I could go."

He took her hand as she spoke, and told her soothingly, "We'll go one

day together and I'll show you my country, as you've shown me yours."
Shannon did not respond, but smiled and leaned back in her seat, letting her imagination take hold.

"I'll write to you and I'll call you," he reassured her. "And I'll be back before you know it. Nine or ten days, maybe two weeks at the most."

Chapter Fifteen

The next day Jack slept late and awoke to a cool, sunny day. He got up and dressed, then descended the stairs and built a fire. Papers in hand, he sat down in his high back chair. A warm glow radiated from rocks in the the fireplace. He began reading the latest draft of his book.

> It made no difference to her what perils or tragedies he had known, she was going to go with him to Europe. The thought of a new land and of living with him meant everything to her. She had become his slave, his servant, his lover. This, then, was going to be her life. The die was cast. At thirty-seven, she felt that it would be her final commitment. It made little difference to her that his character had changed, even though his position and fortune had improved.

Jack took out a pad and pen and made a few notes. He had just laid them down when there was a knock at the door. He opened the door and was pleasantly surprised to see Shannon.

"Shannon!" He took her by the hand and led her inside. After closing the door, he gave her a long, warm hug and then kissed her gently.

"I just wanted to see you," she said. "I started to call first, but then…" she paused.

"What?" asked Jack.

"My mother. She had another talk with me, about you. About us. Oh, Jack, hold me," she reached up on her toes and put her arms tightly around Jack's neck, and he stroked her hair.

"Come, sit by the fire, now. Tell me what this is all about."

"Well, my papa went outside to the barn, and my mother asked me to sit with her. So we sat down at the kitchen table and she said that she and pa were concerned that we had been spending too much time together. She asked me what your intentions were." Shannon leaned forward to warm her hands against the fire.

Jack sat motionless, just looking at her. She continued, "I told her that we are in love. Then she asked if you had talked about getting married? She asked about America, and would I be moving there."

Jack pulled his chair closer to hers and sat facing her, holding her hands tightly and looking directly into her eyes. "What did you say?"

"I didn't say anything. I didn't know what to say, Jack." The pain of dealing with her parents' oppression showed clearly on her face. "My ma has never been one to cry very much, but I thought I saw tears in her eyes. She got up to get a cup of tea, and when she returned she told me that pa was beginning to get very concerned that I was making a big mistake, just what they had warned me about."

"Do you think that we are a mistake?" Jack asked for his own sake as well as to help her sort out the situation. He needed her reassurance.

"No, no. Not at all. You are the best thing that has ever come into my life." She reached up and placed her hands against his cheeks, and held his face in her hands, looking at him. "I love you, my darling. We'll just have to work this out. I'm a grown woman and I have to live my life, not theirs. My own dreams, not my parents' expectations. They are living in a time that has gone by. I respect that, truly I do. And I love them so. I'd like to make them happy, but I've already given them a great deal of time and consideration. I wonder how much more I can do and still have a life of my own."

There was a somber feeling in the air as Jack and Shannon sat talking. Outside a slight wind blew in gusts, and now and then the old windows of the cottage would rattle. Sitting there, watching the slow smoke rise from the fire, Jack and Shannon fell silent. They both stared into he flames for a very long time.

Finally Jack spoke with all his heart. "My sweet Shannon, my lovely Shannon." The words rushed from deep inside his being. She was crying now, and he pulled her close to him and kissed her. The glow of her magical kiss lifted the heaviness. "Hush," he said softly. "It will be all right, I promise. I'll go speak with your father and your mother. I'll make them understand. They like me, Shannon, and they will like me even more when they get to know me better. You'll see. It's just that they love you and they are concerned for you."

Shannon pulled away slowly and sat back in her chair.

"Jack, listen to me. I need to tell you something, something that I promised my pa I would never talk about, but you need to know. I think that you have a right to know. And besides, I don't want to keep secrets between us."

Her words riveted his attention. He saw her eyes begin to mist.

"Jack, do you remember the day I told you that my sister died when I was young?" He nodded. Shannon pulled her hair from her face and sat up very straight in her chair. "You asked about my brother, Brien, and I changed the subject. I have to tell you about Brien. He's in the IRA." She bit her lip a little and stared directly into Jack's eyes, then looked down.

"What?" Jack gasped, clearly shaken.

"Jack, please don't yell. Words carry their own power."

"I'm sorry, Shannon, you took me by surprise. Why did you wait so long to tell me? How long have you known this? Surely your parents' worries have a lot to do with this. How could you not see that? How could you not tell me such an important thing?"

Shannon paused, breathing heavily as she tried to frame an answer to his frenzy of questions. "Jack, please, my darling. I couldn't. I promised my father," she said presently. She stood and began to walk around the room, and he followed her with his eyes. She stopped in front of him, then sat down. "Brien moved to Dublin four and a half years ago. He found some type of work, and that only lasted about six months, then he moved to Belfast. He got a job in a metal factory. When my mother fell ill three years ago, Brien came home for a visit to see her.

"While he was here, he and my papa got into a very bad discussion. Finally, Brien lost his temper and told my papa that he was working with the IRA." Jack felt a rush of anger. So this wasn't only about himself, he thought. Shannon continued, "My brother tried to explain that he had never been involved with the bombs and the killing or anything like that, but nonetheless he was a member of the IRA. He tried to tell my papa that it was for the good of Ireland, the good of everyone. He said he needed a sense of place."

"This makes no sense. I don't believe this," said Jack wearily.

"My father told Brien that he no longer had a son. That no son of his would be involved in killing." Jack stood up and began pacing the floor as she talked. "In other words, my papa said, as long as my brother was involved in the IRA, he was not welcome in his house."

"What did you do?" asked Jack.

"What could I do? Oh, and it hurt my mother so very much. I would dare say that my mama and papa have never been the same. Don't you see? My sister died, then this business with Brien, and now all they can think of is losing their only daughter. Papa and I are all that mama has left. I've heard her pray, 'God what am I to do when Shannon is taken from me?'"

Jack sat down and took her hands in his. "How do you feel about all of this? Have you heard from Brien?"

"I have, yes. Brien called me at the bank one afternoon last year. We did not talk long. He asked how we were all getting on. I have not heard anything now in ages."

"How do you feel about all this?" Jack repeated his question.

"I worry, of course, for Brien and for my parents. It truly defeated me at first, until I decided that I can't live my brother's life for him. But, Jack, I worry for my little brother. I love him so much, but this is bigger than me. It's not in my control."

"How old is Brien?"

"Twenty-six. "

"Twenty-six!" Jack repeated. "He's only a kid." With that, Jack realized that Shannon was just twenty-eight herself, although she had never seemed so young to him. She took no notice of the irony.

"I know," she said quietly. "He's never been a hothead. I just pray that he doesn't get mixed up in something far more serious with this IRA business."

She looked at him a moment longer, then said in a hard quiet voice, "There. I've told you. I feel much better. I want no secrets between us, ever." She could not have known how important her trust was to Jack.

Shannon turned and walked outside, and Jack followed her to the shoreline. Jack took her in his arms. "Shannon, you don't have to bear the whole burden yourself. You've got a right to your own life. You can't live anyone else's life for them, any more than they can for you. I think that you have done remarkably well to balance it all and to be of so much help to your family."

He continued to hold her close. Somewhere far away, he could hear the sound of a bird song. Shannon at last broke down and began to sob. He cradled her in his arms for a long time, until her tears subsided.

They stood by the sea in sunwashed silence. Shannon lifted her head and looked at him. In that brief moment, she wanted to reveal that she was falling in love with Jack. She felt a strong impulse to submit to him completely. Then her sense of Irish rule and judgement took hold, and she pulled back and headed toward the house.

Chapter Sixteen

"There is a peculiar lightness in the air in Ireland, which brings healing on its wings to the over-excited mind, as well as to the exhausted."

Jack had read this passage in a magazine while he waited for his car, and now he thought of it again as he drove along the highway. He felt as if the words were written for him and him alone.

His trip to Cork had worked out perfectly. He had found a very satisfactory car that he could lease for a year and then continue on a month to month basis thereafter. Now his first major outing with Shannon could be set. She could ride back to Cork with him on Saturday to pick up the new car and drop off the rental. He was excited with the thought of it.

Jack was becoming much more in tune with Ireland and her people. He was beginning to understand the way in which they meet strangers with an eagerness to pass the time of day. The Irish would make the effort to spend time with you, he learned, whether it was in a pub, on a busy street, or in a remote village. He had also found that one could get away from everything just as easily by going out into the countryside. Its cozy homesteads, its rivers and lakes, its shining fields of rich soil, and its slumbering mountains filled his dreams. Jack said out loud, "You have not been in love until you have been in love in Ireland." He took out the pad and pen that was always with him and wrote down his thoughts.

"Céad Mile Fáilte. Welcome to Kenmare." The sign sped past as he headed to his cottage to call Shannon. He had gotten up very early so that he could finish his business in Cork and be back in Kenmare near lunch time. He called the bank and was connected.

Shannon picked up the phone to be greeted by Jack. "I'm coming over to take you to lunch, okay? I want to talk with you about going to Cork with me on Saturday. I've leased a new car, and I need to pick it up and turn in my rental car. Will you go?"

"I don't know, Jack, if I can."

Jack realized he was being presumptuous, and began choosing his words more carefully. "Shannon, not only do I want you to go, but I need you to go. I need someone to drive the rental car, that is, after we pick up my new car. We could drop it off, then have lunch and head back. Please, say you'll go."

"Let's talk about it over lunch today, all right?" she asked at length. Jack agreed.

There was talk in the village about a major storm coming their way. It was expected to hit the coast Saturday afternoon or evening, bringing lightning and the kind of wind and rain that can make the coast look like a wind-torn flag. The worst storm in recorded history was that of 1839, known locally as the Big Wind. Most of Ireland had felt the fury. Roofs were blown off, and some homes were completely destroyed. The rains come down sideways, cutting across the countryside like thousands of small spears cast off by the gods, leaving the land soaked and silent.

Shannon's great-grandfather had passed down many tales of the Big Wind, and she had told Jack some of them. He had heard others as well. More than anything else, they gave him that sense of history he was looking for. He was just now beginning to see how important history was to the Irish, and how it was interwoven with legend until it became something more. He was starting to accept this as somehow more real than the mere facts, this convoluted history of Ireland, of the people of County Kerry, and of Shannon and her family.

Jack went into the bank and found Shannon sitting at her desk. She smiled at him, arranged a few items on her desk, got her hand bag and sweater, and moved to greet Jack.

Once outside, Jack took her hand and held it in his for a long time. He just wanted to look at her. Then he smiled and said, "Where would you like to eat? Anywhere at all is fine with me." They decided on a pub just around the corner from the bank.

He had meant to be calm, he really had. But the thought of a real trip with Shannon made him as excited as a kid. They ordered their meal and talked about the trip to Cork, and at length Shannon agreed to go.

Jack was overjoyed. He was about to take her hand when a voice called out, "Shannon." An unkempt fellow moved closer to the table and called out her name again.

"Bruce," she said, surprised. Jack turned to face Bruce.

"Bruce, this is Jack Murphy," Jack put his hand out to Bruce, who did not respond or even look at him.

"Well, is this your latest blow-in?" he asked Shannon rudely. She could tell that he had been drinking quite a lot. He snorted and glanced at Jack, who sat motionless.

Shannon stood up. "Bruce, please. Just go about your business".

"You think I don't know about you and this rich American? You think I haven't heard the talk?"

"Bruce, my friends are none of your business. Now, be getting on." Her voice took on a harder edge.

The bartender and two other men sitting at the bar were watching and listening. Finally the bartender called out. "Come here, lad. Bruce! Shut your gob."

Bruce looked over at the bartender, then back at Shannon, then at Jack. He stood silently for a long while, swaying slightly, then took a deep breath. "What the hell," he muttered, and walked away.

Shannon and Jack stood up, gathered their wraps, and left the pub.

"I'm sorry, Jack. I'm truly sorry."

"There is no need to apologize. Bruce was drunk. And there's no doubt he was hurt when he saw us together."

"I'm still sorry it happened." She took Jack's hand as they walked. "Bruce has always had a bit of a temper, especially when he's had a few too many pints. I can remember one night in a pub when he was so wild with jealousy that he struck this poor man just for looking at me. It was after that night that I really started to look at Bruce, and at the idea of us getting married. A few weeks later I broke it off with him."

"Has he bothered you since then?"

"Not much. For awhile, he would call me and try to see me. Once he came over to the house and tried to get me to go for a ride so that we could talk. I didn't go. Finally, my father asked Bruce to leave and to please respect my wishes. Since that afternoon, Bruce has not called or come around. Once in a while I have met him on the street and he has just nodded and said hello under his breath. I don't know what got into him today."

Jack was quiet for awhile, then said, "I was so proud of you back there in the pub. You handled that with such dignity." Shannon nodded in thanks. "Bruce looked so pathetic," he added.

"Oh, but he's a big, strong man," she cautioned him. "I don't want you ever to get into it with him, Jack. Do you promise?"

"Shannon, I'm not a fighter. And I do promise." His eyes showed that she had surprised him with her concern, and that he was touched.

"Let's don't talk about it anymore."

Her words made Jack feel better. "Done!" he said, and changed the subject. "I'll pick you up early on Saturday, say about seven a.m. We'll have a lovely lunch in Cork after we get the car business done. Then we'll see some countryside on the way back, and be home well before that storm they're talking about." She looked at him with gratitude for cheering her up.

CHAPTER SEVENTEEN

Finally Shannon realized that sleep would not come to her this night. Seeing Bruce that day had stirred up memories of her days with him, and other unresolved sorrows as well. She got up from bed, put on her robe and sat down to try to read a book. At length, she gave up and simply allowed her mind to drift back and forth, not necessarily trying to make sense, but watching for patterns and listening for echoes.

Jack's dear, familiar face came into her thoughts, and she let her feelings for him rise. She remembered old times with Bruce, before his drinking and his temper got the better of him. There was Stal, whom she normally tried to avoid thinking about. She thought of everything and nothing in particular, of hopes of things to come and of long ago dreams. Flashes of the past illuminated the present like summer lightning.

Shannon's life had not been easy. Often it had been painful and many times difficult. Always, she had worked very hard at it, striving to stay clear and do her best. No matter how emotional she became over the stormy course of events, there was a calm place deep inside her where she could go and restore herself.

Several years before, Shannon had had a romantic affair. She had fallen in love, or so she thought, with an American from California. He was the assistant director for a production company that was shooting a film on location in Ireland. Stallard Hopkins was his name, though most people called him Stal. She allowed herself to picture him, his face, his light blond hair, his tall strong body, and his easy way with people.

She remembered how they had met. It was in the bank in Limerick. He had come in to exchange currency and ask directions, and Shannon assisted him. He was one of the most charming men she had ever met. That day, when she got off work, he was outside the bank waiting for her.

"Hi, remember me? I'm Stallard Hopkins."

"I do, yes," Shannon replied.

"Call me Stal. Would you like to go across the street to the pub and have a pint with me?" He did not wait for an answer. He took her by the arm, and before she could respond they were crossing the street.

Shannon sat there in the quiet of her room thinking of these events. She reached up and turned off her light and sat in the dark, her mind racing back in time. Stal had swept her off her feet. She remembered talking and talking that night, more than she had talked to anyone in ages. She was free with Stal. She told him about Kenmare, about going to college in Limerick and working part-time at the bank, and then getting a job there after she graduated. She talked about her mother and father.

Shannon recalled the first night that she and Stal had made love. She had gone with him one Saturday to watch how a movie is made. It was exciting, meeting movie stars and watching people set up shots. In the evening, they had gone to dinner and then to Stal's hotel for a drink. It was after that drink that Stal invited her to his hotel room. She smiled in spite of herself. It had been purely fantastic.

Aloud, she said, "Why am I awake at three in the morning, sitting here thinking about Stal and Jack and everything else under God's blue sky?" She turned the light on in her bedroom and reached over to the bookcase, pulling out a small box. She took out several photos.

Most of the pictures were of her with Stal, and each carried with it memories of the past. One reminded her of the day Stal was packing to return to California. He was first going back to his home in Philadelphia to visit friends and relatives, he said, and then on to Hollywood. He told her that he would call her from Philadelphia. He never did. He said that he would write to her from California. He never did. He told her that he would return to Ireland for a visit. He never did. In the past, Shannon would cry when she looked at these old photos. Even after she had moved back to Kenmare and started dating Bruce, she would find herself looking at these pictures, these two happy people living and loving in Limerick, and she would cry.

Shannon realized that night, as she looked at each photo very carefully, that she was not crying. This was the first night in over three years that she had been able to revisit the past and not break down. Very slowly, with no anger, she placed each photo back in the box. Then she closed the lid and walked downstairs. There was still a small flame flickering in the fireplace. She stood for a moment looking at the hot coals, then sacrificed the box to the fire. As the flames caught hold of the dry cardboard box and devoured it, an overwhelming sense of relief came over her. The shame of playing the pitiful fool suddenly vanished. She could feel the plunge back into innocence, into trust. She had escaped that bit of her past, and now she had a wonderful feeling of well being. She returned to her bedroom, crawled under the quilts, and fell asleep.

The next morning Shannon awakened to the sounds of birds outside her bedroom window. Her dreams lifted slowly enough for her to capture a waking memory. She had been on a magic flying carpet, high above the Irish coastline. The rush and hiss of tides, the layers of foam pouring over the rocks, and the miles and miles of beach were as vivid as any day. She saw the sun blazing down and filling every crack of the rocks along the shore. It had lighted up the countryside, the birds and animals, and the working farmers. It dipped under the trees and created patterns of light on the mountains. The sun turned the rivers and lakes into molten silver, and moved across the fields weaving patterns of beautiful shapes and colors. Like an impressionist painter, the sun had warmed the whole of Ireland, filling all the spaces with its beauty. The world was perfect. It was a wonderful dream.

This feeling she had was special, and she knew it had a great deal to do with Jack. She had always known that one day she would experience such an emotion, and now here it was, with all its wonder and its magnificent kind of strangeness. Yet, it was as familiar as an old friend. Something had bloomed within her, she knew.

As she readied herself for this day, Shannon paid special attention to what she was going to wear, for it was today that they were going to Cork. She decided on a straight, form-fitting dress with scooped neckline. She picked out simple earrings, a scarf and her favorite cardigan sweater.

She lingered at her bath, scenting it with a few garden herbs that perfumed the air around her. She washed her hair and brushed it until it shone, then put it up in a soft French twist with a little left hanging down her back. She paid close attention to every detail.

I must hurry, she thought. Jack will be here soon. Excitement and anticipation lifted her spirits high, filling her with triumphant confidence.

Jack hardly said a word to her when he picked her up, but he never took his eyes off her. Once they were on the road, he turned to her with a stunned expression. "I've never seen you this way," he said softly.

"And what way might that be, Mr. Murphy?" she responded, even though she knew perfectly well.

"I don't know exactly. I can't put my finger on it. There is something very different about you today."

Shannon brushed her hair with her hand and flashed him a smile, nestling down a little in the seat. She felt liberated, full of life. She was free to love him now, she thought to herself, smiling inwardly. She would tell him soon, but not right this minute. She wanted to savor the feeling a little while longer.

"You're like a schoolgirl with a secret," Jack said, looking over at her. Then he put his eyes back on the road. "You have a constant grin on your face, as if you've done something but you can't tell."

"Is that so?"

"What is it?" Jack finally asked, seriously.

"Mr. Murphy, you just mind the car, now." She sat up straight and cracked the window just a little to allow some fresh air into the car. It had started to rain slightly and she could hear the tires splashing, the unique sound that tires make when they come in contact with water on the pavement. Like the sound of the surf rolling in against the coastline.

"Look," she pointed at an old ruin on the hillside.

"Shall we buy the old place and restore it and move in?" Jack asked, half kidding and half serious. Shannon did not respond, but continued to look as they drove past. She turned her head and followed the ruins until they were out of view.

"I love old ruins," she remarked. She fiddled with a strand of hair falling across her brow. "I especially love to visit Glanworth Bridge. Do you know it? It spans the River Fushion with twelve huge arches. It is outstanding."

"Where is this old bridge?" asked Jack.

"Glanworth is near the village of Fermoy, actually not that far from here. The bridge was built around 1450 or so. Actually, it's the oldest standing bridge in Ireland. And just above the bridge are the ruins of an ancient castle of the Roche family."

The rain began to fall harder and Jack slowed the car a bit. Finally, they reached Cork and found their way to the auto dealership. Jack concluded his transaction and they headed out to the rental car agency to return the vehicle he had driven since his arrival in Ireland.

Shannon followed him at a close distance in the new car. The storm was making her nervous. She waited outside the rental car office, and rejoiced inwardly as she Jack heading her way.

"Wow! Some rain," he said, jumping into the car. There were reports on the TV back there in the rental office. They say it could be the worst storm in twenty years." Shannon did not speak but instead just looked at Jack, then at the sky, and back again.

The darkness was gaining on the sky now, and there was just a touch of light off to the east. The rain began to fall like pellets. The storm was coming on very quickly. In a matter of moments the whole sky was overtaken by sheets of rain.

Shannon was beginning to be really afraid. In a low voice that trembled ever so slightly, she said, "This is a bad one." There was an uneasy silence as the wind battered the car. With the increasing darkness and the heavy rain, it was growing harder to see by the minute.

Finally, Jack pulled over to the side of the road. He tried to remain calm, not wanting her to know that he was as scared as she was. "Let's think about this," he told her. "I don't want to take a chance on driving in this storm. The report is that we may get wind gusts up to seventy-five miles an hour. It doesn't sound so bad when you hear it on TV, but out here in the thick of it, it's real enough."

She nodded in agreement, her eyes fixed on the raging storm outside. "Shannon, there is no need to risk our lives. We will just stay here overnight until the storm passes." At that, the fear left her face.

Jack pulled the car onto the road slowly. He motored along with extreme caution until they came upon a small hotel sitting just off the road. He felt fortunate to find one so soon, and a real hotel at that, instead of a bed and breakfast. They were both flooded with relief when he pulled into the parking lot. The mood changed subtly. Moments before, they had been in real danger, and it was not funny at all. Now they had reached safety. There was a sense of adventure, underscored rather than dampened by the untamed storm roaring about them.

Jack stopped the car just short of the front entrance. They sat for a moment in silence. He looked directly at Shannon. Finally he broke the silence. "Shall I get one room?"

She did not speak at once, but returned his look with a steady and meaningful expression. Then she simply said, "Yes."

Chapter Eighteen

Jack took Shannon by the hand and they walked toward their room. He stopped at the door before placing the key in the lock. He took Shannon in his arms and pulled her toward him. She did not resist. Rather, she melted into his arms. He gave her a soft, warm, gentle kiss. They stood for a moment at the door, just holding each other and looking into each others eyes.

They entered the room and locked the door behind them. Jack started to turn on a light, but Shannon stopped him. There was a soft glow through the curtains from the outside lights, and it was enough for them to see one another clearly.

She reached up to let her hair down, allowing it to fall freely over her shoulders. Then she looked deeply into his eyes. In a moment more, their lips met as he gathered her in his arms and pulled her close.

Shannon responded as she had never responded to anyone before, giving up her whole heart to his kiss, meeting his desire with an intensity of her own. Jack gently placed her on her back and lay across her, still kissing, letting the passion build. She made no pretext of hesitation now.

"Jack," she said with a husky sob, "I love you." And again, "I love you."

"Shannon. My Shannon. I love you." He kissed her cheek. "I love you." He kissed her forehead, then her chin. "I love you." Then he returned to her lips.

Jack slowly moved down her neck and kissed every area around her neck and shoulders, gently pulling back her sweater. He pulled her dress off her shoulders and kissed her there, and finally moved down and buried himself in her breasts. He was consumed by this moment.

Shannon arched her back and pulled her dress further off her shoulders. She sat up, reached around behind her back, and unhooked her bra for him, exposing her breasts fully to his lips, wanting him with all her being.

The dim light cast beautiful shadows on Shannon's naked shoulders. Outside, they could hear the storm rage. The wind moaned and slammed into the wall, echoing their passion. He stood up and pulled her to her feet, unzipped the back of her dress, and allowed it to fall to the floor. She slid her hands down her hips and let her lace panties fall on top of the dress, watching him intently as he looked at her body, shivering as he ran his fingers lightly across her breasts and belly.

Shannon reached up and unbuttoned his shirt, pulling it off as she went. Her hands were wild on his chest. "Jack, my darling," she whispered with her mouth against his ear, "please, let's get into bed."

Jack pulled back the blankets and removed the rest of his clothes, then followed Shannon as she slipped under the covers. Now, the moment he had dreamed of so many times. He felt Shannon's body next to his, her heart beating as ecstatically as his own. She was more than he ever expected or dreamed. She was incredible.

He moved his hands ever so tenderly across and around every inch of her. He explored her back, her thighs, her breasts and between her legs. Then he started to kiss her and follow with his lips the same path he had taken with his hands. The smell of Shannon was everywhere, the green and amber scent that can only be described as love. In a way that was new to each of them, they understood the strength and the beauty of love.

Then it happened. They came together. They were one. Every song that had ever moved him now began playing for him alone. Every crashing wave Shannon had ever heard, she now heard anew. Every sunbeam that had ever gladdened her heart was inside her at this moment.

Together, they moved past the boundaries of ordinary experience. They released love stored up from every dream either of them had ever known. The overgrowth of the tropics and the magical fragrance of a flower garden blended in their senses with the taste of rich Burgundy wine and the smell of fresh cut fields. Together they voyaged down a vast river, walked slowly along the fault line, lay perfectly still on a hot August afternoon.

Their union went beyond words. Raw emotion was their world at this moment. Inside and out, they were wetter than the rain that ripped through the trees outside. Every dream, every instinct, every internal force that either of them had ever felt now overwhelmed the solitary mysteries of separateness.

Jack looked into Shannon's eyes and saw a perfect ecstasy of love. He moved her hair away from her face and kissed her just below the chin, where her pulse was just beginning to subside a little. "I love you," he said softly. Shannon did not speak, but pulled him into her bosom and ran her hand through his hair. They lay together in silence.

After a very long time, the rain and wind began to let up. Slowly, they drifted back into the present, and began to take notice of ordinary things. She remembered something and looked at the clock. Kissing him gently, she said, "I know my mother will be worried about the storm. I must tell her I am safe." She paused. "I am far better than safe at this moment, and beyond happiness, but that is only for us to know."

"Yes," said Jack. "Yes." He was utterly at peace. "I'll get dressed and walk down to the restaurant. You go ahead and place your call and then meet me."

Shannon smiled and nodded. "Mind the door," she said.

Chapter Nineteen

Shannon and Jack had a quiet dinner and returned to their room in a peaceful state of mind. They didn't talk much, but gave each other a loving glance, a slight kiss or a soft touch as they prepared for bed. They made love again that night.

They were not conscious of the world outside, but only of each other and of being together. Their love was not as before. Then, they had won their first release from the chains of the past. The second time, each tender kiss was orchestrated. The random passion was replaced by a delicious, slow awakening of their senses. Each touch was carefully placed. After a long, dreamlike time, they fell asleep in each other's arms.

The next morning they dressed and left their hotel. The cool, misty air jolted Jack into wakefulness. Shannon greeted the morning with a smile, and took a deep breath before getting into the car. The storm had passed, leaving the world washed clean. "What a glorious morning," she sighed.

"Shannon." Her name dropped musically off Jack's lips. "I love you."

"And I you, Mr. Murphy."

A light wind fanned over the hillside, and there was the sweet odor of green fields in the air, the smell of Ireland. Down the road a straggling group of cows grazed on the roadside. Once again, Shannon was listening to the sound of the tires on the road, which was still wet from the storm. Today it sounded to her like a waterfall, and she pointed this out to Jack.

He lowered his window and listened. "Sounds like bacon to me," he said with a guileless look.

"Bacon?"

"Bacon. Can't you hear that hissing sound of bacon frying in a pan?" He laughed, and Shannon caught on that he was teasing her. She gave him a big smile.

"I suppose, Mr. Murphy. I guess that's the imagination of a writer. Writers, painters, poets, you all see things a little differently than us common folk."

"Common? You are anything but common." Jack reached over and touched Shannon's hand. "Now you're the one putting me on."

"No, Jack. I'll say it again. I truly loved your books. You are a very good writer. No, you are a superb writer."

"Thank you. That means a lot to me."

They did not speak for a long while after that. The sun had burned off the morning fog and patches of blue began to peek out behind the clouds. The clouds were moving quickly.

"I think it's going to be a bright day." Jack said, coming out of his reverie. Then, in a more serious tone of voice he asked her, "Shannon, do you want children?"

She did not answer.

"Would you like to have a big family? One or two, maybe? Five? Twelve?"

"Jack," she said in a strained voice, a tear forming, "I can't have children."

Jack rubbed his forehead. Of all the things he could have said, trying to make her happy, he had chosen the worst. He took her hand. "I'm sorry. I'm so sorry," he said softly. He felt that he should not press the matter.

Shannon did not respond, but turned and looked out the window and willed the tears away. Then she turned toward him with a serene look.

"It's okay. Let's not talk about it just now."

They were very quiet then, as the miles flew by. Jack could feel her heavy heart, and had no wish to add to her pain. After a time, she put her head back against the seat and dozed. Jack gazed out at the random images before him. The sun began to brighten the green limestone pastures. He could see the lush farmlands that lay beyond, outlined with ancient patterns of carved stones. He passed an old church. Macroom was not far away. The mountains would be next, he thought, then Kilgarven and Kenmare.

Shannon stirred, opened her eyes and sat up in her seat. She ran her hands through her hair and rubbed her eyes.

"Good morning, Mr. Murphy."

"Good morning. Did you have a nice rest?"

"I did, yes. Where are we?" she asked, looking out the window.

"Almost to Macroom."

"Oh. Can we stop and get something to drink? I can wash my face."

Before long they reached Macroom and Jack pulled into a small restaurant. It was nearly empty, so they chose a small table in a cozy corner. Jack ordered coffee and Shannon asked for tea and scones. Their conversation was relaxed. Voices and laughter drifted from a table on the other side of the restaurant. Music from a radio in the kitchen was playing softly, and the cook rattled the dishes in accompaniment.

Jack and Shannon considered how comfortable their being together was this day. It seemed as though neither of them had any reservations. Wonderful memories of the night before ran through their minds. Jack moved his coffee aside and reached out and took Shannon's hand in his.

He sat quietly, looking at her in a way he never had before. He saw a lighter green in her eyes, which he had never noticed. It was a cobalt green color that danced next to her pearly white skin. Astonishing, he thought to himself. He followed her full, rosy lips all the way around and back again, and then moved up to her high cheek bones. She was more beautiful today than ever.

A warm smile tugged at the corners of her mouth. She tried to appear serious, but her eyes gave her away. Cheerfully she asked, "So, tell me, Mr. Murphy, do you not miss seeing your relatives back in the American South?" He could see that she didn't expect an answer by the way she asked. "Where exactly is Clyde?" she continued gaily.

"Clyde, my dear, is a very, very small town in the mountains of North Carolina. The nearest large city is Asheville. It is very beautiful there, but it is not a place I would like to live today. I liked it as a kid, before we moved to Florida. I have many fond memories."

"Is Clyde very far from Florida?"

"To Miami, where I live now, it's about seven or eight hundred miles."

"That far?" she asked, surprised. "And California, where your sister lives. How far would that be?"

"About two thousand, five hundred miles."

"No," she exclaimed. "I had no idea America was so enormous. When you study America in school or look at a map, the size doesn't register. I dare say, you live in a very large place."

"Yes, America is big. Over two hundred and fifty million people."

"You must think that our little baby island is nothing more than a dot."

Jack parried the comment with a chuckle. "I think your little baby island is wonderful. You have more history in this little restaurant than we have in our entire country. We may be large in size, but in history, we are still in our infancy." Then a question occurred to him. "Have you got relatives in America?"

Shannon thought for a minute. "We do, yes. My great-grandfather's two brothers went to Boston, but none of his kin ever made it back to Ireland, not as we know at any rate."

"What about other relatives, here in Ireland?"

"Well, there were five brothers and sisters on my mother's side. Their children live all abouts. Some in London, three in America and two in Dublin. My mother is the oldest. She had me very late in life. Her brother, my Uncle Liam, was living with us at the time. He had been on the dole. He was not my favorite. The fact is, I couldn't stand him. He was mean to me, to my mother and even to my father. Finally, my father ran him off the place. He died a few years later in Cork. My mother is the last of her brothers and sisters living. And my father, you may find this strange for Ireland, but he had no brothers and sisters. After he was born, my grandmother could no longer bear any more children."

"You were like an only child, right?" he asked.

"Not really, though it may seem that way now. I had my sister until I was fifteen. And, of course, my brother, Brien."

"That must have been hard on your parents. And on you."

"It was a nightmare. I don't think that my mother is truly over it to this day. She was never the same after Bridget's death."

Jack was glad to see the waitress returning to the table. She poured more coffee for Jack and asked if they would be having anything else. He looked at Shannon, who shook her head, and then responded with a no, thank you.

"How's the book coming?" Shannon asked, changing the subject.

"It's coming very well, it is," he put on an Irish accent for her amusement. "The book is writing itself. It's amazing. My first two books took great labor, and this book is flowing so easily."

"May I read some of it?"

"Not yet. Please wait. It is so crude just yet."

Shannon did not press the issue.

Jack added, "I think that any writer, or painter, or even someone who writes music is always on a journey of discovery. We write out of our own life and our own experiences, but to transcribe one's life in a literal sense is near impossible. Artistic creation kicks in."

"What do you mean?" she asked in a serious tone.

"Well, it's that the creative portion of writing alters many facts. It blends with the truth to the point where one cannot tell what part of the book is fact and what part is fiction. I even find myself believing that the fiction portion of my book is fact."

Shannon understood completely. It was evident as she said, "Is that not much like life itself? Don't we alter many facts in our own lives, and doesn't there come a time when they become truth? We begin to live a myth of our own making." She paused, then continued. "And what about the quality of our memories? Have you noticed how our minds block out certain things, while retaining others?"

"You sound as if you're speaking from a great deal of first hand knowledge."

Shannon looked him in the eye. "I am, Jack." And then, "I think I should tell you more about Stal and me." She took a deep breath. "I met Stal while living in Limerick. I've mentioned his name to you before. What I didn't tell you is that that relationship nearly destroyed me. For months, I did not want to work. But I did. I did not want to go out with friends. But I did. I would find myself crying over nothing, and over everything."

Jack nodded his head in understanding. "God knows, I tried to get over Stal," she confided, "but everywhere I went, he was there. I would see a couple walking in the park, and I would so want it to be me, with him. I would go home and look at old photos and break down. I was so sad, so lonely. So hurt."

Leaning against the table, Jack looked down at Shannon's hands in his own, then back again at her lovely face. "And now?" he asked.

"I have you, my love," she answered with no hesitation.

Troubled and a little afraid, Jack asked again. "Are you sure, Shannon? Are you sure of us?"

Shannon stared at Jack, then blinked. "Yes. I was afraid at first. I held back and would not allow myself to get close to you. All I could see was a terrible and savage picture of sadness, a kind of grief which I knew I could not cope with again."

Her voice changed then, losing its sorrow and taking on a quiet note of respect and affection. "I love you," she said tenderly. "I have turned myself over to you completely. Did you not feel that? After last night, is there any doubt of my love for you?"

"Shannon," Jack broke in. "I'm not questioning your love. It's just that I need to hear you say it, and it makes me feel so good. You see, I have been thinking about my own past. It is full of tears and bitter memories not unlike yours. I have been remembering Helen, a girl I loved once when we were both just kids. It was a wild, young time, my first true love. It took me a long time to get over Helen. Looking back now, I don't think that I truly accepted the idea of loving another woman until I met you. I know that sounds crazy, because Helen and I had our love such a very long time ago."

"What happened? Where is Helen now?"

"She killed herself. She was with child. My child."

"Oh Jack. Oh, no. I'm so sorry, for the both of you. I'm so sorry."

"Perhaps one day, if you want to know all the details, I'll tell you about Helen and me." His emotions were running high, both in pain from his memories and in relief at having voiced them. At last, he had broken through his fears and his silence.

Now he could think and feel only one thing, and he said it. "Shannon, the important thing is that I love you. Today. Now."

She nodded in agreement.

"We were meant to find each other, Shannon. The lonely years are gone. It is our time now, for peace and love and each other. Right this moment, I feel that we are the luckiest people on earth. We have our health, and our interest in life. I have more income than we will ever need. And even if we had none of those things, we still have our love. We have our love."

Chapter Twenty

Jack started out early in the morning for Shannon Airport, en route to America. Remembering the events of the previous day, he drove along the highway feeling very peaceful and happy with the knowledge that his life with Shannon was unfolding in a way that he could hardly have hoped for.

It seemed to Jack that even the weather this day was tuned to his wishes, as if it knew of his happiness. Traffic was very light, the air was still and the whole of Ireland appeared settled. Nothing could disturb his calm certainty of the future with his beloved Shannon.

The charmed day continued. Everything went perfectly. His plane was on time, and the flight to America was smooth. Even the airline food tasted better than usual.

Sometime after he landed in California, and before meeting his sister Sylvia, Jack felt a rush of confusion overtake him, as if America itself had brought him back to earth. Flashes of his past filled his thoughts, and random fears rose up as he tried to get in touch with the meaning of it all.

He recalled the afternoon Shannon asked him why it had been so long since his last serious relationship. Helen was not the total and complete answer, and both he and Shannon knew it. It was something far deeper, something Jack was unable to talk about at all. It was a fear of abandonment, this much he knew. Since his mother's and father's deaths, there had been a vacancy in his whole being. He was marooned, isolated in a place that had no roots and no boundaries, and he could not connect with any place beyond.

With the loss of Helen, such emotions were sharpened. He had almost gone under from the weight of them. But slowly, over the years, he had learned to stifle those feelings. He was well aware that his record of success in all that he attempted was a substitute for human bonds. A living part of his survival was in winning a series of women who came in and out of his life without really touching him. These women had offered Jack a form of absolution. He could not, he must not fall into that familiar pattern with Shannon. He felt literally that his life was at stake.

He roused himself from his gloom long enough to greet his sister with warm affection. He noticed that she looked somewhat drawn, and attributed it to her concern about Terri, as well as her hectic American lifestyle. After a brief visit with her, he went to his hotel to let his mind and body adjust to the time change. Later that night, his spirits began to lift a little. He took a long bath, then sat down at the table with a pen and paper.

My dearest Shannon,

I write this letter to you from the confines of my hotel room. Nothing is right, being here without you. I don't eat well, I don't sleep well, and I miss you with all my heart. I visited with my sister today, and she seems sad, but otherwise okay. We will be flying to Las Vegas in the morning. Our plan is to meet with Terri, hopefully alone, with the idea that we can be of help to her.

Then I'll fly to New York and meet with my publisher. I'll call you from New York in a few days' time. I expect to be there no longer than a week, or eight days at the most. It all depends on the final approvals we have to make in our meetings. There is the dust jacket design, and some details concerning book signing dates and things of that nature to deal with as well.

Shannon, my love, I need your love more than ever. I need your love more than I need fame or money or getting my book published. God has made no other person more perfect than you. I am in such a mood tonight, missing you. I can feel your body wrapped in silk, next to mine. I have memorized you. I know every inch of your gentle beauty. I see your hair falling over your shoulders, and your lips parting to meet mine. If I were a painter, I could never be able to capture your essence. There is no way I can write the words to match my love for you. If I were to name you, I would have picked Shannon.

Night is all around me and I am here without you. Shannon, my love, you are my purpose. You are so beautiful in love. I am lost in this land I used to know, with an ocean between us. I'll think of you and miss you.

With all my love, Jack

The meeting in Las Vegas went well with Jack and his two sisters. He thought perhaps Sylvia had exaggerated the seriousness of their younger sister's situation, and guessed that what Sylvia really wanted was to spend time with both of them, and especially him. Perhaps she was a little depressed. He did not force the issue. Instead, he used the opportunity to give both of them his support, advice and encouragement.

It was heartening for Jack to witness his sisters getting on together so well, and he hoped that this would be a new beginning for the two of them. He felt that they needed the family support he was offering. It had not been easy on any of them. As children in high school and college, they had all had the usual troubles, and not having parents to lean on had only made matters worse. Maybe now, as adult siblings, they could forge a family unit and help each other. So he hoped.

Jack rose early the next morning to catch his flight for New York. Arriving at the airport, he glanced down at his watch and calculated the time change from California to Ireland. Shannon would still be at the bank. He dialed the number and waited eagerly for the lines to connect.

"Good morning, the Bank of Ireland. How may I help you?" a voice said. Just hearing the Irish accent on the other end made Jack feel better. "Good morning. May I speak with Shannon Kelly, please."

"You can, of course. One minute, sir." There was a long silence on the line and then a voice came on.

"I'm sorry sir, but Shannon Kelly is not in today. Could someone else help, or would there be a message?"

Jack thought for a second and then said, "No, thank you. I'll call back." He considered calling her at home, but just then his flight was announced, so he boarded the plane for New York. The ride was uneventful—the only kind of good plane trip, Jack would always say. He landed at JFK to a wet, chilly day, then made his way to his hotel.

He had wondered all day why Shannon was not at work, and where she might be. He decided to call her at home. By now, he thought, the family would have finished their dinner and would be sitting by the fire. The phone rang and rang, but there was no answer. He hung up and sat on the edge of the bed. He asked himself out loud, "Where could she be?" Now he was truly concerned. Then his imagination took hold and he began to feel desparate.

Tormented by worry and fatigue, he did not know what to do next. Not knowing Shannon's whereabouts, he thought of every grotesque possibility. He began pacing the room. He went to the window and looked down on the tiny people moving about like worker ants. His mind was racing. Unconsciously, he fiddled with the blinds. He ran his hands through his thick, dark hair, and rubbed his eyes.

Then he made his way to the bar in the corner of his room. He took out a small bottle of Scotch, found a glass, and poured himself a drink. There was no ice in his room, so he took a tentative sip without it. Then he consumed the entire shot in one gulp. He immediately took out another small bottle and poured it into his glass. This time he sipped it slowly as he sat on the bed and looked at the wall. He lay back and tried to doze, then turned on the television and watched some newscaster recite the irrelevant events of the day, then turned it off and tried again to settle himself down and get some rest.

During this strange spell of time, Jack became totally aware of how much of his life was wrapped around Shannon. Unknowingly, she had put her enchanting spell on him. He was frightened at the thought of not having her. What would sleep be like, he thought, and how would I work? Could I write if I were filled with desolation and despair? There is no way I could work again. I could not handle the suffering, the maddening passion, the hunger to be with her.

His feverish imagination would not let him be. Where was she? Where could she possibly be, if she were not at work and if no one were at home to answer his call? Once again, he thought of all the terrible options. He saw himself condemned by fate to live out the rest of his life without Shannon, without love. He would be neither awake nor asleep, ever again. Rather, he would be a man obsessed, hopeless, exiled, banished. He saw himself as totally incurable, with no hope of gaining back his life.

Jack went to his bar and found another Scotch. He took his ice bucket and went down the hall to the ice machine, then returned and fixed himself a Scotch and water. He was startled when the telephone began to ring. He looked at it as if it were an intruder, distracting him from his agitation over Shannon. It continued to ring and ring until at last he picked it up.

It was A.J., his editor. She asked how he was doing, and if he liked his room.

"A.J." He regained his composure. "I'm fine. The room is fine. And how are you? How have you been?"

"Great, Jack, just great. God, it's good to hear your voice. I have so much to tell you, and so many things about the book to go over. Can we have dinner tonight, a few drinks? What time?"

Jack thought for a minute. He knew that he did not want to see anyone tonight. Especially, he did not want to see A.J., to talk business, and then go out for drinks. Most certainly did not want to return to the time and place when he had once taken her to bed.

However, he also knew that there was business to conduct. He must look to his career and his future, and he needed to eat something tonight anyway. And, after all, A.J. was his editor. "How about eight p.m. in the lobby bar?" he finally said.

"Perfect. I'll see you then. I can't wait. Later, Jack." There was a click. Jack sat holding the phone, just looking at it, then very slowly he placed it back on the receiver. He finished his drink quickly and said out loud, "Get hold of yourself, ol' boy. Everything is just fine." He started taking off his clothes as he headed to the shower.

After cleaning up and getting dressed, Jack tried to call Shannon one more time. There was still no answer, and he started to panic. He gathered his coat and started toward the elevator. He could not even think straight. "If it's eight p.m. here, what time is it in Ireland? Is it one a.m.? Yes, that's it. One a.m. It's after midnight and none of the Kellys are at home."

The thoughts were wrung out of him in a kind of insanity, and his mind swarmed with fears for Shannon. He felt as if he were losing control, as if he were no longer master of his emotions and his actions. He had never experienced this in his life, not even when he had heard the news about Helen. Nothing had ever affected him this way. God, how he wished he were back in Ireland.

A.J. was standing by the doorway leading into the lobby bar when Jack approached. "Jack," she called out, and ran to greet him. She tossed her hair back and threw her arms around his neck, pulling him toward her and kissing him on the lips.

"Let me look at you," she said standing back. "Well, you still look pretty good to me. Are you ever going to age? My God, you look thirty-five." She gave him a bear hug. "Oh, you feel good. Damn, it's good to see you." She continued to chatter. "So tell me, what have you been up to? I want to hear everything. Don't leave out a thing."

A.J. was one hundred percent pure New York. She was tall and slender, and had a nice figure if a person took the time to get by the style of clothes she wore. No matter what the fashion of the moment decreed, A.J. would wear it whether it suited her or not. She practiced looking youthful, but Jack could always remember her age exactly, as they were born the same year, the same month, and one day apart.

A.J. had brown hair that was cut short in the back and longer in the front. Jack had never liked a woman's hair that fell in front of her eyes in such a way that she needed to throw her head back constantly in order to keep the hair off her face. But he knew that that, too, was a New York mannerism. Still and all, she was rather attractive. He had noticed that the first time he met her, when they were working on his first book.

"Alice," Jack said now. "It's good to see you."

"A.J.," she corrected him. "You know I hate to be called Alice. Alice Cohen sounds so ordinary." Her thick New York accent sounded suddenly strange to Jack. "Now, darling, what have you been up to?"

"Well the book, of course. It's coming along quite well."

"Quite well? That's an interesting way to put it. When do you plan on getting the first draft to me?"

"A few more months, I should guess."

"A few more months? Jack! You klutz, you. Come on, now, baby, you can do better than that. Of course, you did this to me on your last book, and you ended up several weeks ahead of schedule. I think you just like to make me worry. Right, my darling?" She lit a cigarette and, holding it behind her, blew smoke up in the air.

"How's Ireland?" she asked in such a way that Jack didn't feel a need to answer. He sensed that she was going to continue, and she did. "I'll bet you have a house full of Irish ladies." She winked and smiled. "What's it like? I've never been there. Does it rain all the time? Oh God. I couldn't stand to live someplace where it rains all the time. God knows, New York is bad enough."

"I like it, A.J. I really do. I love the people, and the food, the countryside, the history. I really do like it."

"Interesting, Jack. Very interesting. And what about this little town, Kenmare? What on earth do you do in a Godforsaken place like that? Shit, I would go crazy."

"Well, A.J., after all, I am working. I'm not on holiday."

"On holiday? You're starting to sound like them. I think I detect a little Irish accent now and then," she laughed heartily as she put her cigarette out in the ash tray, leaving the ash burning. Jack reached over and completed the job.

"Another drink, darling," A.J. said as she lifted her hand in the air and motioned with two fingers for another round. Jack did not want another drink just now, but he didn't say anything.

"I ran into my first husband the other day. Abe, remember Abe?" He nodded. "Oh my God, you should see him. He's gained thirty pounds, and he's lost almost all of his hair."

"And your second husband," Jack said politely. "What was his name?"

"Carl."

"Carl," Jack repeated. He was doing his very best with the small talk, but his mind was on Shannon. He couldn't wait to get back to his room. He so much wanted to place another call to Ireland.

"Oh, Carl is doing fine. You know he will always do great in business. Everything he touches turns to money." A.J. continued as if Jack wanted to be brought totally up to date. "My daughter is still married to the doctor. Doing great. My son moved to Israel and joined the army. What's a mother to do?" She smiled and shrugged her shoulders.

The bar was beginning to fill up and the noise level increased. Jack looked around at the faces of the people, at their dress and their mannerisms. The weariness of the night wore on his nerves. A.J. continued to talk, and talk, and talk. She went on and on about every person at the office. People were hurrying by their table, and now and then someone A.J. knew would stop to say hello. Jack would have to stand, shake hands, make small talk about how great Ireland was and how his new book was coming. This was the drill, he reminded himself. He hated it.

"I love this bar, don't you?" A.J. asked brightly. "All my friends at work and in the biz come here. Look. Over there sits one of the new head men at Doubleday. You wanna meet him?"

"No. Please A.J., I'm too tired to meet him now. Another time, okay?"

"Sure, my darling, whatever my new star wants. You know, everyone at the shop is really excited about your new book. The company is getting behind this one and I think it's going to be a smash hit." She raised her drink, as did Jack, and tipped glasses. "Here's to Jack Murphy, the fastest rising star at Kingdom House Publishing. And here's to *The Fields of Sensation.*"

Jack smiled and took a sip of his drink. "Thanks, A.J. Thanks a lot. I hope I can live up to everyone's expectations."

"You will, darling, not to worry. Your new book will go into a second printing for sure, maybe even a third. I know that, sweetheart. That's my job and I'm damned good at it. Just you wait 'til tomorrow, when we show you all the plans we have for you. But that's enough for now. You look like you could use a bite to eat. Where do you want to go?"

Jack looked at A.J. "What?" His mind had been drifting.

"What are you in the mood for? A good steak? Lobster? You call it."

"Can we just have something here? I'm really beat. And we have an early day tomorrow."

Jack's mind was bound up with his concern for Shannon. Now and then he would think that he was overreacting, and that there must be a very good explanation for the fact that he couldn't get in touch with her or her family. Then anxious thoughts would swarm over him, back and forth. Back and forth. He wished again that he were in Ireland.

Chapter Twenty-One

Rain moved in on New York. The far darkness closed in, and the steady drizzle danced with the city lights, making haloes around each separate window. Jack could not sleep. He felt the old wildness that had overcome him each time an adored person had suddenly disappeared from his life, never to return. And now he could not find his Shannon. Her parents were gone, too. Why? He thought of calling Mr. Mullins, but reconsidered.

He lay across his bed, fully clothed, and let his mind take him back to the last night he and Shannon were together before he left for California. He could feel the weight of her on his body. He could feel her warm young face against his. He thought of how she loved to thrust her fingers through his hair and pull him close to her and kiss his eyes and his lips, and then move his head down between her breasts. She would sigh with pleasure.

Jack could almost hear the sounds of lovemaking with Shannon. He could feel the intensity, the complete closeness, the way they devoured each other until there was no separateness at all. Then, deeply at peace with themselves and each other, they would just lie in each other's arms, talking softly. They would discuss so many things in these quiet moments. Shannon would caress him and pull him close to her. And always the soothing kisses, so many soothing kisses.

Jack did not know what time he fell asleep. When he awoke, it was still dark. He turned on a light and looked at his watch. It was five a.m. Should he try another call? He decided to wait. He lay half asleep and half awake, and time passed.

When next he looked at his watch it was after six. He was finally awake enough to want a cup of coffee. He stumbled across the room to the cupboard, assembled the packet of coffee and the water, and started the coffee machine. He glanced out the window at the smoky dawn, then turned the shower on hot and stood under it for five minutes.

He shaved and got himself presentable, put on his socks and underwear, and lay back on the bed briefly, getting his thoughts together. Now, he thought. He phoned Shannon at home. No answer!

Three cups of coffee later, Jack stood in front of his hotel. He was wearing his city armor, a fashionable suit, and he was intent on getting his business out of the way and getting back to Ireland as soon as possible. He climbed into a taxi and directed the driver to Kingdom House Publishing.

Inside the sleek lobby, he boarded the elevator to the thirty-fifth floor. He stepped off, strode through the imposing double doors, and announced himself to the receptionist. She was new and did not recognize him. He asked for A.J., and in a moment she came briskly out into the lobby to meet him.

"Darling. My darling Jack. Good morning, sweetheart." She gave Jack a kiss on each cheek, informed the girl at the desk that he was their new star, then took his arm and escorted him to the conference room.

"Coffee, darling?" she asked as she poured a cup. "Let's see. No cream, no sugar, right?" She set the coffee in front of Jack. "You got a good nights sleep, right? And now you're ready to get down to work." Not waiting for an answer to any of her questions, she picked up the phone and called someone. "We're ready."

The meeting went as Jack expected, and it lasted past noon. They ordered out for corned beef on rye, took a short break, and continued to work. By three o'clock, they had decided on a design for the book jacket. They had gone over other details concerning layout and printing.

Several dates were set for book signing parties, the biggest and most important being in New York, Chicago, Boston, Dallas, Los Angeles and San Francisco. The schedule would be crowded, with the book signings set only a few days apart. During the tour, Jack was to appear on three different TV talk shows, two in New York and one in California.

There was a big advertising campaign laid out, which A.J. covered in detail at the meeting. They planned full page ads in the New York Times and ads in several national magazines. For the major book stores, they were fabricating a massive display of an Irish castle with a life-size cardboard Jack Murphy standing in front of it. Jack was nonplused by the publisher's expensive investment. A.J. was right. Kingdom House was truly behind his project.

During a break, A.J. leaned over and whispered to Jack. "Listen darling, you seem to be getting a cold. When we're done here, let me take you down to Second Avenue Deli, fix you up with some matzo ball soup. It'll be all right, not to worry."

"Thanks, A.J., but I'm going to turn in early tonight. We'll go another time."

"Okay, darling, but I asked," she replied with a smile.

"You're a sweetheart. Thanks for thinking of me."

"Honey, I just love thinking about you," she said with a grin, raising an eyebrow. "Oh, well, okay. Back to work."

A.J.'s assistant stood up with a sheaf of papers. "We have two movie companies wanting *The Fields of Sensation*," she reported. "Right now we're trying to wrap up a deal with the highest bidder. Both of these deals are big. Really big. One has James Marshall interested."

"You're kidding," Jack interrupted.

"No darling, she's not kidding," A.J. said quickly. "Go on, honey."

"Yes, Ms. Cohen. The other company has not reported to us on exactly who they have in mind for the script, but they love the story line and the first four chapters. However, they want to wait until the book is completed."

"I say no way," A.J. said. "This is too big. We want to come out with the paperback right after the hard cover, and we want to be able to say, 'soon to be a major motion picture starring James Marshall.' Right?" She looked around the room and received a nod of agreement.

Jack just sat in amazement.

"I say we take Golden Pictures. Get Marshall, and cut a deal. Anybody disagree?" She looked around the table, but no one said anything, so she went on. "Look. Golden loves the story line. Ireland is hot right now, and they know it. They also know that we are behind this project one hundred percent, and that the book will be a tremendous success. They see money written all over the cover of 'Fields of Sensation.' We may not get as much as we want for the movie rights, but we will more than make it up in paper back sales here and internationally. We have three deals working to go to press in French, Spanish and Greek, and I'm working on China. Think about that. Do you realize how many people live in China?"

Everyone cheered. "God, I love this business," A.J. beamed. "Let's have a drink." She opened the bar in the conference room and took out a bottle of champagne. "See this, fellas? This we open the day the book comes off the press. Of course, we'll have more than one." Then she laughed and asked what everyone wanted to drink in the meantime.

Throughout the day, Jack looked for an opportunity to slip away and call Shannon, but none came. He realized that many people were involved in this campaign, and that his presence was necessary, so he forced himself to work along with the rest. After the meeting, A.J. insisted that she, Jack, the Vice President and his wife, the art director and several others on the staff go out to dinner, despite his earlier protest that he needed to retire early.

Jack was trapped. He asked if there were and an office where he could use the telephone. He tried to reach Shannon once again. Still no answer.

"What's wrong, Jack?" A.J. asked when he returned. "You look drawn. Is all this too much for you, darling? Perhaps what you need is a little play time." She said all this in a whisper, as she took Jack's arm and led him toward the elevator.

To the rest, she said over her shoulder, "I've made reservations at a great new restaurant everyone is talking about. We'll stop at Harry's for a drink or two on the way. How does that sound?"

The cocktail party from Hell, Jack thought. Two nights in a row.

It was still raining as the group got into several cabs and started out toward Harry's. A.J. sat close to Jack. Rubbing her hands along her waist and down her thighs, she laughed and said, "Not bad, huh, Jack?" She flipped her hair away from her eyes. "I'm still pretty good for my age, wouldn't you say, darling?"

"Oh, yes. You've stayed in fine shape, A.J." Jack tried to sound convincing. After all, she was finely molded, and not an ounce of fat anywhere. But her features were a little coarse, he had always thought. He always got a little angry with himself for even looking at people this way, and more so for being judgmental.

"Jack, darling. You didn't say anything about my boob job." She lifted her breasts up with both hands. "Whadda ya think? Pretty good job, and what the hell, they only cost $4000 each," she said, laughing. "You might say it was an investment. An investment in my work. After all, a gal has to look her best. Right?"

Jack smiled. "You're right, A.J.," he said dutifully. "They make you look great."

The rest of the staff was waiting when the cab finally arrived at Harry's. The party was just about what Jack expected. Many toasts about his book and the new rising star of Kingdom House. Rosy forecasts. Lots of industry gossip.

Jack played the role assigned to him. Brilliant, confident, yet becomingly modest. He said all the right things, but he was not really there. The noise of the bar, the tinsel-faced people, the meaningless conversations tested him beyond his strength to endure. His emotions were on edge as the gallery of faces blurred and swam in his vision. If I could only get out of here he thought. Right now. But the next party from Hell was just beginning. Dinner!

Somewhere in all the noise and smoke and nonsense of that endless evening, there was a sea change within Jack's mind. He did not know exactly when it happened, but all at once he became aware that this very scene, once so familiar and now so bizarre, had forced him out of his habitual way of thinking. In a strange way, it had liberated him.

He knew then what he was going to do. When he returned to Ireland, he would go at once to Shannon, and he would ask her to marry him.

Chapter Twenty-Two

Another rainy day. It was nine a.m., and Jack planned a quiet breakfast alone. There were no meetings today. He smiled inwardly at the thought of being free from publishing details and, especially, from the endless drinking and dining and empty talk.

After breakfast, he spent the morning walking the streets of New York, looking for a special gift for Shannon. He had several more days in New York, and he was determined to find the perfect gift. Then it hit him. A ring. Yes, of course. An engagement ring for Shannon.

It was starting to rain harder now. Jack was not prepared. He had no raincoat and no umbrella. He decided to return to his hotel, place a call to Shannon, then have a light lunch. He went to his room and called her home. The phone rang and rang. No answer. Then he dialed the bank, and was connected straight away.

"Would this be Mr. Jack Murphy?" a voice finally asked. He guessed that it was Mrs. Martin, whom he had met and liked early on. Jack knew just about everyone at the bank by now.

"Mr. Murphy, I have this message from Shannon for you. Her mother fell ill, so Shannon and her father took her to the hospital in Limerick. They decided to transfer her to Dublin for more testing. Her mother is much better now, so Shannon and her parents will be returning home tonight. She will be at work tomorrow, and wants you to call her."

"Thank you. Thank you, Mrs. Martin. Did she leave a number in Dublin?"

"She didn't, no. I'm sorry."

"Mrs. Martin, I can't thank you enough. I was worried when I couldn't reach her. I am so relieved. I hope her mother is all right. Oh, and by the way, here is the name of my hotel in New York, and the telephone number." He gave Mrs. Martin the information. "Thank you again."

Jack sat on the side of his bed and felt like saying a prayer. A huge weight was lifted from his mind. Just then the phone rang.

"Jack, darling, how are you?"

"A.J. Great, honey. I'm great."

"Listen, sweetheart, here are the plans for tomorrow. I have a very full plate in the morning. After lunch we'll send a courier over with some papers for you to look over. You have an appointment with me and several others at four o'clock tomorrow afternoon. Sound okay, darling?"

"Perfect. What time will the papers arrive?" he asked.

"About two, okay? Gotta run. 'Bye, love. See you tomorrow, and stay out of trouble. Ciao, darling."

At last, he thought here was the break he needed from the round of meetings. Shannon was all right. He could breathe again. He spent the afternoon relaxing, then had a quiet dinner alone in the hotel dining room, which had decent food and not a trace of a social scene. Then he watched a little TV and fell off to sleep.

By the next morning, the rain had lifted. Jack had an early bite of breakfast and headed out to find Shannon's ring. New York was alive with traffic and the smell of gasoline, alive with the honking of horns. Taxis were everywhere, and people were dashing about on their way to work. A breeze kicked up as he walked the streets, and it blew away the cobwebs. He remembered what he had always liked about America, before he fell in love with Ireland.

He looked into a display window of a jewelry store, and saw a wide variety of diamond rings. This was his third stop already this morning, and he had yet to see the perfect ring. He walked into the store and was greeted with a wide smile by an elderly man with a slight paunch and a round, beaming face.

"I'd like to see some engagement rings," Jack told him.

"Engagement rings. Of course. Over here, please. What price range are you considering?"

"Price range? I hadn't thought about that. I'll know the ring when I see it."

The black-vested little man pulled out a couple of trays of rings and placed them on the counter. Jack peered down to find that they looked pretty much like all the rest he had seen. He shook his head, and glanced over the other trays in the case. Then he saw it. "That's it," he smiled at the man and pointed to a large diamond with a simple, graceful setting. "That one."

The man took out the ring and held it up to the light, then handed it to Jack to inspect.

"This is a beautiful ring. How much is it?"

"$6500." The man watched him to see what effect the price would have. Seeing that there was no problem, he added, "This is a lot of ring for $6500."

Jack's mind was filled with happiness at the thought of getting a ring, this ring, for his Shannon. "I'll take it," he said decisively.

"Great," the old man was pleased. "I know the little lady will love it. When are you getting married?"

Jack considered the question. He had not proposed yet, so he did not know how to answer. At length, he replied, "Well, we haven't set a date yet."

The transaction was concluded and Jack walked back to his hotel with a spring in his step. The air sparkled after two days of rain, and the roar of the city filled him with energy. He went up to his room. There was one message, from A.J. "I'll bring the papers over myself, about noon."

Jack placed the ring in his hotel room safe and went down to the restaurant for a cup of soup and a light sandwich. He finished them and looked at his watch. It was nearly noon, and A.J. would be along any time. He still needed to shower and dress for the late afternoon meeting. He dashed from the elevator toward his room.

He found a clean white shirt and tie, and laid them out on the bed. He dusted off his black shoes and arranged them beside his socks and underwear. He had just gotten undressed and turned on the shower when he heard a knock.

"Jack. It's me, A.J." He covered himself with a robe and opened the door.

"Oh, honey. My timing is perfect," A.J. said with a good-natured leer as she walked in. Jack smiled, knowing that her mind was strictly on business.

"I want to go over a few of these items with you. How about you get dressed and we'll go down for a coffee. Hurry, darling," she said, not giving Jack a chance to answer.

"Make yourself at home," he told her. "I'll just be a minute." He gathered up his clothes and jumped into the shower. A.J. opened her briefcase and took out some papers. The phone rang, and she picked it up with a cheery, "Hello. Jack Murphy's suite."

"Hello." There was a pause. "Hello, may I speak with Mr. Murphy."

It was Shannon.

"Who's this?" A.J. asked in her flippant manner.

"My name is Shannon Kelly. I'm calling from Ireland. I'm a friend of Jack's."

"Well, honey, he's in the shower. Can I have him call you back?"

"No. No, thank you. That won't be necessary. It can wait."

There was a click.

Jack came out of the bathroom, dressed and ready to go. They were already in the elevator when A.J. casually said, "By the way sweetheart, you had a phone call. Some little sweet thing from Ireland. Said her name was Shannon."

"What?" Jack almost shouted. "When? What are you talking about."

"Just now, when you were in the shower."

"What did she say?"

"Not much. She asked for you, said it could wait. Is this one of your little girlfriends checking up on you? Well, whadda ya know? Jack has himself a girlfriend. Right, Jack? I should have known that you would get yourself an Irish speaking guide," she laughed. She was enjoying herself hugely. "Tell me about her, Jack. Does she have red hair? And can she dance the jig? There you are, poor Jack, all alone in Ireland. Just you and your native guide, Shannon."

"A.J., it's not like that. Please." He looked pained, and she knew she had struck a nerve, so she moved in on him.

"Oh, honey. I think you're hooked on this little lass. How old is she? She sounded pretty young on the phone. Come on Jack. You can tell A.J."

"Please, A.J.," he said again. "She's a very good friend. She works at my bank. We've gone out a few times. She's a good friend," he repeated, and left it at that. When they were seated and had ordered coffee, Jack excused himself. "I'll be right back, A.J." He did not wait for a response, but rushed back to his room as fast as he could. He dialed the bank and waited what seemed like an eternity for the connection.

"Mrs. Martin?" He did not go through the usual pleasantries.

"Yes, this would be Mrs. Martin."

"This is Jack Murphy again. How are you?" he added distractedly, aware that he was being abrupt. "May I speak with Shannon, please?"

The line went silent.

"Mr. Murphy. I'm so sorry, but Shannon can't come to the phone just now. Would there be a message?"

"Mrs. Martin, are you sure Shannon can't come to the phone? This is very important."

"I'm sorry, Mr. Murphy, but Shannon is in a meeting."

"Can you tell her that it's me calling?"

"I did, Mr. Murphy. I'm sorry."

He was silent. Then he said, "Thank you, Mrs. Martin," and hung up and sat motionless for a moment. How had this happened? What had A.J. said to her? "God damn it!" he cried out in anger.

He spent a few minutes getting himself under control, then returned to the coffee shop and A.J. He managed to get through the discussions and the review of the various papers. A.J. informed him that the four o'clock meeting had been changed to nine the next morning, and departed for the office.

Jack was thankful that A.J. had not pressed the issue about Shannon, and he was more than grateful that the meeting had been postponed.

Now he must find Shannon, talk to her, make her understand.

Chapter Twenty-Three

A period of bad weather had settled over County Kerry, and it added to Shannon's state of depression. After a simple dinner with her father, she went to her room with an excuse that she was not feeling well. She did not turn on her lamp, but sat in the lonely darkness. There was no moonlight, no light at all to relieve the gloom.

Her mind raced as the hours moved slowly. She sat thinking, wondering, worrying. Why was she distrustful of Jack, she asked herself. Was it related to her past, and to that other American, Stal? Back and forth, back and forth went her memories, from one man to the other. Scene after scene from her life passed through her mind as she sat numbly, staring into nothingness. She questioned her own perceptions. Was there a side to Jack that she did not see? Were all men alike, or was it just Americans?

Pools of water in the road shimmered with light from the house, and a gentle rain danced against the glass. Shannon stood at her window, just looking out. She had felt this pain before. It remained buried deep within her, and it filled her with fear. An awful pressure began to build up inside her. The rain continued and she could hear the high notes of water falling on the roof. What was this overpowering echo in her heart? She began to cry, and even though she tried to stop, she couldn't.

Shannon did not want this battle to be raging within her. She was exhausted from the struggle, and by her conflicting emotions. Her senses were functioning at their highest level. She wanted to believe that the answer to her phone call to New York had some logical explanation. She wanted to be comforted, reassured. She wanted Jack.

She was blind with love. She wanted to drown in his embrace. She wanted his warm breath against her skin, and his smothering kisses. She wanted to be with him this very moment, to hear him say that he loved her and that all her fears were ungrounded.

This scene reminded her again of how she felt the night Stal left Limerick, only now she was not guilt-ridden as before. She blinked her eyes rapidly and wiped the tears away. Unconsciously, her shoulders straightened. Deep within her heart, she suddenly grasped the true meaning of her feelings. Why think the worst of Jack? Shannon, my girl, she told herself sternly, this is not about Jack. It is about you. Your lack of trust in him is just that foul atmosphere that occupies you when your own self-esteem is challenged.

She caught herself smiling, then laughing out loud. She was struck by the absurdity of this uninvited delusion that had gripped her all day. She had allowed herself to obsess over the image of Jack with another woman. She had feared the worst, which was the loss of Jack. It had grown into a drama of confusion and self torture, and she had wallowed in it. She was ashamed of herself for behaving in such a childish fashion. Shannon, she told herself, not trusting Jack is just the half of it. You haven't been trusting yourself, either. Now snap out of it at once. At that, the swarm of painful emotions subsided, and she began to feel like her real self again.

Her reverie was interrupted by the ringing of the telephone down in the kitchen. She could hear the muted sound of her mother's voice speaking to someone, and then her slow footsteps ascending the stairs. There was a knock on the bedroom door. "Shannon, the telephone."

She sat very still for a moment, then jumped to her feet, calling out, "I'll be right along." She wiped her eyes and she rushed downstairs.

"Hello, this is Shannon."

"Shannon, my darling. This is Jack. Please don't say anything. Just listen. Please."

"All right," she answered, looking over at her mother standing in the kitchen.

"Shannon, that woman who answered the phone in my room. That was my editor, A.J. She had brought me some papers to sign and I was in the shower when she arrived. I asked her to come in and wait, and that is all there is to it." He sounded apologetic. "A.J. is a New Yorker through and through. She may have been rude to you. I don't know. Maybe that's what makes her such a good editor. It's a pretty harsh world over here."

Then his tone of voice changed. Tenderly, he said, "Shannon, I know that you believe me. I want no other woman but you, so much so that I went shopping in New York and I bought you an engagement ring. We're going to get married. Will you marry me?" There was a very long silence.

"Shannon, are you there?"

Shannon believed him. This was a never to be forgotten day. Jack had asked her to marry him! Inside, she felt bathed in light. She wanted to shout, to sing, to dance about the room. But she hid her emotions from her mother and simply replied, "I'd like that, Jack. Can we talk about that upon your return?"

He understood at once. "Is your mother listening"? he asked.

"Yes, I think so," was Shannon's immediate reaction.

"I see. We will have to find a way to tell them, won't we?"

"Yes." She took a deep breath and rubbed the back of her neck.

"And not this way, right?"

"Yes, Jack, that is right."

"Then you will marry me?" He immediately continued hurriedly.

"I will. Yes." A tear began to form in the corner of Shannon's eye, but she held back from crying. She knew that it would be difficult to explain all of this to her mother and father. But, more importantly, she realized that she had finally won her freedom. She had made the decision and had gained her own release from the duty that bound her too long to her childhood home. She was a woman now, about to make a life of her own.

When she hung up the phone her mother looked at her, then bowed her head over her task once more. She was baking a pie for tomorrow's bake sale at the church. Shannon helped her mother clean the kitchen and tidy up the house. Not a word about Jack was spoken by either of them.

Shannon's father came in from the barn and walked into the kitchen, hanging up his hat as he entered. He took a piece of brown bread and a glass of milk and sat down in front of the fireplace. The house was very quiet as each person moved about doing their customary things.

Finally, Shannon bid her parents good night. Ah, she loved them so, and always would. Things would work out so that she could continue to help them. She knew that. She went upstairs to her room and closed the door behind her. Now she didn't have to be discreet, so she let the joy rise up within her.

Turning on a small lamp near her bed, she sat down at the dresser and looked into the mirror. She saw a bride, Jack Murphy's bride. She was in an exalted state, yet with it was an awareness, a wisdom about her thinking. If ever two people were meant for each other, it was she and Jack. Every minute since they were born they had been moving toward the point where they met and fell in love. They were both ready for this love and the sharing that only love can offer.

The soft lights at night, the beautiful music they shared, the moments of tenderness together were never to be forgotten. They talked of poetry and art in their conversations. There were the long drives to explore the history of Ireland, and the glorious walks by the sea. They had developed a bond and a friendship beyond the normal sex-love relationship of most people.

She liked their childish moments as well—the joking and kidding around, the deep laughter released by their love for each other. There was something at once innocent and fiercely ambitious in the way that they stole every possible minute to be in each other's company.

Shannon took off her dress and shoes and lay down across her bed, wearing only her white slip. Her magnificent hair tumbled across the coverlet. Still thinking of Jack, she said, "I'm getting married" in a loud whisper.

"Mrs. Jack Murphy," she murmured very softly, under her breath. "Mrs. Murphy. Shannon Murphy." A succession of feelings coursed through her. Doubts and fears of the unknown territory she was entering. Wonderment at the beauty of it all. Liberty, a loosening of the chains that held her to the past. Happiness beyond telling. And, finally, an overwhelming love for Jack, greater than she had ever felt before.

She dreamed of life with Jack. Breathing in deeply, she could smell hot coffee in the morning, bacon cooking on the stove, bread baking in the oven, and scones browning to a crisp golden color, the way Jack loved them. She savored the image of clean sheets on a freshly made bed, the pungent aroma of freshly cut fields and flowers blooming in the spring, the simple odors of fresh fruit on the kitchen table and meat cooking in the oven, and the smell of making love.

Shannon stretched her arms high above her head, then brought her hands down across her breasts and ran them across her stomach and down her thighs. She rolled over on her stomach and rested her head on her arms. "I'm to be married, married to Jack Murphy," she said again, softly.

She began to plan her new life. We'll build a small house near the water, she thought, picturing it in her mind. Jack can have his work studio facing the ocean, and on the same side of the house, at the other end, we'll put our bedroom so that we can see the water as we lie in bed together, and listen to the ocean sounds filtering into our window. I can hear Jack working at his typewriter as I go about the house.

I'll plant flowers everywhere, and tend a small garden in the summer. I'll be the woman of the house. I'll be Mrs. Jack Murphy. In the dead of winter, when the icy storms come, we will take a holiday to Spain or Greece. We'll bask in the sun together, run on the beach, and make wild, mad passionate love until the sun comes up.

Dreaming of her marriage to come, she fell asleep, and the dreams took on softer colors and more fanciful details. Sometime in the middle of the night, she awoke feeling cold. She got up, changed into her nightgown, crawled under the covers, and fell off to sleep again.

Chapter Twenty-Four

The next evening, Mrs. Kelly was waiting just inside the door for her husband when he came into the house after working all day. The sun was about to set on a partly cloudy day, and there was a slight chill in the air. She did not say anything when Mr. Kelly first entered, but waited for him to hang his hat on a peg and sit down in front of the fireplace to take off his boots. This is what he would do every day when he came in from work. Taking a seat across from him before the fire, she told him that Jack wanted to ask for Shannon's hand when he returned from New York.

His broad forehead and his neck were covered with sweat from the day's labor. He sat without speaking for a long time, staring at the fire. Mrs. Kelly could tell that he was riled. He fumbled with the button on his sweater, pulled it off, and dropped it on the floor. There was a faint sound of something boiling on the kitchen stove, and Mrs. Kelly got up to tend to it.

Finally, he called out to her. "I knew this were bound to happen. 'Tis exactly what I told you would happen, I did." He rubbed his head with his huge hands and ran his fingers through his hair. He sat brooding for a long while as Mrs. Kelly continued fixing supper. Now and again he would glance up and watch her as she moved about the kitchen. Then he did something that he very rarely did. He went to the chest under the window and took out a bottle of whisky, then went to the kitchen and poured himself two fingers.

"Let's drink to our little Shannon and her happiness," he finally said. "That's all there is to be said, and I won't hear of anything else." He tipped the glass up to his mouth and, in one fast gulp, finished off the shot of whisky. He wiped his mouth on his shirt sleeve and returned to the chair next to the fireplace. Mrs. Kelly stood for a long time, motionless, staring out the kitchen window.

Mr. Kelly sat looking at the glow of the fire. "She's a grown woman," he said in a subdued voice. "It's not her doing that her brother is off with the IRA some place in Belfast, and certainly it's not her doing that God took her sister Bridget's life. You can't hold on to her, woman, you've got to let her fly. God knows that I have thought about this hard and long, I have, and prayed for understanding. I think God has answered my prayers and told me what to do."

"Papa, God's got nothing to do with this," Mrs. Kelly flashed back. "Jesus, Mary and Joseph! She'll marry and move off to America. Mark my words." She made the sign of the cross and sat down at the kitchen table.

"Ah, still, Shannon is a woman now." His eyes crinkled with a fond expression.

"She can't have children," she reminded him, hunching her shoulders as she spoke.

"She can't have children?" he repeated in bewilderment.

"Papa, we tried to tell you that years ago, but you wouldn't pay any mind." That seemed to stagger him. She continued, "You know well how you are when it comes to setting your mind. If you don't want to think of something, you act as if it never happened. I'm telling you now. You know in your heart that you already knew. Shannon can't bear children. I'd sooner her not have children than move off to America with Mr. Murphy."

"As if it were one or the other. What makes you think she'll move to America?"

"More fool her," she muttered sourly, not caring to explain herself.

He got up from his chair and crossed the room. In the glow of the firelight, she saw a look of pain on his strong, gentle face. He looked out the window as a car pulled up. It was Shannon home from work.

"I declare to God, you have a tear in your eye," he said to her. "Not to be letting Shannon see that, mind you."

Shannon stepped into the door, light as a feather, took off her coat and went to the fireplace to warm her hands. She gave her father a hug as she passed. "Chilly evening," she said, not to anyone in particular, but as a statement of fact.

"It is, the wind shifted today. May blow a storm tonight," her father answered.

Shannon's mother continued to work in the kitchen finishing dinner, not saying anything for now. In her wisdom, she had noticed many changes in Shannon. A mother knows when her daughter is in love, the Irish would always say, and Mrs. Kelly was more intuitive than most women in the village. Once, she had predicted that a local priest was having an affair with his housekeeper, and it turned out to be true. Deep within her she could sense a change in the priest and the housekeeper when she would be in their company, and no one else in the village had ever noticed this.

The three of them were very quiet during their meal. After supper, Mrs. Kelly began to clear the table. "Many hands make light work," she said pointedly, looking in Shannon's direction. Shannon did not get up from the table, but sat straight in her chair looking at her mother and then her father, "Jack has asked me to marry him," she said.

"I know," her mother answered.

Shannon was a little puzzled by her mother's response. She had watched her words so carefully when she was on the phone with Jack. But of course her mother would see right through her.

"I told him yes, mama."

"I see," she said. "And when is this to happen?"

"Jack called me at the bank today and we talked a long while. We agreed on July. We talked about the twenty-fifth. His book will be coming out the end of September. We will take our honeymoon, then return home."

Her mother interrupted. "Home? Is this to be your home?"

"Yes, mama. I want to look for land down near Tahilla. Now, there is a pretty place. I've always liked it, and you know, mama, it's only a thirty minute drive from here." Shannon could see that both of them were relieved and pleased with her news of building a house, and so close by at that.

"Anyway, after our honeymoon, we will have to go to America for a few weeks. Jack will have much to do concerning his book. Then I want to start work on our new house. I'll do most of the planning. Naturally, I'll resign my position at the bank, for I'll be busy with Jack and his book, and working with the builders on the new house." She found herself talking faster, sharing her excitement and happiness.

"Will you stay on at the Mullins' place until your house is built?" Shannon's father asked, not so much as a question, but as if he already knew the answer. Shannon nodded.

"Jack can work on his next book, and I can work on building the house." Shannon walked over and gave her mother a hug. Her mother turned from the stove and put her arms around Shannon and kissed her on both cheeks.

"I'm happy for you, my dear child. Jack's an all right kind of lad, I guess, and I know that he will be good to you and you'll never want for anything. Just don't run off and move to America on us."

"Not to worry, mama. Jack loves Ireland, and besides, a writer can write anywhere. Isn't that right?"

Shannon's father walked over and put his arm around her shoulder.

"I agree with your mama. I don't think Jack is like some lads I've heard tell of. Sometimes a man who has all that money will have two graves, one for his money and one for himself. Your Jack is the sort who will take good care of you. Just make sure you keep him happy at home, so he doesn't go chasing after some little American lady."

"Oh, shh," her mother motioned with her hand. "Watch your mouth. 'Tis a naughty thing to be saying to your own daughter."

"Well, I'm only telling her that men can change. I've seen what happens to some when they get all that fame and fortune. They become different sort of people. Or," he added slowly, so they would not miss his point, "they become what they always were in the first place."

"Jack's not that way, papa, and you know it. Besides, we love each other too much for anything like that to happen."

"Well, Shannon," her father smiled on her fondly. "I hope you're right. Now. What would you be wanting for your wedding? Keeping in mind, would you, that I'm not a wealthy man."

"Nothing, papa. Just your blessing will be more than enough."

"Na, your mum and I must get you something special."

"How about a piece of Waterford crystal? There is nothing as pretty as the sound of Irish crystal when you tap it."

"Done. Crystal it is."

After a while, Shannon went to her room. Shortly, her mother followed her upstairs. Shannon had left the door open, expecting her, so she walked in and sat down on the edge of the bed. "Come." She patted her hand on the bed for Shannon to sit next to her.

"Do you love him, child?"

"Aye, I do."

"Is there any doubt?"

"No. None," she answered.

"Not even a wee bit? For if there is, I'll tell ye to be holding off on the wedding." She looked at Shannon with kind eyes. "Getting married is not something to do if there are any doubts."

"I have no doubts," Shannon said quickly.

Shannon's mother looked at her approvingly. Shannon had been taught since childhood to answer questions with a full sentence, and to present her thoughts clearly. It was considered bad manners to answer any question with a simple yes or no. Most Irish children have been trained to use words and very few gestures when speaking, and Shannon was no exception.

"Child. You're a grown woman, you are, and I don't want to be telling you how to live your life any more than I can help. I want you to be happy as can be. If you're sure of this, and Jack Murphy is the kind of man you say he is, then I guess you're doing the proper thing."

"I am, yes. I know Jack loves me, and I him." She paused and gave her mother a warm, understanding look. "And I won't be running off to live in America. I promise." This seemed to be what her mother truly wanted to hear, for with that she gave Shannon a hug and left the room.

Chapter Twenty-Five

Jack was getting dressed when A.J. phoned him the next morning. She reminded him that they had another early meeting, nine o'clock sharp. Before she hung up, she added, "By the way, darling. Forrest Dodson is having a little get-together at his home tonight, and told me to make sure you were invited. Black tie, if you have one. The company is throwing a party in honor of John Savage's new smash hit, *The West Turns Gold.* Turns out it was aptly named. I'll pick you up in the limo at eight o'clock tonight. You can't say no. Gotta run, sweetheart. Don't be late for this morning's meeting. This is a big one. We got the okay on the movie deal. I'll tell you right now, don't hold out for more money. We did just fine. Gotta go now. Later, darling."

Jack thought about all she said as he ate his breakfast. This is the big time, he reminded himself, and all the partying and politics are just part of the territory. Today, he didn't feel so disgusted with it all. He had found his Shannon, and she had agreed to marry him. He didn't feel so alone now. Let them dish it out. He could take it.

He grabbed a taxi to take him to the meeting. Again, the session lasted nearly all day. By the time it ended, the light was growing pale against the tall buildings of New York. It was a very good meeting. The movie contract promised to launch Jack's career into the Hollywood writing elite. With the celebrities involved, and the top quality directors and producers suggested for the movie project, it was evident that the film company considered it a major motion picture. They had also included in their contract a clause that gave them first option on Jack's next three books, which was unusual even by Hollywood standards.

In the taxi back to the hotel, Jack sat in amazement as he thought about the turn of events in the last few days. He felt as if he were finally realizing all the dreams of his youth, dreams that had been shattered by the hard lessons of life. Now, all of a sudden, his fondest hopes as a writer and a man were within his reach. He had the book, he had the movie, and most of all he had the girl. His sweet Shannon.

Everything was moving so quickly in his mind. The past days' events had bolstered his confidence. In the past, though he had hidden it very well, he had had moments when blind fear would consume his thoughts and plummet his self-esteem. He would always stifle these thoughts and move steadily forward. Now the discipline was paying off.

Jack was eager to return to his hotel room. He couldn't wait to call Shannon and share the good news about the book and the movie contracts, and he wanted to impress upon her what this could mean for their future. When he called the bank, however, she was at lunch. He left a message that he was going to a publisher's home that evening, and would call the next day regarding travel plans for his return.

Surprisingly, the limo was on time. Traffic must have been light that evening in New York, he reflected. On the way to Dodson's home, he and A.J. reveled in the string of successes that had lofted his career and his forthcoming book into orbit.

They arrived at the party a little after nine. They were greeted at the door by a stunning brunette who introduced herself as Forrest's oldest daughter, Kevan Vassar. She was visiting from Boston while her husband was away on business. Kevan was exquisitely dressed in a long, tightly fitted black dress with a low neckline. She wore a simple strand of small pearls and single post pearl earrings. Her hair was pulled up and secured in a chignon that accentuated her brown eyes and full lips. It appeared to Jack that she was in her late thirties. Tall, dark and deadly, he thought admiringly.

A.J. introduced Jack to Kevan, who kissed the air beside his face in the typical Hollywood salute. "So this is the infamous Jack Murphy I've been hearing so much about," she said with a knowing smile. "My father speaks very highly of you, Mr. Murphy. He says that you are the heir to the title of Master Storyteller at Kingdom House Publishing. Is that true, A.J.?" she asked, keeping her eyes on Jack.

"Oh, darling. You just don't know how true," A.J. responded with a laugh. Kevan motioned for one of the servants to take their coats and led them into the bar, introducing them to a few guests along the way. Jack casually glanced around the first floor of the house, taking in all the details. The writer's habit, he supposed. Each salon and dining room had a grand cathedral ceiling and two fireplaces with mantels of Italian marble. Overstuffed leather chairs and couches were arranged in comfortable groupings, while a scattering of antique cabinets, tables and mirrors conveyed discreet opulence. Off in another room, he could hear music from a string quartet.

The art collection was superb. Jack recognized several fine French Impressionist and Post-Impressionist works and a score of important American pieces. Each was framed in heavy, antique gold leaf and set off by its own light recessed in the ceiling just above. He reflected that Kingdom House was obviously not on a tight budget.

Jack sipped his first scotch and water, while A.J. ordered her usual martini. Kevan asked for a glass of Pavilion Blanc, a wine Jack had never heard of, then raised it to tip with Jack and A.J. in a toast. "To your new book, and to the beginning of a lasting new friendship." It sounded well rehearsed. Kevan tasted her wine and remarked to Jack, "I love this wine, don't you?" Jack nodded sagely, as if he knew all about it.

"Excuse me, you two. I see someone I must say hello to," A.J. said, darting into another room. Kevan drank down her elegant wine in one swallow and ordered another. Her cheeks slightly flushed, she took Jack's arm and announced to Jack that they must find her father. "We can walk around this way and I can show you a little of the house," she added, being the gracious hostess. "I think Dad is in the library."

Jack was a bit intimidated by Kevan's assertive manner, and by the fire that smoldered just beneath her sleek appearance. But her attentiveness, as well as the drink in his hand, soon loosened his reserve. He found himself feeling very comfortable in this wealthy environment, with a lavish woman on his arm. He loved the house, the art, and the rich feeling.

As they toured the house, Kevan discussed some of the objets d'art. They exchanged small talk about Ireland and his book. He learned a bit more about Kevan and the Dodson family. They finally found Forrest Dodson, who was talking with the guest of honor, John Savage, and several other men. Jack exchanged greetings and said the expected things, practicing his new role of brilliant but modest author. He had always hated this kind of thing, but it was starting to become routine.

Kevan had left his side to greet another guest. Upon her return, she whispered to Jack that dinner was being served, and that he must sit next to her. She was a charming partner, and the food was extraordinary. She confided to him that her father retained the best caterer in New York.

After dinner, the guests returned to the main rooms and broke up into small twosomes or foursomes. Then, like clockwork, they would exchange places and reassemble into different groupings. It was like a state occasion orchestrated by Amy Vanderbilt herself.

Kevan suggested to Jack that she show him the gardens. As they moved slowly along the lighted pathway, Kevan clung to his arm and described the landscaping in such a low voice that he was obliged to lean close in order to hear. He felt an unmistakable warmth about the entire evening. He didn't know why, but not once did he mention to Kevan that he was recently engaged to be married. In fact, for reasons he could not quite fathom, he talked very little about Ireland and did not mention Shannon at all.

Why? Was it the glorious night air or the drinks, Jack wondered as they walked. Like time, he thought, was it all an illusion? Was it the riches and fame that awaited him? Or was it this woman, a luxurious creature of wealth and charm who was moving in on him none too subtly?

As they wound their way back toward the main house, Kevan asked Jack when he was returning to Ireland. "Day after tomorrow, on the early morning flight," he said matter-of-factly, relieved to have a bit of reality to stand on.

"I am going into the city tomorrow to do a little shopping," she said. "Could you join me for lunch?"

He didn't answer at once. He saw where this was going, and he reminded himself that she was the publisher's daughter. After a pause, he said, "Kevan, that is very kind of you. However, tomorrow is a full day of meetings and my last day in town. I can't. I'm sorry."

"Well, dinner, then." She pulled herself closer to Jack so that he could feel her bare breast under her dress, pressing against his arm. She whispered, "Tomorrow?"

"Kevan, I truly can't. I just don't know how long the meetings will run. You know how these things go." He wondered why he could not give her a definite no. Why was he making these excuses? It wasn't just the politics of the thing, and that frightened him. There was an easy familiarity between them, as if they had known each other for a long time. There were no barriers. Jack felt very comfortable, almost playful, in Kevan's company. She was so open, so lovely, a mischievous vamp with angelic qualities.

He tried again. "Kevan, I really cannot meet you tomorrow. I think it would be grand to have dinner, but honestly..."

She interrupted and got to the point. "Jack, I like being with you. I would like to see you before you leave. Perhaps I could stay over in New York and we could have a nightcap. Please don't make me beg." She pouted prettily. About that time, as they neared the edge of the garden, Jack realized that he had had too much to drink. He began to feel dizzy.

A.J. came out just as they were walking up the stairs. "There you two are! I've been looking all over. What have you darlings been up to?" she asked in a loud, cheerful voice.

"Oh, A.J., I was showing Jack the garden."

"Well, I hate to break up this little quinella, but our limo is here and we both have an early day tomorrow. We're going to have to bid adieu. Kev, it was a great party. But then your father always throws great parties."

He was being rescued. He knew he must play his part. And so, after three scotch and waters, a glass of white wine and a glass of red with dinner, and a cognac and coffee after, Jack took hold of himself. He turned to the ravishing Kevan with utmost courtesy and said, "I'm really sorry that I can't get together with you tomorrow."

A.J. jumped in as Jack had known she would. "Not on your life. We need him tomorrow. He's ours!" Then she took Kevan gently by the arm. "Besides, honey, you don't want to get mixed up with these writer types. You know they're different from us normal people. They ain't Yankees, and they ain't Southerners. They're adrift from some other planet."

"I don't know A.J.," Kevan said, sizing up Jack. "I think he's kind of cute."

"Cute? Jack's gorgeous, but tomorrow he's mine. We have to be going now. There'll be other times," she said, laughing as she kissed the air by Kevan's cheek.

Jack was quiet on the drive back to the city. A.J. kept going on and on about the party and the many influential people she had met. She talked about the writers, the movie stars and the producers.

The drinks had caught up with Jack. By the time he reached his door to his hotel room he was already half asleep. Yet as he lay in bed, caught between slumber and consciousness, two points occurred to him. One was that he did not have a photo of Shannon. The other was that he wanted very much to hear her voice at that moment. He dropped off to sleep, numbed by the alcohol and the evening's events.

At some point during the night, he sat up, fully awake. His mind retraced all the events of the past few days. With Jack, everything had to be formulated. It had to have hinges, to be articulated. Perhaps it was the writer in him. In any case, he was able to sober up and to think clearly.

On this night, he put in order his pending marriage. He resolved that no one would stand in his way of making Shannon his. Not her mother or her father, not Brien, no one.

Nor would he allow himself to repeat his old mistakes, for Shannon was not like any other woman who had ever come into his life. Jack knew that he had idled away much of his life and squandered precious time and energy on far too many passing attractions, women who were in and out of his life in a moment. One such opportunity had presented itself this very evening, and it was a clear warning that he must heed. He needed to focus on Shannon, to remain clear about her. He could not allow himself any mistakes concerning his Shannon.

BOOK TWO

"The now,
the here,
through which all
future plunges to the past."

James Joyce
(1882-1941)

Chapter Twenty-Six

At the sight of Shannon's tears, Jack was filled with an emotion that sent him reeling back in time. He understood loss all too well, and he longed to comfort her. At the same time, he knew that only in inner solitude can a person come to terms with death. Drop after drop the tears rolled down Shannon's face. Inwardly, she repeated that she could not allow herself to be ruled by her sorrows. She had been brought up to have the finest self-control, a trait she learned from her mother.

Jack looked at her with deep anxiety. Finally, she stopped crying, leaned back in her chair and took a deep breath. "There," she said. "I think that I have finally accepted it." She said the words in a monotone, as though she were speaking at a bank meeting. "I'm fine, Jack. Just fine," she added. She was not, and he knew it. Shannon's father had died only one week after their return from their honeymoon in Greece. It was a sudden death caused by a stroke.

For a moment Jack was tempted to express his thoughts. Before he could, Shannon put her tears behind her and changed the subject. She jumped to her feet and walked over where Jack sat, and kissed him on the forehead.

"Jack, I know what would cheer me up. I want you to drive me somewhere, right now. I've found the perfect place to build our house, and I would like to show it to you. All right?" She looked at him for a reply. "Jack, it's so perfect."

"Sure," he said to her soothingly. "We could do that. Where is this perfect spot?"

"In Tahilla. You remember Tahilla. It's twenty-five kilometers from Kenmare. We passed by it on the way to Sneem."

"Yes, I remember now. It's there at the old church, near the sharp curve."

Shannon reached up on her toes and kissed Jack gently. "Come, let's go now."

On the way to Tahilla, Shannon carried on about the land she had found. Jack was pleased when they arrived at the spot and saw the beauty of the location. Shannon was right. It was perfect. They decided to make an offer on it the following day. Jack stood with his hands in his pockets, looking out toward the water. He was trying to think of the right thing to say to her, to draw her out of herself. He knew that she was trying to bear her grief alone, and had bottled it up inside. He turned to her, took her by the shoulders, and looked directly into her eyes.

"I'm sorry that your father couldn't see this place."

She looked at him gratefully. "I know, Jack. It's hard to believe that he's gone. My poor mother, Jack. I don't think she's going to live much longer. With papa gone, she has no desire to do much of anything." She put her arms around him and buried her face in his chest. "I'm trying to prepare for it, as much as anyone can. And, Jack, thank you for understanding."

On the ride home, they were both quiet. Then Shannon fell to talking about her father, and as she talked, her sorrow began to lift. She told Jack what her father had been like when she was young. "He would say, 'Won't you give us a song yourself, Shannon.'" She smiled fondly at the memory. "He said it each night after supper, until I was sixteen. Then I would sing a little song, and he would tap his foot."

Shannon also told Jack about a recent day when she was at her mother's home. They were in the kitchen cooking together, and her mother was doing her own kind of reminiscing. Of course, she was much more stoic. That was her way.

Mrs. Kelly was standing over the counter preparing plaice in herb butter. Scattered about over the counter top lay finely chopped parsley, chives, fennel, and thyme leaves, and, of course, the ever present flour, butter and lemon juice.

"The thing that counts most about the fish is the freshness," Mrs. Kelly said calmly. "That's what your father always said. He said that anyone living over a hundred miles from the sea should never eat fish older than one or two days old."

Then she picked up the heavy frying pan and covered the bottom with melted butter. "Too much butter will delay browning," she said, surveying all the other ingredients. "Your papa always liked his plaice very brown." She turned her head toward Shannon. "Add a little more butter when you turn the fish, mind. Papa always liked his fish cooked in a pan. It was all I could do to get him to eat it baked." Mrs. Kelly wiped her hands on her apron. Very seldom would Shannon catch her mother in the house without her apron. Once she had even gone to the market in Kenmare wearing her apron, and only noticed it as she was leaving the store.

Shannon kept silent throughout her mother's explanations of the lore of cooking fish. She sensed that her mother was merely going through the motions, since she had never heard her talk so much before.

"Now, crabs are another thing altogether, child. Always choose heavy ones. Those caught by potters off the rocks are far better than crabs caught in a trawl off a sandy bottom. Mind you, never steam crabs longer than twenty minutes."

"I know," Shannon said in a low, obedient voice.

"Papa loved crab mayonnaise on brown bread, with a just a little grated onion. Put on a little watercress for decoration."

As Shannon repeated this conversation to Jack, she confessed that she was surprised at both her mother and herself for the way they were holding up after the death of Mr. Kelly. Everything had changed for Shannon, and perhaps doubly so for her mother. Shannon's father would say grief was a ghost wind. Now, many weeks later, grief seemed to fill the house like an old friend, and loom around them as if comfortable in these now familiar surroundings. Especially in the evenings.

As she talked with Jack, Shannon told him how she hated to leave her mother alone with her grief in the evening. On that day, she had delayed going as long as possible, and then had said, "I need to be getting on." Her mother nodded, but did not speak. "Why don't you come and stay with Jack and me? We have plenty of room."

"No, child. It's a thing I'll never do. Do ye see? This is my home. 'Tis where I belong. I could never make do living in somebody else's house. Do ye see?"

With that Shannon had smiled and had given her mother a long hug. "You will call if you'll be needing anything." It was a statement rather than a question.

"I will, yes. Now be off. Jack will be wanting to eat. It's important to make your husband a fine meal. I always saw to it that papa had a good meal on the table, no matter how bad the times got. Like the time we lost our twenty-pound cow. Now that was a blow to your papa."

"Mother, exactly what is a twenty-pound cow?"

"A twenty-pounder? Well, for a long time, all the milk we couldn't use here at home, we'd thicken it and churn it. Any butter left over, we'd salt, then store it in the butte. We'd take the butte into Kenmare to sell to the butter buyers, by the pound they would buy it. A good cow will give you ten or twelve pounds, some maybe fifteen or sixteen. But a twenty-pounder! Now, that was the talk of the village. Of course, most of that kind of butter is just for using at home, with the big dairy farms and fancy creameries these days."

Shannon looked at her mother as she continued to tell her about the old days. She went on and on about how to churn butter. "In hot weather it comes in an hour, but in cold weather it takes half the day." Finally, Shannon had to interrupt, saying that she must be on her way home.

It was like that every time she went to visit. Her mother continued to tell stories of the way it was, many of which she had heard often times before. But she listened to her mother as if it were the first time she had heard that particular story.

Deep within her soul, Shannon was convinced that her mother would not live very much longer, mainly because she didn't have the desire to do so. She was more overcome with the loss of her husband than she would allow anyone to witness. Shannon knew that once she was alone, her mother would no doubt break down from the pain of the loss of her beloved husband. Sure enough, a few months later her mother died in her sleep. There were no signs of physical sickness. Most people in the village said that old friend, grief, was to blame. She was buried alongside Mr. Kelly in Kenmare, next to the church.

Shannon had tried to locate Brien when their father died, but with no success. This time she didn't even try. She always kept in her heart the hope that one day she would find her brother. She dreamed he'd come strolling in as if he had never left. She knew that it would hurt him that both his mother and father died and he did not attend either funeral.

The bond between brother and sister had grown stronger since Bridget's death. Before that, the two sisters were very close. Brien spent his youth doing what all young boys do in Kerry. He played sports, went fishing and hunting, and helped his father with the horses and cattle and tending to the farm. After Bridget's death, Shannon and Brien learned to lean on one another for support, sharing secrets of girlfriends, boyfriends, and all the magic of young blind confusion. Brien loved to sneak into Shannon's room at night. The two of them would sit by the window talking quietly. Brien would tell Shannon of his new girlfriend in school, and Shannon would confide to Brien her dreams of having a husband, a home, and a family.

It was truly a sad day when Shannon's mother died and Brien could not be at the funeral. It took Shannon a long while to recover from the grief of the past events. Finally, she managed to throw herself into her marriage and her home, and slowly she recovered from the depression that had overcome her.

Jack had come up with an idea that he thought might comfort Shannon somewhat. He suggested that they fix up the old homestead, telling her that he wanted to spend the money and the time to make the old place really shine. He saw that this pleased her a great deal. He knew that her emotional threads had been strained severely by the deaths of her parents and by Brien's absence. Jack was the only true support system she had.

It was shortly after Shannon's mother's funeral Jack received a phone call from New York. It was A.J., giving him an update on the book. The movie contract was still on. There was also an agreement to have his book published in three foreign languages. The Spanish edition would be distributed throughout South America, Mexico, and Spain.

Very excited for Jack, Shannon suggested they go out to dinner to celebrate.

"Where do you want to go?" Jack asked.

"How about Tahilla Cove?"

"Perfect," Jack replied. "Listen, I'm going into the village to run a few errands. Perhaps I'll stop off at the pub on the way home. I feel like talking with some of the old guys down there. Maybe I can keep quiet and learn something for once."

"All right, my love. But don't be late. I think we should have an early dinner tonight, if you know what I mean."

"I'm not sure I understand," Jack said jokingly. "Please explain."

"Begone with yourself, Mr. Murphy. Allow a lady to get dressed and get some housework done."

Jack drove off in the direction of Kenmare. Shannon stayed home and didn't do much of anything all day, but, as she would say, she did it very well. She took her time dressing for dinner, but the dinner hour came and went. It was long past dark when she heard a car outside. It was Jack. He had run into a bush down at the foot of the driveway. Shannon stood watching out the window as Jack stumbled up the walk toward the door, singing some old country and western song he had learned as a youth in America. He would sing a few lines, forget the words, laugh, and start over.

Shannon opened the door, went outside, and took Jack by the first place she could grab. She led him towards the house. "Mr. Murphy! Are you drunk?"

"No, my sweet. I'm not drunk. Just a couple of pints with the old guys down at the pub. My pub. Murphy's Pub. You know, I tried to buy it tonight," he said, laughing to himself. "Not for sale. Do you believe that? Can't even buy my own pub."

Shannon took Jack inside and closed the door. "So you've been to the pub, drinking, have you? It looks to me like you've been there all afternoon."

"Let's have a drink, my sweet."

"I wouldn't be having any drink myself, Mr. Murphy."

"The pub was fantastic. We did what any good Irishman would do. We talked treason."

"Mind your tongue, Jack Murphy," Shannon said with her hands on her hips. "You haven't seen the likes of the fury of a red-headed temper."

"Well, it's true. The Irish sit in pubs talking politics, religion, poetry and treason," he said. She glared at him. "Ha. You know what you get when you have four Irish together in a pub? You get five political parties." Jack slapped his hand on the side of his knee laughing. "Oh, long life to man who invented potheen. Sure and the Pope ought to make a martyr…"

"Jack."

"What, my sweet turtle dove?" He tried to put his arm around her shoulder, but she moved backwards. He changed his tactic. "Now get yourself ready," he said. "We're going out to dinner."

"No, Jack. We are not going out tonight. I have eaten already, and your own food is on the stove. Come. Take your coat off. Let me make you a cup of coffee."

"No. No. Get me a drink. I don't need coffee."

"No, sir, Mr. Murphy. No more drinking tonight, mind you. You've had plenty."

"The spirits have called me out of exile, my sweet Shannon, my sweet Minerva. My senses have deserted me in this time of need. You are the Goddess of Triumph. Save me."

"Oh, Jack. You are hopeless. I'll make some soup and hot coffee."

"No. No. A thousand times no. I'm taking you to dinner. And right now I want a drink. My kingdom for a drink," he declaimed, raising his arms in the air.

"No, Mr. Murphy. No more drinks. Please."

"Get thee to a nunnery, my fair Minerva." Jack made his way unsteadily to the chair in front of the fireplace. He slumped down and allowed his arms to hang over the sides, and within a moment he was sound asleep.

Shannon stood looking at him. Then, grabbing her sweater, she headed out the door. As she walked along the road, she heard the faraway sound of a lone dog barking at the moon. Then nothing, only darkness and the hush of the night.

She thought of how happy Jack had been earlier that day. She had wanted to make love with him, and she had been bold to ask him to have dinner early so they could get to bed straightaway. For some reason she didn't understand, he had not come home to take her to dinner at all.

Even more baffling to her was the sure knowledge that she didn't care. He had behaved like a common lout, and her desire for him had left her, at least for the time being. She stopped in the road and looked up at the sky for a long while. Then she turned and headed toward the house.

Chapter Twenty-Seven

On a rainy day in Belfast, Brien Patrick Kelly stood by the window of his studio apartment, waiting for a telephone call. On his bedside table was an old photograph of him with his sister, Shannon. They were carefree school kids then. Lord, he thought, how he wished he could see her. There were times when he wanted to catch the first train to Dublin and go home. He had visions of offering flowers to his sister, a box of sweets to his mother and a fresh can of pipe tobacco to his father.

Brien had known the secret dreams and joys of being a young boy in County Kerry. He had known the triumph of a young boy's first catch, the big one. He could recall the passion he felt for his childhood sweethearts. The rich fragrance of freshly cut flowers was a familiar memory to a boy from Ireland. He often dreamed of clouds moving across the horizon, leading him home.

Brien looked around his tiny apartment in Belfast. He saw depression reflected from the peeling walls, the filthy windows, and the bleak furnishings. He had thought about buying a bucket of paint to try and brighten the place up, if only to please Margaret Winslow. She was his new British friend and his special secret.

Brien jumped when he heard the phone ring. He pulled his long hair away from his handsome young face and stood looking at the phone. After too many rings, he picked up the receiver hesitantly.

"Hello."

"Brien. This is nightwatch."

"Yes."

"Meet me at one a.m. We'll give you the flashlight."

"Sure."

"Come the long way 'round." With that, the phone went dead.

One a.m., he thought. He looked at his watch, it was merely eleven-thirty. The time dragged as he thought of tonight's mission. How had it come to this? He began to question his motives for becoming involved with the IRA. His life had become the antithesis of all he had hoped it would be. He felt a heavy energy cooking all around him, invading his mind, making a mockery of the youthful ideals that had brought him to this sad state of affairs.

Brien was haunted by the stories of injured men and women, of dead children who had been victims of bombings. Both sides were guilty, he understood that. He also knew that that didn't make it right. Tonight, he was going to walk out into the rainy darkness to begin a journey which would change him forever. It would even affect Shannon, and everyone else who knew him or cared for him. He centered his mind on Shannon and his mother and father, and he began to weep.

The overwhelming feeling of loss made him think of the new love he had discovered in Margaret. His hopes for a joyful life with her vanished, like a flame suddenly extinguished, not to be rekindled.

He had sensed from the beginning that the inevitable would happen. Gone would be the stuff poets were made of. Gone would be the glory that once filled his dreams. The paradox, for him, was the realization that he had always been a person who loved life. He knew that real human joy came from giving. His soul was good. But somewhere between County Kerry and Belfast, the hopes of a young boy had been replaced by ugliness and desperation. He wanted his dreams back.

Brien felt betrayed by life. He felt betrayed by school, by the government, by his family, and most of all by the IRA. He felt betrayed by truth. He had felt this way many times before, but never so strongly as right now. In this time of darkness and confusion, Brien considered ending his own life.

Out of that same darkness within him, he called upon his ancient faith, and it did not desert him. His life was ruined, but somewhere deep inside his memory, a small river flowed with promise of a new beginning. He thought of his unshakable love for his sister and mother and father. If he could just get through this, he truly believed that one day soon he would awaken to a bright, shining morning. His dear family would be around him, and Margaret would be at his side.

Brien looked at his watch. It was time. His heart began to pump rapidly. He descended the stairs and walked out to embrace the cold night. For a moment he felt weak, then with each step he became stronger.

Echoes of his father's words rang through his head while he walked, and he could smell his mother's cooking, fragrant as ever. The sweet voice of his sister lingered in his thoughts like background music. Unnumbered thoughts hurled through his mind as he continued to walk.

There were few people about. The street lights were dimmed by the fog, casting a faint glow from their haloes of mist. An old car drove slowly, crossing Brien's path, and a man came out of a doorway to a pub and disappeared down the block. Brien continued to walk, picking up his pace. He turned the corner and started toward the boat docks. He wanted with all his being to turn around, to go back. He could not. His choices were up.

Just ahead, a black van was parked to the side of the building. Brien could see the glow from a cigarette through the window. As he approached, two men got out of the van holding a small briefcase. They handed it to Brien and said, "Go home. We'll be in contact. Don't leave the house."

Brien took the case and turned to walk away. As he put some distance between himself and the van, he heard one of the men call out, "And don't do anything stupid." At that moment, the only thing Brien could consider was keeping his own heart steady and beating. He could not lose control, no matter how frightened he was. He dared not show any confusion at this crucial moment.

Then he heard the van pull away. He turned his head slightly and watched over his shoulder as the dim red glow of the rear lights disappeared into the dark night. Brien was now moving in long, hurried strides, covering the sidewalk at a high rate of speed. He finally reached his building, and made his way upstairs. By the time he reached his door, he was out of breath. He placed the briefcase under the bed. He knew there would be no sleep for him tonight.

The light of reason had failed him, and the minions of chaos came crashing into his soul. He was night's child now. He was a messenger of darkness, a symbol of evil. He had come face to face with his demons.

Brien thought of his childhood, and how simple life had been. There were rainbows in his life then, and he would be forever chasing the pot of gold that was said to be at their end. Young and free, he ran through the meadows of memory. He wanted to go back in time and hide there, to start over and direct his life toward someplace other than this. He realized that he had taken his life for granted, and had all unheedingly let himself be led down this shadowy path. A hundred thoughts raced through his mind, until at last he was exhausted enough to sleep.

Chapter Twenty-Eight

There was a cool breeze coming off the water. Shannon stood watching the regular pulsing of the waves as they flowed in and out. Now and then, she glanced over at the workmen. The past few weeks the weather had smiled on her building project. Construction was ahead of schedule, even with the many changes that she had instituted. Jack had insisted on a larger bedroom than originally planned, and so she had also enlarged the bath.

Their new home was nestled into a small hill facing the ocean. Of all the possible sites on the ten acres, Shannon found this one the best. She had designed the main floor with four large rooms, each facing the water. The master bedroom and bath had a dressing room and two walk-in closets, Jack's idea. There was a spacious living room, a combined sunroom and large kitchen divided by a storage wall, and a formal dining room with crystal chandeliers, another of Jack's ideas.

Both Jack and Shannon loved fireplaces, so she had designed a fireplace for each of the rooms on the main floor. This allowed for a fireplace in each of the upstairs rooms, another of Jack's ideas.

Jack had purchased a four-door Mercedes Benz sedan for Shannon. Today, as she looked about the shore, a young man working on the job walked over to take a closer look at the new car. He called out. "Is this your new car, Mrs.Murphy?"

"It is, yes," she answered, turning back toward the car.

"It's a fine car," he said.

"It is, a fine car indeed, thank you." She paused, looking at him politely.

"Paddy, ma'am. The name's Paddy."

"Nice to meet you, Paddy. And no need to call me ma'am. Do I look that old?"

"Oh, no, ma'am. No, Mrs. Murphy, I didn't mean that," he said, embarrassed. Then he asked, "Didn't you work at the bank awhile back? I used to go in there to cash my payroll checks."

"I did, yes. But I resigned when I got married."

Shannon regarded Paddy, standing before her now. She guessed that he was about twenty-nine or thirty years of age, certainly no older. His face was lean and browned by the sun, and was set off nicely by long, thick hair that he had pulled back out of his eyes and tucked under a cap. He was shirtless, with the kind of strong, alert figure that one often finds on a ballplayer. And there was something else about him, a mythical quality, an intelligent look in his dark eyes that seemed somewhat out of place on a construction site.

"I don't know you, Paddy. Are you from Kenmare?"

"I'm not, no. I'm from Cork. I moved here to be with my girlfriend, and then she left for London. So here I am, working for Mr. O'Shea. A fine chap, he is, and it's good work."

All around them the workers were speaking the universal language of a construction project. A voice called out, "Morning, Mrs. Murphy."

"Good morning," she replied.

"Paddy, come give me a hand."

"Right away Mr. O'Shea." Paddy shook Shannon's hand and smiled. He held her hand for what seemed like a very long time, but she did not pull away. Paddy looked into her eyes a moment longer, then turned and walked away. She watched him as he moved about his work. When he glanced over toward her, she turned her head away and walked back to the water's edge. She could feel his eyes on her as she moved down the hill.

Shannon stood watching the blue and green light bounce off the water. Foam floated about like white diamonds on the ripples, making evanescent designs that skittered among the waves.

On the hill, a car pulled up. She turned and saw that it was Jack, and she watched as he got out and spoke with Mr. O'Shea. She could not hear them, but guessed at their conversation. They patted each other on the back as they talked, laughing now and again. Paddy was standing next to Mr. O'Shea. He was introduced to Jack, and they shook hands. Paddy glanced over toward Shannon before returning to work, and he managed a partial smile.

Jack waved and called to Shannon, and she walked up the hill to meet him. He gave her a big hug. Over his shoulder, she saw Paddy staring at them, so she pulled back quickly and gave Jack a kiss on the cheek.

"I have great news," Jack exclaimed. "I am now an official citizen of Ireland." He handed her a piece of paper which had arrived from Dublin.

Shannon beamed. "Oh, Jack, this is fantastic." She put her arms around his neck and embraced him warmly.

"It's more than that," he said into her ear. Then he took her by the shoulders and looked earnestly into her eyes. "This can be a very good tax advantage, you know, with the amount of money I'll be making from the book sales and the movie rights and all the rest."

Shannon knew, of course, but she was a trifle disappointed in his priorities. She was more interested in his commitment to Ireland, to her, and to their new life together. "Jack," she said in a soft voice, "do you realize that this very spot where we are standing has been here since the beginning of time? The cliffs, the sea, just look at them. This place, where we will live, is everlasting, like our love."

Jack pulled her close to him. "I love you, Shannon. I love your Ireland. My own Ireland now." She laid her head on his shoulder, contented, and listened to the sounds of the waves and the seagulls. Out in the ocean, a ship's bell rang faintly, echoing the busy sounds of the workers as they went about building her new home.

"Tonight we celebrate," Jack told her. "Let's go out for dinner."

"That would be fine. But mind you not to get drunk this time," she laughed.

Jack stood with his hands in his pockets and a big smile on his face. "If someone had asked me several years ago where would I be and what would I be doing now, the last thing I would have told them is that I would be married to a beautiful woman, I would be rich, and we would be building a house in Ireland." He looked at Shannon, took a deep breath, and said, "Wow."

She kissed him gently. "And you, my love. Without you, I would not want any of this. Don't let the honeymoon stop. Let's keep it going forever."

Jack nodded in full agreement. "Come let's go. Follow me home."

They turned and went to their cars. As Shannon passed by Paddy, he stopped working to watch her. He stood motionless as she opened her car door, and he caught a glimpse of her thighs as her skirt lifted when she got in. As she drove off, she looked into her rear view mirror. She could see Paddy, still leaning on his shovel, still looking at her.

The next morning, Shannon got a call from Mr. O'Shea. "Mrs. Murphy," came his cheerful voice. "How are you keeping this fine morning?"

"Very well, Mr. O'Shea. Very well indeed. Now. How can I help you?"

"Can you go to the new house today?"

"I can, yes. What time?"

"In about an hour's time. We have some questions about a few things that you need to make a decision on, plus we have a couple of suggestions. I won't be there when you arrive, but if you will ask for Paddy, he will take care of you. Will that be all right?"

"It will, yes. Thank you Mr. O'Shea. I'll be along directly."

Shannon hung up the phone, curious as to why she suddenly felt nervous about going out to the new house. Yet, she was oddly delighted. She wondered if she were feeling this way because of Paddy, and the thought frightened her just a little. She had always had the habit of analyzing herself, and today was no exception.

There was a light mask hiding the mountains as Shannon drove to Tahilla. The sun had not burned off the morning fog, so the entire area seemed to be filled with steam. She stopped at the only store in Tahilla, a tiny gathering place with a single gas pump. It was also the village post office.

"Top of the morning, Mrs. Murphy. Come to check on the house?"

"I have. It's coming along very well indeed. With all these bright days, the workers have made good progress."

"How's Mr. Murphy keeping?"

"Very well, thank you. He's very busy with his new book and all."

"It's a lucky day for Tahilla to have you and a professional writer living here. Lucky day, indeed."

"Well, thank you, Colin." Shannon said, getting into her car. From where the road turned and crossed the bridge to her island, it was exactly three kilometers. As she passed the old church, she could see glimpses of sunlight starting to break through the mist, turning the whole world into gold. She took the narrow dirt lane to her building site at the top of the small hill.

Their land was only ten acres, but it felt much larger due to the vast water that lay before it, and the mountains to the left. The island was about seventy-five acres in all, and there were only three other homes on it. One of those was a summer home for an American couple who only spent two or three months out of the year in Ireland. Shannon learned from Mr. O'Shea that from time to time the couple would allow friends or relatives to use the home for holiday. She had yet to see anyone there.

However, she did meet another neighbor, an old Irish gentlemen who had been born and raised on this little island. He was the fifth generation to live in that same house. He was the last survivor except for a sister who lived in London. The third house was at the far end of the island. It was owned by a man and a woman who kept to themselves, and Shannon had not met either of them.

As Shannon parked her car and got out, Paddy greeted her. "Morning, Mrs. Murphy. Fine day." She smiled and returned the greeting, then they turned and walked up the road to the top of the hill. Paddy was very attentive, and she found herself a bit flustered by his direct gaze.

He took her to the other side of the house, and unrolled the blueprints he carried. "This is the place where we planned the stairs to the patio. Mr. Murphy calls it a patio. Notice the layout," he said, pointing first at the site and then at the plans. "We want to know if you would like for the stairs to curve, as they do now in the blueprints, or if you would like for them to go straight down with a landing, like this."

Shannon listened to his explanation and looked at the plans. Paddy's eyes took in the way her hair fell forward as she looked down, and the soft outlines of her figure beneath her jacket.

"I like the curve myself, if you don't mind my saying so."

"I agree, Paddy. Let's do the curve."

He nodded with satisfaction and then took Shannon by the arm. "Mind your step," he told her and led her to the front window of the bedroom. "Mr. O'Shea thinks that we should make these windows here about four or five inches lower." He placed his hand on the spot where the window would be. "It would be very easy to do at this point. The adjustment would allow more light into the bedroom and give you a better view of the water."

Shannon nodded her head in agreement. "It is a very good idea, yes. Please inform Mr. O'Shea that I agree and that he has my permission to enlarge the windows. And thank him for me, too, for the sound suggestions." Her voice was formal.

As they turned to go, Shannon lost her balance on an unsecured stone. Paddy grabbed her as she fell. He held her tightly and said, "Mind your step. I don't want you to get hurt." She looked at him curiously, without uttering a word, keenly aware of his strong arms and his tight, muscular body against hers. Then she pulled away. With crisp assurance, she said, "I'm fine, thank you."

He continued to look at the beautiful face before him. "Would you be having any more questions, Mrs. Murphy? Is there anything I can do for you, anything at all?"

"No questions right now, Paddy."

In an effort to regain her composure, Shannon made light conversation as they walked back toward her car. With a casual glance at him, she asked, "Where do you go from this job, when my house is finished?"

"Mr. O'Shea says we have a new job to start in Kenmare. An American bought a cottage just west of the village, and says he wants us to restore it."

"Kenmare!" Shannon repeated in a surprised tone. "I grew up thereabouts. We have a cottage in Kenmare that we are going to restore one day. Perhaps you can do ours next?" Despite herself, she smiled and tilted her head coquettishly.

Paddy took her hand. "Thank you, Mrs. Murphy, for coming out today, I can't tell you what it means to me."

"You're welcome." Shannon returned his handshake. Paddy could not stop looking at her. He was under the spell of the green fire that danced in her eyes and the music that filled her voice. She was extraordinarily graceful, yet her manner was correct and sophisticated. He wanted to touch her shining hair and run his fingers through it. He wanted to sink into the very heart of her.

"I have to be getting on." Shannon said.

"What? Of course," he said, coming back to the here and now. His dark eyes glowed as he opened the car door for her. "We'll be seeing you again soon, I hope. Still lots to be done." She nodded, started the car, and headed down the hill. Over her shoulder, she saw the pensive expression on his face. He stood at the top of the road and watched until she was out of sight.

There can be no greater affliction, Paddy thought, then to place your heart in the hands of a married woman. In one day's time, she had taken him hostage. He was her bewildered servant. His life turned on that day. He knew that his memory would forever hold her scent and the sound of her laughter, and the delicious feel of her as he had steadied her from falling. His very dreams would be filled with Shannon.

Chapter Twenty-Nine

Before dinner, Jack brought out a letter to read to Shannon. He took a pair of reading glasses from his pocket.

"Jack, the glasses. When did you get glasses?"

"Today. I finally had to bury my vanity and buy a pair of reading glasses. I admit it. I can't read small print any longer in dim light. I used to say that my eyes were okay, but my arms were too short. What do you think? Cute? No?"

"They look good, Jack. You truly look like an Irish writer now."

"Well, then."

Jack began to read the a letter from A.J.

> Dear Jack,
>
> Darling, how are you? Here is the schedule from our travel agency for you and Shannon. By the way, I can't wait to meet her. I'm also enclosing some other papers that are a summary of the details concerning the movie sale. Notice that I got you $300,000 for this book and $400,000 each for the next two books. You asked me about control over the script. Jack, you give up control. Trust me, these people are good, really good. You will have input on the screenplay but they will have final say. Don't worry, darling, A.J. is looking out for you. The foreign

contracts are completed, and a copy is there for you to keep. Just sign the power of attorney and have it notarized, then send it back to me. We can go over all these things when you arrive in New York.

Gotta run darling, duty calls.
See you love,
A.J.

Attached to the letter was the itinerary. He leaned over the kitchen table and laid it all out for Shannon to view. Peering at her intently through his new glasses, he said excitedly, "This is going to be the greatest trip ever. Look at this! New York book-signing. Dinner with people from the New York Times. TV interviews. And the next day, we fly to Boston and do it all over again."

Shannon looked thoughtful. "Jack, what do I do during all this? Perhaps I should fly home after New York and mind the new house."

"No, I want you with me. I want this to be something we experience together. Please, Shannon."

She put her hand gently on his face, "All right, my love. I'll be going with you."

Jack reached over and kissed her. "I love you," he said. "I love you, Mrs. Murphy."

"And I you, Mr. Murphy." Shannon returned to preparing dinner and setting the table. Although it was still daylight, she set out candles for the dinner hour. In this old farm cottage they would often eat by candlelight. She said it made her feel like they were still on their honeymoon. She glanced over her shoulder, "You know, Jack, our wedding day and honeymoon were the happiest days I ever, ever had. I didn't want it to end."

Jack did not look up from the papers. "I agree," he said absently.

"Jack."

He looked up. "I'm sorry. I heard you. Yes. A thousand times, yes." He got up from the table and gave Shannon a bear hug and a long kiss and whispered, "You are right. It was fantastic. All our days will be one long honeymoon."

Jack went upstairs to change his shirt, while Shannon continued to cook in the kitchen. She glanced over at the table and saw a photograph of her family when they were all together. She was with her mother and father, her brother Brien and her sister Bridget. She picked up the photo and studied each person carefully. She noticed that her hair was shorter then, and she thought how it made her look younger.

She placed the picture back on the table and wiped a tear from her face. She suddenly realized how much her life had changed. She was married. Her family gone. A foreboding rose within her, the same ghastly feeling that she had when her sister died, and then again when her brother, Brien, left home. The same distinct emotion she had suffered when her mother and father died. Almost incidentally, she remembered Stal and the aftermath of that relationship. Why? She asked herself. Why do I have these feelings now?

Perhaps this is normal, she considered. It might be what all newly wedded women felt. It could be bound up with a loss of freedom and perhaps a bit of her identity. Her visions at that moment came from a hundred random sources. Her past loves, her family and growing up in Kenmare, her happy days in college in Limerick, and now, here, her life with Jack.

"Oh, God, I miss my family," she said under her breath.

Shannon was startled when Jack entered the kitchen. "Something sure smells good in here," he said appreciatively.

Shannon did not turn from the stove until she had gathered her senses. She said over her shoulder, "It won't be long, now." She took hold of herself sharply, realizing her many blessings. She could hardly believe she had been married eight months. She chuckled to herself as she looked out to watch the clouds drifting along the mountaintops. Sunlight came rushing through the cottage windows like music, transforming everything into an incredible splash of color. Winter was gone, and the weary earth gathered up the sun. It pierced her heart with a fresh new hope, awakening in her the sensuous desires of a newly married woman. Spring flashed before Shannon like a glorious jewel. She did not want to miss a moment of it.

Chapter Thirty

Brien Kelly walked into the noonday sun. It was a bright day, and the streets were alive with people. Spring had come to Belfast in a blaze of glory. The air was filled with a spirit of unity and hope. The sounds and smells of the city delighted him. He had made his decision. He felt an uplifting sense of joy, almost like being in love.

The aroma of the day's joint of meat cooking in a nearby pub, the sweet scent of the bakery breads, and the fragrant flower beds lining the street all added to his inner triumph. He turned the corner and walked along the river. Young leaves were sprouting on the trees, and it filled his heart with new life.

He thought of his father and longed to see him. As he walked the back roads and fields, he listened to his memories. He could see his mother in the kitchen preparing his favorite pie. The thought of his sister's gentle ways brought back the magic feeling that only she could stir in him. He smiled to himself at the thought of walking along the Kenmare River and feeling the breeze from the water on his face. He pictured the clouds changing shape over the mountains, and how the mighty rocks would rise to greet him.

Brien clutched the briefcase tightly as he hurried along. Up ahead he saw the train station. An hour's ride, he thought, and I will be rid of this burden. I'll be free again, truly free of guilt and pain. He went over in his mind what he was going to say when he confronted his leader in the IRA. He reviewed again and again the way in which he would tell them of his decision to leave Belfast and return to his homeland in County Kerry. They would understand. They must understand. After all, he had been of great service to the IRA. He had a passionate interest in their cause, but now it was time for him to leave. He could not, he would not be part of the bombings.

Brien reached the station and stood watching the train come in. He thought of the journey ahead. The train came to a stop and Brien rushed to purchase his ticket. People were moving about, getting ready to board. Some were saying good-bye to loved ones, while others turned quickly away to avoid saying anything at all.

Brien found a seat, and before long the train pulled out of the station. Light came into the car in random flashes as they passed through tunnels and between buildings. Brien's mind centered on Margaret Winslow, a quiet, peaceful girl whom he had met some time back. He was having a drink at a local pub when three girls walked in, and something moved him to strike up a conversation. During the evening, he and Margaret were drawn together, and gradually began to talk only to each other. Finally, her two friends left the pub.

"So, tell me, how long have you been in Belfast?" asked Brien.

"About a year. I work for an insurance company. And you?"

Brien paused, thinking over his answer. "About a year as well. I'm from County Kerry, in Ireland."

"I see. Well, I'm from London. Does this mean we can't see each other again?"

Brein liked her frankness. She seemed real to him. "I should say that that is up to us, wouldn't you?"

"I would indeed," Margaret answered. And then added after pause, "I take all people as they are, Catholic or anything else, for that matter. Are you Catholic?"

"I am, yes."

"Good. Now I have someone to talk with and learn more about the Catholic religion."

Brien liked Margaret immediately, and he especially enjoyed her light-hearted ways. He found her small frame a perfect match for her bright, upbeat personality. They met again several times over the next few weeks, until they both realized that they were falling in love. Without saying it in so many words, they simply knew that one day they would move in together.

Margaret told him she had even considered going to Ireland, should Brien one day want to return. This thought became central to Brien's mind as he pondered his future plans. Soon, he would be at his destination, and his two leaders would be waiting for him. He knew that there is a time in every young man's life when ignorance gives way to understanding, when arrogance gives way to common sense and humanity, and when even a fool must listen to the voice of God. This was his time. This was his moment to step out into the light. He thought of his small universe waiting in Ireland and the pivotal point of his life about to unfold.

Brien was sitting very still, his head resting against the glass, when he was startled by a loud voice behind him. He sat up straight and looked about. It was a woman scolding a small child. He turned back to the window and saw the sign for his station. He clutched the briefcase as the train slowed to a halt.

Out the window, he could see his leaders standing near the station. He descended the steps and walked in their direction. When he reached them they did not greet him, nor did they smile. They turned and walked toward a parked car, and he followed them.

"Give me the case."

Brien did as he was told. "I'm leaving Belfast. I'm going home," he said forthrightly.

"Going home? This is home," one man said.

"I mean, back to Ireland."

"What do you mean, Ireland? This is Ireland."

"I mean that I want to see my family. My parents are old, and my mother is not well. She has been sick off and on for years. I want to help on the farm. My papa can't do it alone."

He paused. "And I can't be part of the bombings. I told you that from the very beginning."

"Listen to me, Brien. We have one thing which we're counting on you doing. We have it arranged for you to be transferred to the plant in London. All we need for you to do is pick up three people in the south of England and drive them to London. That is all. No more."

"Then what?" Brien asked.

"You can go home to County Kerry."

"When?"

"In about six weeks, you'll move to London and go to work at the steel plant there. When we tell you, you will pick up a car at the airport and drive south. We'll tell you where at that time. Pick up three people and drive them to London, leaving the car with them. Then you can get on a plane the next day and return to Ireland. You will turn in your notice at the plant two weeks prior, giving some excuse that your mother is ill or something like that. You will do it, right? Before you answer, just let me say that things will not sit well with everyone here if you don't."

Brien sat very still. Finally, he said, "I will do it. But that is all. I won't do anything else except pick up these people and turn the car over to them."

"Good. That's very wise of you, Brien. We'll take you back to the train station and you'll hear from us. Just go about your normal business. Do not call anyone in Ireland or try to get in touch with any of your family. There'll be time for that later."

"Okay," he answered.

"Brien. Look at me," one man said. "Don't do anything foolish. This is very important to us. Don't tell anyone that you are moving to London. Clear?"

“Yes. I told you, don’t worry.”

“I’m not the one who should worry, Brien. Understood?”

“Yes. Yes. I understand.”

On Brien’s mind the entire way home was Margaret. He knew that he could not discuss any of this with her, but he must find a way to let her know that he planned to leave Belfast. He finally arrived at a workable solution. He would simply tell her that his company was sending him to London for a spell because they were short handed, and that in a matter of a few weeks he would return to Belfast. Secretly, his plan was to take her with him to Ireland upon his return.

Chapter Thirty-One

The final draft for *The Fields of Sensation* was complete, and the word from New York was that the publisher was extremely pleased. The galleys were being readied for Jack's approval. Now he turned his attention to the details of their new house.

Spring had been a blessing for him and Shannon. It was one of the warmest and driest years in more than a decade, and the sunny weather filled them both with energy. Shannon was especially happy now. Her life seemed to be a symphony. Each morning she would awake full of the joy of her life and of her love for Jack.

She had never seemed more beautiful. She was more attractive to Jack than ever before. As he watched her move about the cottage, he would get lost in her charm, and would fall in love with her all over again. Their love-making filled their nights, and their dreams filled their days.

On one such enchanted afternoon, Shannon returned from the market with fresh meat for dinner. She rushed into the house and flung her arms around Jack's neck, then kissed him boldly.

"I could devour you right now," she said. "I could just eat you up." She kissed him several times again.

"This calls for a drink," Jack said heartily. He went into the kitchen and opened a bottle of wine. "Let's go out to eat."

"Not tonight, Jack Murphy. I'm cooking you a great dinner, and afterwards we are going to sit by the fire. Then I think I'll be taking a hot bath and we'll be going to bed early. How does that sound, my love?"

With that, she put on an apron and began to prepare dinner. Jack grinned like a schoolboy, then took his place in front of the fire and picked up his newspaper. From time to time he would look up and watch Shannon moving about in the kitchen. He thought of this whole scene as a beautiful painting, with the loveliest woman in the world cooking a meal just for him. It was a masterpiece. He smelled the wonderful aromas coming from the kitchen. He feasted his eyes on the outline of Shannon's full breasts and round curves under her cotton dress.

Jack walked over to the kitchen, pulled in by her subtle seductiveness. Standing behind her, he slipped his arms around her waist, then allowed one hand to cup her breasts and the other to slide down between her legs. She pressed her body back against his. There was a hunger in her with every move. She could not contain herself, and turned to kiss him passionately.

This fired their emotions to an even higher pitch, and Jack could not restrain himself. He pulled the front of her dress up and plunged his hand down between her thighs. She was warm and moist at his touch. He gripped her tightly as she devoured him with kisses, her hands crushing his hair. Shannon's heart was beating rapidly as the exuberance grew into a physical frenzy. She pulled away.

"Jack, my God!" She could barely speak. Her face was flushed and she laughed out loud. "Look at you, you're covered in flour." Still trembling, they both laughed as she brushed the flour from his shirt. Shaking her head, she scolded him. "Look at what you've made me do."

In a teasing voice, he replied, "I know, it's my fault. Please don't have me flogged."

"Out of my kitchen. What's a woman to do?"

They talked quietly during dinner. From time to time they would mention the new house and their ideas on how to furnish it. They would talk of the weather, and of their trip to America. They expressed their love for each other. In the unspoken language between lovers, they knew what was to come later in the evening. Each could read the other's mind.

After dinner, Shannon undressed Jack very slowly, as if she were opening a special gift. She touched him here and there, tilting her head to study his reaction, going further with the things that pleased him most. With erotic precision, she focused all of her being on the lovemaking, and the hunger that began before dinner was satisfied in a flood of pleasure.

"I adore you," Shannon whispered, just before falling off to sleep.

Chapter Thirty-Two

The next few weeks were busy. Jack and Shannon filled their days working on the house. They decided to use mostly antique furnishings from Ireland, and Jack offered no resistance to the cost. They drove the countryside looking for unique items, and even went into Limerick and Cork to the larger antique dealers. They completed the master bedroom and the kitchen first, and then began to fill in pieces around the rest of the house.

Meanwhile, all the dates and plans were finalized for their working holiday to America. On the eve of their trip, Shannon experienced some misgivings. She could not understand why she was not more excited about going to America. She thought of her family a great deal while packing. She knew that if her mother were alive, she would insist that they have their journey blessed by the priest, and she felt the burden of guilt that was her Irish Catholic birthright.

By the next morning, Shannon's spirits had lifted. Most of their early morning trips started in near silence like this, and their conversation would unfold with the day. As they passed through Kenmare, Shannon looked over her shoulder at the vanishing buildings, then at Jack, and finally at the road ahead. Ireland began to come to life. The feathery light underneath the clouds ripened into full midday sunshine that brightened the road all the way to Shannon Airport.

As they boarded their plane in early afternoon, the morning sun was just beginning to warm up the day in New York. A.J. was at work early, as usual. She was sitting at her desk with a cup of black coffee when the phone rang.

"A.J., this is Manny Freeman. How are you?"

"Manny, darling. It's good to hear your voice. I'm great, darling, just great. Are you back in New York?"

"No, I'm calling from California. It's still dark outside."

"What's it been, darling, three or four months?"

"Yes, at least."

"Remember that last night? That dreadful dinner party at the Four Seasons? Oh, my God, darling. Did I get drunk that night. I was stuck next to that couple from one of those Godforsaken places down south, or out west. Hell, I don't remember."

A.J. took a sip of her coffee and lit a cigarette as Manny began talking. "We are all very excited about Jack's story," he told her. "I've hired two of the best screen writers in Hollywood, and get this. Remember that young director, Stallard Hopkins, who worked with me on my last movie, *Blue Sage*?'"

"Stal. Yes, I remember him. Good looking kid, if I recall."

"Well, he has agreed to be my assistant director on Jack's picture, and will be ready to start when we are ready. This kid is so talented. He called me last night and accepted the position. Oh, and I think I can get Victoria Steele as supporting actress."

"That's great, Manny. But then, I knew that if anybody would pull together a top-notch team, it would be you." As an afterthought, she added, "Jack is coming over from Ireland with his new bride, Shannon."

"Jack Murphy, married? What do you know about that?"

"Yes, darling, and get this. His new bride is twenty-five, twenty-six, something like that. Whadda ya think?"

"Hey, what the hell, A.J., Jack isn't exactly over the hill, you know. And besides, you only live once, so why not?" Manny paused. "Look. I've been married three times myself. I'm finally happy with Sally. Maybe this is the perfect match for Jack. Who knows?"

A.J. took another puff of her cigarette. "Honey, it's none of my business. Right? What do I know, anyway? I'm happy for Jack, if he's happy. They'll be here soon. What's today?" she rattled on without pausing for an answer. "What am I saying? Jack will be here this afternoon. They've already started out from Ireland. We'll see him tomorrow."

As a matter of fact, Jack and Shannon were just finishing their meal on board the plane. Shannon asked the airline stewardess for a blanket and a pillow. Jack looked around the cabin as he always did. The writer's habit. A woman across the aisle looked very familiar, but he couldn't place her. Finally it came to him. Just then she turned and he saw that he was mistaken. But he realized with a start that he had never told Shannon about the woman he had thought he recognized.

He turned to her impulsively. "Shannon, there's a woman over there who looks a lot like someone I used to know," he told her. "It's not the same person. I checked. But I just realized that I never told you about her. It was so long ago, I guess I just forgot. It was a girl I knew at work, even before I met Helen. I mean, we were really young. And foolish. What I want to tell you is that we got married and, well, we had a child. A little girl."

"Jack, why haven't you mentioned this to me before?"

"I just didn't think about it. Honestly."

Shannon took her hand from Jack's and folded her arms. "Where is this daughter of yours now?"

"I don't know."

"You don't know? You have a daughter somewhere and you have no contact with her? None at all?"

"No. I only saw her once. Her name is Elizabeth. Her mother remarried right away and, from what I was told long ago, she had more children with her new husband. Elizabeth was raised with many brothers and sisters. Very happy, I might add. My agreement with her mother, Lou, was to stay out of the way. Lou said that one day, when Elizabeth was old enough to understand, she would tell her about me, and if at that time she wanted to look me up, she would."

"I don't believe this story, Jack." She looked at him as if she were trying to decide if it were a joke. "This is preposterous."

"I know, Shannon. I know. But I'm sorry to tell you every word of it is true."

"Where do they live now?"

"I have no idea."

There was a long silence between them. Jack could hear the low murmur of people talking business somewhere behind them. The flight attendant appeared. "Can I get you anything?" she asked Jack.

"Yes, please. Give me a scotch and water."

"And you, madam?"

"No. Nothing, thank you." Shannon sat up very straight as the flight attendant left. "What else haven't you told me, Jack? What else have you left out?" Jack had never seen that fury in her eyes. "Jack, I still can't believe you waited until now to tell me. It's not so much that it happened, or even that you had a child. But, you didn't share something like this with me? Don't you trust me?"

"Of course I trust you. Shannon, look at me. I love you. You are my wife. Nothing is more important to me than you. I've been so in love with you ever since I met you that the past just doesn't seem real to me sometimes. Long ago, I accepted it that incident as a major youthful blunder. My daughter was happy. What else could I have done?"

"I don't know, Jack. Nothing, I suppose."

The flight attendant returned with Jack's drink. He thanked her, then looked at Shannon again. He saw the anger still in her eyes. They did not talk after that. He sipped his drink. She put her seat back as far as it would go and closed her eyes.

Chapter Thirty-Three

It was just after three-thirty p.m. when the plane touched down. Shannon took Jack by the hand, and in a few short words brightened his day. "Jack, my darling, everything is all right." He smiled with relief. They proceeded through customs and found a taxi into New York City. "Jack, this place is huge," she said, looking out the window of the taxi. "So many tall buildings."

Jack leaned over and kissed her cheek. "Shall we move here?"

"Move? Here? Come, Mr. Murphy." She continued to stare out the window. "So many cars, everywhere."

"This is light traffic for New York," Jack explained. "Wait until you see the rush hour."

"Whew! And I thought Cork was big."

"You're cute," Jack said, laughing.

"Where are you folks from?" the driver asked.

"Ireland."

"Ireland. I had some people in the cab last week from Ireland. Or was it Scotland? They are the same, right?"

"Not exactly," Jack said. "But they aren't that far from each other."

"Never been overseas, myself," the driver said. "I'm born and bred in America. In fact, I think I'm the last American cab driver in New York," he said, laughing.

They reached their hotel, the Waldorf Astoria. Shannon was amazed. "Look at this lobby, would you?" she said softly to Jack.

"I know. It's something. I wanted to bring you to one of the grand old hotels of America. This is where the President stays when he's in New York."

"It's beautiful. Like the inside of one of our castles."

They checked in and were shown to their room. On the table sat a basket of fruit, some fresh cut flowers and a bottle of champagne in an ice bucket. The card said, "Welcome to New York. Love, A.J." Shannon went to the window and stood looking out at the city below. It was a clear day, so she had a panoramic view of the skyline. She turned when she heard a popping sound. Jack was opening the champagne, and he filled two glasses. Handing one to her, he raised his glass. "Here's to the most wonderful, beautiful, and charming lady in New York."

She smiled graciously and took a sip. "Hmm. Very good. Very good indeed." She sat down and started leafing through a magazine from the stack of entertainment and advertising material on the table. "What's the plan for tomorrow? When do you have the book signing? and New York Times interview? and, oh, the T.V interview?"

"Day after tomorrow. But tonight and tomorrow are ours. What would you like to do? A museum? Or perhaps a Broadway show. Go shopping? We must go shopping in New York."

Shannon stood up and walked around. "Jack, this is a very nice room, or should I say a suite?" She sat down on the edge of the bed. With a schoolgirl grin she said, "Nice bed."

Jack missed her sly suggestion because he was pouring himself more champagne. Then he topped Shannon's glass off. "I think I'll unpack," he said. He took out a copy of his new book and placed on the bed. Shannon picked it up. "You know, this is a very nice picture of you on the back. Don't you think?"

"I suppose."

"Really, Jack. It's very becoming." She held the book, looking at it as if it were the first time. "I love the cover. It makes you want to open the book and see what's inside." She flipped through the pages. "Jack, this is a wonderful book. I think you have yourself a masterpiece."

He laughed. "A masterpiece? Come now."

"Jack, don't be so modest. Don't sell yourself and your work short. It's a fantastic book. A true work of art." She hugged the book to her breast. "When they start filming the movie, will they be filming in Ireland?"

"Most likely. The entire book is set in Ireland. Oh, they may do some scenes in the studio, but most of it will be on location."

"Can we go one day when they start filming and watch?"

"Of course. Not only that, but we will have some of the cast, directors, and special members of the production company over to the house for a big party."

"Oh, that will be exciting," she said with a big smile. "How long before they start filming?"

"I'm not sure," he said. "I'll ask A.J. tomorrow if she has the schedule. She did tell me that they want to start quickly, so that the movie comes out during the peak of book sales. Or as near to that as they can manage."

"Jack, this is all so exciting. I'm so proud of you."

"Shannon, I know what we should do tomorrow. Let's go find you two or three new dresses. One for the cocktail party and a couple for running around New York. I know the perfect place. Saks Fifth Avenue."

"Saks Fifth Avenue? Isn't that a little expensive?"

Jack took Shannon by the shoulders and held her tight. "Listen. Money is not one of our problems, and the real money hasn't even begun to come in yet. I'm talking worldwide book sales. And after the movie comes out, the sales will start all over again. Plus the movie rights. My dear, don't worry about shopping at Saks Fifth Avenue. I want to buy you the best they have to offer. I want Mrs. Murphy to be the Queen of the Ball. I want to show my new bride off to these American bums."

"Jack. Don't talk about your countrymen that way."

"Only kidding. Only kidding."

"Well, all right," she said gleefully. "Let's go shopping tomorrow, then."

That evening, they had a nice dinner and retired early. The next morning, they were wide awake at five a.m. They tried to go back to sleep, but couldn't, so they got dressed and went down for breakfast. At ten, they took a taxi to Saks Fifth Avenue.

Everything Shannon tried on was stunning. Jack couldn't believe how glorious she looked. Dress after dress, one after the other, each more beautiful than the last. Shannon was absolutely striking in each and every outfit. Then she tried on a black, low cut cocktail gown. Jack stood speechless when she came out of the dressing room. "My God," he breathed. "You are so beautiful."

"Thank you, Jack," she said softly. Then she looked at the price tag on the sleeve. $2,000. "Did you see this?" she asked him.

"No, and I don't care. This gown was designed for you." He took her by the arm and turned her around. The outline of her full breasts, and the way the dress hugged her in the back, was too much for Jack to take. He whispered, "Damn. You are one sexy woman."

"Jack, please," she said sternly. He knew that when he got that look from Shannon he had better leave it alone.

"Shall we take it?" he asked her.

"Well, I guess so. Are you sure?"

"I'm sure. Now we'll need shoes, an evening bag, earrings and whatever else this nice lady thinks would go well with this gown." Shannon beamed as they walked about the store. By the time they left, they had three huge shopping bags and two hanging bags filled with clothes and accessories. Jack had insisted that they stop off at the perfume counter. There he helped her select three fragrances, all French, all exquisite.

"Now," he said, as they climbed into the cab with their purchases. "We'll go back to the hotel and make an appointment to have your hair and nails done, while I go over and meet the manager of the book store. I want to speak with him before tomorrow's book signing." He helped her to the room with the packages, then headed for the book store. Afterwards, he went back to Saks Fifth Avenue and purchased a new tuxedo, then rushed the alterations through. He wanted to surprise Shannon. He intended to look good when he escorted her to the cocktail party in his honor at Forrest Dodson's home. He couldn't wait to introduce her to everyone at Kingdom House Publishing. He wanted to show off his bride, his Irish beauty, his Shannon.

Chapter Thirty-Four

When Jack came out of the bathroom wearing his new tux, Shannon was sitting on the bed. At the sight of him, she gasped, "Jack! My God, you're beautiful. Let me take a good look at you. Turn around. Well, Mr. Jack Murphy, you are going to be the most handsome man at the party." She walked over for a closer inspection. "Just look at yourself. Where did you get that tuxedo?"

"I wanted to surprise you. I spotted it when we were shopping at Saks, so I went back and bought it. Like it?"

"I love it." She reached up on her toes to give Jack a quick kiss. "Now, be gone with yourself. Go down to the bar and have yourself a drink, not too much, mind you, while I get dressed. A lady needs her privacy." He gathered her up in a happy hug and kiss, then left obediently. He returned in an hour, giving her ample time to dress. When he walked into the room she was standing in front of the mirror, putting on her last earring.

Jack stood looking at this vision, speechless for a long time. This was the woman he knew so well, he thought, yet there was an added dimension to her in the long black evening gown. He had never seen Shannon in a low neckline quite like this one. The décolletage cradled her magnificent breasts and displayed them in a way that was both elegant and slightly immodest. Jack had sensibly decided to splurge on a fine pair of diamond and emerald earrings and skip the necklace. If anyone wanted to ogle her beautiful bosom, he reasoned, he was not going to give them the excuse of staring at a piece of jewelry.

The construction of the dress exaggerated her small waist. It carved out her hips and poured over her back with utmost refinement, yet at the same time somehow exaggerated the sheer erotic splendor of her curves. At that moment, she was the most ravishing woman he had ever seen in his entire life. He was simply overwhelmed.

Shannon watched him in the mirror as he took her in. The magnetism was almost unbearable. With a slight stammer, he confessed, "I am flabbergasted. I cannot find words to tell you how beautiful you look to me."

Shannon twirled about the room, showing him every angle. "So you like it?"

"Like it? Darling, I could eat you up. Bite by bite."

She laughed, "That's later."

When they arrived at Forrest Dodson's home, the party was already in full swing. A.J. was watching for them, and came hustling forward to greet them at the door. "Jack, darling. Our man of the hour! How good to see you." She gave him her standard greeting, a kiss on the cheek always a bit too close to his lips. Then, turning with a flourish, she said, "And you must be Shannon. My God, darling. Jack said you were beautiful, but he didn't do you justice. Welcome. I'm A.J., the other woman in Jack's life, the one who stays up late at night working on his career."

"I'm happy to meet you. I've heard so much about you," Shannon said.

"Well, darling, if it's good stuff you heard about me, then it's probably rumor." She turned to Jack. "Come on. I'll introduce you to a few people." Slipping between them and linking arms, she guided them into the party. "Forrest, look who's here," she said to their host. "Jack and his new bride, Shannon, all the way from Ireland."

The urbane publisher extended his hand to Shannon and then to Jack. "Welcome, and congratulations on your marriage, Jack. Well done. Tell me, Shannon, how did Jack ever hook you, anyway? Was it his money or his charm?" She smiled but did not answer. A waiter appeared with a tray of champagne, and they each took one. "Excuse me, Jack," Forrest continued. "I'm taking Shannon and introducing her to a few of my guests. If we're not back in an hour, send the dogs."

Shannon did not want to leave Jack, but graciously accepted. They had just moved away when Kevan Vassar walked up. "Jack. It's good to see you again. Remember me? I'm Kevan, Forrest's daughter."

"Of course, Kevan, how are you?"

"I'm much better now that I've seen you. How have you been? How's Ireland?" She didn't allow Jack to answer, but put her arms around his neck and pulled him close against her body, kissing his lips. At that moment, Shannon glanced over and saw the exchange between them. She quickly turned her head back to the conversation. Kevan put her arm inside Jack's and stayed close, talking. They were still in that position when Forrest and Shannon returned.

"Oh, there you are," Forrest said to his daughter. "Shannon, I would like for you to meet my daughter, Kevan Vassar." Shannon extended her hand to Kevan.

Kevan looked her over appraisingly. "Jack, your new bride is a perfect doll. Now I see why you're so anxious to stay in Ireland." Jack put his arm around Shannon's waist and smiled proudly.

"Listen you two, I'll see you later. I've got to say hello to a few people." Kevan walked away.

"Friend of yours, Jack?" Shannon asked calmly.

"Not really, I met her once before, on my last trip to New York."

"I see. Very attractive, she is. But then, so are you. I can't blame her for taking a liking to you."

"What? What are you talking about, darling?"

"You can't fool another woman."

"What does that mean?"

"It means that a woman knows when another woman has taken a liking to her husband, that's all."

"Don't be silly," Jack responded.

Shannon leaned over to whisper in his ear. "Not to worry, darling. I'll keep my Irish wits about me, if she keeps her American mitts away from you."

"You're not kidding, are you?" Jack looked at her closely.

"I'm not kidding." She glanced around the room. "Excuse me, love. I'm going to freshen up." She set her glass on the table and made her way to the powder room. As she returned, she saw Jack across the room talking to a group of people.

A huge, ruddy-faced man stopped her. "Hi. I'm Todd Taylor. You must be Shannon."

"I am, yes. I'm Shannon Murphy, Jack's wife. I'm happy to meet you."

"Well, little darlin'—I knew when I saw you that you must be the gal from Ireland that everyone's talking about. You are for sure the best lookin' thing here, so I knew right off that you must be Shannon." She did not reply, but took another glass of champagne as the waiter passed by. "I can't drink that stuff," Todd said to the waiter. "Get me a C.C. and Coke, little buddy. And here, this one is dead. You can have the glass." Shannon turned to go, but Todd started talking to her again. "Boy, I'll tell you, I never thought anyone could hook ol' Jack baby. When he and I worked together in Miami, why, he was the ladies' man of Florida. He could of had any woman he wanted. They flocked to him like bees to honey. I sort of lost track when I took this job here in New York. How's the ol' boy doin'?"

"He's been fine, Mr. Taylor."

"Todd. Call me Todd. None of this Mister stuff. Where I come from, East Texas, everyone is on a first name basis. My dad is Mister. I'm Todd. Know what I mean?" He gave her a nudge.

"I think I do, yes," she said with a forced smile. "Please excuse me, Mr. Taylor, Todd. It was nice meeting you. I think I'll find my husband."

"Yeah, you keep an eye on him. Nice talkin' to you. Maybe we'll all go out sometime and I'll show y'all some real fun spots in New York. There are a few, if you know where to look for 'em."

She smiled graciously and moved away. When she found Jack, he was engaged in a worldly conversation about writers, publishers and the American public. Shannon took his arm and he stopped to introduce her to everyone. Immediately the same chitchat began. "How are you? How's Ireland? Aren't you gorgeous. How did Jack ever land you? Are you planning to move to America?" And on and on.

"Oh, my God," she thought to herself as she smiled and made appropriate murmurs. "And I have to do this for two more weeks. How will I ever make it?"

The remainder of the night was much of the same. Forrest Dodson stopped the music at one point to introduce to his rising new star and his rising new star's wife from Ireland. Then the band played again and people danced all night long. The waiters circulated with yet more drinks, and the small talk got smaller and smaller. Shannon wondered if all American cocktail parties were filled with such idle babble.

Kevan Vassar stood across the room with a group of Hollywood socialites. "Look at the figure on that little Irish doll, would you?" one of them snickered. "How old do you think she is?"

"She's about twenty-nine," Kevan said.

"Damn, she doesn't look it."

"Rich and famous gets 'em every time."

"Hey, Jack's a handsome man, and brilliant besides," Kevan said defensively.

"If only I had known he was available," one said wistfully.

"Sorry, honey, but you don't have the material to compete with that," Kevan said, adding quickly, "Just kidding." She looked at the other women with a knowing expression. "Don't be surprised if they have a falling out and Jack ends up in New York one of these days down the road. When that young ass wears off and he gets tired of that down home Irish cooking and those old country ways, he'll be back. You'll see."

"Yep," one added. "I've seen it over and over again. Older men get tired of their trophies and go looking for a real woman with some experience."

"Like you?"

"Maybe."

"Jack's not that old. He's not even fifty."

"Really. Wait a couple of years. My husband's not much older than that, and all he wants to do is sit in front of the T.V. and watch football and baseball and God knows what. And he plays golf on weekends. Is that going to satisfy a high-spirited young filly like her?"

Kevan stood quietly studying Jack and Shannon. "She is beautiful. I'll say that for her."

"Bitch." Another woman wisecracked.

The party was winding down as Jack and Shannon thanked their host walked out the front door. In the limo, Shannon rested her head on Jack's shoulder, saying, "Jesus, Mary and Joseph, that was a long night."

Chapter Thirty-Five

Their whirlwind trip continued from New York through the great cities across America. Jack worked hard to publicize his book at the receptions, book signings, television interviews, and press conferences. Evenings were also devoted to promotion, in the guise of that popular American pastime, cocktail parties. Jack and Shannon attracted a great deal of notice as a good-looking couple, and they functioned smoothly as a team.

Shannon managed the elegant parties and the rich hotels with the ease of a natural aristocrat. She thoroughly enjoyed the occasional symphony or ballet that would be arranged for them by a thoughtful book store owner. In the daytime, while Jack was preoccupied with business, she set out to explore his country. She went on as many guided tours as she could find. History museums became her passion. Popular culture intrigued her, and she investigated everything from tourist traps to shopping malls. She wrestled with the unfamiliar accents from coast to coast, considering all of them rather flat.

As much as she tried to embrace America, she was still mortally homesick. She felt lost in the impersonal monotony of the cities. She was pained by the constant struggle she saw all about her. She longed for Ireland incessantly. In her memory, the things she loved all seemed to appear in perfect form. She envisioned the rock cottages set into the noble green earth, the sound of the ocean crashing against the rocky cliffs, and the magnificent beauty that illuminated all of County Kerry. She was torn by these conflicting emotions, but she kept them to herself.

Then a wonderful thing happened. On the last day of their trip, they awoke very early. Jack reached over and gave Shannon a slight kiss, then said, "I'm ready to go home. I miss Kerry and our new home. I miss the pub, and the music, and the people. I miss being alone with you in our world."

Shannon smiled through a sleepy-eyed daze. He pulled her close, eased his hand down between her legs and gently moved them apart, looking into her eyes as he touched her. "Jack," she whispered, "I love you. Let me just go to the bathroom and brush my teeth."

When she returned, they took each other fiercely, urgently. It was not the kind of lovemaking they had experienced in their most exalted moments. They were simply starved for each other. Fearlessly, they pillaged and plundered to the point of exhaustion. If there had been any remaining barriers between them, they fell now.

Jack and Shannon were very quiet and subdued on the drive to Los Angeles International Airport. While all of the meetings, interviews and book signings had been very successful, they had taken their toll. It was not until they were settled in the first class cabin of their transatlantic flight and had received their drinks that they began to relax. "Thank God, we're going home," said Shannon, lifting her glass. "As my grandfather used to say, 'East is our future, West is our past.' He had many old sayings like that. I believe they came out of the Great Famine."

Jack seized upon the topic. He had always loved to listen to her tell of Irish history. "Was it as bad as they say?" he asked, drawing her out.

"It was, yes. I can remember when I was smaller than a pin box, I would hear tales of the Famine. The stories passed down to us were more dreadful than any written accounts. Entire families wandered the roads in total despair, their little children leaning against trees, for they couldn't stand.

Even those who had a plot of land and seeds had no strength to plant and till the earth.

"When conditions were at their worst and most fearful stage, with the uncoffined dead all over the roadside and in the trenches, the British advanced a loan for relief. Some relief. No farmer could benefit unless he first forfeited all of his land except for a quarter of an acre. The British sent troops to seize the sheep, the cows, the oats, the furniture and the horses from the starving people. Those with nothing left to seize were thrown out by the landlords."

Jack sat very still, concentrating on every word. This was living history he was hearing. The books he had read had not conveyed the human side of the Famine. He tried to grasp the enormity of what she was telling him. "But surely someone sent food for help?"

"True enough, they say. The British sent Indian corn, but they took all the corn that was grown in the fields of Ireland and shipped it to England. There was more corn going out of the country in one month than the British shipped into Ireland in an entire year. And of course, there were no potatoes at all."

"Shannon, that is unbelievable."

"It is, yes. Unbelievable but true. English traders, speculating in Irish corn, continued to ship out our corn, while tens of thousands were dropping dead for want of food. They were dying in the fields and in the streets of Ireland, while shiploads of corn crossed the Channel. Jack, in those times, the world was not Ireland's friend, and certainly not the British."

Gently he asked, "Does that have anything to do with the troubles in Northern Ireland today?"

She considered his question. "Technically, no. After all, the Famine happened in the middle of the nineteenth century. But if you want my personal opinion, I would say that it is one reason why the British government is regarded with distrust. I would never condone the actions of the

I.R.A., but I must admit that I understand their sentiments up to a point."

The airline stewardess asked if they would like another drink, and they both accepted. Shannon paused to collect her thoughts. The drinks arrived and she took a sip, then continued.

"In all, a million Irish died, and a million more left their country. Hundreds of thousands flocked to the boats that were heading to America or Australia. Our poor little bays were floating with human cargo. To compound matters, many of the people were sick with famine fever. They carried the fever aboard the ships, and thousands never saw land again. That is why they were called coffin ships.

"Wherever the tide of emigration extended, they found an unbroken chain of graves and not a stone to mark it. To think how they must of felt, huddled together in misery without any expectation of ever revisiting their native soil. Such a long and dreary voyage it must have been."

Shannon sat very quietly. Jack took her hand and held it for a long time. She said, almost in a whisper, "May the bright angels watch over Ireland and its people until the day cometh." Then she turned a tearful face to Jack. "I miss my mum."

"I've never heard you call her your mum," he said, putting a protective arm about her shoulder.

"I called her that until I was about sixteen. She was mum to me. She would sit at my bedside and read poetry to me, even before I was old enough to understand. it. To this day, I can recall her favorite poem.

> She stepped away from me and moved through the fair,
> and fondly I watched her go here and go there.
> Then she went her way homeward with one star awake,
> as the swan in the evening moves over the lake.
> I dreamt it last night that my young love came in.
> So softly she entered, her feet made no din.
> She came close beside me, and this she did say,

'It will not be long, love, till our wedding day.'"

Shannon smiled a small smile. "She loved that poem then, as I do now." She rested her head back on the seat and closed her eyes. Soon she was asleep.

Chapter Thirty-Six

Brien Kelly arrived at the airport in London and found his way to the parked car. He threw his small duffel bag in the back seat, then looked in the glove compartment. There was a map and an envelope containing five hundred pounds. His instructions said that he was to go to the town marked on the map and proceed to a callbox at a certain address. The instructions gave the time he was to be there. Upon his arrival, he was to receive a telephone call with additional instructions.

As he worked his way out of the parking lot, Brien watched the nameless people hurrying about on the dreary, chilly evening. Loneliness filled his heart as he ventured into the face of darkness. This was his final task. His heart pounded and his mouth was dry with anxiety. Fear was his only companion.

He set his mind on the end of his journey, when he would be free. His one spark of hope, as he drove through the night, was the wild belief burning inside that told him he would return home to the security of County Kerry. There, he would be reunited with his mother and father and his sister, once this horrible adventure was through. He could almost feel the warmth of his lovely Margaret at his side and the comfort of his friends at the local pub.

He pulled to the side of the road to study the map and find his route. Lighting a cigarette, he cracked the window to allow the smoke out. Raindrops pelted his arm as he located the correct highway, turned on the windshield wipers, and pulled back onto the road. Fog began to move in, and he sat up stiffly as he peered ahead at the bright lights from oncoming cars.

Carefully, Brien continued forward until he reached the village marked on his map. He located the callbox. He was thirty minutes early, so he sat across the street, looking at his watch every three or four minutes. The time arrived and he walked across the street, filled with misgivings. The knot in his stomach told him not to do this thing. He dared to hope that he had missed the connection and could just abandon the car right here and go home. But the telephone rang exactly on time. Brien picked up the receiver after the first ring.

"Hello."

"Good lad. You made it on time. Good lad." Brien's hands were shaking as he tried to hold the receiver still. "Is there anyone nearby?"

Brien looked all around him. "No. I don't see anyone."

"Good. Listen carefully. Get in your car and drive exactly four blocks north and turn right. On the next corner you will see a parking lot and another callbox. Get in your car and drive there now. Make sure that no car is following you. Is that clear?"

"Yes. Perfectly."

"Good. Now go." The person hung up.

Brien did as he was told. By the time he arrived at the next telephone, he was somewhat more relaxed. He parked and went to the callbox. In a matter of minutes the phone rang.

"Hello?"

"Fine. You've done just fine. Now look around and make sure no one has followed you."

"I don't see anyone," Brien said calmly.

"When you return to the car, take out the map. On the back of the map is a list of villages. One of the villages is marked with a line drawn under it. Drive to that village and find The Town Pub. Go inside. Sit at the bar and order a pint. Then say to the bartender, "Have you got change for a ten?" The bartender will give you your next instructions."

"I've got it." Brien said.

"You should be there in about thirty minutes. The bartender will be expecting you." With that, he hung up.

Brien drove to the marked village and located the pub, then parked and walked inside. The place was nearly deserted, with only a few people having a drink and talking quietly. There was only one person behind the bar, so Brien considered that this must be the man. He found a stool and sat down, taking out a cigarette. The bartender approached with a match.

"What will it be for you, lad?"

"I'll have a pint, and have you got change for a ten?"

The man looked at Brien and with no display of emotion replied, "Of course, lad. Let me get your pint started."

Brien glanced around the room and back again. He felt warm so he removed his jacket and placed it on the stool next to him. The bartender returned with his beer and change for a ten. Brien handed him the money, and the bartender gave him his change.

"Count it, lad."

"What?"

"Count the change."

Brien looked at the money and inside, folded up, was a piece of paper. He opened it and read it. 'Finish your pint and then drive to the rear of the pub,' it said. Brien folded the money and the note, then shoved it into his shirt pocket. He drank his beer quickly, took his jacket, and left the pub.

He spotted a small alley next to the pub as he walked to his car. The street was as nearly empty as the pub. The black of night was undisturbed with the exception of a few lights to mark the way. Brien got into his car, turned into the alley, and pulled to the back of the pub. He turned his lights off. In a moment, three people appeared out of the darkness, two men and one woman. One man got into the front seat and the other two in the back.

"Hello. My name is Brien Kelly," he said.

"No need for names, lad. Just drive."

"Where to?" he asked calmly.

"Take the main road to London. Make sure you stay at the speed limit. Not any slower, but doin' the speed. Understand?"

"Yes," Brien responded.

They reached the main highway. There was no conversation. The only sounds came from the hum of the engine and the outside traffic.

"Oh, my God," Brien said suddenly. "The garda is behind us."

"Don't panic. Just continue," the man in the front seat said sternly.

"They want me to pull over."

"Go ahead. Don't do anything stupid. Just *be calm*."

Brien pulled over to the side of the road. The police car pulled in behind him and an officer got out of the car and approached the driver's side. "May I see your drivers license?" he said in a friendly voice.

"Sure." Brien reached for his license.

"Belfast," the officer said.

"Yes, sir. I've recently been transferred to London. My company moved me." He paused. "I haven't had the chance to get a new license."

"What company might that be, lad?"

"Briton Metal and Steel," Brien answered.

The officer peered inside the car looking at the other people. "You have a tail light out, lad. Did you know that?"

"Oh, no sir. This is a rental car."

"May I see your papers?"

Brien located the rental papers in the glove box and handed them to the officer.

"Who is Bob Ward?"

Brien thought quickly. "He is a friend who works with me at Briton Medal. We rented the car together. I'm staying with him until I locate a flat of my own."

The officer folded the papers and handed them back to Brien, along with his license. "Get that tail light fixed right away, lad, do you hear? It's not safe driving at night in the fog with only one light."

"Yes, I'll do that, right away. Thank you, officer."

"Good night to you, now. Drive carefully," the officer said as he turned and walked away. Brien waited.

"You did just fine, lad, just fine. Now let's be on our way," the man in the back seat said. There was no more conversation. When they reached London, the man in the front seat gave Brien directions. At length, they reached a small hotel near the boat docks. "Park over there." Brien did as he was told.

"Get your gear and follow me. Lock the car and give me the keys." Brien followed the man up a flight of stairs to the second floor. "This is your room. Go in and go to bed. Tomorrow morning we'll be gone. Don't leave the hotel until after eight a.m. Understand?"

"Yes," said Brien, standing in the hallway in front of his room. "Then what?"

"Then, nothing. You have a ferry ticket to Ireland, don't you?"

"I do, yes," Brien answered.

"Well, take a taxi to the ferry and go home. It's County Kerry, isn't it?"

"It is, yes. Kerry. I was born there. But my ticket is for the day after tomorrow."

"That's not a problem. You stay here at this hotel until then. Just don't do anything foolish. Stay out of the pubs. Stay close to the hotel. There is a small cafe across the street. You can eat there, but no place else. Got it?"

"Yes."

"Good luck to you, lad."

Brien went inside his room and sat on the edge of the bed. He was free now, he thought. He was going home. He lay back across the bed and fell asleep.

Chapter Thirty-Seven

Shannon was gone when Jack awoke in the morning. He looked out the window and saw her sitting on a huge rock down by the water's edge, staring out to sea. This spot had become one of her favorite places. He pulled on his pants and sweat shirt and walked down to join her. He slipped up behind her and wrapped his arms around her waist.

"Oh, Jack. You startled me."

"Good morning," he said, grinning.

"Would you be wanting breakfast?" she asked. "I'm not hungry, but I could make you something."

"No. I think I'll just have coffee and a scone."

"I was just thinking. It doesn't seem like we've been back a week already, and then in some ways it's like we never left at all."

"I'm going into Kenmare today. Do you want to come?" Jack asked.

"No, not really. I think I'll stay at home. I have much to do here."

He took her hand and they walked back to the house. "I've to take my car in for service soon. I thought I'd plan a trip to Cork later in the week. Damn, I wish we had a dealership here."

"This is not America, where there are ten or fifteen dealerships per town."

"Tell me about it, Shannon. It's getting old going into Cork every time I need some little something done to the car."

"I don't mind it," Shannon said, a trifle defensively. "I rather like the drive when I have to take my car in. It's a pleasant trip. My, you're getting peevish lately."

"Peevish?"

"Yes. You seem annoyed at so many things since we've been back home."

"Like what?"

"Oh, I don't know. You complain about the muddy roads, or having to drive so far for supplies, or the power going off."

"I wouldn't call the power going off a little thing, Shannon."

"I didn't mean that, darling, I just meant that you seem edgy."

Jack got his cup of coffee and scone and sat down at the table. He had more to say on the subject, and wanted to air his grievances. "Well, you have to admit it, Shannon. There are some things lacking in Ireland. Like hot water all the time. And roads at least big enough for a car and a truck to pass. How about something simple, like a movie theater? To go see a decent movie we have to drive to Limerick, for God's sake."

"Jack, what is troubling you?" Shannon asked, putting her arms around his neck.

"Oh, I don't know. I'm all right. Maybe it's jet lag," he laughed. "Maybe I'm going through the change of life."

"Oh, Jack, be serious."

"I am. Maybe we need a little excitement in our lives."

"Excitement? We just came back from two weeks of every minute, every day, filled to the brim with activity."

"That was work. It's not the same."

"Maybe work is what you need. You always seem to be happy when you're writing. When you get started on your next book, you'll feel much better I'm sure."

"I'm not ready to start my new book. I can't just turn on creativity like a light bulb." He took a sip of his coffee. "Let's go to Europe on holiday. A real holiday."

"Jack, we can't. You know that. We're starting to remodel the old farmhouse next week."

"So? They can start without us."

"They can, yes. But it would be better if we were here." Shannon poured herself a cup of coffee and sat down at the table. "Listen. It will be fun, remodeling the old place. We'll do it together. Buy new furniture, redo that old kitchen. And then once Mr. O'Shea gets a good start, we'll take a holiday to Italy or France. How does that sound?"

"Okay, I guess." He stood up and reached for his coat, and gave her a kiss on the cheek. "I'm going into town. I'll see you later. Sure you don't need anything?"

"I'm sure." Shannon took his hand. "Jack, I love you."

"I love you, too," he said, going to the door. She watched as he got into his car and headed down the road.

A short while later, the telephone rang. "Shannon? This is Mrs. Connely."

"Mrs. Connely, how nice to hear from you. How are you? And the bank?"

"Well, Shannon dear, very well. Listen honey, I think that you should turn on the news. There's talk about your brother."

"Brien? Is he in trouble?"

"He is, yes. I'm sorry Shannon. I hated to be the one to bring you such bad news. Go now and turn on the news. And if there is anything I can do..."

"Thank you Mrs. Connely." Shannon rushed over to the TV and sat on the edge of the chair. The news was just beginning.

"Another bombing in London. Five members of the I.R.A. were arrested last night as suspects of yet another bombing in London. The five in custody include four men and one woman, all reportedly from Belfast. They are under suspicion of placing a bomb on the front steps of the Union Credit Building. Arrested were Nan Philbin, age 41, Pat Connegan, age 29, his brother Liam Connegan, age 37, Brien Patrick Kelly, age 27, and Richard O'Shaughnessy, age 49. The five are being held in custody in London. No charges have been filed as of this hour. This is Jean Sims returning now to our studios in London."

"Thank you Jean. We are pleased to report that no one was killed or injured in the bombing. There was however, extensive damage to the Union Credit Building. Had the bomb detonated an hour later, the building would have been filled with workers and visitors. In other news..."

Shannon turned off the television and sat staring at the black screen. Then she began to wail and run about distractedly. She could not stop weeping. Finally, she managed to gain enough control to sit down at the kitchen table. "How I wish Jack were here," she said aloud. She was fearful for her brother, fearful for herself. This was the only time that she was glad her mother and father were not alive. I've got to go to London, she thought. I'll hire someone to help Brien. We'll get him out of this. Oh, God, she prayed, please help me.

She jumped as she heard the phone ring, and rushed to pick up the receiver.

"Shannon. This is Brien."

"Brien. My love, are you all right?"

"Yes, yes. They allowed me to make a phone call. I didn't know who to call. I tried the bank and they gave me your number. Did you move?"

"Never mind that. Tell me about yourself."

"I didn't do it, Shannon, I swear. I told them that I wanted out. I told them that I wouldn't be part of the killing. They agreed if I delivered a car, I would be allowed to go home. No more than that. That's all I did. I picked up three people and they dropped me off at the hotel. I was getting on the ferry to come home to Kenmare, to stay, and they arrested me at the boat dock."

"Oh, Brien. My dear, sweet brother. Not to fret. I'll be in London on the next plane. I'll get help and we'll get you out of this mess. Do you hear me?"

"Yes. Oh, yes. How I have missed you. How's mum? And papa?"

Shannon could not bring herself to tell him at that moment that they were gone, dead. "Fine, dear. I'll tell you all when I get to London. Now, not to worry. I'll be there soon. Are you listening?"

Brien was crying on the phone. Then Shannon began crying, too. Through her tears, she said, "I love you. I'll see you soon."

"Shannon, I'm sorry."

"I know Brien, I know. 'Bye, my love."

Chapter Thirty-Eight

Shannon looked out the window at the silvery water, but she did not see it. She turned away and walked through her beautiful home, now and again picking something up and putting it back down without noticing what she was doing. Her thoughts were many miles away, in a grimy cell in London with her beloved brother Brien. With that intuitive closeness she had felt with him since childhood, she now took on his loneliness and fear. He could go to prison, she knew. And if he did, her heart would go with him. She was beside herself.

She reached the airline and made reservations to London for the next day. She had not spoken with Jack, but she booked two fares anyway. She began to pack a small bag, then she made herself a cup of tea and sat down in the living room to await Jack's return from Cork. It would be a long day, for he had only just left.

With a chill, she realized that she had no family to turn to. Her mother and father were gone and her brother was in jail. There was only Jack now. There was nothing she could do but wait through the day for his return. She sat in silence broken only by the faint splashing of the ocean against the rocks and her own heartbeat in her ears.

Shannon found herself in another dimension, somewhere between the past and the present, and it did not sit with her. This was not proper. This was not how it was supposed to have turned out. She had a clear picture of her brother when they were children. She could see his bright and smiling face, and could recall his mischievous ways.

He was all boy, she remembered with a fond smile. A rawboned country lad with happy eyes and an unruly mop of dark hair. Despite his rambunctiousness, he was always kind to his sister Shannon. She remembered how they would stay up late, whispering so as not to let their mother and father hear, talking about their youthful hopes.

Brien was an idealist even then. He would share his wild dreams with Shannon. He would talk of being a great leader, perhaps president. He loved Ireland as fiercely as she did, and he wanted somehow to better the lot of the Irish people. So young he was, yet already wanting to do something important.

Shannon would tenderly confide in Brien her awakening female desires to be married and have at least six children. She longed for a time when her life would be filled with the work of it. She would cook their favorite foods, wash their sweet little faces, laugh and cry with them, carry them, and play with them. She would fall into her bed tired from the day and drift blissfully off to sleep with her husband by her side.

During those sessions of quiet sharing, they became forever bonded as their young souls soared and sang with the happiness of youth. Where had it gone? Shannon watched the afternoon shadows lengthening. She stood up and walked to the window. There was no sign of Jack's car. She began to pace the floor. She made another cup of tea. She looked at the clock. She walked to the window again.

"Oh, please hurry," she said out loud. Her mind raced from one thought to another. Everything has changed, she screamed inside. Brien's life, my life, Kenmare, the whole of Ireland and perhaps the world. Where did my life go? How did I end up with this life instead, in this big house with Jack? What happened to time? Brien is in serious trouble! I need my father and my mum, and they are both gone.

The early hours of this day had thrown her into a state of confusion.

Even her memories of a childhood filled with happiness did not to belong to her. She felt oddly detached from it, a witness rather than a participant. She tried to focus her thoughts, but they would diffuse and scatter.

She realized that her innocent days were over. She was a woman now, living in a modern world. The sweet honeycomb of her youth had been rifled by adult sorrows, by death and terror and pain. Yet, from a tiny corner of her internal universe, she saw hope. She had relentlessly pursued her perfect dream of a happy home with six small children playing on the grass outside. Some of it would not come true, she realized, but perhaps some of it was still possible. Then it occurred to her that maybe there was no such thing as happiness. She sat at the table, her head in her hands, seeking a meaning to it all. Could such sadness be overcome if the soul finds happiness and peace late in life, she wondered. Do I not love Jack, and he me? I know my brother and I love each other very much.

Shannon heard a car coming up the road. She rushed to the window. It was Jack. "Thank God!" she said aloud. Then, "Oh, God, what will I say?"

Jack came in and Shannon immediately sat him at the kitchen table. She was surprised at how calmly she managed to address the subject. It was not as difficult as she had expected to explain the details of Brien's situation. Now it was their problem as well. She took control of the conversation, speaking softly and confidently. "We will go to London and get Brien help. He didn't do it. I believe him."

She noticed one nagging thread moving in and out of her thoughts. Kenmare. She repeated over and over to Jack that there would be no repercussions in the village, but she was only trying to convince herself. She had her doubts that anything could be the same in the village, especially after this.

She wanted to believe that they all could come back to Kenmare and put their lives back to normal, but common sense told her otherwise. She knew the talk was already about, of how she had married a Yank and he had built her a big house and given her a fine car. In Shannon's mind, her rich new life was just a natural extension of her marriage to Jack, and she felt no personal compromise. But if the village people wanted to make up some disparaging image of her, they would. She knew that. She should not fear their opinion, but in fact she did. And now there was Brien.

"I'm afraid, Jack. I can't tell you exactly why I feel this way, but, yes, I'm concerned for all of us. This is our home. I know we'll be just fine, but we have to find a way to carry on after this is all behind us." She could see the hurt waiting for them in the days and weeks ahead. There would be time when fury would fill their lives, when the familiar friendly faces would scowl and sneer behind their backs.

Shannon knew that her people and her native land could be cruel, but she also knew that her countrymen forgave the innocent. Her ancestral land had seen far too much savage treatment. It had been torn apart by countless murders of the soul, of the heart, of childhood itself. Shannon had faith in her people and in her God. They would see in time that Brien had done no wrong, and that she had married for love. They would stand by her in the end. She and Brien could weather this storm. As she knew well, Ireland itself had weathered many before.

Chapter Thirty-Nine

Jack and Shannon arrived in London on the early flight and checked into their hotel. Shannon asked Jack if he would allow her to visit Brien alone initially. He agreed that it was a good idea, and said that he would begin calling law firms. She gave him a grateful hug, then walked out into a foggy London morning. She felt tired and depressed, but she pulled herself together. She knew that she could not allow Brien to see her in this condition.

At the police station, Shannon was escorted to a visitors' room. She sat looking at the cold glass cage before her and waited to see Brien. The door opened and he appeared, escorted by two guards. It was the first time in many years that she had laid eyes on her brother. It was all she could do to hold back the tears. His face was drawn, tired and thin. He seemed so lost, so out of place. He looked to Shannon as if his very life had been destroyed. As this man approached, she thought, is this poor soul my brother? Unable to hold back any longer, she broke down and began to cry. Through her tears she cried, "Oh, my poor Brien. I wish I could hold you and tell you everything will be all right. What have they done to you?"

"Shannon. Hello, my girl. It is so good to see you. Thank you for coming."

She wiped the tears away from her face. "Are you all right?" she asked as she regained control of herself.

"Yes, I'm fine."

"Brien, Jack has begun looking for help. We will get you a good barrister."

"Who is Jack?" asked Brien.

"He is my husband, Brien. He is an American. Well, actually he's Irish, but he's from America. His name is Jack Murphy. He is a writer. We were married last July."

"Well, congratulations. My big sister, married?" Brien seemed happy for her, she thought. "How are mum and papa?"

"Brien, I did not want to tell you over the phone." She paused.

"What's wrong?" Brien asked quickly.

"Brien, they're gone. They both died last year. There was no way to find you. We tried everything." Brien did not blink. He sat very still. A tear formed in the corner of his eye. Shannon sat with her hands against the glass and started to cry. "Oh, Brien, darling. I'm so sorry."

"It's okay, Shannon. I'm glad that they aren't here to see me like this. It is a disgrace to the family, to you and to myself."

"Brien, everyone makes mistakes. We are going to get you out of this mess. You'll see."

A guard appeared behind Brien, saying their time was up. "One minute, please," Brien asked, and turned back to her.

"Brien, don't worry. I'll be back soon. Okay?"

Brien nodded as he got up to leave. He looked back over his shoulder and said, "I love you."

Shannon could not hear the words but recognized the phrase in her heart. As she left the visitors' room, a guard asked her to step into the office. There, the chief introduced himself and asked Shannon to take a seat. "Mrs. Murphy," he smiled kindly. "I'm sorry about your brother. He seems like a good lad, and you seem like a fine lady yourself. I can see that the boy comes from good stock."

"Thank you, Lieutenant," Shannon replied.

"I believe the boy's story. I don't believe he had anything to do with the bombing. He gave us many eye witnesses who said that they saw him the morning of the bombing. There was a hotel clerk, and a waitress at a nearby cafe. He could not have been at the Union Credit Building."

"Oh, God, what good news to my ears," Shannon exclaimed. She could feel the color coming back to her cheeks as she relaxed a little.

"That does not mean that he can be released at once, mind you. But it does mean that they may give him a very light term, perhaps only a few months. When you come back tomorrow, I'll try to have more information for you."

"I can't tell you how good that makes me feel, Lieutenant." She smiled at him in gratitude. "Can I ask you something?"

"Yes, ma'am."

"If I agree to accept full responsibility for my brother, and take him back to Kerry in Ireland, and promise that if he leaves Kerry I will call you, do you think they would allow him to go home in my custody?"

"They might. He doesn't have any prior record. I fully believe that what he's saying is the truth, that he only picked up three people and transferred the car to them. But if they did the bombing, then he is an accessory. And by law, he is as punishable as they are. He will be tried lighter, but can be found guilty just the same."

"I understand, Lieutenant. Thank you, and thank you for your kind words. Until tomorrow, then."

Shannon returned to the hotel and found Jack asleep on the bed. He opened his eyes and looked at her with fond concern. "How did it go?"

"Oh, Jack, Brien looked so pitiful. It was heartbreaking to see him like that."

"Did you tell him about us, and about his mother and father?"

"I did, yes. He was happy for us, but oh, it was so hard on him to hear that mum and papa have died."

"What did you think of his situation? I mean, do you believe him?"

"Oh, yes, I do, and so does the officer I spoke with. They know he was not at the Union Credit Building, and it could go very light on his time."

"That's good news," Jack said soberly. "I want to go back with you tomorrow. I want to meet Brien. Okay?"

"Of course. I want you to meet him."

"By the way, I talked with several law firms today. I was recommended to call one firm in particular. They are Irish, but well respected in London. They agreed to meet with us tomorrow afternoon."

"That's good news. Thank you. Jack, I've got to lie down a wee bit, do you mind?"

"Of course not, my darling. You take a nap, and I'll go down to the pub for a drink. I'll come back in a while and we'll go get something to eat."

The following morning, they took a taxi to the station. They checked in and were escorted into the visitors' room. In a few moments, Brien was brought in. He smiled lovingly at Shannon as he walked toward his chair. "Good morning, sister."

"Good morning, Brien. You look much better today. This is my husband, Jack Murphy." Brien smiled and nodded.

Jack greeted him warmly. "I'm happy to meet you, Brien. Your sister speaks very highly of you."

Shannon continued, "Brien, I have good news. Jack and I have a meeting today with a law firm we believe can help. Also, I talked with the Lieutenant yesterday, and it may go better for you then you think. They have proof that you were not at the Union Credit Building." He listened to her intently. "Brien," she asked, "What are your plans when you're released?"

"Released?" he was startled. "When do you think that will happen?"

"I think it will happen very soon, Brien. I mean that."

"I was wanting to come home to Kerry," he said, with just the beginnings of hope in his voice.

"Ah, good. Jack and I are remodeling the old home place, Brien, and it's yours if you want it. You could get a job, work the land a little bit, or just take it easy for awhile if you need to. You decide."

"That's right," Jack agreed. "We are starting work on the cottage right away. We're putting in a new kitchen, reworking the old floors, and refilling all the stone inside and out. It's going to be much more comfortable, but still like home."

"That's sounds good, sis. Really." Brien spoke humbly. "I want you both to know how sorry I am about all this, and I appreciate what you're doing for me."

"We love you, and we want what is best for you. It will work out. Keep your chin up, as papa would say. Don't give in to hard times."

"I'm trying. Truly, I am." Brien said sadly. "But it's so hard. This is an awful place." He looked down at the floor.

"Listen, Brien, we'll back tomorrow with news about our meeting. I'm sure it will be good news. Try to rest, if you can. You've been through the worst of it now."

Shannon put her hand to the glass as Brien did the same. They gave each other a deep, loving, loyal look, then Brien was led back into his cell. On the way out of the visitors' room, Shannon looked for the Lieutenant. She couldn't find him, and when she asked about him, she was told that he was not in the building. She left her name and their number at the hotel.

They talked very little on their way back to their room. They were mentally drained beyond the ability to carry on a conversation. They seemed almost in a state of trance, their minds floating someplace between opaque and transparent. They stopped in the hotel restaurant for a cup of soup and some tea, then went to their room and fell asleep.

They awoke refreshed in time for their meeting, which turned out to be the high point of their trip. The law firm insisted that there was no way Brien could be booked on anything. He had broken no laws, and there was no evidence to prove he was involved with the bombing at all. The fact that he had given three people a ride in his car was not, in itself, a reason for a prison term.

The three others arrested admitted to knowing each other, but they all had alibis for the day of the bombing. They insisted that they did not know Brien, nor had they ever met him or seen him before. This strengthened his case further. It began to look as if all of them might be released. Brien could not be held more than twenty-four hours without a charge filed against him, and that was not likely to happen now. Shannon believed in her heart that Brien was going to be set free, and she prayed to God that she was right.

Chapter Forty

There was a message waiting for Shannon at the hotel. It was from Lieutenant Morrison. She rushed to her room and called immediately. "Hello, Lieutenant? This is Shannon Murphy. You rang?"

"Yes, I did. I have wonderful news for you and your brother. He is not going to be booked. He will be released tomorrow at ten a.m."

"Oh, thank God, thank God!" Shannon cried.

"What is it Shannon?" Jack called out.

"Oh, thank you, Lieutenant. Thanks so much. We'll see you tomorrow at ten." Shannon hung up the phone and threw her arms around Jack's neck. She was crying with joy.

"Jack, darling. They aren't going to book Brien. He will be released tomorrow at ten. We can pick him up. Is that wonderful news?"

Jack held Shannon tightly, kissing her hair and putting his cheek against hers. "This is wonderful, yes. I know it is a heavy load off your mind. We should celebrate. What if we go out to dinner tonight? We'll go to Rules, the oldest restaurant in London."

"I would like that, yes. Let's go out." She paused. "I can't believe it's over."

The next morning Jack and Shannon arrived just before ten. Brien was waiting in an outer office. When Shannon spotted him she rushed up and gave him a big hug. She placed her hands on his cheeks, and stood just looking at him for a very long time.

Brien took Shannon in his arms and pulled her close. "Thank you," he said as tears formed in his eyes. Then, looking over at Jack, Brien put his hand out, "Good morning, Mr. Murphy. How are you keeping?"

"Much better now, Brien," Jack said graciously.

"Come," Shannon said. "How about we all go find a nice restaurant and get Brien a real meal. I bet you're ready for that," she said, almost laughing.

"Oh. I am, yes. That stuff they serve here is fit for my dog." The three of them located a restaurant and ordered lunch. Then Brien looked at Shannon very seriously and said, "I've decided not to move back to Kenmare, at least not right now."

"Brien, why?"

"I was thinking that I'll go visit my friend in Dingle. Do you remember Mac O'Grady?"

"I do, yes," Shannon said. "I always liked Mac."

"I saw him some time back, when I was in Dublin. Mac owns two small fishing boats in Dingle. He offered for me to come and work with him. I was thinking that I'd go to Dingle and look him up, maybe stay on a while and work. It's that I don't feel right going back to Kenmare, at least not now. With all the news, and there's bound to be talk, I think it would be better for everyone if I get work in Dingle for a spell."

"I think you're right," Jack added, "Let some time pass."

"I dare say that I don't agree," Shannon said sternly. "Brien was released. He's innocent. He can hold his head up and not run from anybody."

"He's not running, Shannon. He's just allowing some time to pass and let this thing blow over."

"Blow over, my eye. He should hold his head high and walk right down the middle of the street. I'll be walking alongside him, shoulder to shoulder, on that you can bet." She paused. "Besides, we have the farm, and his home, our home."

"Shannon, Mr. Murphy, I know you both mean well, but I've made up my mind. I want a change. I have a lovely friend, Margaret, and I want her beside me. I want to work with my friend Mac, and to work the sea."

"What the sea gives, the sea takes away," Shannon said. Brien could almost hear his father in Shannon's voice.

"Truly, Shannon. But I will be all right. It will be for the best. I know it."

"Listen, Shannon," Jack interjected. "It's only a few hours drive. We'll see Brien. And as he says, he'll return to his home, but not right now. He's right. There's no need to rush. The important thing is that he's coming home, to Ireland."

"I suppose you're right, the both of you." Shannon took Brien by the hand. "The main thing is that you're safe. And you'll be home again in Kerry." She looked at Jack, then back to her brother. "We'll help you to get a start. Won't we Jack?"

"Of course."

"We'll get you a nice small car, and enough money to tide you and Margaret over till you get on your feet. And there'll not be a word out of ye either. Ye'll take it." Brien smiled a sheepish smile. "Now. We should eat, and then we'll all go shopping and get Brien some new clothes. Then we'll check him into our hotel. And tonight, we'll celebrate with a big dinner, someplace really nice." She started talking faster as she took control of the situation. "We'll get three tickets to Shannon Airport. We'll pick up our car and drive to Cork, get a hotel room, and look for a new car for Brien. Then, the next day, we'll head to Kenmare, and Brien to Dingle. There. Everything's in order." Shannon sat back in her chair, folded her arms, and smiled merrily as she looked at the two of them. "Say no more, for that's the way it will be."

Chapter Forty-One

Shannon had been watching Jack for the past few weeks since they had returned from London. She thought perhaps he was homesick for America. He was finding fault with everything he once found charming and delightful. She wondered if she would be next. Today, for the first time, she saw a kind of anger in him, an anger at nothing in particular but many things in general.

"Damn," he said aloud.

"What is it, Jack?"

"The damn bank. I was going into Sneem to the bank. But no, they are only open Thursdays for three hours. And of course, there is no office in Tahilla. Which means I have to drive all the way in to Kenmare."

"What's so horrible about that?" Shannon asked laughingly.

"It's not funny." Jack snorted.

"Shall I ride with you, to keep you company on such a long journey?"

"Don't make sport of me, okay?"

"Very well, then. Be off with yourself. You'd be no fun today anyway. Besides, I'm going to bake a pie." She kissed him lightly, and he grabbed his coat and marched out the kitchen door in a huff.

She was busy about the house all day, humming happily to herself. She decided to polish her Waterford crystal. She held it up to the sunlight and looked at the fire within the intricately carved design. She watched the prismatic reflections it cast on the wall. She tapped it just to hear it ring. Aloud, she said, "I'll make ye happy, Jack Murphy. I will."

She put clean Irish linens on the bed, then plumped the pillows and the eiderdown and carried them outdoors to air. She made brown bread and a couple of pies, filling the house with wonderful aromas. She did not notice the gathering dusk until she saw a seagull fly close by the kitchen window. She stood very still, her eyes shining, as she watched the bird make a turn and fly out of sight across the water toward the mountains.

She wiped her hands on her apron and put on a kettle of water to make tea. The room was growing dark, so she went about the house turning on lights. She couldn't stand a dark and dreary house, especially when she was alone. She glanced out the window to see a car approaching. Looking closely, she saw that it was Mr. O'Shea. She watched him get out of his car, then went to the door and opened it before he had a chance to knock. "Hello. Come in. I was just about to have a bit of tea, would you join me?"

"Oh, I would, yes. Thank you, Mrs. Murphy. How are you keeping these days?"

"Grand, Mr. O'Shea. Milk?"

"I would. And sugar, if you please."

"What brings you out our way this fine afternoon?" Shannon asked.

"Well, we will be finishing our job this coming week, and I wanted to know if you are ready to begin the farmhouse."

"Oh, I am, indeed." Shannon said, smiling.

"That's fine, ma'am. We know what there is to be done. 'Tis a nice old cottage, too. Worth saving, I'd say." Mr. O'Shea took a sip of his tea.

"Would you be caring for a piece of fresh apple pie? It's just now cool enough to cut." Shannon held it out for him to see.

"No. I mustn't be spoiling me supper. But thank you, Mrs. Murphy." He took another sip of tea and wiped his mouth. "A lot of talk in the village about Mr. Murphy's book, and everybody's excited about the movie. How about that? His book being made into a movie and filmed right here in

Ireland. You know, my uncle Pete was in a movie once, a long time ago. It were no speaking part or anything like that, but we all sure did have a fun time watching the movie and seeing him in it."

"Well now, Mr. O'Shea. A wee bit more tea?"

"Ah, you may so, indeed. Are you going to market tomorrow?"

"I am. Are you?"

"I am. What time do you plan to be back home, Mrs. Murphy? I'd like to have Paddy stop by to show you some samples of sinks for the kitchen and bathroom. They're only photos, mind you."

"I should be here by two," Shannon replied.

"Very well. Two it is. Have you any news from your brother?"

"I have, yes. He moved to Dingle."

"Dingle, you say. What's Brien doing in Dingle?"

"He is working on a fishing boat with an old friend. Remember Mac O'Grady?"

"Oh, I do yes. I knew his father well. He died last year, you know. A good man, he was." Mr. O'Shea paused. "Mrs. Murphy, I'm sorry to hear of that business in London, with Brien and all. I'm glad for you and for him that it's over."

"Thank you. I, too, am glad. It was all a mistake, you know. He did nothing wrong. He is a good lad, not one to harm others. He is doing fine now, working with Mac over in Dingle." She went into some detail, knowing that word would travel in Kenmare.

Mr. O'Shea glanced at his watch. "I dare say, 'tis time I be going. Thank you for the tea, ma'am. Paddy will be out tomorrow about two, then."

Mr. O'Shea had been gone just a short while when Jack pulled up to the house. "I saw Mr. O'Shea on the road just now," he said walking in the door and dropping a kiss on her forehead. "He said he was up for a visit and that they are ready to begin on the farmhouse. That's good news. It'll be nice to get the old place fixed up and rented."

"Rented?" Shannon asked with a frown on her face.

"Sure. Brien won't be needing it for some time, and there's no point in letting it sit. In the summer the Americans would pay top dollar. I was talking to Matt at the pub the other day and he says that he gets $500 a week for his cottage."

"Jack, I don't like this at all. You said nothing to me about renting it, and it's not as if we need the money. Jack, that's my home. I was born in that house. My father was born in that house, and his father."

"This is your home, Shannon," Jack said shortly. He poured himself a Scotch with a splash of water. "Want a drink?" he asked, as an afterthought.

"I do, yes. I think I'll have an Irish whisky." Shannon took a sip of her drink. It made her shiver a little at first. "Sit down, Jack, I want to ask you something."

They sat down across from each other.

"What?" he asked.

"I have a question for you, Jack. Answer me straight. Have you cast America out of your head, or do you long to return?" Jack stood up and walked to the window, looking out into the darkness. "Well?" She pressed him, but he did not answer. "I've felt for some time now that you've been, shall we say, somewhat disenchanted with small village life here in Tahilla. Is that true?"

Jack swallowed his drink and fixed himself another, then sat down and looked at her. "You may be right," he finally said, his face utterly expressionless.

"You act as if you're giving up something. Is that not so?"

"I guess so," he managed to say lightly. Then he took on a paternal attitude. "You don't understand. How could you?"

"What do you mean, Jack? That I'm just a country girl from a wee little village in Ireland? Never been around the world as some? That all I know how to do is bake pies and keep a man happy in bed? Is that what you mean?" She was astonished at herself. She had never talked like that to anyone. Where did these words come from? Had she read them in a book?

Inside, she liked her words. She was speaking the truth, and it made her bold, so she flung herself into it even more. "Listen to me, Jack Murphy."

"Shannon, this isn't like you."

"Well, excuse me. Perhaps this is like me. Or like I have become, or will be tomorrow. Maybe you don't really know me."

"Shannon. Please, let me explain. I don't want to fight."

"Fight? We're not fighting."

"Listen," he demanded, with an air of authority. "Calm down. I've thought about what you're saying. Sure I miss some things back home. So would you, if you lived some place else. You'd miss Ireland no matter how nice the other place was. Is that not true?"

"I suppose so, yes," she had to admit.

"Well, then that's all there is to it. Every now and then I long for a corned beef on rye, or a good football game between the Dallas Cowboys and the San Francisco Forty-Niners, or the hot, hot, sunshine in South Florida. Can't you understand that?"

"I can, yes. I can. But it's more than that, Jack. It's . . ." she paused, thinking.

"It's what? Say it."

"You've changed since your book came out. Is it the new found money, or the idea that you'll one day be famous? Or is it that you're tired of your little Irish country girl? Maybe that's it, Jack. Maybe you want someone more exciting in your life. That woman who kissed you in New York, the one with the man's name? Kevin, was it?"

"Shannon, don't be silly."

"That's the way you've been acting lately."

"Shannon, did we not have a great time in America? Did I go with you to London to help with your brother? And aren't we going to have fun together fixing the old farmhouse?"

"Yes. But, now, you want to rent it out. My house."

"Okay. We won't rent it, okay? Like you said, we don't need the money.

I just thought that renting it was better than it just sitting there."

"Well, perhaps we should move in."

"In the old farmhouse? You are kidding. You would give up this," he waved his arms around, "for that little old farmhouse?"

"Jack. What are we doing? What are we talking about?"

"I wish I knew," he said angrily.

"Jack, I'm only interested in us. Our happiness. Can't you see that?"

Jack did not answer, but finished his drink and got up to replenish it. "Want another drink?"

"No."

"Come on, have another drink with me."

"No. I don't care for one. Please."

"I think I'll go down to the pub. I'll get something to eat there. We'll let things cool off a bit." Shannon did not respond. Instead she got up and left the room. Jack got his coat and yelled out as he left, "I'm gone. I'll be back in a while."

She heard the door slam. She walked to the sunroom and sat down, staring out into the dark of night. A quiet despair was in her heart, and an overall feeling of weariness seized hold of her as the hours of the night lengthened. She sat motionless, thinking of the ugliness of their conversation. For just a very brief time, she thought of Stal. "Why would I think of an old boyfriend at a time like this?" she asked herself. Tonight, her house and everything about her seemed very strange and unearthly, even the ideas running through her mind. Finally, she said out loud, "I've a right to my thoughts, to my own life. I've a right to be happy, the same as anyone else."

For a long time she sat without moving, curled up protectively on the sofa in the sunroom, thinking. The most important thing, she knew, was to preserve her spirit and her integrity, and never to betray herself. On this evening, Shannon set these goals as her compass, and they brought her some measure of peace.

After awhile, she fell asleep on the couch. Sometime during the night she pulled a quilt over her. She was awakened the next morning by sounds in the kitchen. Jack was up. She had no idea what time he came home. Shannon walked sleepy-eyed to the bathroom, brushed her teeth, washed her face and put on a robe. Her back was stiff from the way she had slept during the night. She could smell the aroma of coffee throughout the house as she walked into the kitchen.

"Good morning," she said politely.

"Good morning," Jack said. "Do you feel better this morning?"

"I do, yes," she poured herself a cup of coffee. "Jack. Last night should never have happened. I was judgmental, I was. I have been thinking that perhaps the great enemy of life is within ourselves. We store up all these assumptions about life. Have you ever thought that we fill our hearts and our minds and even our soul with dreams, and most of them can never be fulfilled? We look for others to be perfect, and we think that we, ourselves are perfect. We're not, Jack. None of us. The world is not young and beautiful. Life is not perfect."

Jack sat quietly looking at her. "Shannon," he said.

"Don't say anything just now, Jack. Let me finish. I need to say this. I need you to understand." Jack was silent, listening to her. "My family was not rich. We worked very hard for everything, and there were times that I didn't have a clean dress to wear to school. But we were not poor, not truly, in spite of the hypocrisy and the cruelty life often handed us. We were much the same as many families all around here. I was lucky. I managed to go to college, to better my lot. Perhaps that was my destiny, to return here for a reason. I remember the night before I left for college. My mother came into the room to talk with me."

"What did she say?" Jack asked.

"She said, 'God is the hand that shapes.' She told me to look for beauty in all things, and never to lose my integrity. To do something useful with my life." Shannon smiled, remembering the homespun advice. "Mind your meals, make sure that you eat proper." She laughed out loud.

"What?" Jack asked.

"Oh, I remember she was standing there, holding a white shawl and a hot water bottle. She handed me the shawl and said that it belonged to her mother, and that she wanted me to have it to keep my head warm and to wear to Mass. She was very old fashioned in that way. She believed that if a woman didn't cover her head in Mass, it was a disgrace to her and to God. Then she handed me the hot water bottle. It was to keep my feet warm in bed on cold nights." They both laughed.

"Did you take it? The hot water bottle?"

"I did, of course. But I must admit I never used it."

Jack walked over to Shannon and put his arms around her waist, saying, "Shannon, I'm sorry about last night."

"As I. Enough said." Then she asked calmly, "You're going to Cork today? I think I want to take up painting again. I was thinking about getting an easel and setting up a place in the corner of the sunroom. Would you get supplies for me, while you're in Cork? You know what I need. I think that I want to work in oil."

"Shannon, that's a great idea." He kissed her gently, then he said softly in her ear, "If I don't get home too late, perhaps you should take a hot bath about bed time. Know what I mean?"

"I do. We'll see about that," she said in a whisper.

"I've got to get going. It's getting late. Are you going into Kenmare today to market?"

"Yes. I planned on it."

"Are you sure? I mean about Brien and all. Seeing all your old friends."

"I'm sure. I'm not hiding my head in the sand. Besides, Brien was not booked on anything. He is innocent. I will stand up for his name."

"And what time is Mr. O'Shea coming?"

"He's sending Paddy at two. I'll be back in time. Not to worry. I'll meet with him. This is woman stuff, anyway. Sinks and the like."

She offered her cheek to Jack and he kissed her as he left.

Chapter Forty-Two

Shannon returned from market about one o'clock, as a light rain began to fall on Tahilla. She looked all around before she entered the house, thinking a storm might be coming. Off across the water, the sky was getting darker, and she could see bolts of lightning streaking across the dark clouds. Her father could have told her exactly what time the storm would reach land, she thought fondly.

After a while, she saw a pickup truck coming up the road. It stopped and Paddy got out, moving toward the house in a slow, powerful stride, looking down at the ground as he walked. She watched him as he approached the kitchen door. He stood there for a moment, wide-shouldered and a little burly, then he knocked two times.

"Paddy. Come in. It's good to see you."

"Afternoon, Mrs. Murphy. Looks like it's going to storm pretty soon. The sky is getting awful dark."

"It does look that way, yes," she said, nodding. "Would you care for a cup of tea?"

"Oh, no, thank you, ma'am." He held up a folder. "I brought these photos of sinks for you to see," he said. His eyes were fixed on Shannon.

"Please, sit," she said, moving toward the kitchen table. Paddy sat down and laid the folder on the table, inspecting the photos carefully as he handed them to her one by one. He nervously rubbed his hands over his forehead.

Shannon was flipping through the pages when Paddy pointed at one. "I like this for the kitchen," he said with a quick jerk of his head. He turned the page, and his hand stopped on Shannon's. "And I think this one would be nice for the bathrooms," he added. He did not move his hand but allowed it to rest on hers. He stared at her burnished hair and her delicate skin. He noticed how her firm breasts rose and fell with every breath. Her eyes, fixed on his, were bright and alert. Paddy cleared his throat. "What do you think?"

Shannon stood up and walked to the stove to pour some hot water for tea, asking Paddy, "Sure you won't have a wee bit?"

"I'm sure, thanks."

She tossed her hair from her face and slowly returned to the kitchen table. Picking up the folders she looked at all the options again. "You know, Paddy, I think you're right. I like these two, here," she pointed at the ones he had suggested.

"There's a lot of talk and excitement in Kenmare about Mr. Murphy, his new book and all, and a movie."

"There is indeed," Shannon said smiling. "You know, Jack's a very good writer."

"Where is he today?" Paddy asked.

"He's gone to Cork. He doesn't especially like doing this sort of thing anyway. He doesn't really care which sink I pick out. It's not the sort of thing Jack pays attention to."

Shannon looked out the window. The storm clouds were rising higher and higher, and the sky was much darker now. The lightning zigzagged across the sky, close enough now that she could hear the rumble of thunder. The wind shifted and rain began to fall sideways, pelting the windows as the storm moved inland.

Shannon sat up in her chair, pointing out toward the ocean. "My. Look at that rain." Then she jumped when a bolt of lightning and a crash of thunder hit nearby. "Jesus, Mary and Joseph," she cried. She and Paddy walked to the sunroom and stood watching the storm as the rain began to pour and the wind grew stronger and stronger. A whirlwind of grass and leaves moved in a mighty surge toward the back of the house, tossing small tree limbs like toothpicks. Suddenly a larger limb crashed against the top of the window. Shannon jumped and grabbed Paddy's arm.

"Did you see that?" she exclaimed, as she held on tightly. Now, as if he felt no danger for himself, Paddy turned and looked at Shannon. He placed his arms around her waist and pulled her to him. She was stiff in his arms, but she did not pull away. The rain and wind slashed against the windows, and thunder and lightning crashed all about. Shannon's emotions rose to a fever pitch. She saw before her, reflected in Paddy's eyes, the same naked longing, the same stripped-down thirst that she had felt with Stal when she first came into young womanhood.

Her hunger frightened her, but she could not stop herself. Paddy pulled her closer and kissed her. Her body relaxed and molded to his as she returned his kiss. She could feel his strong arms around her and his hard body against hers. She felt cheap doing this, but she was too excited to care. She recalled the trashy women she had seen in college, their raucous laughter hovering above the smoke filled pubs, and the thought stimulated her. She remembered the party in New York, where the gorgeous brunette had draped herself all over Jack and kissed his mouth.

Shannon pulled Paddy closer and thrust her hips against his. She kissed him madly, wildly and without hesitation. Paddy moved his hand down her shoulder and across her breasts, then, pulling up her skirt, eased his hand between her legs, stroking her gently.

She almost fainted then with desire, but she managed to pull back. "No, Paddy. We can't do this. Please." Shaking with thwarted passion and covered in sweat, she moved away from the window. Her face flushed, she straightened her dress and pulled her hair back from her face. She turned her back and took a deep breath. Standing in the middle of the room, her arms folded, she whispered. "Paddy. I'm sorry. This is not right."

"Shannon," Paddy started to say something.

"Paddy. Please go, and I promise you this will never happen again."

"But, Shannon."

"Paddy, please do as I ask. Please."

Paddy turned and walked toward the kitchen. The rain still coming down in sheets and the wind was howling even harder. The waves hurled themselves against the rocks with brute force. He watched for a break in the storm, but none came, so he braved the outside and worked his way out to his truck. Shannon drew back in the shadows beside the kitchen window and watched him intently.

Paddy stood by his truck, looking back at the house. The gale rocked him on his feet, and the torrent of rain soaked him to the skin. Still he did not move. He stared at the window where she was hiding, trying to see her. He seemed to her like a wind-ridden ghost, grieving as he stood transfixed in the roaring storm.

"God. Get in your truck, Paddy. Please," Shannon beseeched him silently. After an eternity, he turned and opened the door and climbed into his truck. She watched as he drove slowly down the hill and out of sight.

Trembling, Shannon sat down in the darkened living room. Terror overcame her. My God, what if she had gone through with it? What if she had allowed herself to make love to Paddy? She could not imagine what the outcome would have been.

Then she gave herself over to the rapture she had felt. During those moments with Paddy, her buried memories of raw desire had returned to her. She could not help wanting to devour the succulence of the fruit that lay before her. The tragic beauty of this brawny Irishman's touch had reawakened in her that invisible light that comes with pure passion. The fabric of her life became unwoven to the pulsations of her senses. She had become a woman bursting into life once more, and she felt more beautiful than any flower. She allowed herself to exist in that state, to imprint it on her reverie.

At length, the storm blew itself out, and Shannon sat motionless in the silence it had left behind. A sunbeam broke from behind a cloud. She watched as the shadows dissipated and the flickering light came and went. She sat back in the chair and stretched her legs, as if arising from a long night of sensual dreams.

Chapter Forty-Three

Sometime in the early evening, Shannon got up and went into the kitchen. She looked at the clock on the wall. It was nearly eight o'clock, and she realized she was starving. She fixed some left over soup with brown bread and a tall glass of cold milk. Then she washed up the dishes and took a hot bath. She was exhausted. She went to bed and fell fast asleep, never knowing what time Jack returned from Cork. She did not even hear him come in, nor did she stir when he crawled into bed at eleven.

The next morning, Shannon was up long before Jack. She was greeted with a nice tall wooden easel, several paint brushes and a huge box of paints. There was a red ribbon tied around the top of the easel. She went to the kitchen and made herself some tea, then returned to the sunroom to watch the light come up on the sea. She noticed a lot of leaves and twigs littered about from yesterday's storm.

At about six o'clock, the phone rang. It was New York calling for Jack. She woke him up and he stumbled into the kitchen and took the phone. Shannon handed him a cup of coffee.

"Darling, this is A.J. How are you?"

"A.J." Jack mumbled. "I'm fine. What's up?"

"Are you all right darling? Are you sick?"

"No, I'm still asleep. I was up late last night. You know it's early morning here."

"Well, darling, it's the wee hours of the morning here. I just came in from a wild party myself, and I'm going to be as hung over as you are. But I just had to call you and tell you some good news. Manny Freeman called, and they are about ready to begin work on the movie. They're sending over three advance people to meet with the Irish Film Industry. They'll organize cars, trucks, hotels, and all those things that advance people do, whatever that is. God knows, it takes a million people to make a movie nowadays."

"A.J., will I have some input?"

"Of course, darling. Manny Freeman told me that he wants your input. But, now, honey, it's their movie. They have the final say on everything, you know that."

"I know. But at least I'll have some of my thoughts about the script and design considered, right?"

"Exactly, darling." A.J. said breezily. "Now, sweetheart, when can you make a trip to New York? We have lots to do, darling, on your next book and your next movie, or movie contract, I should say. We need additional photos of you. And a bunch of other things. Now, where did I put that laundry list? Here it is." She was thinking out loud. "Let's see. Oh, Manny Freeman asked me to ask you if you would like to try your hand at writing a made-for-TV movie script. How about that one? Don't have to make a decision now. That one is down the road. Hmmm, oh, yes, one other thing. Kevan Vassar was in the office the other day. She was in town to do a little shopping, stopped by to say hello to her father, then she and I had cocktails after work. She's getting a divorce. So what else is new already. Annnd, darling, she asked about you. Wanted to know when you would be back in town. Well, you know me, honey. I told her to forget it, that there was no way she could compete with that sweet little thing you have in Ireland. Was I right, darling?"

"Absolutely right on that one!" Jack looked at Shannon standing by the sink, and motioned with his hand that he wanted more coffee. "I'll think over a schedule and call you back in a few days," he added.

"Don't put it off, darling. We have a lot of important stuff here, and all of it makes you dinero, moola, yen, pesos, you get my drift. Hell, Ireland to New York is about as quick as me trying to fly to one of those Godforsaken western towns. I had to go to Phoenix a few weeks back, yippee-yi-yo. I couldn't get a direct flight and it took me all damned day to get there. Hell, I could have gone to Paris in the same amount of time."

"Not to worry, A.J., I'll work it out and call you back."

"Great. Say hello to your cute little wife. 'Bye, love."

Jack hung up the phone and looked at Shannon. "Wow," he said. "That lady never stops. That was A.J. She needs me to come to New York."

"Really?" Shannon said coolly. "When?"

"As soon as I can. She has a long list of items, including paperwork on my next book, a movie contract, and maybe a made-for-TV movie script."

"Well, congratulations. When are you going?"

"When am I going? You mean you don't want to go?"

"Jack, honestly, no. Not this time. We're starting work on the farmhouse, and I want to spend some time with my brother. I'd like to go over to Dingle for a couple of days, and well, you understand. You'll be in meetings all day, and I've already seen New York."

"Shannon, you could do some shopping."

"I don't really need anything, Jack."

"We could hit a couple of shows, go out to a few nice restaurants, a museum or two. It would be fun, not like the last trip."

"Jack, really, I don't think I need to be going just now."

Then he said jokingly, "I know. Tell me the truth. It's the cocktail parties from Hell that really bother you. Right?"

Shannon laughed sheepishly. "There is that, yes. No offense, Jack, but all that baby talk at your American cocktail parties is something I can live without."

"Baby talk? Come now Shannon, it's not that bad."

"I guess not," she said unconvincingly.

"You know Shannon, you've been taking a lot of pot shots at America lately."

"I have not, Jack. That's not true." She wondered why she was defending herself from his accusation.

"You have, I tell you, you have. You've made fun of, well, not just our cocktail parties, but our restaurants, our overcrowded cities, the traffic, the noise. And you're always saying that Americans always seem to be in a hurry."

"Well, Jack, most of what you've said is true, isn't it?"

"Don't be so critical."

"Critical, you say? Come, Jack, if anyone has been censorious lately, it's been you about Ireland."

"Censorious? Wow, where did you come up with that five-dollar word?"

"What's that supposed to mean? Am I supposed to act like a little ol' Irish country girl with half a brain? May I remind you that I am a college graduate, and that you yourself admire our universities?" As soon as it was out of her mouth, she wondered why she was participating in this infantile conversation, this witless exchange of words.

"It's not my fault that you are a serf bound to Ireland."

She almost laughed. "Oh, come now, Jack. If I'm the serf, does that make you the master and lord?" Disgusted, she tossed her apron on the counter. "Enough, Jack. This conversation is fruitless."

"Ha, ha," he said under his breath.

"And what does ha, ha mean?" Shannon asked looking straight at Jack, her hands on her hips and her head tilted slightly back.

"It doesn't mean anything. Ha, ha, that's all," he blustered.

"Jack, stop it!" she said loudly.

"You're right. Why are we doing this? We're babbling on about America, about Ireland, I have this and you have that, I think this and you think that. You're right. Come here, my sweet, and give me a hug and a kiss."

Shannon looked at him a long while in silence. Her face showed no emotion. Finally, she walked over to the table and put her head down next to his, and kissed him gently.

"I love you," he said. "Don't you know that?"

"And I you, Jack," she paused and said softly, "Let's stop all this gibbering, shall we? We've had far too much of it lately." She turned and walked toward the sink, picking up cups and glasses along the way. He followed her with his eyes, and then he gave her body a long, appraising look. He noticed that her movements were slow and very sexy this morning, and she seemed especially pretty in a tousled sort of way.

Jack thought he might get back in her good graces. "They're going to be getting ready to start filming the movie pretty soon. A.J. said that the company is sending over some advance people any day now. Isn't that great? I think it will be exciting to go watch them film. Think about it. They will be shooting my story. It still hasn't sunk in yet. I don't guess it will hit me until we are sitting there seeing it on the big screen for the first time." Shannon glanced over her shoulder and smiled. He got to his feet and started toward the back of the house, "I'm going to shower and dress now."

When Jack returned to the kitchen, Shannon had begun to scrub the floors. She was on her hands and knees when Jack walked in.

"You, Shannon, I think maybe its time we got a cleaning lady to come two or three days a week. She could help with the cooking, too."

"I won't be needing any cleaning lady, Jack. I'm perfectly healthy and I can manage the cooking and cleaning," she said, without looking up from the floor.

"I'm only trying to help. Give you more time to do your painting and work on the farmhouse, and we could do more things together."

"Thank you, Jack, but I don't feel that I would be happy with someone here, in my house, cleaning my clothes and my things, cooking my food. I know it's hard for you to understand, but I like taking care of my house, I do." She stood up and wiped her face with a towel, surveying the spotless kitchen. "Now," she said simply.

"One last question about New York. Are you sure you won't go with me?" Jack asked.

"I'm sure. Please try to understand. I want to see my brother."

"Well, I guess I could make it a quick trip. I could be back in a few days."

"Yes. Go take care of business. You'll get a lot more done without me. And then come home. Now, won't that be all right?"

"Sure. Look, I'm going in to Kenmare to visit with an attorney. What do you call them here? Solicitor? Barrister? I can never keep the two apart. I'll be back in a couple of hours." Jack left Shannon standing in the kitchen. She had just put on the kettle for a cup of tea when the phone rang. "Hello," she said cheerfully.

"Shannon? Mrs. Murphy?"

"Yes."

"This is Paddy."

Instantly, she was on guard. "Paddy, did Mr. O'Shea ask you to call?" Silence. "Paddy, if it's what I think it's about, that was a big mistake. There's nothing we have to say to each other, except that should have never happened and it won't happen again."

"Shannon, I can't stop thinking about you. Please. Can we meet?"

"We can't, no. Paddy, look. I've got to go now. Please don't call here again." Shannon hung up the phone and stood frozen in place, staring at the phone. She was startled when she heard the teakettle begin to whistle. She moved slowly to the stove, took up the kettle, and filled a cup with hot water. She dropped a tea bag into the cup and sat down at the table. She just sat there, looking at the tea. She did not move for a very long time.

CHAPTER FORTY-FOUR

Four days later, Jack left for New York. Shannon packed a small bag and started out for Dingle to visit her brother. She had always liked Dingle, even though she had never spent much time there until she was grown. She loved the unspoiled valleys and the purple mountains watching over the hedgerows ablaze with fuchsias. She liked to walk the golden beaches, which stretched for miles. The Dingle peninsula seemed to dart out into the sea, forming Ireland's most westerly point. Two miles beyond Dunmore Head lay the Blasket Islands where she and Jack had first explored their love together.

When Shannon arrived in Dingle, Brien was out to sea. He was expected to return before dark, so she drove at a leisurely pace out to the shore, within sight of The Great Blasket Island. She pulled into a standby and got out of her car. She found a huge rock which made for a perfect spot to sit and take in the beauty of the rocks, the cliffs, and the ocean below.

Shannon sat quietly for a very long time. She watched the tourists as they would come and go. Most of them were couples on holiday, and most seemed to be from America. Now and then she would be asked to take a photo for them, the way all tourists do when they want to get everyone in the picture. One couple, whom she guessed to be in their late forties or early fifties, stopped to look out at the island. All the while, the two were taking verbal jabs at each other. After a very brief while, the husband yelled,

"God damn it, come on, let's get going. I hate traveling with you sometimes. Takes forever to get anywhere." The woman did not respond, but made her way to the car like some hurt puppy. Shannon could see the man still yelling at her as they drove away.

Are Jack and I getting to be like this? she asked herself. She recalled her father quoting Aesop's Fables when the neighbors weren't getting along. "Familiarity breeds contempt," he would say. She hadn't understood it then. But there are many kinds of familiarity, she thought. Familiarity can mean everything from knowledge to intimacy to impudence. Anyway, she asked herself, why such heavy thoughts? Why waste such a beautiful day?

She glanced at her watch and realized that she should be heading back to Dingle. When she pulled up to the docks, she saw Brien walking toward her. Shannon got out of the car and ran to greet him, giving him a big hug and kiss.

"Now. Let me take a look at you," she said, standing back a little. Brien's face was browned from the sun and the sea. He looked rugged, but fresh and healthy. His eyes were bright, and he had a big smile on his face. Shannon stood taking in her brother, and was happy for him.

"Come," he said. "Before it gets totally dark, I want to show you Connor Pass. Then we'll drive to a favorite village of mine, Cloghane, and we'll eat a little pub grub there."

"What about Margaret? She'll be coming with us?"

"Oh, no. I'm sorry. Her mother fell ill and she had to go visit."

"Oh, Brien. I was so looking forward to meeting her."

"I'll tell you what. She'll be back in a week or so, and then as soon as we can get away, we'll drive over to Tahilla one Sunday for a visit."

"Lovely. Promise me it won't be long."

Brien put his arm around her shoulders and gave her a small hug. "I promise. The past few weeks we have been working hard, very hard. Mac needs extra money right now for repairs on both his boats. But things are getting better, so it won't be long."

"How are you and Margaret getting on?"

He smiled jubilantly. "I love her, Shannon. We have talked about getting married."

"Oh, Brien! I'm so happy for you," she beamed at him.

He slowed the car and looked over at her. "And you. How are you and Jack getting on?" She did not answer, but looked straight ahead at the road.

Just then, they reached the summit of Connor Pass. "This is the highest mountain pass in the whole of Ireland," he said. As they descended the other side, they gazed at the magnificent view which lay before them.

"I had forgotten how extraordinary this place is," Shannon said. "It has a majestic quality. It gives me a sense of pride. Does it you, Brien?"

"Oh, it does, yes. Just the measure of it alone is awe inspiring."

They reached Cloghane just as it was getting dark, and made their way to the pub, which consisted of two small rooms, with a fireplace in each room. The dining room was nearly empty, and they sat at the far end. After they ordered their meal, Brien looked pointedly at Shannon. "What's troubling you?" he asked. "You seem, how shall I put it, unhappy."

"Unhappy? I don't think that it would be called unhappy, my dear, but I am confused, you might say."

"About what?"

"My life. My marriage. My relationship with my husband. Something has changed in the last few months. Perhaps it's Jack's concern for his new book, or the movie. I don't know for sure. I do know that Jack misses America, or he is tired of Ireland. I'm not sure which it is."

Brien sat very still, listening, considering what to say to her. The pub began to get busy. Two men entered, with a small brown dog trailing behind. The men found a seat at the bar and ordered a pint, while the small dog found a spot underneath the bar stool and lay down. The bartender came in and placed two pieces of peat on the fire, then walked over to their table. "Would you be wanting another pint?" he asked.

"We would. Thank you."

"Fine day it was," he said leaving the room.

"It was indeed, a very bright day indeed," Brien answered.

"Brien," he called out from behind the bar, "this is one of God's days, when he smiles on you fishermen. No one knows that better than you."

"How true 'tis. How true," Brien answered him with a smile.

"Do you come here often?" Shannon asked.

"I do. Once a week or so, I guess. Most of the pubs in Dingle are always crowded. I like the people here, and the small pub reminds me of Kerry." Brien lit a cigarette, offering one to Shannon.

"I never have and I never will," she said. "And you should quit. You know it's not good for you."

"You're right. Perhaps I will one day," he answered. The bartender returned with two pints and two plates of food.

"Now. First things first. Here's your two pints," he laughed. "And here's Kate's fresh baked chicken, potatoes, carrots and brown bread. Would you be wanting anything else?"

"No, thanks." Brien picked up his glass and took a big swallow, then set it down and threw his cigarette into the fireplace. "You're not thinking of moving to America?" he asked, returning to the subject at hand.

"I'm not, no. I can't leave my home, and you, and Ireland. I would be a fish out of water over there."

"The real problem is here," Brien said tapping his heart. "You've always had a dream in your heart, Shannon. You've always known who you are. Lord knows we've been through much. We've known the bitter cold kind of loneliness that gnaws at your insides, but we've also known the joy that comes come from a loving family. We were so lucky to have such a strong papa, and a very wise mum. We cannot root from our souls that great quality of love they gave us. 'Tis the very backbone of our being."

"Tis true, Brien. And that's what I want in my marriage." She pointed toward his plate, saying, "Eat your food, before it turns cold."

"You know, sis," Brien spoke with a mouth full of food, "You always did mother me. I always thought of you special. You took care of me." He smiled. "Keeping me out of trouble, you were. Say, did you ever hear any more from that fella, Stallard?"

"Stal? No. Never again." She paused. "What made you think of Stal?"

"We were speaking of trouble, so naturally I thought of him," Brien laughed. "Stal. Now, there's a name you can never forget. So American. Gosh, I remember when you came home one weekend, and you were in love. Remember? You had met the man of your dreams."

"I loved him, I did. 'Tis true. But it wasn't meant to be, Brien. That's all. It wasn't meant to be." Shannon looked down at her plate and sat very still for a moment. "I'm not a child any longer, Brien. I've truly grown into a woman. It's as if I awoke one morning and an iron gate had opened. Suddenly, I realized that the very fabric of my life had been woven out of dreams. When that iron gate opened, I saw a vision of reality. I thought then that I knew exactly who I was and where I was going and where I belonged. Now I'm not sure, except that I know that I belong at home in Ireland."

"How serious is this problem with you and Jack?"

"I'm not altogether sure." She fell silent. She heard the distant barking of a dog, and the small brown dog jumped to his feet and ran to the door. Then he returned to his spot under his master. Shannon watched the little dog as if in a trance, her thoughts many miles away.

Then she looked at Brien and said cheerfully, "Enough, as our father would say. This is a happy day. We're together, you and I. And this business with Jack and me, well, I'll just have to work that out, now won't I? Let's finish eating and head back to Dingle before the fog rolls in. That little winding road scares me even in bright weather."

They ate the last of their supper and drove back across Connor Pass into Dingle. Shannon stayed in a small bed and breakfast and spent the best part of the next day with Brien. Then she headed home to Tahilla. As she drove along the water's edge toward home, she looked about her attentively.

Nothing has changed, she thought. It looks just the same as it did the last time I was here, and the time before, and time before that.

This web of life, Shannon thought as she drove along in silence. Who am I, truly? I was once a child, a new-born babe with tiny little fingers and not very much hair. All I wanted to do was to sleep, eat, and cry. After that, I became a young girl, and I did the things young girls do. I learned about cooking and cleaning and going to Mass on Sundays. I noticed boys for the first time, and I put on lipstick in secret. Then my breasts developed, and my desire to be with boys.

I learned about jealousy, hate, love and wonder. I played games, tried to write poetry, dreamed. Then I went to college, dated boys, studied, drank pints of beer, worked, lost sleep, didn't eat proper, and I fell in love. Made love, got hurt, cried, wanted to die. Dreamed. Went to confession. Painted paintings, studied, worked. Discovered for myself my own sensuality, my own feelings.

Then I became a woman. Fell in love, married, slept beside my man. Washed, cleaned, cooked, dreamed some more. One cannot scorn this creature, Woman, she told herself. Woman is love, and without her there can be no love on the face of this earth. Woman is frail, and tough, the worst and the best. She is immortal, high-minded, the keeper of the flame. She is the defender of the home and the Irish ideal, obedient to duty, with a devotion to family, home and God.

What makes Woman? What thread binds this fabric of our lives to contain forever our customs? Tiny cardboard boxes, filled with bundles of lost dreams. Remembering the smell of bread cooking in the oven, clean sheets, and fresh flowers on the table. The sounds of little children. Woman is the very root of durability, she thought, from which springs all of God's love, all of life, and all that is good.

Shannon continued to drive and to ponder the past and the present. In this single hour she raised so many questions for herself. One can live for years sometimes without living at all, she mused, and then all of life comes crowding into one single hour.

She reviewed her life carefully. She knew that she had a fine, healthy body. More importantly, she was mentally healthy. She would protect her good mind from anything that threatened her inner security. Brien was right. Shannon still knew who she was. She resolved to put an end to the petty little mind games that she and Jack had been playing. Perhaps he had a need that had nothing to do with her, she considered. Perhaps his need stemmed from some hidden feeling of abandonment, as a child who lost his parents when he was a young boy.

Her thoughts drifted back to her own childhood, when she was kicked by a horse and had to undergo surgery. Later, she was told that she could never have any children. It didn't register at the time. The awful reality did not dawn on her until many years later, the terrible fact that a family of her own would be denied her forever. Yet, from a place deep within her, she found the power to maintain. She accepted her life as it had been given her to live.

In this single hour driving along Dingle Bay, back toward the main highway, Shannon realized that for her life to be whole, it must be within the confines of her home, her mate, her lover, her friend, her husband. She made a bargain with herself. In this hour, she concluded that there must be a change, and that the change must begin with her. She could not and would not accept any superficialities in her relationship with Jack. In this single hour, she finally said it aloud. "If Jack and I can't repair our marriage together, if we don't recover our bond as true soul mates, as *anam cara,* then I am prepared to leave him."

Chapter Forty-Five

The weather was already turning cool in New York, especially in the evenings. Jack was sitting in his hotel room reading *The New York Times* when the phone rang.

"Jack," a sultry voice said. "This is Kevan. How are you?"

"Kevan. I'm great. How have you been?"

"Better than nothing, I guess. You know I got divorced."

"I heard that. Is everything okay?"

"Oh, sure. Everything turned out just fine. I got the house, my car, and plenty of money. As if I needed it. My father was more upset than I was, I think. How about joining me for a drink? I could use some company. I'm at the Plaza. Why don't you hop in a cab and meet me in the lobby bar, say in about thirty minutes or so?"

Jack thought for a minute. "Sure, why not? I'm bored just sitting here. I'll see you in the bar." He dressed quickly and jumped in a cab. He walked into the glamorous surroundings of the Plaza and made his way to the bar. He looked around for Kevan. She had not yet come down, so he found a corner table for two and ordered himself a scotch with a splash of water.

He looked up to see Kevan coming through the doorway. She was stunning, he thought, better looking than he had ever seen her. He stood by the table when she approached.

"Hi, darling. You look marvelous," she said, giving Jack a kiss on both cheeks.

"Well, look at you," Jack said holding her hands in his. "Divorce agrees with you. You don't look at all like a long lost divorced woman in mourning."

"I'm not, darling. You have my word on that."

"What will you have to drink?" He raised his hand to catch the waiter's eye.

"Martini, very dry," she said, smiling.

"Vodka or gin?"

"Vodka."

"Well. Are you Ms. Kevan Vassar or are you Kevan Dodson these days?"

"Vassar. I love the name. It's so snooty, darling. Besides, all my credit cards, passport, drivers license, all the rest are under Vassar, and what a pain it would be to change everything back."

"Well, you always were one to take control. Making a decision has never been one of your shortcomings." He looked at her carefully, taking in her simple, elegant dress and her polished makeup. "You've changed your hair."

"Oh, thank you, darling. You noticed. Do you like it? I love the color. Chestnut, I think they call it. I think it makes me look ten years younger. Well, maybe five," she said, laughing.

"Whatever it is, you're certainly vibrant these days. I wouldn't change a thing if I were you." The waiter arrived with her drink, and Jack placed an order for a refill. Raising his glass to hers, he said, "Cheers, and here's to the new Kevan Vassar."

"I'll drink to that." Kevan took a sip of her drink. "Boy, that's perfect, nothing like a good martini." After a second sip, she set her glass down on the table, took out a cigarette, and offered one to Jack. He accepted, telling her, "I stopped smoking years ago. But, you know, you never get over wanting one, especially when you're having a drink."

"Or after sex," she added teasingly.

"Right you are." Kevan held a match over and lit Jack's cigarette. He took a long drag. "My God, I think I'm going to pass out."

"That would be all right," she said with a wink. "I'll take care of you, darling."

"So, fill me in on all the news," she said, placing her hand over his on the table. He did not move away, so she wrapped her fingers around his and held his hand tightly. "Tell me, how have you been?"

"Really good. They're going to be starting the movie soon."

"I know," she replied, "A.J. told me all about it. How exciting! Oh, and I hear your book sales are going out of sight. Isn't that wonderful? I'm so happy for you, darling. You deserve it."

"Thanks." Jack drained his glass quickly as the waiter arrived with his second drink. He stirred it and took a big swallow. He put his cigarette out in the ashtray and asked, "Are you ready for another martini?" Kevan nodded. Jack raised two fingers in the direction of the waiter.

"So, how is married life?" Kevan asked in an even tone.

"Oh, fine. We finished our new house. Now we've started, or should I say Shannon has started remodeling the old cottage, the farmhouse that belonged to her mother and father. And she's taken up painting again."

"Painting? Really, how interesting. Does she work? Of course not. Silly question."

"Well, she did work, at the Bank of Ireland in Kenmare. She resigned when we married."

"Oh. A bank teller," Kevan said curtly.

"No. She has a degree in finance. She worked on loans, new accounts, things like that. It is a very small bank, so a few people do a lot of different things. Kenmare is a tiny village, but beautiful. Very authentic."

"I'm glad you met me for a drink. It's truly good to see you," Kevan said, clearly not interested in hearing about Ireland or Shannon. Jack did not respond. Then the waiter returned with their drinks. "You're going to get me drunk, Jack. You know how wild I can be when I've had a few drinks," she said, laughing a little too loudly. "I may attack you right here at the bar."

Jack could feel the alcohol beginning to have an effect on him, especially since he had had a light lunch and nothing to eat since. Everything began to seem just a little blurry and feverish. Kevan looked over toward the end of the bar when she heard the sound of a piano. "Ah, music," she said. "Now all we need is a little candlelight." Almost as if he had heard, the waiter returned and lifted the glass top from the candle on the table, lit it and replaced the cover. "There. Say the magic word and poof, we have music and candlelight." Kevan raised her glass to toast Jack. He did the same. They took a sip without speaking. Kevan did not take her eyes off Jack.

They finished their drinks and had one more each. Now, feeling weightless and giddy, Kevan suggested that they leave. Jack ordered the bill and paid it. As they passed the elevators, she took him by the hand and pressed the button to go up. Jack looked at her, not speaking. Kevan moved in very close until she was glued to his side. He could feel her breasts against his arm. She was not wearing a bra. Her breasts felt larger than they looked.

"I need to go to the room and powder my nose. Do you mind?" Jack shook his head mutely. They stepped back as three people got out of the elevator, then they boarded. Kevan reached past him and pressed number eleven. She looked at him and smiled. The elevator arrived quickly and they walked down the hallway as Kevan fumbled for her key. "Here we are," she said as she unlocked the door to her suite. "Jack, darling, fix us a drink over there at the bar, while I use the washroom." It seemed to him that she was gone for a fairly long time. Then she emerged, wearing a cashmere robe. Her eyes seemed very bright.

"Let's eat in, shall we? I'll just order something up later. I really don't feel like going out, do you?" She walked over to Jack and stopped directly in front of him. Their eyes locked. She moved closer and parted her lips. He took her in his arms, pulled her close, and kissed her fully for a very long time. She kissed him back wildly, all the while pushing her body against his.

Then he pulled back and handed Kevan her drink. She took it, keeping her eyes on his, and looking over the top of her glass, she took a long drink. Jack did the same. "Give me that," she said, taking the drink from his hand and putting it on the counter along with her own. She took him by the hand and led him into the bedroom. She drew him toward the bed and they sank down into it. Jack gently pushed her against the pillows. Hovering over her and looking deeply into her eyes, he reached down and kissed her. He slipped his hand under her robe. She was not wearing anything underneath. He let his hand slip across her breasts, then he opened her robe to expose her full rounded breasts. He moved down her neck, kissing all parts of it.

Quickly, he undressed and slipped under the covers and began kissing her again. Kevan began to moan. Jack ran his hands over her entire body, across her breasts, around her shoulders, down her back, across her buttocks, and finally between her legs. She felt very warm and moist. Suddenly she thrust her hips upward as a wave of pleasure came over her. She arched her back and moved to his touch. Finally, she couldn't stand it any longer, so she took him and thrust him deep inside her. She began to move against him, panting and moaning as she moved higher and higher until finally she nearly screamed. Just then, Jack let himself go completely until they had reached the crest of their encounter. Exhausted, they lay quietly side by side.

"Wow. You're something, Jack, darling. I'm going to get a smoke. Do you want one?"

"No thanks," he answered, his head against the pillow, his eyes closed. Kevan got up, put on her robe, and found a cigarette. In a moment, she returned and crawled into bed. Jack got up and went to the bathroom. He stood in front of the mirror looking at himself.

"You bastard," he said under his breath. "You rotten bastard." He washed his face and hands and returned to the bedroom. He gathered up his clothes and started toward the bathroom.

"What are you doing, darling?" Kevan asked, startled.

"I'm getting dressed. I'm going, Kevan. This was a mistake. This should never have happened."

"Darling, don't be silly. It was wonderful. Look. You and me, we're two of a kind. So we like each other and so we made love. What harm can it do? People do it every day." Jack did not answer. He went into the bathroom and dressed as quickly as he could. When he came out, Kevan was sitting on the side of the bed.

"Okay, Jack. I understand. But if you change your mind, you know where to find me. I'll say this for you, darling. You're good. Real good."

"Kevan, please. Just forget this happened, okay?" He was putting on his coat as he started toward the door.

"Jack, darling, don't take it so seriously. And please don't hate me."

"I don't hate you, Kevan. I hate myself." He turned and looked at her. "Good night." In the hallway, Jack felt a rush of relief to be out of her den. He stood waiting for the elevator, a lost and lonely man. How cruel, he thought, was the enigma of the human male, filled by a brutish hunger, an uncontrollable beast. He stepped into the elevator not looking at the nameless faces before him.

Jack walked out into the night and felt the crisp air hit his face. He was angry with himself. He was angry at New York, at the world. There was no gratification in what he had done, only a feeling that he had known before, that there is nothing honest or sacred in life. Every temporal being he had ever known had been consumed by power, money, lust, greed, and above all sexual gratification. He looked sorrowfully out the window of the cab. He did not see the energy and exuberance of a bustling city. He saw only the lost, savage creature within himself.

In those moments, Jack saw with absolute clarity that he had in Shannon a person who was not of this synthetic world before him now. Shannon was his magic light, his best hope, his last and only chance for his dreams to be fulfilled. In Shannon, he had an opportunity to have a life that he had only written about. And he was driving her away. And he couldn't help himself.

Here was truth staring him in the face. More than anything in his life, he longed to live in the enchanted world that was Shannon's birthright. Here, he believed, he could recover a youth that he had never really had, and be a part of a real place, where he had never been allowed to go.

He left the cab and raced toward the elevator. He needed the sanctuary of his hotel room, a place of refuge where perhaps he could regain control of his faculties. He could not stand the thought that he had returned to the stale world of his past, yet why had he thought he could escape it? He had just proven to himself yet again that he was powerless over his own cravings. He had failed his marriage, himself, and his lifelong dreams.

And now, he thought, I have to go home and face Shannon.

Chapter Forty-Six

What a beautiful Irish morning, Shannon thought as she pulled out of the yard and headed down the hill. The fog had lifted and the sun was making its way through the broken clouds. It was the kind of morning fisherman prayed for. The wind was calm, the ocean was smooth, and the day promised to remain in a state of peacefulness. Shannon lowered the window of her Mercedes to allow the fresh air to hit her face. Her spirits were high. She was excited to be going to work on her family farmhouse.

It always made her feel comfortable inside when she turned the corner and saw the old cottage at the end of the road. She would be filled with fond memories. She could almost see her mother in the back yard hanging clothes to dry, or puttering about in the garden, or simply taking in the air.

Shannon had left the big house in Tahilla spotless, with a pie on the kitchen counter and a fire laid in the fireplace. She expected that by the time she returned this afternoon, Jack would be back from New York. He would have driven in from Shannon Airport unless the fog had caused the plane to be diverted to Dublin, which was often the case. Shannon Airport was very near the bay where the Shannon River emptied into the Atlantic between Loop Head and Kerry Head, often causing the fog to linger around the airport. Travelers would have to land in Dublin and then go on to Shannon, usually causing a two hour delay.

Shannon pulled into the road leading to the old cottage, parked her car, and walked toward the front door. Several workers were outside tending to the rock walls. Two were up on a scaffold and one was mixing mortar and handing it up. They waved and smiled. "Top o' the morning, Mrs. Murphy. A fine bright day 'tis, and a grand day to be alive."

"It is indeed," she returned their good cheer. She was met by Mr. O'Shea when she stepped inside. The place was a mess, she saw. Sawdust, dirt, pieces of wood, tools and a general state of disorder caught her attention. All necessary, she knew, to bring the old house up to a modern standard of comfort.

She looked in toward the kitchen and saw Paddy working. He turned and nodded. She greeted him civilly. "Good morning, Paddy, how are you keeping?"

"Fine, Mrs. Murphy," he answered, almost under his breath. Shannon stood talking with Mr. O'Shea, answering several technical questions concerning the remodeling. After a time, Mr. O'Shea excused himself, saying that he had to drive into Kenmare and pick up some supplies.

Shannon walked upstairs and roamed around the rooms. She stopped at the doorway of her old bedroom when she heard footsteps behind her. She turned to find Paddy standing in the hallway. "Hello, Paddy," she said, calmly enough, yet feeling a bit nervous.

"Good morning, Shannon," Paddy murmured familiarly. "How are you?"

"I'm fine, Paddy," she said, a little confused as to how to act. She felt as if she didn't know what to do with her hands. "I came up to look at my old room," she finally said, walking in and smiling, in spite of herself, at the sight of the familiar furnishings.

Paddy followed her into the bedroom and stood looking at her, feeling awkward also. Then, with a friendly look, he said, "I have the new stove in the kitchen, and it's working now. Can I fix you a cup of tea?"

Shannon nodded, considering that it might be helpful to have tea with

Paddy and to explain her feelings about the events of the other day. They went down to the kitchen and he put some water on to boil, then sat down on a wooden box. Shannon sat down on an old chair nearby. "Paddy," she said softly, so as not to be heard by anyone outside, "about the other day at my house. That was my fault, not yours. I should have never allowed it to go so far. I'm married and I love Jack very much. I'm truly sorry."

He did not answer or comment in any way, but sat very still, just looking at her. Then he got up and rinsed out two cups, put in tea bags, and poured hot water over them. "I don't have any milk, but we do have sugar."

"This is fine, the way it is," she answered. Paddy walked over and handed her the tea. He could smell a light scent of French perfume as he moved past her. She was wearing a white dress with a huge Aran sweater which fell far below her waistline, almost like a jacket. A bright blue scarf was tied around her neck and flipped back over her shoulder. The morning sun, streaming in through the kitchen windows, gave her face a soft pink look against the scarf.

"Don't you have a girlfriend?" Shannon asked.

"I did. But there hasn't been anyone in my life since my old girlfriend left for London."

"I would think a nice looking man like yourself would have dozens of girls." She was trying to lighten the conversation and to make him feel better.

He looked her full in the face. "Shannon, I'm sorry about the other day. I had no right. It's just that I find you so very attractive. And I can't stop thinking about you." He looked away quickly, then back at her, meeting her eyes.

Behind his simple words, she saw that he truly cared for her, and that his longing caused him great pain. She felt much calmer, and her shoulders relaxed as she sat back in her chair. She chose her words carefully. "Paddy, thank you telling me this. I know that you didn't mean any harm, and that you're a good person. Thank you for understanding."

Paddy nodded. “I’ve never met anyone like you, Shannon.” He looked down at the floor. “Sure, I’ve had a lot of girlfriends, and I’ve been close to one or two of them.” Then he looked up. “But you’re different. There is something about your way, how you sit and walk, and even how you talk. You have such nobility. I can’t explain it. And how beautiful you are. You are the most beautiful woman I have ever met.”

“Paddy, I thank you for all your kind words, but you’ve got to put me out of your head. Find a girl that you like, that likes you.”

“Shannon, if I can’t have you, I don’t want anyone.”

“Oh, come now. You don’t even know me.” She spoke with authority, but at the same time she was keenly aware of his sexuality. He was a very handsome young man, and his direct gaze reassured her by its honesty. “You’ve only seen me a dozen times or so. We’d only talked a few times before that day.” She stopped, aware of what she had been about to say.

“’Tis a shame. I’m just a work hand, with no money, no position. I was lucky to have two years of college. I’ve nothing to offer anyone such as yourself.” He shook his head. “What was I thinking? How did I expect to get a woman like you? You’re beautiful, wealthy, married to a very famous writer. I lost my head, I did.”

Shannon interrupted him. “Paddy. Don’t say those things about yourself. Another time, another place, I would have been honored to be your friend. You’re a sweet person. You have no right to speak of yourself in that way.”

Paddy looked surprised, but pleased. She could see that in his eyes. After a moment, he said, “You know, I used to try my hand at writing poetry. Sometimes I still come up with something to read to the lads down at the pub.”

“Really. And who might your favorite poet be?” She was relieved that he had changed the subject.

“Oscar Wilde is one of my favorites. ‘I’m not in favor of long engagements. They give people the opportunity of finding out each other’s character before marriage, which I think is never advisable.’” They both laughed.

"I like Wilde," Shannon said. "We had to study him a great deal in college."

"Can you remember one of his?"

"Oh, I can, yes. This is one of my favorites; 'There is nothing in the world like the devotion of a married woman. It's a thing no married man knows a thing about.'"

"Why did you choose that one?" Paddy asked jokingly. "Do you think it fits today's conversation?"

"Perhaps." She was more pleased with his quick intelligence than she let on. In a light voice, she said, "I'm glad we had this talk, Paddy." She looked at him with soft eyes. Her voice was calm and her manner relaxed. "This is a good thing."

"Yes. I agree. Shannon, can we be friends?"

She sat very still, thinking. She felt that she understood him without really knowing him. She wanted to be very thoughtful of his feelings. Her own self confidence had been shattered in the past, and she was sensitive to it in someone else. It had taken her a very long time to recover from her affair with Stal. She did not want to cause any kind of emotional damage to Paddy, no matter how slight.

"I would like that, Paddy. Of course we can be friends." She stood and extended her hand to shake his, saying, "I need to be getting on now." She left the cottage feeling much better for having established an understanding with Paddy. She had been suffering from guilt, and though she knew it was a false emotion, it had bothered her ever since the night of the storm. Now she felt free.

Shannon glanced over her shoulder as she headed down the road. Paddy stood in front of the cottage. He waved, and in reply she honked the horn with two quick taps.

Chapter Forty-Seven

When Shannon arrived home, she was greeted by a box of perfume sitting on the kitchen counter with a note. "I've gone into Kenmare, will be back soon. I missed you. Love, Jack." Shannon picked up the box and looked at it carefully. She did not know the name. She opened it and took out a small dark blue container with a large gold cap. She tried a little of it on her wrist. Very pleasant, she thought.

It seemed like less than thirty minutes when she heard a car pull up. She looked out the window and saw that it was Jack. He came briskly up the path and into the kitchen, calling out, "Shannon. Shannon, I'm home." He saw her standing in the hallway, smiling.

"Hello. I'm glad you're home," she fairly sang. She threw her arms around his neck and gave him a big hug, then kissed him for a long time.

"Oh, you feel good," he said in her ear.

"And you, as well," she said softly. "Thanks for the perfume." She pulled back and put her wrist up to Jack's face. "Like it?"

"Oh, yes. Makes my knees knock," he said with a laugh, as he stepped back and shook his knees playfully. "You make my knees knock," he added, grabbing her and pulling her to him again. "Let's go out to dinner tonight."

Shannon hesitated. "Aren't you tired?"

"A little. But, hell, I'm getting used to this jet set business. Whadda ya say?"

"Yes. I suppose we could. I had thought we would spend a quiet time at home tonight."

"We will. We won't stay out late, okay?" With another impulsive kiss, he went to shower and change clothes. He called out from the back of the house, "I think I'll take a little nap." Shannon did not respond, but continued to straighten out the kitchen and put away some dishes.

Along toward dusk, Shannon went to bathe and dress for dinner. She stopped by the guest bedroom. Jack lay across the bed sideways, fast asleep in his bathrobe. She took a quilt and covered him, deciding not to get him up after all. She gently closed the door and returned to the kitchen to fix herself a bite to eat. For the remainder of the evening, she moved quietly about the house so as not to disturb him, then found a book and went to bed early.

Jack slept through the night, and did not awaken until after five the next morning. It was still dark when he came into the bedroom. Shannon stirred and saw his shadow outlined against the window. "Jack, what time is it?"

"I don't know," he said, turning on a small light in the bathroom. He looked at the clock by the bed. "It's 5:15. Did I sleep all night?"

"You did, yes. You were very tired."

"I'm starving."

"I'll get up and fix breakfast."

"Sure," he answered as he went in to brush his teeth and use the bathroom. In the dim light, Shannon put on her robe and went to the kitchen. Jack had already started the coffee and she could smell the sharp aroma.

In a few minutes, Jack came to the table. He seemed refreshed by his night's sleep, but still in an edgy, big city frame of mind. "So. What's happening with the cottage?" he inquired briskly.

"I was there yesterday. They are coming along very well. It's going to be quite nice. The kitchen in nearly finished. Mr. O'Shea is happy altogether, I should say."

"And you?"

"Yes. I'm very happy. It's nice to see the old house come to life again. We never had enough money to fix it up proper. My father always talked about what he wanted to do. To fix this or remodel that, always adding, 'God willing.' Of course, we never saved enough money. It was always something that he was going to do one day."

Jack moved to the kitchen window, "Looks like a heavy fog this morning. How's the weather been?" he asked.

"Grand. We've had several soft days now."

"It was a little cool in New York."

"How was New York? Did everything go well?" Shannon asked, pouring herself another coffee. Without asking, she poured coffee in Jack's cup as well.

"Everything went off without a hitch. We got a lot done in a short period of time. Book sales are fantastic, and it seems like everyone at Kingdom House is hyped on my next project. They suggested that perhaps my next book be set in a tropical area."

"Tropical?"

"Yes. Like the Mediterranean, or the Caribbean, or even some exotic place like Bali or Java."

"And how do you feel about that?" Shannon asked as she took out eggs and bacon from the refrigerator.

"Well, as you know, my notes and outline all have the next book set in Ireland again. Moving its locale would mean a lot of changes, but it wouldn't be too hard to do. We would have to go wherever the book is set, for a few weeks at any rate. I can't just write the whole thing from research books out of the library. I need to feel the place first hand. I've got to see the people, understand the customs. And, as they say, smell the roses."

He took a sip of his coffee and started to elaborate when she interrupted and said, "How do you want your eggs?"

"Any way. However you fix yours." He got up and paced the room as he talked. "I would start changing the book here at home, because I want to be around while they are shooting the movie here. Maybe not for all of it, but a good portion. Then we could take a working holiday to Bali or wherever, and I'd put some finishing touches on the book. After the first draft, we'd return home and all the major work would be done here in my office."

"All sounds very interesting, but complicated," Shannon said as she dished up the eggs. She took some brown bread and scones off the top of the stove, got the butter and jam from the refrigerator, and set everything on the table. "Come. Sit. Breakfast is ready." He left off his pacing, sat down at the table, and began to eat quickly, talking as he did so.

"Jack, you'll choke to death. Mind your food and slow down."

"I'm famished."

She watched him for a few minutes. "Did you miss me, Jack?"

Jack stopped eating and looked up at Shannon. She sat looking at him, a slight smile on her face. "Of course I missed you. You should have gone with me. It was lonely in New York without you." He began eating again.

Shannon did not finish her food. She sat with her hands folded on her lap as Jack worked his way through the plateful of food. They were quiet for a long while.

"I went to see Brien," Shannon said breaking the silence.

"Oh? How is Brien?"

"He's getting on real well. He loves his work. Says that perhaps he was meant to be a man of the sea. And he likes Dingle, as well."

Jack reached over and took Shannon's plate. "I'm going to finish your bacon, okay?" She nodded, helping him with the plate.

"Brien says that he may come for a visit soon."

"That'll be nice," Jack said quickly.

"He looked real good. He has gained some weight. His eyes were bright and he seemed very happy, indeed."

"I'm glad to hear that. Is he making any money at this fishing thing?"

"I couldn't say. We didn't talk about that."

"How's his car? Running all right?"

"Oh, it is, yes. He loves it."

Jack finished his meal, went to the kitchen sink, and washed his hands. "Sun's not up even yet," he observed, looking outside.

"I started a painting."

"Really. What of?"

"I'm doing the sea, right out my own window." He did not respond as he walked to get his coffee cup and pour himself a refill. He sat down again. "Jack, what's wrong? You seem very distant, or distracted. Is something on your mind?"

"What do you mean? No, nothing is on my mind. Just thinking about my book project, I guess. Or jet lag. I don't know."

"Something's wrong. What is it?"

"Shannon, nothing is wrong." He got up and walked around behind her, putting his arms around her shoulders and giving her a kiss on the top of her head. "Nothing's wrong. I promise," he repeated.

Shannon moved his arms and stood up to clear the table. "I'm going back to the house this morning," she said in a businesslike tone. "Mr. O'Shea has a couple of things he wants me to approve. Do you want to go?"

"No, not today. I want to get caught up on a few things. I have to go into Kenmare to the bank, and pick up a couple of items at the store."

Shannon went to the sink and started to do the dishes. Jack stood by the counter, watching her. "You know, I don't understand why you don't use the dishwasher. You have not used that dishwasher one time since we moved in."

"I guess I'm just old fashioned. I don't mind doing dishes. I've done them all my life. I enjoy it."

"I can't understand you sometimes," he said as he turned to walk away. "Well, I'll be in my office. Oh, and I may get a phone call from America today. I'm expecting a call about the movie. You know, I wish that phone line worked in my office. Why can't they fix it?"

“The phone man said that he has to run a new line, that something is wrong with that one. Perhaps it got cut, or something. He said to just let him know what we want done.”

“Sure,” Jack said, walking away. “Sure.”

Chapter Forty-Eight

The soft warm day descended upon Tahilla, and a mild breeze filled the air. A memento of summer, it fooled the heart. The landscape was changing like a Monet canvas still being painted. The roads were quiet now, with the tourist traffic gone, and Shannon made good time into Kenmare.

She arrived at the cottage to find Mr. O'Shea standing out front talking with one of the workmen. When she got out of her car, she stood beside the door until he finished his conversation. He waved as if to say that he'd only be a moment. Then he turned to her. "Top o' the morning, and such a bright day 'tis. A beautiful day altogether."

"It is that, Mr. O'Shea." She smiled up toward the sky. "What a glorious day, indeed."

"A great day to be alive," Mr. O'Shea replied, "but hold on to your hats, mind you," he continued in a single thought. "This time of year, the fall's twilight is short-lived. We have no enemy but time. The weather will change, I dare say."

"How right you are," Shannon said.

"Mrs. Murphy, I'll just go and get Paddy. He has several questions that he needs to ask you. It's about the fireplaces, and if you want him to build a larger stone base around them." Mr. O'Shea walked to the back of the house, calling for him.

In a few moments, they appeared at the side of the house. Shannon felt a secret delight to see Paddy, as if he were a long lost friend.

"Good morning, Mrs. Murphy," he said with a smile. She noticed the high color in his cheeks, pushing up toward his eyes, which were dancing just now.

"Hello, Paddy."

"Please follow me, Mrs. Murphy." He led the way into the living room. They walked to the fireplace, where he had laid out some stones to show her the shape and size of the base that he wanted to build. She stood looking at them thoughtfully, then raised her head.

"I like what you've done. I would say to build it just this way." She waved her hand above the stones.

"Fine. I'm glad you like it, Mrs. Murphy," Paddy said, raising his dark eyebrows. "We'll get right on it."

"The upstairs fireplaces will be the same?" asked Shannon.

"They will, only a little smaller. We haven't laid them out as yet." Paddy took her elbow. "Can you follow me out back? I want to show you our idea about the store room."

She nodded an assent. As they reached the door, they heard Mr. O'Shea and two of the masons talking about the fine points of caulking the stone walls. They did not notice when Shannon and Paddy came out of the house and started toward the back.

Paddy pointed out how he would like to tear down the old shed and build a new, larger one, much closer to the house. His enthusiasm ran high, as if he were building it for himself. He showed her where he would put the new garden, and how he would move this wall to here, and that stone wall there, and replace this fence, and so on.

Shannon watched and listened with delight as he took such pleasure in explaining what he would like to do and why. They walked down toward the creek and crossed the garden, now overgrown in weeds. At the far edge, Paddy halted and turned to Shannon. "I would start here, at this point, and bring the garden all the way to that tree," he said, pointing. "It would take some extra work to clear off all the stones, but what a grand garden it would make."

"Oh, I agree, Paddy." She looked at him wistfully. "You know, you're a lot like my father was. He had great vision. He could get past the ugly, and he had the ability to see the finished thing, even before it was begun. Ah, a fine man he was, indeed."

Paddy smiled. He sat down on a low stone wall, picked a piece of tall grass, and placed it between his teeth. He sat quietly looking about. "This is a beautiful place you have here, Shannon. Mrs. Murphy."

"Shannon," she said gently.

"Beauty is truth," he mused. " I mean, well, truth is self-respect, you might say, and beauty comes from imagination. James Joyce believed that beauty is the splendor of truth, to put it in short words."

Shannon looked out over the land, pondering his thoughts, remembering the long ago. "When my father died," she told him after awhile, "Jack recommended that we sell our cattle and other animals. I guess he was right, but it hurt me to see them go."

Paddy surveyed the fields and meadows, thinking of how to comfort her. He knew she was sad for the passing of her parents, and the changing of her life as she had known it when she was a young girl. He looked at her kindly. "Sometimes it's wise to let things happen in a natural way," he explained. "Like this land. It hasn't been worked now for a long time. It's good to let the land rest. The land needs rest, the same as a man. One day, when you plant it again, and put cattle back into the pastures, it'll be ready."

He waved his hand at the whole place, the house and the farmlands. "One day this place will be full of life again. Crops in the fields. Children running about. Do you like children, Shannon?" he asked in a very direct manner. Shannon did not answer right away.

"I do. I love children," she said at last. Then she became quiet for what seemed to Paddy a long time. Finally she asked, "Do you like children, Paddy?"

"Oh, I do, yes, I love children," Paddy paused. "Can I tell you something very personal, that I've never told anyone?" He took her hand and she did not pull away. She knew he was about to share something with her, and his holding her hand was an act of friendship.

"You can, yes, Paddy. You can tell me anything, in confidence."

He held her hand tightly as he started to speak. "Remember when I told you that I had this girlfriend, and she left for London? Well, what I didn't tell you is that she later wrote to me and said that she was going to have my baby." He looked down at the ground, then up again into Shannon's eyes. "She returned to Dublin and had the baby there, a little girl."

Shannon just nodded, then asked gently, "What is the child's name?"

"Maura. She was named after her grandmother."

"How old is she now?"

"She just turned three."

"Three," Shannon said in a surprised voice. "Do you ever see her?"

"I do, yes, as often as I can. I don't have a car. The pickup truck I drive belongs to Mr. O'Shea. I would never ask him to let me take it to Dublin, and I don't think it would make it there and back anyway." Paddy stood up and walked about, then turned toward Shannon. "I love that little girl, and some day she's going to live with me. You'll see. Her mother is no good for her, and she's been sick a lot lately besides."

"Who takes care of Maura?"

"Well, my old girlfriend has a sister in Dublin who helps. That's where she and Maura are staying. I hate going there. I guess that's why I don't go more often. Besides, it isn't easy to get to Dublin and then to get back in time for work."

"Paddy. I'm proud of you. You love your little daughter and you care what happens to her. I know that it will work out."

"That place where she lives is no good. It's a poor, rundown apartment building in the very worst part of Dublin. The streets are lined with whores and drunken sailors. I hate for Maura to be living there, and some day I'm going to get her away from all that."

Shannon looked at him with new respect, and when she spoke her tone had changed completely. "I wish there were something I could do to help," she said softly. They were quiet together, listening to the sounds of the workmen back up at the house. Then they heard Mr. O'Shea calling for Paddy as he came through the garden.

"Oh, there you are. Come, lad, we need a hand. Will you excuse us, Mrs. Murphy?" Paddy smiled and gave her a nod, then followed his employer to the house. She kept her eyes on him as he walked away.

Sitting there on the rock wall and looking out into the open field, she felt deeply moved by what had just been revealed to her. She saw now the kindness and wonderful heart of Paddy O'Corry. Patrick Henry O'Corry, she had learned was his full Christian name, was no ordinary lad. He was a sincere human being, intelligent and full of poetry, and he had spoken with his heart. She felt honored by his confidence. If more people on earth were like Paddy, she thought, then much of the confusion and ugliness of this life would vanish.

Shannon heard her name called. It was Mr. O'Shea, standing just at the corner of the house. She waved her hand in acknowledgment and started toward him.

"I'm going to be off now," he said when she got close enough to hear. "Would you be needing anything else today, Mrs. Murphy?"

"No, thank you, Mr. O'Shea. I have to go meself," she said, slipping back into the country ways of Kerry. "I must be tending to dinner and the ways of a married woman," she said gaily. She passed by the front door of the cottage where Paddy was standing. "I'll see you again soon."

"Sure thing, Mrs. Murphy. You take care, now."

Shannon drove home to Tahilla, all the while thinking of young Maura. She wished that she had asked to see a photograph of Paddy's daughter. I will, she resolved, when next we meet.

BOOK THREE

"The innocent and the beautiful
Have no enemy but time."

William Butler Yeats
(1865 - 1939)

Chapter Forty-Nine

Everyone on the streets seemed as happy as Shannon, now that Spring had arrived in Ireland. All the girls were prettier and the young men more handsome than ever. The town seemed elated as Spring burst out of earth in a blaze of color. The cold heavy rains were gone and everyone seemed to have grown younger all of a sudden. Shannon felt like her old self. The townspeople treated her just the way they always had, as their own special darling.

The old farmhouse was for the most part completed, with only a few finishing touches left to do. Then the furniture could be brought down again, and dusted and polished and set in place. Shannon had purchased a couple of antique pieces to fill in, but, for the most part, she was going to leave the homestead intact.

Jack had begun to work at a fierce pace on his new book. He had decided that it would be set in the Caribbean, on the islands of St. Thomas and St. John. The main reason for his choice was that he was already familiar with St. Thomas and St. John, having visited them many times while he had lived in Florida. He said he could do the story far more justice using the Caribbean. Shannon thought secretly that he also wanted to spend several months there the coming winter.

They had fallen into a kind of routine. Jack worked on his book and spent more and more time in the local pubs. Shannon fixed up the family cottage and got on with her paintings. They would take walks along the shore, and would go out to dinner more often than Shannon wanted. Occasionally, they would make love.

Sometimes in the night, she would hear her mother's voice. "Daughter, my sweet Shannon. Patience. A woman must always have patience, especially when it concerns her husband and her marriage." Her mother's advice was bound in tradition. "There will be trying times, maddening times, but have patience and any grief in your life will pass. Go to Mass, and pray to Mary to guide you and keep you from the confusions and the dark moments of despair found in this world."

Then she would think of her father's practical wisdom, and it strengthened her will. He would always say to her, "Shannon, you are too pure for this world, for you thirst for beauty and peace. People such as you will hurt more than the others. You have a vision, and you must stay true to that vision."

The days went by in a placid procession until at last the movie production was ready to begin. There had been several delays, but now everything was in place. The company had made the decision to film most of the movie in and around Kinsale. Jack was pleased because it was only a two hour drive from Tahilla.

The staff and the cast were ready, and shooting was scheduled to begin in one week. Jack was busy planning their welcome party. It had been decided to have it before the shooting began, which left Shannon little time to prepare.

Jack was very much into the party, and was actually doing far more than Shannon wanted. He had hired three bartenders and two servers. The wine he had ordered was quite costly, and the food much too lavish in price, style, and quantity, to her way of thinking. "Jack's Bash," as she had come to call it, seemed to be getting out of hand. She was troubled over the entire affair. She knew that she would be able to calm herself, and would be totally collected when the day arrived. But she was equally certain that Jack would be worried and uptight.

The guest list for Kenmare, Tahilla, and Sneem was so large that she wondered where Jack had come up with all the names. To compound her anxiety, she had no idea who or how many of the production company were coming. She finally put her foot down on the subject of valet parking. Jack was concerned that many of the people would have to park a considerable ways down the hill, and that the road might be muddy, but she would have no part of it.

In truth, Shannon was more concerned with the aftermath in her own village than with the event itself. Kenmare had never seen a party such as the one Jack had planned. The townspeople still thought of her as one of their own, especially with her keeping the family home. She cared for them, and did not want them to withdraw from her because they thought she was trying to act like a rich American.

All during the remodeling of the cottage, she had taken time to be out and about in Kenmare, keeping up with her old friendships. Her new bond with Paddy was a source of joy to her. They had seen each other on a regular basis during construction work, and an understanding had developed between them. She had asked Paddy to show her the photo of Maura that he always carried with him. Shannon was stunned by the beauty of the child. She was even more surprised when she saw Maura's light red hair and green eyes. Maura was the very image of Shannon when she was that age.

Shannon had not seen much of Paddy in recent days, as she had so much to do to get ready for Jack's Bash. One morning about eleven, as she returned home from her errands, he surprised her by calling. Jack was out of the house playing golf, something he had taken up again these past few months, and she planned to get some housework done while he was gone. She had just placed her bags of groceries on the counter when the phone rang.

"Hello, Shannon. This is Paddy. How are you?"

"Hello, Paddy. I'm well, thank you. And yourself?" He did not answer, but asked a question instead. "Can you meet me on the strand near Sneem

in about an hour? I have something very, very important to show you."
Shannon thought for a minute. Paddy had never called her again at home, so she considered that it must be important.

"What is it, Paddy?"

"Please Shannon, don't ask me any more. Just meet me, will you?"

"I will, yes. I'll be there in an hour." She hung up the phone and began putting away her groceries, wondering what this emergency could be about. Paddy's voice had not sounded harried in any way, just mysterious. She was caught up with a feeling of expectation. She finished her tasks and made ready to leave. Her excitement built as she drove down the hill and onto the road that led to the church at Tahilla.

Turning left onto the main road, she picked up her pace, only slowing as she went through the village of Sneem. She waved to a couple of people whom she knew as she passed by the Sneem square, then she was over the bridge and out of town. It wasn't long before she reached the turnoff to the strand. She saw Mr. O'Shea's car parked on the side of the road, and she pulled in behind it and walked down the path toward the strand.

The ocean was rather calm today, she noticed as she looked around for Paddy. Then she spotted him. At his side was a little girl. She knew right off that it must be Maura, and her heart leapt as she waved to the two of them. She rushed up just as Paddy was picking the little girl up in his arms.

"Hi, Shannon. I want you to meet Maura."

"Hello, Maura," Shannon smiled at her. She held out her arms and the child came willingly. "My, you're a big girl. Won't you just look at those lovely green eyes. And all these curls," she added, as she smoothed Maura's hair. "Your daddy must be very proud of you. He has told me that he loves you very much."

Paddy beamed at them. "Mr. O'Shea gave me a couple of days off and said that I could borrow his car to drive to Dublin and get Maura. I have to take her back tomorrow, but we've had a great time together. We went to the zoo in Cork yesterday, and we had ice cream and went looking for a stuffed bear for her."

"Is that right, Maura?" The child smiled shyly and nodded. Shannon set her down, and right away she took off running toward some birds.

Shannon stood still, looking at Paddy. "She's precious, she is." She reached over and kissed him on the cheek.

"Thank you, Shannon. I wanted her to meet my best friend." At that, Shannon was overcome. To hide her tears, she turned her head away and looked after Maura, who had slipped and gone tumbling in the sand. She was covered in sand. It was all over her clothes and in her hair. They were all three laughing as her father helped her to her feet and began brushing her clean. Then he put her down and she ran off again.

"Her mother is not well," he said as he watched her at play. "They think it's cancer. She has been to the hospital for tests, and is going in again in a week or so."

"Oh, Paddy. I'm so sorry to hear that. I truly am."

"We shall see."

"I'll pray for her this Sunday at Mass. I've been going to the little church in Tahilla, rather than driving into Sneem or Kenmare. Everyone asks about Jack, but he hasn't been going with me for a long time now. He'll go on some holy days, but that's about all."

Paddy did not reply. He looked at her tenderly. "I've missed you, Shannon," he said, touching her cheek with his hand.

"I've missed you as well." She looked at him in silence. Then she glanced away and started walking toward the water's edge, laughing as she said, "Maura, mind you watch the water. Not to be getting your clothes all wet now." She picked her up in a swinging motion and carried her back to her father.

"Daddy," Maura said, throwing her arms around his neck and kissing him on the cheek. Shannon stood watching the love that was being exchanged between the two of them. How beautiful, she thought. If only the whole world could be this way.

"I should be getting on, though I don't want to," she said. "Let's walk up to the cars." They started up the hill. Maura danced between them, holding first Paddy's hand and then Shannon's. "We have our big party day after tomorrow," Shannon continued, "and I have much to do. Oh, God, how I dread that party. I can't wait till it's over. And Jack, he's so excited about it all. He's like a schoolboy, worse than on my birthday."

"When did you have a birthday?"

"A few weeks back. Jack took me to dinner. Oh, sweet Jesus, did he get drunk. The truth is, the night was a disaster."

"Why didn't you tell me it was your birthday?"

"Well, you know. You might have made a fuss."

"Might you tell me how old you were," he said with a laugh.

"I shall not. But I will say this—I'm not a girl in my twenties any longer."

"Nor am I a lad in my twenties," Paddy replied. "I was thirty-one six months ago. I can't believe it. I'm going on forty."

"Oh, you are not. I hardly think thirty-one is going on forty," she said playfully.

He winked to show her he was joking. Then he put his hand on her shoulder. "Thank you for coming. I'm glad you could meet Maura." She took the child in her arms and kissed her good-bye. "You take care of your daddy, now, little miss Maura," she said with a big hug. "And come back to see me, will you?" She returned their waves as they drove away, brushing a tear from her cheek.

Shannon got into her car and sat behind the wheel for a very long time, just staring out to sea. Paddy's daughter is a miracle, she thought. Now she's come into my life. What would become of little Maura, she wondered, if something happened to her mother? She did not want to think about the dangers that faced the child.

She sat very quietly and watched the waves roll in and hit the rocks. Then they would become still, and in a moment another would crash in. The rocks were painted silver as the water smashed against them and splintered into a thousand colors and designs.

When youth is gone, she mused, we look back at what happened to our lives, sometimes in bitter sorrow, full of regrets, and sometimes with feelings of love, full of wonderful memories. Which will it be? A woman's youth is a glorious thing, even if most of it is filled with doubts, guilt and anguish. She smiled to herself. There was magic, too, like the ocean waves before her, and like this strange miracle called life.

A young woman is like these waves, she thought, forever exploding, only to grow still and calm as she learns about herself. A young woman is so certain, yet she can be filled with doubts. An older woman is never certain, but she has few doubts. As her youth passes, she looks back and wonders what happened to it.

There is something in the very nature of our being young that causes the time to be misspent. Or does it? Perhaps this misspent time is what molds one into a mature woman, she reflected. At what point does youth end, and can one lose it prematurely? Can youth be recovered if it is caught in time? And if one precipitates maturity, then what? When I married, did I give up my youth even as my father gave Jack my hand?

Is it at this moment that we suddenly realize what our life is to be, in this strange and wonderful journey from birth to death? Can anyone really know? What if I had not married Jack? I never wanted wealth and power, or did I? When youth has vanished from your life forever, is that what remains?

Shannon concluded that her days of innocence were gone forever. Memories of youth belong to the heart alone, she realized. They become a part of the web of life that grows larger with every passing minute, yet the inner person continues to grow as a unique soul. This, she thought, is the eternal fact of youth. As the ocean waves rolled before she was born, so they surged unceasingly now as she saw that her youth was gone. The ocean had always been the same, and always would be.

She made of her mind a clean canvas, and allowed her impressions to dance on it like dappled sunlight on the water. "I have so many questions, so many doubts," she said aloud. "Why is this? We can have everything and yet have nothing. We can have nothing and still have everything. How does it all fit together?"

Shannon suddenly realized that she had sat there for nearly an hour. She glanced down at her watch. "Jesus, Mary and Joseph," she exclaimed. She started her car and headed toward home. As she drove towards Sneem she recalled a recent conversation with Jack. That difficult conversation had thrown her problems into sharp relief, and she suddenly realized that it was the very reason for her long reverie today.

She had initiated it. She was trying to articulate what her intuition was telling her about their marriage. That seemed to be the only thing in her life that lacked substance, yet, to her, it was the most important thing. Their relationship felt like a deception. Finally, one day last week, she had confronted Jack with her thoughts.

"Jack," she began, "I need to know something. Something which has been on my mind a great deal lately." She spoke with authority, in a calm, direct manner. "Help me to understand how it is that when you are in Ireland, you long for America. Then we go to America, and you can't wait to get back to Ireland. What is behind this unrest?" She did not wait for an answer. "I want to be of help, truly I do. I feel that something is driving a wedge into our closeness, and that our marriage is coming apart."

Jack jumped into the conversation on the defensive. "I think that you resent Americans and America." He did not know exactly why he was saying that, so he said it very loudly.

"Resent America? No, Jack, truly I don't. But I suppose I do resent the effect that the American way of life has on Ireland. I resent driving down a beautiful lane into a village, and turning the corner to find a charming old stone church, and right in front of it is a petrol station with huge red signs on all four sides, when one small sign would identify it and still blend with the old architecture. But no thought is given to history or beauty, only to money."

She continued, picking up the speed of her words. "And I resent what is happening to Cork and to Dublin. I feel they will one day look like Los Angeles. I resent people coming to marvel at the splendor of my country, and then ridiculing our customs, our food, our roads, our weather, and our traditional ways, as if that were not the very essence of what makes Ireland great."

"Shannon, that's not fair. That's not true."

"Oh, 'tis, Jack. I've seen it and heard it all my life."

"Are you talking about me?"

"Not exactly."

"What is 'not exactly' supposed to mean?" he demanded testily.

"Please don't raise your voice, Jack. Words carry their own power. I am trying to show you that you have started to pick apart the very things that drew you here in the first place. You came to Ireland because you had this vision. Then you met me, and I seemed to be everything you imagined. Everything was so charming and cute in the beginning, like a fairy tale. You got caught up in me, and I got caught up in you as well. So we both jumped on this yellow brick road and began a journey, and it gets less real as it goes on."

Without raising her voice, she made her point. "Don't you feel the loneliness in our lives? It's as if everything is being held in abeyance. Jack, face it. We have a patchwork marriage." She squinted a little as she talked, something her mother would always do when she felt uncomfortable during serious discussions with her father.

"It sounds like nothing but nonsense to me," Jack said in an official bass tone.

"It's always nonsense when I bring up something that you don't want to face."

"What do you want from me?" Jack asked icily, although he was not really interested in finding out.

"I was hoping that we could make some ground, come to some understanding. I want to know how all of this is going to end."

"End? That sounds so final," Jack threw in.

Shannon was beginning to get upset. "I can't talk about this any more right now."

"I don't understand you, Shannon."

She turned her head away. "You said that, not I, but 'tis true."

"Are you going to weep?"

"No," she snapped defiantly. They both fell silent and looked at each other. And that's how the conversation ended, as had so many before. For a very long while, Shannon neither spoke nor moved. Then, ever so gently, she rose to her feet with apparent composure. She was, herself, surprised at how she managed to control her emotions.

And nothing has come of that conversation, she thought now as she turned off the main road and started up the hill toward the house. She directed her mind to the upcoming party. So much still to be done, and Jack was changing his mind about something every day. She was filled with dread. Something deep inside told her that the party would end in disaster.

Chapter Fifty

Everything was in order. The long buffets were loaded with delectable food. Battalions of champagne glasses stood at arms, awaiting the invasion. Flowers filled every room in the house, which had never looked quite so magnificent as it did just now. It would be a matter of minutes until the first guest arrived.

Shannon walked through the main rooms checking everything out one last time. For this grand occasion, she had selected one of her New York purchases, a long, elegant evening gown. It was a rich, slinky knit, mostly bare on top with very slim straps. The lower part of the dress had side slits, which showed off her legs in sheer black stockings and black high heels. On anyone else it might have seemed trite. On Shannon, with her radiant fall of hair and her sumptuous curves, it was simply spellbinding.

Jack came out of the dressing room wearing a black suit and a bright red tie.

"My God!" Shannon exclaimed upon seeing him.

"Thank you. I thought you would like it."

"Turn around. Let me see you." She eyed him appraisingly, then asked him to get her a drink. "I believe I will just have an Irish whisky," she said. "I feel like a modernist painting tonight, loaded with vanity, pride and conceit."

He was surprised at her sophisticated repartee. "You're kidding, right?"

"Am I?" She struck a pose. "Now. How does A.J. say it? Jack, darling, could I bother you for another drink?" She was playing with the New York accent, putting on a hard, slightly blasé act. For some reason, Jack was faintly shocked. He felt that such pretentious behavior was inappropriate for his genteel Shannon, even as a joke. But he couldn't very well object, so he went to the bar, where the young man fixed a Black Bush with a splash for Shannon and a Scotch and water for Jack.

She raised her glass to her husband. "Here's to your party, darling."

"Our party," he corrected her.

Shannon finished her drink with unaccustomed speed. She went to the bar for a refill, then answered the doorbell. It was a couple from Sneem that Jack had gotten to know, a chemist and his schoolteacher wife. She greeted them pleasantly and directed them to the bar, where Jack found them and began a conversation. Jack had a way of winning people over, of making them feel very special.

Soon more began to arrive, including many people that Shannon had never met. There was a couple from Germany who owned a house about two miles down the road. There were owners of restaurants, pubs and other businesses, all the people Jack had met since arriving in Ireland. She knew most of the townspeople from Kenmare, of course, but very few from Sneem, and only a handful that she had become acquainted with since moving to Tahilla.

Shannon stood in the doorway greeting people as they made their way up the steps to the front door. Jack had met some Americans at a pub in Sneem and invited them to join the party. The two couples had come from Pittsburgh on holiday and had rented a cottage for several weeks. Another American couple arrived. They owned a home in Kenmare and spent six months of the year in Ireland. The man was retired from a large corporation back in America, he told her. "You and Jack will have to come over some time for drinks and dinner," his wife said as she pumped Shannon's hand in a rather forceful manner. "We just love Jack's books. We have all three of them. Isn't it exciting about the movie? Jack said this party is in honor of the movie, and that some of the cast and crew would be here." While she was talking nonstop, her eyes roamed around the house. "Oh, there's Jack. Let's go say hello." They walked away.

"Nice meeting you," Shannon said under her breath. "Welcome to my home."

All around the house, small groups were starting to form. A larger number of people had gathered around Jack. She watched as the talking, smiling, hand shaking, laughing, eating and drinking continued. One man was describing to a cluster of fellow Americans what he had done since arriving in Ireland. He carried on monotonously about the bad roads, and how he couldn't stand Guinness beer, and how he wished people would get over their quaint expressions and speak normally. Now and then his wife would break into his monologue and fill in some part of the story.

"When are you two going home?" one American asked as she found an opening and jumped into the conversation.

"In about two weeks, now. Don't you just hate that plane trip back?"

"Oh, its not so bad. You should have been on the New York to Jordan trip last year. Oh, my God. I never want to go through that again." The woman took an hors d'oeuvre off one of the trays as it went by. Shoving it into her mouth, she continued her complaints. "And the stewardesses these days make you feel as if they're doing you a favor to allow you to pay money and fly on their airline."

Shannon stood at the door, watching and listening. She noticed that now and then some couples would change places, rotating from group to group according to some invisible plan. Sometimes they would graze at the buffet, but more often they would stop at the bar for refreshers on the way to their next position.

"Hello, Mrs. Murphy." She turned to see Mr. O'Shea as he reached the doorstep.

Shannon clasped his hand in both of hers. "My, my. Look at you." He was wearing dark brown trousers and a green and dark golden brown tweed jacket, and his best wool hat. He had on a white shirt with a vest and tie. He held his pipe in his teeth, off to one side, and it stayed in place even when he was talking.

"You know that there's no smoking in my house, Mr. O'Shea."

"I do, indeed. I never light it anyway. Now and then I'll sit by the fire and smoke a bowl."

"Where's Mrs. O'Shea?"

"Under the weather, she is. Bad cold."

"Mr. O'Shea, I want you to know that was a very nice thing that you did, allowing Paddy to use your car to go to Dublin."

"Ah, Paddy. He's a fine lad, he is. He'll be back tomorrow, God willing."

Shannon looked out to see two cars coming up the road. They passed all the other vehicles and pulled directly in front of the doorway, or at least as close as they could get. One of the cars parked on the edge of the front lawn.

"This must be some of the production company and cast," Shannon said to Mr. O'Shea. "Perhaps they were expecting valet parking."

"Exciting times," Mr. O'Shea said. "A movie and all."

"Mind you, now, you'll be needing something to drink, and do help yourself to the buffet," she told him. He walked in and headed for the bar, shaking hands with friends as he passed.

The two groups started up the steps toward the front door. Shannon recognized the movie stars right off. She could not help being a little excited to see such famous people coming to her own home.

Connie Lange was dressed down in a casual pants suit that did nothing to hide her allure. James Marshall had on dark slacks, a sport coat, and a white shirt and tie. Shannon thought he was more handsome in person than on screen.

"Hello," said the other man. "My name is Manny Freeman. I'm the director of *Fields Of Sensation.* You must be Shannon Murphy."

"I am, yes. Welcome, Mr. Freeman." She extended her hand.

"And, my, how lovely you look tonight," he added. "I already heard that you were a legendary Irish beauty, but I see that it was an understatement. Shannon, this is Connie Lange, the star of our movie."

Shannon smiled and extended her hand. Ms. Lange kissed Shannon on both cheeks. "I'm happy to meet you."

"And this is James Marshall. Jim, this is Jack's wife, Shannon." They shook hands. At that point, Jack noticed their arrival and rushed to the doorway.

"Manny," he boomed. "It's good to see you. Welcome to Ireland."

They shook hands and Manny introduced him to Connie Lange and James Marshall. "I can't tell you what an honor it is to have you two starring in my movie," he gushed.

"It's a great story, Jack. I'm looking forward to doing this one," Ms. Lange said smoothly. Jack thought they were very personable. He had been concerned that he wouldn't know what to say to movie stars.

"Very nice home you have here," Marshall said.

"How about a drink?" Jack asked, taking Ms. Lange's arm and motioning for the others to follow. "I'll introduce you to a few people." Marshall smiled at Shannon as he left.

"My, this is a big party, Jack. I thought it was going to be a small affair." Connie Lange moved easily through the crowd.

"Are you the only ones coming?" Jack asked Manny.

"No. There are a few more coming up the walk and another car back down the road," he replied in a businesslike manner.

Shannon watched as they all headed across the room, then turned to greet four more people. The introductions were made in rapid-fire order.

"I'm Harry. I do lighting."

"Hi. I'm Sam. I work with Harry. This is Barbara. She works on the sound system."

"Hi. My name is Matt Coleman. Some say I'm an actor."

Shannon liked their straightforward manner. She shook hands with each one of them and suggested they have a drink and some food. The party had become very noisy, as everyone was caught up in the excitement of Connie Lange and James Marshall being there. Jack did not leave their sides as he introduced them ceremoniously to each and every guest, saying the right thing, always.

Shannon glanced out the door and saw the headlights of a car that had lagged behind the rest. It must be the remaining members of the movie troupe, she decided. She knew she had guessed right when they pulled in and double parked alongside a car directly in front of the house. In the dim light, she saw a man and a woman get out and start up the path. The woman stepped into the light first. Shannon recognized her as Victoria Steele, an American actress who was very well liked here in Ireland. Then the man came into view.

It was Stallard Hopkins.

Shannon was frozen in place. She could not believe that it was Stal, and that he was actually coming up the walkway leading into her home. They reached the door.

"You!" Stal cried. "Shannon Kelly, is that you? My God, are you Jack Murphy's wife?"

Shannon did not answer at once, but let the silence lengthen between them. She reminded herself that she was the chatelaine of this mansion, and that she looked terrific this evening. When she finally spoke, it was with an edge of icy formality. "Yes. Hello, Stallard. Welcome, Ms. Steele."

"You know each other?" Victoria Steele asked.

"We do," she said distantly. "We met some years ago in Limerick."

"I was working on a film," he put in hurriedly. "How long has been, Shannon?"

"I have no idea." Her eyes glittered menacingly. "Why don't you visit the bar for a drink?"

Stal looked as if he had been caught cheating at cards and was trying to save face. "God, it's good to see you, Shannon. You are really looking great," he said over his shoulder as he and Victoria Steele crossed the room, nodding to people along the way.

Shannon realized with a feeling of relief that she was not in the least hurt by Stal's presence. There was only a healing rage. Stal got his drink and returned to where she stood. She did not acknowledge his presence.

"This is too much," Stal said. "Here I am working on a movie, and of all people, your husband wrote the story." He chuckled theatrically. "Shannon, about what happened a long time ago. I know what you must think of me."

"Stal," she interrupted, "You are mistaken. I don't think of you at all." With that, she turned on her heel and walked away with every bit of her considerable class. She looked for Jack and found him engaged in a conversation with Victoria Steele. She touched his shoulder and he turned.

"Oh, hello, Shannon. Have you met Vicky?"

"Yes, we met," Shannon said with a polite smile. "Ms. Steele, could I borrow my husband for just a moment?"

Vicky smiled and nodded, then walked over to the bar where Stal was talking to Manny Freeman. "Jack," Shannon said softly. "That man standing at the bar, the younger one talking to Vicky and Manny Freeman?"

He looked in their direction. "Yes?"

"That, my dear Mr. Murphy, is Stallard Hopkins. The one and only, the real thing, Stal Hopkins."

Jack glanced casually in that direction. "What? That is Stal? The one you had a schoolgirl crush on?"

There. That does it, she thought. She had realized of late that it was near impossible for them to hold any thought in common. Now it was completely obvious that neither Stal's presence at the party nor her reaction affected him in the least. She took him by the arm and dug her fingernails into his sleeve.

"Jack, listen to me very carefully. Never invite that person into my home again, ever. Do you understand?"

"I didn't invite him," Jack whispered forcefully.

"I know that. Just be certain that you never do. Second, I would like for you to ask him to leave at once."

"I can't do that, Shannon."

"Why can't you?"

"Hold your voice down," he said. "Don't tell the whole party, okay?"

"Jack, I want him out of my house."

She looked up to see Stal approaching them with a patronizing smile. She marched out of the room.

"You must be Jack Murphy. I'm Stallard Hopkins, the assistant director."

Jack put his hand out. "I've heard a lot about your work."

"Thanks. I'm happy to say that I just went under contract to direct my own film when this one is finished. It will be my first head director project."

"Well, congratulations."

"You know, Jack, I met your wife several years ago. We went out a few times. I think she's a little miffed with me. She seemed to think that there was more to the relationship than there really was for me. Know what I mean?"

"I know all about it. Shannon told me." He paused. "It did bother her then, but she's well over it. Hell, Stal that was a long time ago. I would just leave well enough alone. Know what I mean?" Jack sipped on his drink and glanced around the room.

They both turned when Manny Freeman rapped a spoon on his glass for attention. "Ladies and gentlemen, I would like to propose a toast. To our host and hostess, Jack and Shannon Murphy. And to our next hit, *The Fields Of Sensation*." Everyone raised their glass and cheered. Manny walked over to Jack and put his arm around his shoulder.

"You know Jack, I think we have ourselves a real winner here. You are to be congratulated." He raised his glass. "Here's to a superb story, and I know that it will make a hit movie. A lot of people agree with me, for we've gotten a ton of money behind this picture. Everybody is talking Oscars."

Jack beamed. Then James Marshall took center stage and asked for everyone's attention. Jack walked over to stand behind Vicky, picking up another drink on his way. She leaned back into him and smiled famously at the crowd.

Victoria Steele belonged in the blazing glare of her Hollywood. She spoke the language of the actors' tribe, and her every move was calculated for the best camera angle. However false her personality, there was a remarkable charisma about her. She wore her image with pride. Her nails were polished, her hair waved, her waist small, her breasts large, her skin like velvet. Her eyes glittered through her Hollywood mask. She was varnished, gilded, waxed, stamped, glossed, embellished, and adorned in a coat of unreality. She was the perfect model of stardom, however transparent her armor.

Only one thing was missing. Never in her career had she had a major starring role. Never had she been accepted in the inner circle, even though she had schooled herself in its ways. Year after year, Vicky continued to add more diamonds to her hands and more polish to her appearance to hide her discontent and growing unrest.

Over time, Vicky had learned that she could star with men. With men there was no mask. She liked them and she knew that they liked her. She knew exactly when to be arrogant and when to be seductive. She could be the perfect temptress. Tonight, Lorelei she would be. And her target was that best-selling author, the man of the hour, Jack Murphy. She turned her head slightly and smiled up at him.

James Marshall was finishing his speech. "We have an early day tomorrow, so I think we are going to bid you all a good night. I want to thank our Irish hostess, the fairest of the fair, the very beautiful Shannon Murphy." Marshall looked over to the doorway where she stood, and she smiled graciously in acknowledgment.

"In her honor, I'll leave you with this bit of Irish poetry," he continued. Then he went into his acting mode, and his deep, resonant baritone filled the room. "A land whose countryside would be bright with cozy homesteads, whose villages would be joyous with the romping of sturdy children, the contests of athletic youths and the songs of comely maidens, whose firesides would be forums for the wisdom of serene old age."

As everyone applauded, Shannon smiled and glanced over in Jack's direction. He was standing behind Vicky, whispering something in her ear. His arm was around her waist. Each time Jack would lean in to say something, she would laugh and throw her head around and look up at him. On one such occasion, he kissed her ear.

Shannon turned quickly and made her way to the front door to bid her guests good night. Jack escorted Vicky to the door, saying, "Allow me to walk you to your car. It's dark out. I know the way." She took his arm and followed him out to the front yard.

Stallard Hopkins started to say something to Shannon as he left. He thought about it for a moment and just continued on his way out of the house. The party was over.

Chapter Fifty-One

Shannon had noticed that some people just didn't know when to leave a cocktail party. It was especially true of the handful of Americans who still lingered. Their small talk seemed to last forever as they stood at the door trying their best to leave. They just didn't know how. A simple, "Good night, I enjoyed your party," would have done nicely, Shannon thought.

Where are the words and smiles, she thought, that I must say and do? How can I do these things and not be judgmental? This is not my world. The core of my universe is something else entirely, and God willing I shall find it.

The last guest finally left and Shannon closed the door. She leaned her back against the door and stood in that position for a long while. All of the forms and faces of "Jack's Bash" filled her thoughts. Her single most haunting memory of the entire evening was that of Jack, not Stal. As she had suspected, Stal was nothing to her now. No, it was Jack whose behavior bothered her deeply. He was truly an illusionist, she realized. And not until tonight had Shannon seen the entire act.

Turning off the porch light, she walked back into the living room. The help had cleaned up quickly and were just packing the last of their equipment. Jack stood at the bar fixing himself a drink. She asked him to get the checks for the help. "Please, they're ready to leave." He went to his office and returned with the checks, thanking them for a "job well done."

Shannon showed them to the kitchen door and saw them out, then returned and stood in the middle of the room. "Jack, I shouldn't even approach this with you right now. You've had a lot to drink tonight. But did you expect me not to notice or say anything about you hanging all over Vicky Steele? I saw you kiss her good night standing next to the car."

"Shannon, I gave her a peck good night. You know that is perfectly acceptable in some circles, to show people that you like them."

She interrupted him. "You always have a string of words to cover up the truth. After all, that is what you do. You deal in words. And make believe."

"What is that supposed to mean?"

"Never mind. It's fruitless to try to talk with you. I wonder why I'm wasting my breath." There was contempt in every word she uttered. She shook her head. "What's happening to us, Jack?"

Jack rocked back and forth on his heels. Then, waving his arms in the air, he said, "I love you, Shannon. You're beautiful and smart, and now you're rich. But you don't enjoy life like I do. All you want are the simple, meaningless things."

"How dare you say that? I love life. I love people. And yes, 'tis true, I do enjoy the simple things. I don't need to be going all over the world, on permanent holiday, shopping in fine stores for clothes which I don't need nor would never wear. I don't need to eat in expensive restaurants every night, and stay up late at cocktail parties. Speaking of meaningless."

Jack interrupted her. "Did it ever occur to you that perhaps I would like to do more? To have more in my life?" He reached for his drink and took a big swallow. "And when do we begin to have fun again?" he demanded furiously.

"Fun? You seem to be doing quite well in that area." She stopped. She did not like herself at that moment, nor did she need this futile exchange. She took a very careful look at her husband. Behind the dreary, sodden pigment of his face, she saw a totally different Jack from the one she thought she knew. For the first time, she realized that he was indistinguishable from most every other man she had ever met. Like the rest of them, his life centered around a witless preoccupation with himself alone. This realization saddened Shannon beyond measure. She looked at him with a cold, detached affection for what had been and would be no longer. She could envision her future, and he was not a part of it. Mostly by unspoken consent, she knew that her marriage to Jack was coming to an end.

"I'm going to bed," she said. "I'm tired."

"Go on," he mumbled boozily. "Run from it."

"I'm not running from anything, not any more. I'm tired. Good night."

Jack sat at the bar, awash in self pity. His thoughts floated dumbly in a pool of whisky. Without taking his clothes off, he lay down on the couch. In a matter of minutes, he passed out.

Alone in her bedroom, Shannon undressed and put on a simple nightgown. She sat down on the bed and put her hands to her face. She had to admit that her husband did not love her, that perhaps he did not know how and never would. It was something she had not allowed herself to believe until now. Her marriage was ruined. Suddenly, it was final, merciless and complete. Her mind could not connect all the details, only an overview of these painful circumstances. She knew the days ahead would be filled with anger and loss.

She had made many attempts to see clearly and to speak honestly with Jack about their marriage, but they had always ended in furious arguments. Now, the words had run out for Shannon. She had no more energy to continue the fight.

She turned off her light and laid her head upon her pillow. She pulled the covers over her, and then began to cry. She could not control her sobbing. Finally, she cried herself to sleep.

Chapter Fifty-Two

Any time Shannon became upset, it showed in her eyes. The next morning when Jack entered the kitchen, he knew immediately that everything was not back to normal. Today was much different than any other day they had ever spent together.

"Go ahead, Shannon. Spit it out. Are you still upset over last night?"

"I'm not in the least upset, Jack. Would like some coffee?"

"Yes."

She sloshed some in his cup. "All right. Let's cut the I-don't-know-what-you're-talking-about routine and get to the point. I will not live under the same roof with my husband while he makes it with another woman. I won't be part of such a disgrace in my own household."

"Now wait a minute." Jack jumped in. "I think you're a little off base here. I talked with Vicky, sure. And you talked with your old flame, Stal. Hell, at least I haven't been to bed with Vicky. Is my memory serving me right, or not only have I had to endure Stal, but another old flame of yours, Bruce? Exactly how many more will come out of the woodwork?" He had a nasty look on his face.

Shannon glared at him, barely able to control the urge to slap him. He stood up. After a long and furious silence, he snapped, "All right. What do you want?"

At that, she calmed down a little. "I think I should move into the cottage for a while. It will be finished soon. I think that we should get some distance from each other, and take some time to think."

"What is there to think about?" he asked, a little too quickly. "Oh, that's real cute. I live here and you go and live somewhere else. What will that prove?"

"Jack," she said, cutting him off, "you've changed a great deal. Or perhaps you haven't changed at all. Perhaps the real Jack Murphy has shown his face. It could be that you're just tired of me, or that I wasn't what you thought I was, or what you want me to be. Listen to me, Jack. I love you. I've given my all to you. I married you. Damn it," she made a fist, "why am I defending myself? The truth is, Jack, that you have been very selfish. Everything that has happened has been centered around you, your ideas, your wants and your needs. I didn't want this giant house. I wanted a modest home by the sea. I don't want expensive clothes and perfume. That's not me. That is some woman that you want me to be."

"Don't say that, Shannon, please."

She forged ahead. "Is Vicky Steele more your type? That's it. You are bored with me."

Jack rubbed his eyes wearily. "It's true that I like to see you all decked out, and show you off. Hell, you're a beautiful woman. And yes, I like to travel and go places I've never been. For the first time in my life I can afford it. I like going first class. I don't feel like apologizing for it." His face was flushed.

"Fine, Jack. We're not talking about whether we fly first class or coach here. We're talking about our future, if there is one. You know, you've changed since your last trip to New York." She paused, as if something deep inside her said not to ask her next question. "Were you with another woman in New York? Tell me the truth."

"Why would you ask such a thing, Shannon?"

"A woman knows these things, Jack." Now, after she had asked the question, she was certain she was right. "Were you?"

"No, I was not." He glanced away.

"Jack, you've been like a kaleidoscope these past few weeks, all manner of colors, ever changing. You seem on edge. You stay gone a lot, and you spend a great deal of your time in the pub, and you seem to be drinking more than usual." She did not enjoy this conversation, but felt that she must get at the truth. "I'll ask you again, and look at me this time. Were you with another woman in New York?"

"Shannon, I don't like this game that you're playing."

"Game? Jack, I hardly think that this is a game. Perhaps that is what life is all about to you. A game. We'll just change the script as we go along. Is that it?" She saw that it was hopeless. "Forget it, Jack. You're not answering my question. This is getting nowhere."

"Shannon, listen. First, I want you to promise me that you're not going to move into the cottage. Okay, we can work this out, but not if you go over there. Second, we shouldn't make something bigger than it is. I had a few drinks and I acted a little out of line with Vicky. No more, no less. It's not like I went to bed with her, for God's sake." He forced a smile. "Now, look. Today they begin shooting. Let's drive over to Kinsale and watch a little of the first day. Whadda ya say? It'll be fun."

Shannon shook her head, "No, I really don't want to do that. Not today, Jack. You go."

He did not try and talk her into it. "Okay, if you're sure. I'll just run over for a little while, then I'll be home before dark." He got up from his chair and put his arm around Shannon's neck. Leaning down, he kissed her cheek. She did not move.

"Hey, don't worry about this. It'll pass," he waved his hand in dismissal.

God, how she hated it when he took this paternal attitude, this contrived, detached manner. She always felt vanquished by his uncanny ability to be in the right, even when he wasn't. Jack dressed and left for Kinsale, and she stood at the kitchen door and watched him go.

She went into the sun room and sat down, her eyes fixed on the sea. The bit of sun that managed to break through the cloud cover made the day a little brighter. She was desperately lonely, and all the wonderful moments in her life could not help her overcome it. This must be the feeling that Brien had when he was put in jail in London, she thought. She decided to call him. Her spirits rose as she went to the phone in the kitchen and dialed the number. An unfamiliar voice answered.

"Hello, is this Brien Kelly's? Do I have the right number?" She paused. "This is Shannon Kelly. Murphy. Brien's sister."

"Hello, yes, it is Brien's home, but he left a while ago for the boat dock. I'm Margaret, a friend of Brien's. I'm happy to meet you. Brien speaks of you often."

"Margaret, I'm happy to meet you, too. Would you just tell Brien I called? Nothing important. I only wanted to say hello."

"I will, yes. He'll be sorry he missed you. Will you call back?"

"Perhaps tomorrow." Pausing, she said, "Good-bye, then."

Shannon hung up and made herself some tea. She sat reflecting on the events of the morning. How quickly things could change, she thought. She fidgeted with her skirt, settling herself in the sunroom couch, and stared off into space. Darkness moved in on the Tahilla coast, bringing with it a threat of heavy weather. There was no way she could know what was to happen in the next few hours.

Chapter Fifty-Three

The old seaman pulled on his beard with weatherbeaten hands. "Well, lads, what about it?" Brien looked at the overcast skies. "I don't think I'd chance it," the old man cautioned. "Looks like it might blow a good one today." Brien and two others stood said by side, gazing out over the mountains at the ominous Dingle sky.

"Sinister, she is," the old sea captain continued, squinting his eyes as he spoke. He would always talk about the sea as if it were an old mistress that he had courted for years, but could never quite get to marry him.

One of the younger fishermen spoke up. "She doesn't look all that bad. Look," he said, pointing. "The main body of those heavy dark clouds is moving off in that direction, away from the Blasket Islands. Heck, it may be a little rough startin' out, but she'll clear in two hours' time."

"I wouldn't count on it," another sailor ventured.

"I still say she'll be all right," the first man asserted.

Just then Mac, the owner of Brien's boat, arrived. He greeted everyone with a good morning, then went directly to the old sea captain and asked him what he thought of the weather.

"I dare say not to go out today," the old man said with a frown. "Like a woman, 'tis the sea that rules us still."

Brien was the least experienced in the group, although, as Mac's old friend, he was responsible for the second boat. He turned to Mac and said,

"What if we only go just beyond the Blaskets, staying close to shore?" Mac considered his question as he watched the looming clouds and sipped his coffee.

"The wind is fine now," Mac said. "As long as she doesn't change on us."

"Hell, the old man runs at the first drop of rain," said a fisherman.

"Mind you, listen," the old man said. "Don't let that calm fool you. I've seen the likes of this a thousand times, if I've seen it once. She looks like she's going to blow by, then in a flash of a second, the wind changes and she comes back on you like the Almighty himself. Jesus, Mary and Joseph, I can recall losing three boats back in '52, on just a day such as this."

One of the men turned to Mac. "I agree with the lad, here. If we stay close to the Blaskets, watch the sky and the wind carefully—"

The other man jumped in. "And we have our radios. Besides, I could use the money." His hair had fallen down in front of his eyes, so he took off his cap to pull it back. "We've been out in much worse looking skies. What are we, fishermen or women?" He laughed and put his cap back on.

"Better to be a living woman then a dead fishermen."

"'Tis true, lads," the old man agreed, leaning on the railing.

Mac looked down at the dock, then at his crew, then at his newest hand. "What do you see, Brien?"

Brien's curious eyes swept the horizon. "'Tis brighter now. Look," he said pointing. "I say we go, but stay close to the island."

"Lads," the old captain said quietly, "It's yer own business, but I'd say wait two hours, then decide."

"If we wait two hours then there's no reason to go at all," one said sternly.

"Okay, let's make ready." Mac had made a decision. He began giving directions to make way. As the boats pulled away from the dock, the old sea captain stood motionless, watching. In his mind, he saw all the sailors and fishermen of his past flash before him. He recalled the faces of those who had sunk in the salt filled urn of the sea, vanished. Coming back to the present, the old man shouted, "God be with ye, lads."

The two boats made their way out to sea through the foaming water. They passed by the old lighthouse and turned toward the Blasket Islands. "Brien," Mac called out from his boat, "I think we should make way to the other side of the Blaskets. I hear tell that fishing has been good in those waters lately."

Brien waved his hand in compliance. He turned to his mate, pointing off to starboard. "This light chop is not so bad, but look over there. Seems to be getting darker." The mate just nodded his head. Brien shouted to the boat in front. "Mac. Mac. Come alongside." The two boats moved closer. "Whadda ya think, Mac? Should we turn and go back in?"

Mac studied on it, then called out, "Let's continue on for a spell and keep watch. If the weather starts to move closer to us, we'll turn back." The two boats made way toward the Blaskets. Brien noticed that the wind had picked up a little, and the light chop was now small whitecaps. At this point, he was not overly concerned.

There was a ghostly light under the clouds that hung tight to the tops of the mountains. Off in the distance, a maze of darkness filled the sky. The fog did not lift as expected, but began to spread over the water. Ahead, the sky appeared brighter, so they continued. Brien could see Mac in the boat ahead, standing near the rail smoking a cigarette.

Off in the distant sky new colors formed. Although Brien noticed the fast moving clouds, it didn't disturb him. He was confident that Mac was in complete control, and that if the wind changed or the sea became rough, he would turn back. It had happened to them before. Fishing off Dingle, Brien had learned quickly that a fishermen must surrender to the sea.

"Aye, never test the sea," the old captain had always said. "Always give it more than a wee consideration, lads, before going out into her, you know. The worst place ever there was is to be in her core during a blow, for she'll take ye into her hollow where no man returns."

The fishermen had told Brien to pay no attention to the old man, that he was a little crazy. Brien didn't think that he was crazy. He had watched as they made sport of the old wharf rat, offering him his choice of a pound or twenty pence. He always took the smaller amount, telling them he liked the gold color of the twenty pence. They would laugh uproariously. This happened time after time. One day, Brien asked him why he didn't take the pound, and if he didn't know it was worth far more money. "It's like this, lad," he answered. "If I ever took the pound, then they'd stop giving me twenty pence, do ye see?"

The old man was wiser than all the rest, Brien saw. He thought of him now, and began to wish they had listened to him about the weather. The wind was picking up, and Brien pulled his jacket tight around his neck. As the boats moved deeper into the heart of the sea, a wind quickly came upon them. In a flash, the mist took away the visibility. It started to rain in earnest. The wind picked up and the waves got steeper. The storm had gained control of the sea.

Brien turned to see how his mate was doing. "Danny? Everything okay?"

"I guess so, yes. But I must admit I'm a little scared."

"Don't ye worry, Danny boy. Mac will turn back if he thinks it's getting too rough."

"Brien, I think we should turn back now. Look at the size of those waves. Come on, get Mac on the radio. Let's talk with him about it, okay?" There was urgency in his voice.

"Okay, Danny. See if you can find the radio." The waves rocked the boat violently. "Danny, the radio?" He turned as an enormous wave crashed against the boat. Danny was not to be found. He was gone, swept overboard.

"Mac, Mac!" Brien called. "Man overboard! Mac, can you hear me?" He pulled on the bell chain as hard as he could and strained his ears for a signal from the other boat. He blew the horn as the waves moved the boat up and down like a match stick in the wind.

About this time, Brien lost control of his boat. The wind continued to howl and the bitter cold slashed at Brien's face as the boat rose and crashed against the mighty waves. Brien called out again in desperation. "Mac! Mac! Can you see me? Can you hear me? Please, Mac, answer me."

He heard nothing but the unrelenting wind and the waves crashing over the bow. Salt foam covered his face and his eyes were on fire. "Hail, Mary, full of grace," he repeated the prayer over and over. During these wild moments, Brien's brief life flashed before him. He saw his parents and his dear Shannon. He thought of Margaret, waiting for him on shore. He realized in this cold and furious place of violence that sudden death lay before him. "The sea knows no names." That was the last thought that Brien was ever to have.

Chapter Fifty-Four

Shannon stood in her kitchen looking out at the sea, watching the storm that seemed to cover half of Ireland. Suddenly she felt a stab of fear, and could not think of any reason for it. She picked up the telephone and dialed Brien's home again. It was after six in the evening, and she expected he would be home by now. She allowed the phone to ring for a very long time. No answer. She had just looked at the clock on the kitchen wall, but she looked again. It was ten past six, only five minutes since she last looked.

She turned on several lights and sat down at the kitchen table, listening to the wind smash against the window. She thought of calling Paddy, but realized she did not even know if he had a phone. She wished again that she could talk with Brien. Her heart felt battered.

She wished Jack were here. The party and this morning's fight had left her utterly drained, and she longed to make peace. She sat for a long time without moving, her arms stretched out across the table. Above the sounds of the wind and rain, she heard a faint fog horn and the ghostly tolling of a bell. No one should be out in this weather, she thought.

She made herself some more tea and returned to the table, watching the clock and wondering if Jack were okay, and especially if Brien were safe. "I wonder if anyone is all right, even myself," she said aloud. "What's wrong with everybody?"

It seemed a lifetime since she had sat in her car on the strand and looked out to sea for an hour, thinking her thoughts. In fact, it had only been a few days. How clear her perceptions of life had been that day. Now she was right back where she started. "How can I understand another if I don't understand myself?" she asked the silence of her kitchen. The same questions scrolled through her mind in an endless loop. Scenes from her past swarmed before her, and once again she was filled with self doubt. What makes people destroy themselves? She had such grand dreams as a child. She was ambitious to be a wife and mother, of course. But beyond that, her greatest desire as a woman was simply to love and be loved. She had failed.

Shannon picked up the telephone and called Brien yet another time. There was still no answer, and the weather was getting steadily worse. The strain was getting to her. She went to the sunroom, stretched out on the couch and lay motionless. Arms folded over her head, covering her eyes, she listened to the storm, listened for the telephone. Late afternoon ticked into early evening. No message from Brien. No word from Jack.

In a cozy little pub in Kinsale, Jack paid no attention to the storm going on outside. He was not worried. He certainly was not thinking about Shannon. He was thinking about Jack. He was happy. Several members of the production troop sat at the bar talking about how the first day of filming went, and he listened eagerly. They were absolutely elated, by the sound of it.

"So, Jack. How did you like it? Is it what you thought it would be?" Victoria Steele asked, raising her glass to her lips.

"Very interesting. I always thought movies started filming at the beginning of the story. It's amazing how it jumps around. I can't believe how much you can get done in a single day, though I have to admit it was a long one. We'd still be there if it weren't for the weather." He looked at his watch. "Can that be right? Is it a quarter to seven already?"

Vicky looked at the clock over the bar. "Sure is. Time flies when you're having fun."

"Vicky, I need to be getting back to Tahilla."

"Oh, Jack," she pouted. "Not right now. Please, one more."

The production crew started drifting out the door. "Hey, you guys. We're going up the street for a bite to eat. Wanna come?"

"No. You go on. We're going to hang in here," Vicky answered. "Besides, it's raining cats and dogs."

"Nice meeting you, Mr. Murphy. Love your story."

Vicky took Jack by the arm, suggesting they find a booth. She slipped in and pulled Jack in behind her. "Now, isn't this better than those stiff bar stools? Plus I can be closer to you," she said with a laugh. "You know what loose women us movie types can be." She motioned for the waitress to bring over two more drinks.

"You know, Jack, when you kissed me goodnight at the party that I actually got hot. Can you believe that? I was like a little schoolgirl about to wet my pants. And I do mean wet my pants, if you get my drift."

"Vicky, you are a bad, bad girl," he said, but he was grinning from ear to ear.

Vicky leaned over and gave Jack a long, tender kiss. Her mouth was soft and her manner was gentle. "I like you, Jack Murphy," she said. "I don't come on to just anybody. But I'll tell you one thing," she softened her voice. "I do come with a guarantee. A written promise of quality. I'm issuing you a voucher to that effect."

The waitress brought their drinks and left. Jack put his arm around Vicky's shoulder, gazed into her eyes, then leaned closer and kissed her. She let her hand slide down onto his knee, and then a little toward his thigh.

"Vicky. We can't start something like this that we can't finish." He sat up straight and looked at his watch. "It's seven-thirty already."

"Now what?"

"What now is that I've got to go home."

"Just one more drink. I enjoy your company so much, and I'm already bored here in Kinsale. Look at this pub. It's dead. The whole town rolls up the sidewalks by eight o'clock. And listen to that wind. We're better off right here. Please. You still have your voucher you haven't cashed in." She raised her glass. "Two more, waitress," she called out.

"Can I have a rain check on my voucher?" Jack asked.

"Sorry, sir. Company policy won't allow us to extend the expiration date. Must be used by midnight tonight. You understand. Policy is policy." She really was a pretty good actress, he reflected. When their drinks arrived, he asked for the check.

Vicky sat back in the booth, her large and very beautiful dark eyes fixed on Jack. "What color would you say my eyes are?"

Jack looked deeply into her eyes. "Blue?"

"Nope. Try again."

"Black? Dark brown?"

"Nope."

"I give up. What color are they?"

"Believe it or not, they are purple. Just like Elizabeth Taylor's. I'll bet you've never been with a woman with purple eyes."

Jack took a big sip of his drink. He was not as fascinated by her eye color as she seemed to be. "Vicky, come on. Let's go."

"Okay, if we must. Damn, Jack. You're no fun."

"Believe me Vicky, I would like to stay. I could use some R and R."

"What's the matter, sweetheart? Troubles at home?"

Jack did not answer, but started to the door. Vicky followed along behind him. "One nice thing about a little place like Kinsale. Nothing is very far," she said. "Come, I'll walk you to your car."

Jack found his keys and unlocked his car door. He turned and looked at Vicky, then put his arms around her and pulled her close to his body. "It was great today," he told her.

"Don't talk." She pulled his head toward her and fastened her mouth on his, letting her other hand drift down between his legs and do wild things. She could feel him growing in her hand. She fairly squirmed with desire.

The rain pelted down on them. Jack could not remember when he had been so excited. "Please come to my room with me," she whispered. "Don't leave me wanting you like this."

He yielded. He locked the car, took her hand, and walked to the hotel. He had just sense enough to ask himself why he was doing this. Before he met Shannon, this was routine for him. In each and every one of his past relationships, save only Helen, he always needed a little something on the side. In Miami, the last time he was engaged, he found himself with other women in anonymous one night stands. Why?

Vicky unlocked the door and threw her coat on the chair. "Make us a drink," she directed him, pointing to a bottle of whisky sitting on the table. "We'll have to do without ice."

She walked into the bathroom and came out a few minutes later wearing a light blue silk nightgown. In her hand, she carried a small mirror and a plastic vial. Jack knew exactly what it was, and he didn't like it.

"Darling," Vicky said, placing the mirror on the table, "we're going to make love like you've never made love before." With a razor blade, she expertly chopped the cocaine into finer particles, then arranged it into two neat rows. She handed him a delicate gold straw. "Here, darling. You go first."

"I don't know," he paused. "I think I'll pass."

"Don't be silly, Jack. This little bit won't harm you. It will relax you. And, I might add, you'll make love as you've never dreamed." She took his hand and placed it on her breast and kissed him, rubbing her body against him in a slow, pulsing rhythm. He felt a surge of excitement. "Oh, Jack, I want you, please. Go ahead. Do it. Take it all and get ready for a wild ride."

Jack inhaled one line, then handed the mirror and straw to Vicky, who did the other line. It hit them both immediately, electrifyingly. She dropped her gown to the floor and switched on a bedside lamp, showing off her spectacularly maintained body. She undressed Jack with swift efficiency, bending to caress him with her mouth.

Then she dove into bed, rolled over on her back, and spread her legs, looking at him like a jungle cat. Jack tried to control his reaction, but it was too much. He ran his tongue right up the middle of her, all the way up to her mouth and then back down again. He ravaged every part of her. The heat between them was intense. Vicky arched her back and writhed in his arms, begging for more.

Then she rolled him over on his back and straddled him, lowering herself onto him and rotating her hips very slowly, watching his face. She began to move faster and faster, almost sobbing in her urgency, then plunged downward with a throaty yell. He gave himself up to her at the same instant. She was absolutely magnificent. It was an Academy Award-winning performance.

The next morning Jack awakened and gathered up his clothes. He remembered why he didn't like cocaine. It was because when it wore off, everything was uglier than it had been before. He looked at Vicky's sexy body and realized how much money had gone into perfecting it. He looked at his own sorry reflection in the bathroom mirror and saw that he was older than he would have wished. He looked around the room where the energy had been so high the night before. Pathetic.

He showered and dressed and walked over to the bed, reaching down and kissing Vicky lightly. She stirred and mumbled and came awake. "Damn," she said. "What time is it, anyway?"

Jack looked at his watch. "It's a little after seven."

"Oh, thank God. I don't have to be on the set today until nine-thirty." She pulled him down beside her. "I want to see you again. Promise."

Jack nodded. "I've really got to go," he said.

"Call me." She swung her legs over the side of the bed and sat staring at the floor.

Jack headed to his car. He felt sick. He felt hung over. He felt like crying. "What the hell is wrong with you?" he asked himself. He sat there in his car a long while, just shaking his head.

Chapter Fifty-Five

It was after eight o'clock when Shannon finally stirred from her place on the couch in the sunroom. The storm was blowing itself out, though not without a few parting blasts. She looked around. Jack had not returned from Kinsale. She was hungry, but didn't want to go through the motions of fixing anything. She decided on a cup of tea and some brown bread. The telephone rang just as she reached the kitchen. "Is this Shannon Kelly?"

"It is, yes. I'm Mrs. Shannon Kelly Murphy."

"Mrs. Murphy, this is Officer Quinn from the garda in Dingle. Your brother Brien is missing. He and three others went out in two boats, and they haven't returned. There was a terrible storm. We know they were going to fish near the Blasket Islands, and we have a search party down there all along the coast and on the strand looking for them. I'm sorry, Mrs. Murphy, but that is all the news I have at the moment. I will keep you informed."

Shannon thanked him and quietly hung up the receiver. So that was it. Now she understood the reason for her flash of foreboding earlier in the day. Brien! In that strange silence, she saw the face of her brother, banished forever to the bottom of the sea. The image would not leave her mind. She walked slowly to the kitchen window and stared into the darkness. Out there, surrounding the island and claiming her thoughts, was the roaring sea. She recalled the lines she had heard so many times as a child. The sea giveth, and the sea taketh away, it was said all up and down the coast. Shannon did not break down and cry, not just yet. She was still frozen in shock. A single tear formed in the corner of her eye and slid slowly down her cheek.

Shannon felt that she had been here before, had known these same emotions. The first time was when her sister Bridget died. She could still hear her mother's cries late at night above the howling of the wind against their cottage, and her young brother's wailing on the day of the funeral. She could see her father's eyes, sad and dull.

Then, one day only a couple of years ago, her father was gone, too. That day she had awakened in a world of madness. She could not see her life without him in it. A few months later, her mother had followed him in death.

And now Brien, lost in time someplace. They had not found his body yet, but she knew. She wanted to pray, but couldn't. She could feel an empty space inside her heart where he once lived. Her whole family had departed this earth. She was completely and utterly alone.

Suddenly, with a shock of recognition that flashed across her brain like a bolt of lightning, she knew why Jack had not returned from Kinsale. There and then, she made the decision to leave him. She looked down at her hands. Slowly, she removed her wedding band and laid it on the windowsill.

In that instant, she set herself free. With the voices of her family ringing in her ear, she burst forth into life. She would find the calm dwelling of her Ireland again, in the white beaches, the tidy villages by the sea, the faces of beautiful children, and the sparkle of a dancing lake. A scene out of some classic Irish story flashed before her, living, breathing, and very much alive.

Somewhere between the pain of losing Brien and the decision to leave Jack, Shannon took control of her will. She drew upon the strength given to her by her father to shake off the heavy hand of guilt and insecurity, for these things did not have a place among the living. The emotional pressure and inner conflicts began to subside. Finally, she stopped doubting her own worthiness.

Moving away from the window, she put water on to boil, then sat down at the kitchen table. She could almost see her father sitting across from her. "Humility, my little Shannon, is the true road to happiness," he would say. "Humility. 'Tis the virtue that disposes a woman to face reality and change what you can, and learn to make the best of what you cannot change. This is living a realistic life."

She must, she thought, begin a life of renewal, a broader and more inspiring vision of her own happiness. She must strengthen her ability to deal with her own reality. Self-possession and self-management were the only tools she needed. She knew that this commitment would take time and application.

The telephone rang just as the water began to boil. Shannon took the pot off the stove and stood watching the phone. One ring. Then two. Now three. Finally she picked up the receiver.

"Hello. This is Shannon Murphy."

"Mrs. Murphy. This is Officer Quinn, in Dingle."

"Yes," Shannon said softly. "I know. You're going to tell me that you have news of Brien. He's gone isn't he?"

"He is, Mrs. Murphy. They found his boat against the rocks near the Blaskets. His body had been thrown onto the rocks. They never found the other lad. I'm sorry."

Her fears were confirmed. A tear began to fall from her eyes, then another, and another. She wept softly as she tried to speak with Officer Quinn.

"We'll make arrangements to have Brien brought home to Kenmare."

"I'm very sorry, Mrs. Murphy. Will you be all right?"

"I will. Thank you, Mr. Quinn. Good-bye now."

Shannon sat down at the table and bowed her head, crying quietly. She got up and went to her bedroom and found a photo of herself and Brien as kids, and looked at it for a long time. Putting her cheek to his picture, she broke down and began to cry uncontrollably. She tried to bridle her emotions, but could not. She sat with her hands against her face, crying for a very long time. My brother, she thought. My brother!

Finally, she went to the bathroom and washed her face, holding a towel to her eyes for a long time. The soft towel felt comforting. I must eat something, she thought. She returned to the kitchen and made herself hot tea and a plate of leftover meat and potatoes. After one or two bites, she realized that she could not eat, so she cleared the table. Looking at the clock as she passed, she saw that it was after ten. Jack was still not home, and she was positive he would not be this night.

She looked around the house. It suddenly seemed contrived. Its rooms felt even larger than before, and seemed overdecorated. She felt completely out of place. This was a lonely house, she thought, with not an ounce of history. No memories, no family, no friends. It was just a house, nothing more.

Chapter Fifty-Six

The next morning, Shannon was awakened by the telephone. She reached across the bed and grabbed the receiver. Still groggy from sleep, she murmured, "Hello."

"Shannon, this is Jack. Good morning."

"Hello, Jack. You didn't come home last night."

"To tell you the truth, I had a few too many drinks with the crew last night. I didn't think I should drive for fear I might get into an accident. I tried to call you, but then I fell off to sleep. I'm sorry. Are you all right? You sound down."

"Jack. Brien is dead. He was killed last night in a storm at sea."

"What? Brien, killed? Oh, Shannon, oh, I'm so sorry. I'll get right home."

"Don't rush. I'm fine. I wouldn't want you to get into an accident. We have enough troubles for one day."

"Shannon, I'm so sorry. I know what Brien."

She interrupted him. "Jack, I don't feel like talking right now. I'll speak with you when you get home."

Shannon dressed and went to the kitchen. She fixed herself eggs with scones and jam, and drank several cups of hot coffee. Then she called to make arrangements for Brien's body to be delivered to Kenmare, and also discussed the funeral.

By the time she arrived in Kenmare, Father Mulvany was waiting for her at the funeral home. "Hello, my child. I just got the news. I came right over." The priest was a tall, lean man with kind blue eyes and a full head of white hair. Shannon had known him all her life. He had given her first communion, and had been to dinner at their house many times. "God bless you, my child, and God bless Brien," he said softly. Another priest was standing by his side, and he introduced them. "Shannon, I'd like you to meet Father Hennessey. He has just been assigned to us here in Kenmare."

"Pleasure to meet you," he said, extending his hand and smiling sweetly. "I'm sorry about your brother." She looked at him, filled with pain, and nodded. She thought him to be younger than herself. He was a good looking man, with short, dark hair. He stood tall and had a kind face.

After making the funeral arrangements and seeing that everything was in order, she walked out a little behind the others with Father Hennessey at her side. She glanced at him and spoke in a low voice. "Father, I must talk with you about something. May I make an appointment?"

"You can, yes, Shannon. But no need for an appointment. Would you like to visit today? Now?"

"I would. Can I come to your office?"

"Sure," he said, smiling. "We'll go directly." Shannon got into her car and drove to the church, arriving just before the priests. She stood by her car waiting for them to park.

Father Hennessey took her gently by the arm. "Come," he said.

"Will you be needing me?" Father Mulvany asked.

"No, thank you, Father," the young priest replied. Shannon was relieved, for what she had to ask would be uncomfortable in front of Father Mulvany. She already knew what his response would be. The father was from the old guard, and a long time friend of the family. Talking to him would be extremely difficult.

She followed the young priest to his office, and they sat across from one another. Shannon looked him directly in the eyes and said, "I must leave my husband."

"I see," he answered. "Why?"

"He has been with other women, Father. There are other things as well, but I should think that reason enough."

"You know divorce is against the law in Ireland. And against God's law as well."

"I do." She paused. "Can I get an annulment?"

"Perhaps. It takes a lot of paperwork and a lot of time, but perhaps." The priest gave her a cheery smile and lowered his voice confidingly. "The church is changing, and Ireland as well. The day will come, and I fear that it's not too far off, when divorce will be legal in Ireland, God forbid."

"I've read that, Father, but I can't wait on the church, or on Ireland. I simply can't stay with Jack. Let me ask you this. What if he filed in America? He'll be going back there, anyway."

"Well, you would still be married by the eyes of the church, and by law in Ireland as well. You could never remarry unless your marriage were annulled, or you were allowed by the church and by Ireland to divorce."

She dropped her eyes, then looked again at the priest. "Will you help me, Father? Can we at least try for an annulment?"

"I will help you, yes. We'll give it a go." Father Hennessey said with no hesitation. His approach came as a great comfort to Shannon. It raised her spirits and bolstered her confidence. She left the Father's office feeling much better than when she arrived.

On the way out of town, Shannon felt a need to stop by the old farm. When she turned off the main road and started down toward the cottage, she saw Mr. O'Shea's pickup in front of the old cottage. She hoped that it was Paddy. She pulled up next to the pickup, and when she got out she heard a voice. "Shannon."

She looked around but didn't see anyone. "Up here." She looked up to see Paddy leaning out of her bedroom window, a big smile on his face.

"Oh, Paddy, you're a sight for sore eyes. I'm needing my friend just now."

Paddy came rushing down the stairs and met her at the front door. "Hi. I was just doing some last minute touch-up." Shannon threw her arms around his neck and hugged him with all her might. She said softly in his ear, "My brother, Brien, was killed in a storm yesterday."

Paddy took her by the shoulders and looked at her suffering face. "How awful, Shannon. How did it happen?"

"He was out fishing, and they were caught in a terrible wind. I guess they lost control of the boat." She paused, trying to hold back the tears. Paddy spoke not a word, but held her closely to him, feeling her anguish and trying to control his own emotions for her sake. His dark eyes clouded over. How he loved this fine woman, and how he wished he could say something that would ease her pain. He stepped back and looked into her eyes, listening as she told him the story.

"I knew something was wrong, even before the call came in from Dingle," she said. "Don't ask me how. I just knew. I was home alone last night when I received the phone call. Jack was in Kinsale, and I haven't seen him yet today. He called this morning."

Paddy took her inside to sit in the main room. Shannon noticed that all the furniture was put back in place and the room looked organized. It was a great comfort to her to see the familiar things of her childhood, and her tears began to subside.

"Paddy, when did you do all this?"

"Today," he answered.

Shannon looked around the house. She had never seen it look so charming, so fresh and clean. "Thank you, Paddy. That was very sweet."

"I enjoyed doing it." Paddy took her hand in his and sat looking at her with kind eyes.

"How's Maura?" Shannon asked, a little cheer returning to her voice.

"She's fine. I can't say the same for her mother, for I think she is worse off than ever. She's going downhill fast. I talked to her about Maura. It's not good, Shannon. I don't know how much longer it can work. I thought a lot about going and getting Maura's things and moving her here with me. That's something I'm going to work on these next few weeks. I've got to."

"I understand," she replied. Paddy stood up and walked across the room, then back again. She rose and moved toward him. "Paddy, will you please hold me?" He took her in his arms and very tenderly pulled her to him. Shannon put her arms around him and held him tightly. They stood there in an embrace for a long time.

She stepped back from him. "Sit," she said kindly. "I need to tell you something." He sat across from her and leaned forward. "I'm leaving Jack," she told him. He sat very still, just looking at her. "Did you hear me? I'm not going to live with Jack any longer. He's been with other women. I can't live like that any longer."

"Do you know this for sure?" Paddy asked.

"I know it as well as my own name."

"But did he say that he had been with someone else?"

"No, not in so many words. But a woman knows these things," she said sternly. "I'm sure he was with the movie star, Victoria Steele, last night in Kinsale. I know it, Paddy. I just know it." She crossed her arms and sat up very straight in her chair. "He didn't come home last night. He stayed all night in Kinsale, and he didn't even call." She frowned. "Am I supposed to live like that, Paddy?" Then, answering her own question, "No. No, I won't live like that."

She sat still, thinking, then glanced down at her watch. "I must be getting on, Paddy. I have some unfinished business to attend to."

He walked her to her car and put his arms around her waist. "If you need anything at all, you know where to find me," he said sympathetically. "I'll be right here all day tomorrow. I still have some work to do to the house." She nodded gratefully and kissed him on the cheek.

On the drive home the road was nearly deserted. Shannon was more relaxed than she had been in a long while. She was glad of that, for she knew it would take everything she had to get her through the next few days. She was anxious for Brien's funeral to be over. And she had to deal with Jack at once.

She reached Tahilla and turned off the main road, then came to her turnoff and drove up the lane. At the top of the hill, she saw Jack's car. Anger rushed inside her as she got out and started walking toward the house. At the back door, she stopped and stood there with her hand on the doorknob. Taking a deep breath, she went inside. Jack was standing in the living room looking at a paper. He turned and saw her, then came walking toward the kitchen. She put a hand up to signal that she did not wish to be touched.

Jack said, with complete sincerity, "Shannon, I am so very sorry about Brien. I don't know what to say." He tried to put his arms around her, but she pulled away.

"No, Jack, please." She managed to hold off the tears.

"God, what a horrible thing. He was so young, such a great kid."

"Why, Jack? I don't understand it. He never hurt anyone. He loved all things. It's the world's loss. This world is not good enough for Brien." She turned and rushed out of the room and went to the bedroom and closed the door. She was gone a long while.

When she came back out, she had regained her composure. The past few days had been devastating, but they had also restored her innate power to her. She was filled with energy and strength, and Jack could see it.

"Jack, please sit down," she said purposefully. "I have something to tell you, and I need you to hear me out." He sat down at the table and she pulled her chair up next to his.

There was no hate in her being, only sorrow for all that had happened. She had lived with him as if in a dream. None of it had been true. The joys and quiet times she and Jack had once shared were not real. She comprehended that the man who stood before her had no balance or clarity in his life. He judged success and failure on visible results alone, and did not understand the root causes of his deficiencies. Shannon understood this about Jack completely. There could never be any hope of their marriage staying together.

"I'm leaving you, Jack. Not because I'm judging you, but because I cannot live with you. We are all helpless and limited in many ways. We grow up with an idealized image of what we must believe and should believe." Shannon did not know where these thoughts and words were coming from. Jack sat still and listened.

"Jack, our past is not something we can disown, or just erase from our lives. It is built into us. There is this pattern to all human behavior that how we act and what we think in the present comes from our past. You know that so much of what we do is unconscious, that our emotions compel us rather than our minds. If we allow our emotions to guide us we become childish and destructive. Children look at something and act on it in direct proportion to how it will make them feel. Adults value things in proportion to how they will affect their well-being."

"Shannon, please let me say something," Jack requested. She looked at him with agreeable eyes. "I know that crying over spilt milk is a waste of time," he said. "I've always tried to pick up and move forward. I think we have something really good here. Sure, we've made some mistakes along the way. We can fix that. We can try. Look around you. We made this lovely home, we have no money worries. Fantastic sex. We truly enjoy each others company."

"Jack, I find it interesting that the words 'love' and 'respect' were not mentioned once."

"Of course I love you and respect you. You know that."

She held up her hand. "We've said all that needs to be said. I will not get into a mind game with you. You have not listened to a word I have said. Not today, not ever. You have some kind of ideal, some self-image, and so do I. We all have a concept of the person we want to be and the life we want to live. I think that you and I have different goals in life. You know, Jack, sometimes a person's goals turn out to be merciless. Often times, that's the price you must pay. I know that you have been with other women. Something inside you drives you to be with them, to prove something. Don't shake your head, Jack. We both know you slept with Vicky last night."

Jack looked down at the table. He knew it would be futile to deny it. "Shannon, I understand everything you are trying to say. Please give me a little credit."

Shannon sat quietly. "Yes," she said. "Go on."

"We can start fresh, work out all of our differences."

"Jack, listen. We cannot begin a new chapter in our lives without feeling the effects from the previous chapters and dealing with them, and that's not going to happen. I'm not trying to judge you, Jack. I'm stating the truth. You don't need to be married, at least not to me." Shannon stood up and looked at him, not with anger but as a positive woman who was in control of herself and her own life.

"I'm moving back to the old cottage after Brien's funeral. And I have already asked to have the church start annulment procedures for a divorce."

Jack looked at her with concern. "You know, Shannon, they say that of the five most stressful things a person can go through, death and divorce are the top two, and you're dealing with both of them at the same time. Don't you want to put off the divorce thing until we've had a chance to think it through?"

"No, Jack. I've already thought it through and made my plans. I will go back to my family's cottage. And what's more, I don't want you sending money to me for the next twenty years. I will take this house and sell it. My car and a one time cash settlement. Is that agreeable?"

"Damn, Shannon. This is all moving so fast," Jack said numbly.

"All right, Jack. Take your time and let me know in a few days what you come up with. I think my offer is a pretty good one. Clean and simple."

"What if we can't get divorced here in Ireland?"

"Well, you can get one in America, for I know you'll be going back. It's true that we would still be married in Ireland, at least for the time being, but I am confident I can get an annulment."

"I can see that your mind is made up."

"It is, Jack."

He stood up and went to the bar to make himself a drink. She realized that he finally comprehended what she had told him. The hardest part was over. She went to him and put her arm around his shoulder. "You'll find whatever it is you're looking for one of these days, and you'll find a woman to share that with. One who will understand and respect your dream." She looked at him warmly and started back to the kitchen. "I'm going to fix something to eat. Would you join me?"

"No, I think not. I'll go into town and eat alone." She nodded in understanding. He put his empty drink glass on the counter and got his coat. He stopped at the door and stood there for a long while, just watching Shannon. She saw a tear in his eye as he quickly turned and left.

Shannon held back her own tears and watched his car until it was out of sight. Then she began to cry, and could not stop. Near mindless with hurt and grief, she stood at the back door as the tears flooded her face.

Chapter Fifty-Seven

Jack and Shannon moved about the house like roommates in a college dorm. They exchanged polite conversation from time to time, but inside they were aware that it was over. Jack moved about the house in near silence, and Shannon stayed mostly in the kitchen. They were shadows only. The house was totally quiet, save the sound of a light rain on the roof. A dismal gray sky covered the landscape, hugging the sea like a Chinese watercolor. No definition, no color, just gray everywhere. The love and happiness in their lives was out like an extinguished candle, with a trickle of smoke rising into the air to remind them that there once was a flame.

Shannon passed by Jack's office door and looked in to see him sitting at his desk, his back to the door, staring out the window at the gray landscape. If ever she had seen the image of a lost and lonely man, Jack was it. She saw him as a man whose faith had betrayed him, whose inner life had come to nothing.

She stopped at the doorway and called his name softly. He looked over his shoulder, then turned to face her. "Jack, this heaviness will pass," she reassured him. Her faith in herself and in God had taught her to believe that. "I don't want to get into it again with you. Lord knows that we have talked this to death. I just want you to get past all this confusion about yourself. We are both exhausted. It's temporary, Jack. You must believe that."

Jack sat back in his chair and relaxed. He looked at Shannon with a slight smile on his face, and nodded. "I know."

She felt relieved. "I'm getting a few clothes together," she said gently. "I'll be staying at the old place tonight. It will be better for both of us." She started for the bedroom. Jack sat motionless as he watched her leave. He knew she was right. The sooner they could get about their lives, the better.

Jack considered his future. He thought that right after Brien's funeral he would leave for Florida. He had always liked Florida, and had felt at home there. As a warm climate kind of person, he felt that it made sense to go back. Not to Miami, he thought. If there was one thing Ireland had taught him, it was that the fast-paced lifestyle of a large city was not fun anymore.

Perhaps he would find a smaller town on the coast. His spirits lifted. Hell, I can afford to live on the ocean now. A great place to write, he told himself. This very office had proven that. The sea had always been good medicine for Jack.

He knew enough about himself to see that his vanity had been hurt. The rejection and downright loneliness he felt at this moment were giving his pride a drubbing, and he knew that he himself had caused it. In some way he understood that his compulsions had been fueled by vanity, and that having it beaten down could only help him avoid such lapses in the future.

Shannon stopped at Jack's office door. "I'm going over to the cottage. I'll be taking just a few things now, and I'll get more later." He started to get up and go to her. "No, please, Jack, not now. There is nothing to say."

He sat back down in the chair. "Thanks, Jack," she said softly, and turned and left the house.

When she arrived at the old farm, there was no one there. She had expected to see Paddy. She went in and looked around, hoping to find him. On the kitchen table, she saw a note. "Dear Shannon," it began. " I had to go to Dublin. Maura's mother is in the hospital, and it looks pretty bad. I'm sorry I won't be here for Brien's funeral. My prayers are with you. I hope to be back in a few days. Love, Paddy."

Shannon put the teakettle on to boil some water for tea, then stood looking out at the light rain from her kitchen window. The house felt cold to her. She had asked Mr. O'Shea to install a new heating system, so she found the thermostat and turned it on. She poured her tea and, taking her cup, she walked around the house slowly, just looking. The restoration was beautiful indeed, she thought, but the house needed life. Some flowers here, a picture there, but most of all it needed human life. Love. Happiness. Cooking. Cleaning. Music. A fire glowing in the fireplace. Muddy shoes on the floor. Dirty dishes in the sink. The aroma of a freshly baked pie.

She sat down in the living room and sipped her tea. The heater had already taken the chill off the house. Her thoughts turned to Brien. They were not sad thoughts, just fond memories. Images of herself and Brien poured through her mind. She looked out the window and could almost see him playing in the rain. No hat, no raincoat, of course. Rain is just something the Irish live with. Brien was a true Irish lad, he was. Her thoughts turned to her sister Bridget. She saw the two of them playing "grown-up" in their mother's room. Bridget was the mother, and Shannon was the baby. A smile came to her face as she recalled the happy times of her childhood.

Shannon heard the ringing of the steeple bell in the village. She got up and went to the front door and stood, watching and listening to the soft rain. As she gazed into the distance, the whole of Ireland appeared in her mind. The bays, bogs, and lagoons, the beaches, mountains, and islands. The plants and birds, the fishing boats, and most of all the people. With all her senses, she imagined the smell of rain-wet fruit on the tree, a fire in the fireplace, the Irish earth after a heavy rain.

She recalled young schoolgirls in uniforms, walking to school. And little dirty-faced boys in their white shirts and blue ties trying to be noticed by the little girls. She remembered with joy her first kiss, and how she had had to go to confession because she enjoyed it.

About that time, the rain stopped and the sky grew bright again. A sunbeam broke through the clouds and stopped right on top of the mountains. She thought that she had never seen them as beautiful as they were today. She was looking at her world with new eyes.

Shannon pushed her fingers through her hair and drew it back from her face to look up at the sky. Then she began to unpack her clothes. She took out a piece of paper and began making a shopping list. She smiled to herself as she wrote down the words "chocolate cake." Paddy had gone on and on one day about his mother's chocolate cake.

She took out another piece of paper and started a different list. Solicitor. Priest. Flowers. Bank. Then, to her own surprise, she wrote, "Shannon Kelly."

Chapter Fifty-Eight

Over the next few days, Jack and Shannon lived in a state of truce. They treated each other with civility, like old friends would. When they came into contact with one another, there was no sign of hostility in either of their attitudes. Shannon certainly felt no hate toward Jack. However, she would rather not have shared his company. As most married couples, they would mention topics from long ago, which had the potential to become disputes. Shannon never allowed this to happen during these last few days. It was she who kept the relationship on a sane and mature level. Jack tried several times to renew the reason for the break-up, and twice he even tried to suggest that they give it another try, although he knew in the soul of his being that it was over.

During the ordeal of Brien's funeral, Jack had been a saint toward Shannon. She was deeply touched by his show of respect and support. She did not cry once during the Mass, but sat quietly between Jack and Margaret. The church was filled to the brim with village people. Many of Brien's old schoolmates and friends could be heard throughout the church, sobbing. People greeted Shannon with tear-filled eyes. She even saw tears on Jack's cheeks.

Margaret seemed to take Brien's death the hardest. She was a lost child, inconsolable, bereft of the joy and singing that had once filled her spirit. She felt deeply betrayed by life, for it had taken all her dreams from her in one terrible hour.

Later, standing by the grave, Shannon considered why she, herself, was not crying. So many people, she couldn't count them all, stopped to say a kind word or offer a warm, comforting hug. They were weeping, but not one tear had fallen from her own cheek that day. She could place the core of her feelings at this moment. As she stood at the grave site in a state of numb disbelief, she recognized that this funeral was like none other she had known. There, before her, was the mystery of life. She asked herself, is there a next life? Or is it a continuance of this one? Do we take all our errors and confusions with us, or do they vanish into nothingness? A thousand pages from her life flipped through her mind as she looked down at Brien's grave.

Somehow in the midst of it all, Shannon realized that she had made it through. Her spirit was still intact, and she knew that she had stayed true to herself and preserved her integrity. This revelation lifted her spirits as she realized that her bruised soul would endure. At that moment, a bird lilted a song of hope from a tree overhead. Knowing that all people's basic drive toward fulfillment was rooted in love, she realized that now, more than ever, she wanted to embrace life. For her, it must be solid and real. She wanted to share it with a true love who was capable of sincere respect and caring. She wanted two lives to be lived as one.

Shannon was fully aware that the kind of love she wanted was rare. She was deep in thought when Jack pulled her arm. "Shannon, it's time to go." She looked around and most of the people were already gone. She took Jack's arm and started slowly toward the car. When she got there, she stood for a long while holding Margaret, comforting her. With a shy look, Margaret said, "I don't want to lose contact with you. Is that all right?"

"Oh, it is, yes. Please write to me, call me, or come and visit me after you've settled in London."

"I'm not going back to England. I have found a home in Ireland, in Dingle. I have my work. Our little house ..." she paused, unable to go on.

"I understand," Shannon said. "I want to help you, Margaret. I want you to keep the car and the other things. They belong to you just as much as Brien. Are you sure you wouldn't like to come by the house just now and rest a bit?" Margaret shook her head and drove off in the direction of Dingle.

With Brien's funeral behind her, Shannon went back to the task of reordering her own life. She made several trips from the big house to the cottage, carrying a few items each time. She stocked the cottage with groceries and made the place comfortable.

She hadn't seen anything of Paddy. Every time she drove up to the cottage, her heart would jump with excitement at the thought that she might see him. It worried her that she had not heard from him for so long. One day she called Mr. O'Shea asking if he had seen Paddy, saying that she had some questions for him about the house. Mr. O'Shea said he hadn't heard from Paddy, but as soon as he did he would relay the message. Shannon tried to make it sound unimportant, saying that it could wait until he returned.

The following week, Jack and Shannon visited the solicitor to transfer title to the house and work out a settlement. Jack surprised her by insisting on a much larger amount than she had requested, reminding her that he cared for her and was determined that she should want for nothing. They moved a few of the smaller antiques to the cottage and made arrangements for an antique dealer to pick up the remaining pieces to sell at a store in Dublin. Jack took a flight to America the next day, leaving the remaining details to Shannon.

And now she sat at the cottage window, watching the fog invade the shoreline. She leaned forward and allowed her head to rest on the glass. The moisture of her breath made her a ring on the window. She was exhausted.

All this time with Jack, gone, for nothing, she thought. All the energy wasted, all the love vanished. She pulled back from the window and glanced at a nearby table. A small lamp cast a shadow on a photograph in a wooden frame. It was a picture of herself, Bridget, Brien and their father's horse, Nell. It looked as if everyone, including the horse, was smiling, except for Shannon. They were all dressed up in their finest clothes, so perhaps it was Easter, or Christmas, some holiday. She could not remember when it was taken or why. She couldn't even remember who took the picture. Why this block? She reached over and picked up the picture and studied it closely.

In the silence, she realized that she had buried a thousand acts, moments and thoughts from her past. They had become mere shadows in her memory as she had struggled to inhabit a life not of her own making. Now, like a melody not heard in years, it all began to appear in her mind, as real and familiar as it ever had been. The entire, complex structure of her past came into focus before her.

Chapter Fifty-Nine

Jack had just sat down at the bar and ordered a drink when he heard a loud voice from across the room. "Jack! Jack Murphy!" Jack looked up to see Sam Bennett waving his arms as he strode toward the bar.

"My God, it's Texas Sam," Jack said with a broad smile on his face as he reached out to shake his hand.

Sam grabbed him and gave him a big bear hug. Slapping him on the back, Sam asked, "What brings you to New York?"

"Well, first, sit down and have a drink, Sam," Jack motioned for the bartender as he pulled up a stool. "I flew in from Ireland two days ago. I stopped in to see my editor at Kingdom House, and now I'm waiting for a flight to Miami. I've been living in Ireland for the past few years, married to a gorgeous Irish woman, and writing books. My latest is being made into a movie, and they're filming in Ireland right now."

"I've been reading about that, Jack. Way to go!"

"Well, my career is going like a house afire, but I'm sad to report that Shannon and I aren't together any longer. That's why I'm on my way to Florida. I'm thinking about relocating there. My next book is set in the Caribbean, anyway."

"Oh, hell, Jack. When are you going to get your life together, anyway?"

Jack missed the ironic humor and began to explain. "I guess the bottom line is that I'm not good enough for her, or ready for a real commitment.

Hell, I don't know."

Sam interrupted, clearly not interested in his analysis. "I'm finally getting married in a few months myself. Can you believe it? Come to Houston sometime and I'll introduce you to my future ex-wife."

Jack chuckled appreciatively. "That's great, Sam."

"By the way, I'm a big shot now. I'm a State Senator. Now the big boys are looking at getting me elected Governor or United States Senator. What the hell, I may as well run. Can't dance and I'm too fat to fly."

That got a real horse laugh out of Jack. "God, Sam, it really is great to see you. You're looking good. A little extra weight around the middle, but pretty damn good."

"You're not looking bad yourself, old boy." He glanced down at his watch. "Listen, I'd better start walking to my gate. Can't miss the plane to Houston and that hot little piece of ass waiting for me." Jack looked at him with a small smile, thinking, same old Sam. "Look. Here's my card with my new number and address. I've moved my office uptown to a new skyscraper. Hell, I own the building. I'm a big shot these days. Call me, or come see me. I'll bed you and feed you." He handed Jack the card, then, taking it back, he wrote his home phone number on the back and returned it. "Can't believe I ran into you after all these years. Last time I saw you was in Miami, and —oh, my God! What the hell is wrong with me?" He took a frantic glance at his watch and said, "Jack. You must not know. How could you know?

"Jack. Helen is alive."

The floor went out from under Jack and he hung suspended in shock. "Say that again?" he managed to stammer.

"Helen is alive, man. I saw her in Midland. I talked with her. I had drinks with her. Helen is alive and living in Midland, Texas."

Jack put down his drink and held his head in his hands, staring at Sam. "You say you saw her? You spoke to her?"

"I did, just a few months ago. I flew into Midland to look at this small oil company I wanted to buy. I walked into the office, and sitting behind the desk was, of all people, Helen. I damn near dropped my teeth. It bowled me over, I mean to tell you. I couldn't believe my eyes." Jack, still in a near state of shock, pleaded with Sam for more details. "Well, later that night, Helen and I hooked up for a few drinks and she told me the whole story. Oh, and I'm going to tell you something else. Hang on to that bar stool, buddy. Helen has a son, Jason. Man, he looks just exactly like you."

"A son. Are you sure it's my son?"

"Does a bear shit in the woods? Is the Pope Catholic? Hell, yes, I'm sure. He's a clone of you if I ever saw one." Sam looked at his watch again. "Anyway, the name of the little oil company where she works is Midland Minerals. I own it now. Everyone knows where it is. Do yourself a favor. Go look her up, Jack. What the hell."

"I will. I will. Yes, Sam, I will."

"The bottom line of the whole story, Jack, is that it was her mother who told the lies about her being dead. You know, the Bible Belt, bastard kid and all. It seems that Helen moved to California to have her son. Then, after her pa died, her mom talked her into moving to East Texas. Apparently they weren't faring too well in California anyway, so Helen and the kid moved in with her mom. Naturally, her mom told everybody in town that Helen's husband had been killed in an accident while in the military, and that her daughter and grandson came to live with her."

Sam took the last swallow from his glass, grabbed his briefcase, and started talking faster. "Helen went to work for an oil company in East Texas and met one of their geologists. They got married. She said he was a real good hombre, took good care of her and the boy, raised him like his own. Later, they got transferred to Midland. He up and died less than a year later, and Helen stayed on and worked for the oil company. She's still real nice and sweet. Still a little neurotic, thinks she's going to die before her time, you know how she was. Still built like a brick shithouse."

"What about the boy? Jason?"

"Well, I didn't meet him. She showed me a picture. Nice looking kid, I must say. Better looking than his old man, in fact."

"What does he do? Is he married?"

"Don't know about that. He did go to Texas Tech, and he has a good job in Odessa, working for a diamond bit and coring company."

"Jesus. This is too much to take." Nothing in Jack's life had prepared him for this. His mind was racing with a thousand questions. He finally asked the one that was uppermost. "Sam, did Helen say anything about me?"

"Yes, she did. She said that she had read your books and was happy with your success and all, but asked me not to mention to you...well, you know." Sam looked at his watch one last time. "Jack, I'm barely going to make my plane. But do come see me, will ya? Promise?"

"I will, Sam, yes. I promise I will come see you just as soon as I can." He stood up to shake Sam's hand. "Thanks, Sam. I mean it. I really do. Thanks for telling me. Take care of yourself, and who knows, I may even come to the wedding."

Sam took off for his gate, almost at a dead run.

Outside the bar twenty minutes later, Jack started toward his own gate. He got halfway down the concourse, slowed down, and came to a complete stop. People surged around him on either side as he stood there. Then he turned and walked briskly back to the ticket counter. "Hi. I have a ticket to Miami. However, I would like to change this ticket and get the next flight to Midland, Texas."

The clerk didn't bat an eye. "Yes, sir. We have a flight to Dallas-Fort Worth leaving in an hour." She looked at her monitor. "I can still get you on it. And from DFW to Midland-Odessa," she scrolled down the screen, "there are a couple of servers, but I don't have flight times. You'll want to take care of it when you get there. I'll credit your Miami ticket and have your DFW pass in just a moment, sir. Is there anything else we can help you with?"

Jack swung into the routine and got to his destination late in the day. Air traffic was stacked up and the plane circled the Midland-Odessa airport several times. Jack looked out the window at the landscape below. It was as flat as Florida, a uniform brown from horizon to horizon. Here and there, he saw small square patches with pump jacks and tanks, for this was the Permian Basin, one of the richest oil deposits in America. A few farms and the modest metroplex were the only other embellishments.

Midland had a surprising number of tall buildings, for all the major oil companies maintained offices there. Odessa, the working end of the oil industry, had more tool yards full of oilfield equipment. Otherwise, the two towns looked from the air to be much the same.

As soon as they landed, he set about renting a car. The young girl at the Hertz counter talked nonstop, in long vowels that only a Texan could understand. "If y'all will just sign here, you can be on your way, sir."

"Can you direct me to Midland Minerals?"

"Hey, Harry," she called out to the clerk behind the Avis counter next to hers. "Do you know where Midland Minerals is at?"

"Sure. It's downtown where the old junior high used to be. Exit the airport and get on the Interstate east to Midland, take the Rankin Highway exit north. It'll turn into Big Spring Street. Hang a left on Illinois, it's one way going west, and go two blocks." Harry rattled it off nonstop. It was clear that he had had plenty of practice.

"Where's a good place to stay?" Jack asked him.

"We have a real nice Howard Johnson," the Hertz girl put in.

"Nah, stay downtown at the Hilton," said Harry. "It's closer to everything, and there's more going on. Pretty ritzy, too. Go in the same way I told you, but turn right on Wall, go two blocks."

"Thanks, pal."

As the Midland skyline came into view, looking strangely incongruous in the vast sweep of nothingness that was West Texas, he tried to adjust himself to the sharp contrast between this place and the other worlds where he had just been, Ireland and New York. His thoughts turned to Helen. Helen was alive. This was where Helen lived, where Helen worked, where Helen had a son who lived nearby. His son.

"My son," he said aloud, trying on the idea. He liked it. Then he began to worry about what he would say tomorrow. He didn't know how to act. Maybe he should just be himself, he thought. He tried to remember himself three decades ago. Sleep, he thought. I need sleep. It's been a long day.

The next morning, Jack had coffee in the lobby restaurant. He could not help feeling overwhelmed at the prospect of seeing Helen. He thought of the pure, intense love he had shared with her when they were so very young. He thought of his search for her, and his devastation upon hearing that she had died. He thought of his long, aimless years as a journalist when he had one affair after another, all pretty much alike. He thought of his early writing successes that led him to Ireland and to Shannon, miracle of miracles. He thought of the fame and fortune that had gone to his head.

Then his perfect marriage had crumbled, done in by his own belief that he was immune from the unhappiness of mere mortals, and could indulge his every impulse because he was a famous writer. He had won the battle but lost the war. And now. And now. The eternal mystery of time had returned. Helen was alive. Jack's spirit was filled with a whole new set of unfamiliar sensations and emotions.

He finished his coffee and faced his destiny. He retrieved his car from the hotel parking garage and drove six blocks to the oil company. Nobody walked in Midland, and for good reason. It wasn't nine yet, and there were already heat waves rising off the sidewalks. The sun glared off the glassy sides of the tall buildings, and a light wind whipped a film of sand through the streets. Jack found Midland Minerals, Inc., between a bank and a Baptist church.

He pulled into the parking lot and turned off the engine. He sat looking at the entrance of Midland Minerals, Inc. Helen was in there. Okay, this is it, he said to himself. He got out of the car and walked up to the door. He stopped and took a deep breath just before he went inside. He stood in the foyer and looked around the office.

Then he spotted her. There she sat, with that same beautiful blond hair falling down across her face as she worked with some papers on her desk. She had hardly aged. He tried to put on the brilliant but modest personality that worked so well for him in the publishing world, but he could only look at her the same way he did the first time he saw her. His eyes misted up. Then and now, she was heartbreakingly beautiful.

He walked slowly toward her desk. As he drew near, she looked up and smiled politely. It took her three full seconds to register that she was looking at Jack Murphy. Tears welled up in her eyes and spilled down her cheeks as she clasped her hand over her mouth. Then she took her hand away and smiled again.

Chapter Sixty

Shannon walked out of the big house, looking back at the empty rooms. She locked the kitchen door, then turned and started toward the ocean. When she reached the cliff's edge, she stood by her favorite rock. The cool crisp air braced her, lifting the weariness from her as she stood motionless, gazing at the sea. She was filled with an overwhelming desire to possess love and beauty, and to find it in all things. The ocean air filled her with a sense of power. She had found her life again. She bowed her head and thanked God for all His guidance and blessings.

Shannon turned and looked at the house. Today, with the furnishings gone and the real estate agent's sign in the yard, it looked very imposing. It also looked cold, and in need of a family to warm its walls. It was a good house, she thought, and one day it will make a good home for someone. Shannon stood and contemplated the ocean for awhile longer, knowing she would never return to this place again, then walked to her car, not looking up toward the house as she passed. She drove down the hill and onto the main road. Tahilla was deserted. There was no one at the church and the little market was closed. She pulled onto the highway and on to Kenmare. It seemed at that moment that she was leaving a foreign country. Shannon was finally going home, and she felt like crying.

When she reached the cottage, the sun was setting. She went in and turned on several lights, made a fire in the fireplace, and put on a kettle for some tea. She went to the stereo and put on a tape of some Irish country music, then collected her tea and sat down in the big chair in front of the fireplace.

She had not been home long when she saw the headlights from a car shine in through the kitchen window. When she looked out, she saw Mr. O'Shea's car. She wondered what he would be wanting at this hour. She opened the door before she could hear the knock.

"Paddy," she cried. "Oh, Paddy." She was elated to see him. She pulled him into the house, threw her arms around his neck, and hugged him with all her might.

Paddy seemed a little stunned. "Wow. I'm glad to see you, too."

"Oh, Paddy, I can't tell you how wonderful it is to see your smiling face." With that she reached up to kiss his cheek.

With a look of concern, he asked, "How are you? Is everything all right? I called your house, but the phone had been disconnected. I took a chance that you would be here." He looked at her keenly. "Are you all right, Shannon?"

"Yes. Yes. And I'm better now that you're here. I missed you. Oh, I can't tell you how I missed you."

Paddy wondered at the change in her. Even as a good friend, she had always maintained a certain formality with him, befitting her commitment to her marriage. Finally, he ventured, "And I thought of you, a lot. Oh, Shannon, how I thought of you." For a few moments, they gazed into each other's eyes, smiling, taking each other in after a long absence.

Then she took him by the hand and led him to the living room. She sat down next to the fireplace. Paddy stoked the fire a little before sitting down across from her. She took his hands in hers and placed them on her knees. He looked inquiringly into her eyes.

"It's over. Jack and I made the break. He's gone to America. Oh, I'm talking too fast. I'll slow down. 'Tis one of my many shortcomings. I do that when I get excited." After a pause to collect herself, she continued.

"The big house is up for sale. Jack is going to file for divorce in America, and I've asked Father Hennessey to begin annulment proceedings." She did not allow him to get a word in. "Jack and I have made a clean cut from one another, a settlement I guess you could call it. I'm a free woman." She looked around the cottage. "I'm home. This is my home, and I'm here again. Isn't it just grand?" With a big smile, she sank back into the big chair.

He nodded thoughtfully, smiled back at her, then grew serious. "I've some news," he began. "Maura's mother died last week, of cancer. I stayed at the hospital with her. They said there was no treatment. She was too far gone."

"Oh, Paddy. I'm sorry to hear that." She reached over and touched his face. He covered her hand with his own. "And, Maura? What's to become of little Maura?" she asked in a worried voice.

"I'm making arrangements to have her here, living with me, as soon as possible." His voice trembled as he spoke.

"Paddy, I'll help you. We'll work this out."

"You're a wonder," he said affectionately. "I want to make you part of me and take you with me wherever I go." Shannon's face glowed in the firelight. She breathed slowly and deeply. Then she put her arms around his neck and kissed him tenderly. He took her into his arms. "I love you, Shannon Kelly. I love everything about you. I fell in love with you a long time ago. I can finally tell you I love you." Shannon looked at him, taking in all he said. "Do you understand?" he asked.

"I do, yes. I understand," she said softly.

Paddy's eyes were intense. "There. I said it. You don't have to say anything back. I understand."

"No, you don't understand, Paddy." She smiled. After a moment, she said in a voice like an Irish lullaby, "I, too, have fallen in love with you, Paddy. I'm sure of it. I fell in love with your goodness, your kindness, your constant show of respect for me. I've fallen in love with your poetry, and your ideas. And your love for Maura. The honor you have shown me at all times has made me realize you are a noble man. The only man for me."

She kissed him again, more passionately this time, then buried her face in his shoulder. They held each other very closely. The crackling of the fireplace was the only sound. He kissed her hair and breathed in her ear. "I want to be inside you. I want to feel you all around me, to become one with you. I want our love to join. I have longed for this moment."

He did not care what his words might sound like to Shannon. Now his dreams were alive. His thoughts dissolved into pure poetry. She stirred in him the long denied passion of their first meeting. He had adored her from afar, and now she was in his arms. She had been the princess of his dreams, filling his sleep with rapture, and here he was awake and she was real. He could not think of anything except the slow melting of their bodies and souls into one. He felt a great fire inside him, and only Shannon could quench him.

Her eyes smiled at him as she whispered, "I have to go upstairs for a moment. I'll be right back." He released her and went to sit before the fire. As the brilliant colors danced in the flames, he felt in his heart a warm and glowing love for Shannon. When he heard her footfall at the bottom of the stairs, he turned to see the face of an angel, lit by the flickering flames. She had clothed herself in a gown and robe of sensuous black silk, and she walked like a symphony toward him. Her body spoke of promises. Her lips parted as she met his. He did not move except to receive her kiss. He was caught in her spell. He had no will, no reason. He was simply hers.

Shannon stepped back slowly and deliberately, took his hand and led him upstairs to her bedroom. She had lit a fire in the fireplace, and the room was warm and filled with dancing shadows. A golden light shone on her, burnishing her hair and outlining her body as she removed her robe. Ever so tenderly, she pulled him close to her. She kissed his cheeks, his eyes, and then his neck, all the while unbuttoning his shirt and letting it fall to the floor. He gently ran his hands down her back and then found her breasts.

Shannon succumbed to his touch and melted into his arms, allowing herself to feel every emotion. There would be no stopping now, she knew.

Paddy unbuttoned his trousers and allowed them to fall to the floor, then gently removed her gown and laid her on the bed. Poised above her, he moved his hands along her curves, down the silken middle of her stomach, then to the tender flesh between her legs. Shannon grew moist from the wonderful rush of joyful feelings. Paddy continued to kiss her body until finally they could not take it any longer. They joined in the glorious act of making love with one another. Never in her life had she felt this deluge of joy and love, at once so pure and so true. There was no line to mark where one left off and the other began. They were one.

They remained in each other's embrace, still and silent. Their hands moved very slowly over each other, picking out the subtleties. They were both drenched in the sweetness of their love. Tonight, Shannon had regained her youth. And she had given it completely and freely to Paddy.

Chapter Sixty-One

In the woodland, birds fluttered from sleep. The sun moved at a slow pace across the dreaming land. Ireland was awakening with the sounds of seagulls, a moving train, a fog horn off in the distance, cries of children, and the smell of fresh coffee. Shannon and Paddy sat across from one another at the kitchen table as if a painting had come to life.

Shannon had never been more beautiful than she was this morning, nor had Paddy been more splendid. A ray of sunlight came darting through the window, then vanished behind a cloud, then returned. It was a bright Irish morning, a soft day which promised to last through dark.

"Shannon, will you marry me?" Paddy asked directly.

She looked at him with smiling eyes, and in a low tender voice she said, "Paddy." His heart was pounding. She went to the stove for more coffee, and carried the pot over and filled both their cups.

He took the silence as an invitation to speak. "Shannon, you know that I love you, and not just because of last night." He knew that simple words were the language of the heart. "I've loved you since we first met. I want to stay with you, take care of you, be with you every day, always."

She shook her head with a serene expression. "I'm not ready to talk about marriage. I can't marry you now, anyway."

"I'll wait," he said.

"It's not that, Paddy. I'm not saying no, and I'm not saying yes, later." She was focused, her thoughts direct and her feelings genuine. "Time, Paddy. I need time. There is nothing more to say." Paddy sat very quietly, and did not press the issue.

A light wind began to fan the trees. The sunlight came and went, playing hide and seek with the clouds. Shannon took Paddy by the hand and without words they walked out into the fresh morning air. As they moved slowly down the road, he stole sidelong glances at her. She was so lovely, so delicate and fresh, a complete and beautiful woman.

She drew up an inward smile. She and Brien had taken this walk so many times together. She looked out toward the field. In her memory, she could see her father working the land with his horses. He would stop to wipe his brow, always with one hand on the horse's neck. She recalled the time she saw her father kiss Nell on the nose, and then look around to see if anyone saw him.

Paddy and Shannon walked slowly, arm and arm, with no words spoken. Now and then it would flash through his heart that this radiant beauty was his, and he would be overwhelmed with joy.

Shannon looked back at the house and could see her mother and Bridget working in the garden. The garden was her mother's refuge, and no peril ever shadowed her there. She had always been more at peace in her garden than anyplace else on earth.

A wonderful confidence grew in Shannon as they walked. The hinges of her life had not come off, she considered. Hidden deep within her she still held the secret hopes of yesterday, the unspoken desires and aspirations of that sweet song. Her spirit was triumphant.

She stood looking at the cottage and a smile took her face. A small puff of smoke came up from the chimney and vanished into the sky. Shannon thought of the poem her father had written to her mother. "I wish I could send armies of swallows to proclaim my love for you, and the swallows will sing your name."

"The dawn was contagious,
spreading rapidly about the heavens.
Birds were stirring
and the great kingly trees
were being pleasantly interfered with
by the breezes.
My heart was happy and full
of zest..."

Flann O'Brien
(1911 - 1966)